PP

A Man Against a Background of Flames

A Man Against a Background of Flames

by

Paul Hoggart

Cover design by Curious, London
Design and typesetting by Jackson Rees
Printed by Clays Ltd, St Ives plc

First published on Kindle May 2013 ISBN 978-1-906309-26-8

This edition ISBN 978-1-906309-36-7

First published October 2013 by

Pighog
PO Box 145
Brighton BN1 6YU
England UK
www.pighog.co.uk

info@pighog.co.uk
www.pighog.co.uk
Facebook: Pighog
Twitter: @ Pighog

To my parents

Richard and Mary Hoggart

'Cursed is he that putteth his trust in man, and taketh man for his defence, and in his heart goeth from the Lord.'

—*A Commination against Sinners, The Book of Common Prayer, 1559*

'How may a man be taught on Sunday that true Divinitie is manifest in the form of a pippin, then catechised on Monday that it appeareth in the guise of a quince? How may he be told in September that a sheep is his Master, ordained by Heaven, but in January that he must make obeisance to a bearded goat? How shall he put his trust in such Divinitie that men may shift its shape upon a whim?'

—*Sir Nicholas Harker, The Colloquies, Book II, Number 6*

Cambridge

When the landline rang it was so unexpected that it made him jump. As it turned out later this was a rather mild reaction. If he had had the slightest notion of what lay in store as a result of his answering it, Appleby might have wrenched the antiquated handset from its socket, hurled it through the quaint little oriel window and watched with grim satisfaction as it splashed into the river. But having no such clairvoyant intimations, he took the conventional course of action and picked up.

It was a glowing Wednesday evening in late May, and he was installed for the rest of the summer in cosy, if cramped, rooms in Despenser College. Despenser is one of Cambridge University's oldest, smallest and most obscure foundations, and he was in one of the few buildings whose medieval walls are lapped by the Cam. Another man might have been blissfully content in such privileged surroundings, but as one of his closest friends put it, Appleby was 'good-humouredly dyspeptic'. Like most men of fifty he nursed a collection of anxieties; some professional, some social, some sexual. His more exotic demons could even claim to be philosophical or existential, though most of the time this heavy mob remained obligingly concealed beneath the froth of daily life.

At that particular moment his horizon was cluttered with more immediate concerns. A habitual procrastinator, he had to review a book he had barely started reading, write a set of lecture notes, come up with some useful advice for the two PhD students he had been asked to supervise and catch up with his lagging research schedule, all before Friday evening when he would take the train home to York to juggle his love-life. His method of restoring order when life's complications threatened to overwhelm him was always the same. He was playing Spider Solitaire on his laptop.

This phone call was an irksome interruption. Who on earth could be calling anyway? Jenny had the college number. So did Iris, but they always rang his mobile or texted. The indigenous Despener staff barely spoke to him, confining communication to the occasional terse email. So he lifted the receiver with a mixture of irritation and puzzlement. And the rest, in several unexpected senses, has become history.

'Hilloo? Is it possible, please to speak with Professor James Appleby?'

The voice was unmistakable. The curious accent, pedantic manner and reedy timbre belonged to an eminent Dutch archivist called Piet van Stumpe.

Appleby groaned inwardly. Van Stumpe worked at the Renaissance Institute, a small independently run archive in Amsterdam, affiliated to the Dutch national library in The Hague. He had met him several times at conferences and once in his lair at the Institute itself. He found the man excruciatingly fussy and tedious, but he had maintained the connection for professional reasons. Van Stumpe was a walking database of every faded document and mouldering scrap of manuscript in the English language ever found in the Low Countries, dating from the accession of Henry VII to the flight of James II.

Among the hundreds of Tudor ships' manifests and routine diplomatic reports filed away in van Stumpe's brain, lurked tiny nuggets of historical gold. On various occasions he had shown Appleby a letter from an anonymous Scottish clergyman threatening to disembowel Erasmus; scribbled messages from the Earl of Leicester haranguing his subordinates in Holland and a fragment from a begging letter, almost certainly by Guy Fawkes. He even had a list of grocery orders from the household of the exiled Prince Charles (they seemed to get through prodigious quantities of poultry). Van Stumpe's synapses operated a biological database, storing exact details of who had requested access to what, on what date and for what purpose. Appleby suspected he was borderline autistic, the 'Rain Man' savant of Northern Renaissance bibliography.

'Forgive me for making disruptions in your studies, Professor...'

That was another bizarre thing about van Stumpe. Apart from his working knowledge of Latin and Ancient Greek, he spoke at least five modern European languages other than Dutch. But unlike most highly educated Dutchmen, and despite his obsession with exactitude in other areas, his command of foreign tongues was chaotic, bordering on villainous. His conversation in any of them, seemed to Appleby to be a riotous muddle of the syntax, grammar and colloquialisms of all the others.

'...but I was remembering a most fascinatingly, if speculation-making, paper which you were publishing some seventeen years ago.'

'Still Doctor Appleby, I'm afraid, Mijnheer van Stumpe,' Appleby replied, trying to sound breezy. Why couldn't the wretched man remember that? He didn't know which was more embarrassing: the fact that he still hadn't made professor or the way foreign colleagues invariably assumed that he had. 'Now, how can I help you?'

'In matter of facts I am thinking that perhaps I can help you – er – Doctor Appleby. You see we have acquired some documents...'

Van Stumpe paused for dramatic effect.

'Yes?' said Appleby.

'We have found a chest!'

Another pregnant pause.

'Ye-es?' said Appleby again.

'An English chest of late sixteenth century. It has been discovered during the renovatings of a medieval farmhouse near Oosterhout. It was concealed behind a false wall which fell all broken when the builders removed some structural lumps from the flooring. It appears that these workmen found that there was rottenness in five upholding beams beneath. When these were removed, the bottom parts of this wall was crumbled away, and a cavity is so exposed. It contained this chest! Sadly the chest was shut with a most heavy lock which was made in an unusually sophisticated design in that period. I should tell you that it was necessary to request for the services of an expert historical locksmith from a museum of Köln to open it without causing damages to the mechanism, which was most intricate. The lock itself is an historical find of much importance as so it happens, and this process took almost three weeks to knock it on its head…'

Appleby started muttering under his breath, 'Please get to the point...'

'I'm sorry. Were you saying something *sotte voco*?'

'No, no. Go on.'

'So – when the locksmith finally succeeded to open this lock, the chest was found to be containing more than three hundred separate documents, including many manuscripts and several completed books. Happily to say, it was brought to my department at the Renaissance Institute in temporary custodianship. The cavity behind the wall would appear to have remained perfectly dry and free from infestation of insects or rodents for these last four centuries, because the papers are in a remarkable state of good preservation. I am even thinking that one could sell them on some internet market places marked 'As New' without committal of any deception!'

Van Stumpe gave a strangulated little chortle at this pleasing thought, but by now Appleby's attention had wandered. The idea of wading through some expatriate English farmer's account books seemed positively purgatorial, and he was staring through the window at three drunken undergraduates on the lawns of Old Hall opposite. Old Hall had always been notorious for its Hooray Henrys and, for the last few decades, Henriettas. Appleby considered them to be the upper class equivalent of the much-vilified working-class 'chavs', a judgment reinforced by the fact that these three were mooning at a group of Japanese tourists in a punt as it passed beneath his window. On closer inspection he realised with distaste that they each had a small brown bottle, protruding from their bottoms, which they were waving provocatively from side to side. 'Rugger-buggers, no doubt,' he thought. 'How on earth can they think that's funny?'

'Forgive me. I am being frivolous,' van Stumpe continued. 'You see some number of the documents seem to relate to the activities in your paper on Sir Nicholas Harker...'

Oh, that paper! Suddenly van Stumpe had Appleby's full attention. His eyes flashed across the cluttered study to a faded picture on the opposite wall. It was an enlargement of an Elizabethan miniature, a portrait of an elderly gentleman with a long beard, a little severe-looking, in a ruff and the black square-cornered 'Canterbury cap' favoured by clerics, lawyers and academics of that era.

'...and I assure you that they are truly extraordinary! As you are the world authority on this man, I would be most delighted to receive your opinions on their nature and significance, if you could be coming to Amsterdam. I feel you will be most excited.'

World authority? Nobody really knew anything about Sir Nicholas Harker, let alone the terrible events surrounding his death. But van Stumpe was right about one thing: now Appleby was indeed 'most excited'.

By the time the call was over the juvenile self-penetrators had vanished. He spent a full five minutes staring into the distance beyond the postcard vista of weeping willows brushing the river to the plush lawns and the Gothic pinnacles of Old Hall glinting in the low evening sun. What could these Dutch builders possibly have found? Any unexpectedly revelatory documents would have to be treated with extreme caution, of course. They could turn out to be forgeries. What if van Stumpe was the victim of some elaborate hoax? The example of Lord Dacre and the fake *Hitler Diaries* hung like a corpse on a gibbet in the minds of all historians, a ghastly warning of the perils of wishful thinking. But then what if they were genuine? Might they finally answer the tantalising questions which had been simmering in the back of Appleby's mind for twenty years? Van Stumpe might be eccentric, but he certainly wasn't a fool.

The moment required what Appleby called 'liquid acknowledgment'. He went to the fridge in his little kitchenette, placed six ice cubes in his favourite tumbler and covered them in 18 year-old Talisker. He took a particular pleasure in pouring fine single malts over ice, even though he knew it was supposed to ruin the whisky. He loved the combination of the intense, complex flavours with the sharp pang of the ice-cubes on his upper lip. He also loved the way the habit infuriated his brother-in-law, Toby, who considered the practice a sacrilege. For years it had provided one of his mischievous little pleasures during family gatherings with his in-laws.

Ice and fire, he thought, sipping the burning nectar as he went back to the laptop to check flights. Next he rang Jenny. He was terribly sorry but something had come up. He had to go to Holland for an important meeting. Would she mind awfully if he didn't make it home this weekend? She didn't mind, of course. She never did. That was half the problem. She would be busy at the Minster as usual. Then he rang Iris.

'Fancy a jaunt?'

'Where to?'

'Amsterdam. This weekend. I'll pay.'

'Well I'm supposed to be…Oh never mind, I can put them off.'

'Can you get yourself to Stansted by 5.00 pm on Friday?'

'Okay. Sounds fun.'

He hung up and raised his glass to the portrait. Large, limpid eyes stared back at him. To Appleby they seemed full of wisdom, mixed with unfathomable sadness. 'Well now, you enigmatic old bugger, am I finally going to learn your dreadful secret?'

Washington D.C.

Six years later Appleby recalled that fateful phone-call as he sipped a glass of his favourite Maker's Mark bourbon on the rocks and stared through another window, four floors up in the Vacation Lodge in Georgetown. This modestly comfortable chain hotel had been chosen for his visit to Washington precisely because it was the kind of anonymous place where thousands of British tourists would stay every year.

But any illusion that Appleby could lose himself in the herd was shattered when his complete American itinerary appeared on a pugnacious Christian fundamentalist website called www.1willrepay.org. Within hours it had been posted on every Evangelical and Christian right website, newsgroup and chat-room in America. What was meant to be a sedate book-signing-cum-lecture tour had turned into a bumper-car ride of strident radio denunciations, hostile demonstrations, abusive emails and tweets and several detailed and graphic death-threats. He even merited a contemptuous entry in an online Creationist encyclopaedia. The fact that it was extremely Ill-written, as if by a particularly dim freshman, was scant consolation.

The FBI were trying, rather half-heartedly Appleby thought, to uncover the source of the leak, but they had certainly taken the death-threats seriously and assigned two agents for his protection. Forewarned of the demonstration, the DC Metropolitan Police Department had also provided heavily armed officers, most of whom were keeping the crowd away from the hotel entrances while others lurked in the lobby.

Agent Jim Delvaux was an imposing, thick-set black man with a rolling Virginia accent. Agent Ashley O'Malley was a pale, elfin redhead with a well-educated Bostonian twang and a wry sense of humour. They had been with Appleby for a week, and he had grown rather fond of them. He found something gratifying about the easy way they worked together: two such physically contrasting examples of humanity, from utterly different backgrounds co-operating with calm efficiency on a common task. Somehow, he suspected, such a partnership would feel more strained back in England, if it was ever formed in the first place.

His room had twin double beds, and O'Malley was sitting on the edge of the one nearer the window with her legs dangling into the gap between. She was watching CNN.

'You made the news again, Professor,' she said.

Despite the stiflingly humid heat of the outside air, Appleby had stepped behind the net curtain and managed to open the window a fraction. He was trying to catch the crowd's chanting which could just be heard above the low whirr of the air conditioner. Disconcertingly it was a second or two out of sync with the same chanting on the live CNN news report. 'Appleby out!' went the crowd. '...'leby out!' went the TV. 'Jesus lives!' cried the crowd. '...'s lives!' the telly echoed. 'Harkerite Heathens!' '...'ite Heathens!' and a new favourite: 'Destroy the Kindred of Satan!' '...'d of Satan!'

'Step back from the window please, Professor,' said Delvaux from his perch on the suitcase-stand by the door. His tone, while polite, brooked no debate, as if he was a traffic cop addressing a potentially uppity motorist.

'But they're all round at the entrance,' Appleby protested, his eyes scanning across a small side road to a nondescript block opposite. 'Do you think I could go for a swim later? That pool looks so inviting.'

'We need for you to be cautious at all times, Professor,' said O'Malley. 'They estimate there are three thousand looneytoons out there, and they're all baying for your blood.'

'Yes, I do realise that,' said Appleby. He turned his head to look at Delvaux. 'But they can't possibly know which room...'

He didn't get to finish his sentence. A high-velocity rifle bullet smacked through the double-glazed window, scooped a neat little notch from the edge of his right ear, and slammed into O'Malley's temple.

As she slumped between the beds, Appleby and Delvaux dropped to the floor. Delvaux shouted into his radio.

'Agent down! Incoming shots. I repeat – O'Malley is down! We have a sniper!' He drew his automatic and peered over the edge of the vanity unit. A second bullet hit a bedside drawer, which burst apart spilling a copy of Gideon's Bible onto the pool of ice, bourbon and blood on the carpet by Appleby's face. The bullet had drilled a hole diagonally through the spine and out through the back cover.

Delvaux was still shouting. 'Incoming shots from above, and to the left! About eleven o'clock! Someone just stood up on the roof! They're running off!'

A helicopter appeared as if from nowhere and swooped overhead in pursuit of a tiny fleeing figure. Two police marksmen in black flak-jackets and helmets burst into the room, both with sniper rifles, closely followed by three paramedics.

Appleby stumbled to his feet. He was just in time to see the gaping exit wound and O'Malley's auburn hair in a puddle of brains and blood on the carpet, before they pulled a blanket over her head. He vomited suddenly and violently, splashing his favourite deck-shoes, then fainted.

Birmingham

Appleby had never planned to become the world expert on Sir Nicholas Harker. And as his head of department snidely observed, 'It would be hard to imagine a more unlikely instigator of a global cult, let alone the focus of rage-fuelled international controversy.' The whole thing, Appleby would tell his friends ruefully, 'was an accident of history'.

Colleagues knew him as a social historian whose credentials were earnestly left-wing and impeccably 'worthy', but by the time he got the phone call from Piet van Stumpe, he felt he had lost his way in life. He had become a misfit, an intellectual dinosaur.

Yet unlike some of his colleagues, his left-wing views were no trendy middle-class affectation. His father was from a family of northern mill workers, his mother raised on a small farm in north Yorkshire. Both became senior teachers in suburban state-schools in Birmingham. Both were intensely hard-working and idealistic. Appleby and his older sister Kate ingested their parents' socialist principles with their breakfast Weetabix and bed-time Ovaltine. Tom and Barbara Appleby were immensely kind-hearted and could be great fun, but he often complained to Kate that their seriousness and fierce honesty put a moral pressure on him which felt burdensome, especially during his chaotic adolescence.

Despite their egalitarianism, his parents were immensely proud when, at the age of eleven, he won a scholarship to Archbishop Cranmer's Boys', an ancient and prestigious direct-grant grammar which affected the trappings of a grand public school. He never felt he fitted in among the sons of the Second City's solicitors, accountants and 'captains of industry', and found himself in a small, tightly-knit clique of rebellious, piss-taking would-be bohemians. Their rebellions were minor enough. They dodged the Cadet Force and games whenever possible, and played fast-and-loose with the school uniform. They smoked cigarettes and, very occasionally, pot in the 'Out of Bounds' staircases behind the school hall and acquired a reputation for impertinence and insubordination.

The self-styled 'Chief Master' made a point of interviewing every boy before he left the school, taking a last opportunity to give the lad the benefit of a few home truths. 'You're a harmless enough chap, I suppose,' he told Appleby in his strange, breathy voice, 'but essentially you are trivial and flippant. You'll never amount to anything. Goodbye.'

With this valedictory ringing in his ears, he set off to read History at York University. Here the Oxbridge 'near-misses' of the state education system mingled a little uneasily with those from the more idiosyncratic private schools. Once again he found himself in a limbo, this time between fellow students from the state and independent sectors.

It took Appleby a long time to adjust to university life. As Kate was quick to point out, he was immature in every way. He had no real sense of purpose and dissipated his energies performing in Joe Orton comedies and feeble revues, making pitifully inept programmes for the student television service and trying, with decidedly limited success, to get laid.

'That Chief Master was a mean-spirited old bugger, but his prediction about you is coming true!' his father told him sharply after learning of a particularly poor essay grade. 'You've been at York over a year now, and as far as I can see you've just frittered your time away! When are you going to grow up, lad?'

It was in the tiny student TV studio with its three clumsy black-and-white cameras that Appleby first fell under the influence of Tim Farnstable, a young man of positively Mephistophelean good looks and bottomless self-confidence. Farnstable (everyone referred to him by his mildly comical surname) attracted beautiful girls much as a bouncy castle at a school fete attracts small children. They just seemed to tear their shoes off, shout 'Yippee!' and scramble aboard.

Years later Appleby admitted to Kate that, on one level at least, he was deeply jealous and felt obliged to try to play the free-wheeling Casanova himself, part rock-star, part James Bond. Yet on another level he remained oddly untouched. Apart from the fact that he completely lacked Farnstable's sexual self-confidence, this quest for spontaneous promiscuous encounters cut against all his natural instincts which were romantic to the point of being downright soppy. It took him over a decade to work it out, but what he really craved was to love and be loved, to respect and be respected in the uncomplicated way his parents had always seemed to love and respect each other.

Farnstable was a master of the art of aggressive teasing, and Appleby was often his fall-guy. Yet his sense of humour was, if possible, even sillier than Appleby's. At school Appleby had sometimes played Eton Fives, a ball-game like squash where the players wear padded gloves and slap the ball about with their hands. The courts had small Gothic buttresses called 'peps' sticking out from one side, which made the balls fly off at crazy angles. Appleby's banter with Farnstable reminded him of Fives matches. Elaborate puns and rococo innuendos, all delivered in silly comedy-sketch voices, ricocheted about in protracted verbal rallies, suddenly flying off on tangents into chaotic surrealism.

Appleby had no idea how important this friendship would prove in later life, but along with a few schoolmates and former colleagues, Farnstable retained a special place, in a cabinet in his heart where he kept emotional trophies labelled 'Life-Long Friends (Even If We Sometimes Don't See Each Other For Years At A Time)'. After York, Farnstable became a television executive, eventually running his own company, one of many student associates who would flourish in the big wide world. Appleby looked on with a mixture of envy and vicarious pride as they rose to edit sections of national newspapers, direct productions at the Royal Shakespeare Company, run Arts colleges or, at the very least become distinguished professors.

Then halfway through his second year, and much to his parents' relief, the skidding wheels of Appleby's intellect finally achieved traction. As he explained to Kate, ever his confidante, he started to work hard, 'Not because I'm feeling guilty or panicking. I'm really enjoying it.' A determined intellectual sprint in his final year brought a scraped first-class degree, which in those days meant the chance of a subsidised doctorate.

As a boy in the early 1960s he had been captivated by children's books like 'People in History' and 'Our Island's Story' with their glorious British heroes and epic military feats. His PhD thesis began as a nostalgic dive back into those cherished childhood narratives. Looking back, he came to think his original idea was downright nerdish, a study of Elizabeth I's navy, all about Drake's *Revenge*, 'race-built' galleons, demi-culverins and other innovations in naval artillery. 'If you ask me, it's the academic equivalent of assembling one of those Airfix kits you used to make,' Kate told him tartly.

His supervisor, however, was a fiery old-school Welsh Marxist called Ivor Gruffudd. As an undergraduate, Appleby had been somewhat sceptical of his more politically engaged contemporaries. 'Half the fire-breathing Marxist champions of the proletariat went to posh boarding schools,' he complained to Kate, 'And the really prissy posh-sounding right-wingers turn out to be from some local grammar or even one of those new comprehensives! The way these people talk doesn't tell you anything about where they come from any more. It's a declaration of ideological affiliation!'

But under Gruffudd's influence Appleby's dormant inherited idealism was reawakened, and he finally took sides. It was the mid 1970s, and he was soon caught up in what felt like a powerful and exciting intellectual movement, joining the ranks of the bearded, long-haired radical academics, to be found on campuses across Europe and America. In senior common rooms and at national conferences they traded Marxist analyses and the new post-structuralist theories, while scoffing at the short-haired, clean-shaven traditionalists. Not that this bothered these adversaries. They scoffed back at the radicals, bandying the theories of Popper, Hayek, and Milton Friedman and waiting for the counter-revolution, convinced that history was on their side.

Appleby's thesis morphed into something much more suited to this new socialist zeitgeist, a painstakingly researched study of the life of the Elizabethan common sailor. When he finished three years later, it climaxed in an angry exposé of the way the ministers of the Queen – or 'the sly, tight-fisted old witch' as Gruffudd liked to call her – had left the crews to starve and die of disease on their ships after the destruction of the Spanish Armada, in a shameless scam to reduce the wages bill. In a bravura coda, published separately in *Deconstructing History* (Vol.3, March 1977, pp.22-36), he subjected the state propaganda of the period, along with the mythologizing of the defeat of the Armada in popular folklore, to a withering Gramscian critique.

It was a strange experience. Kate asked him if he didn't mind savaging his old childhood inspirations. 'I've finally grown up,' he told her. 'I'm beyond all that now.' His research was exhaustive and meticulous. The external examiner said the theoretical analysis was 'sophisticated, pungent and challenging'. Gruffudd urged him to apply for a temporary assistant lectureship. He got it, and a year later the post was made permanent.

While his old friends built careers in the arts and media, Appleby's new socialist zeal blended with the cosseted life of an academic of that era. He and like-minded colleagues honed their sense of progressive political morality in articles, on demonstrations and campaigns or in impassioned debates at History Workshop conferences. They shared a genuine sense of mission, a belief that their work could transform society for the better. Despite certain reservations, this stirred Appleby's blood. And York's was a friendly little department. The staff mixed genially with the students, while pushing the boundaries of research into previously unexplored territory.

He quickly discovered there were other benefits too. As an undergraduate he may have been a vulnerable sexual romantic. As a popular, entertaining and not unattractive young lecturer, he enjoyed a new status and a rush of self-confidence. He took full advantage. While never becoming another Farnstable, he enjoyed a series of 'non-possessive' liaisons with unattached female colleagues and graduate students.

'Every time we see you you're with some new woman!' his mother told him during this belated period of self-discovery. Like his father, she could be uncomfortably forthright. 'Either you're breaking their hearts like a selfish little so-and-so or you can't hang on to them. Which is it?'

'You're being petit-bourgeois, Mum,' he muttered resentfully. 'That kind of possessive monogamy is an outmoded patriarchal construct.'

In fact almost every intelligent woman he met in those days had become a feminist of some description, though the women he was drawn to, or at least who were drawn to him, tended to be of the less finger-wagging variety. He decided to think of himself as a 'fellow traveller'. He told himself he genuinely respected the anti-phallocratic statement implicit in their hairy legs and armpits, though he was secretly relieved when most of them started shaving or waxing again a few years later.

Meanwhile middle-class lifestyles were changing rapidly. In the comfort of his university flat, he developed a taste for Italian wine, real ale and Indian food. Kate gave him cookery books by Elizabeth David and Robert Carrier, and he learned to cook ratatouille, coq au vin and beef Stroganoff. In term time he was vain enough to replenish the reserve tanks of his ego by seeing how many of the prettier first-years developed a crush on him, though he never attempted to exploit his position by seducing undergraduates. And in those long, long vacations, when he wasn't paid to attend symposia in agreeable university towns in Europe or America, he would join friends in villas in Umbria, Brittany or the Languedoc and work on his first book.

'It's a cushy number, isn't it?' Kate told him drily when he outlined his schedule one summer, 'this freeing the nation's consciousness from the shackles of capitalist hegemony malarkey.'

This barb hit a nerve. Despite his enthusiasm for his blossoming career, Appleby had been ignoring nagging doubts, doubts which began to grow and which would eventually hobble both his sense of direction and his sense of belonging. Now derided as naïve, the progressive ideals of his parents' generation had seemed honest, direct, unpretentious, humane and pragmatic. They spoke to ordinary people in their own terms. The new wave of radicals seemed to grow ever-more extreme and ever-more dogmatic. Worse, what had started as a flirtation with abstract theorising had become a sort of addiction, incomprehensible to the outside world. Appleby was becoming increasingly alienated.

Then the hot, acrid wind of Thatcherism blew through the land, battering and scorching the left. Appleby was dismayed by the failure of his radical colleagues to put up any kind of defence that resonated with the public. He even began to share his sister's genial cynicism about his earlier zeal. And yet through all this turmoil, he never lost his parents' burning desire for greater social justice, and within his own discipline, he held doggedly to the conviction that the shift of focus from kings, wars and treaties to the lives of the common people had been immensely important and worthwhile.

That first book was a study of the conditions of the rural poor in the reign of Elizabeth I, focussing on communal resilience in the face of crop failures, epidemics, inflation, land enclosure and other manifestations of economic hardship and political repression. He conceived it as an antidote to the Merrie England maypole-dancing hey-nonny-nonsense of traditionalist historians like A.L. Rowse.

As the research progressed he became increasingly preoccupied with the way farmers, agricultural labourers and their families had coped with the pressure to conform to the new Protestant religion. How had they reacted to this huge change in their lives? How rigorously had the obligation to attend church been enforced in different parts of the country? How consistently were the punishments applied to those who failed in this duty? How far was enforcement affected by the attitudes of individual clergy or local law officers? Everybody knew about the concealed priest-holes in aristocrats' mansions and the gruesome executions of captured Jesuit missionaries, but what became of ordinary folk who retained their allegiance to the Pope? Or who just hated going to church?

He was scouring the Diocesan Archive in Salisbury Cathedral Close, when he visited the ancient Library over the East Cloister and was introduced to a young art historian called Jenny Webb. She was poring over illuminated bibles for her Illustrated Introduction to Ecclesiastical Art. That lunchtime he bumped into her again in the Cathedral gift-shop, looking at the pictures of medieval stone-masons in a children's book.

'Did you know these places were built by Smurfs?' he joked. She gave a warm little chuckle, and he detected a slight twinkle in her eyes. Half an hour later they had arranged to go for a drink. The next evening they went for an Italian meal.

His friends said they made an unlikely match, and at first he didn't think she was his type at all. She was far too conventional, fresh-faced and wholesome. But there was something open and generous about her manner, an unselfconscious warmth and a kindness in her soft, hazel eyes which he found completely disarming.

They discovered, almost accidentally, that they felt extremely comfortable together. At first he thought her politically naïve, but he soon realised that she was shrewd, broad-minded and very well read. She told him upfront that she was inexperienced sexually and a practising Christian, but to his surprise he found both these attributes refreshing. She was entirely free of the existential self-righteousness, aggressive moralising and intellectual vanity of some of his female colleagues. It was a relief to be with someone who didn't monitor his every remark for ideological error. And she laughed at his jokes.

He didn't hide the fact that he had had a string of partners, that he was a socialist and a religious sceptic. She told him later that she found all that rather exciting. He was 'slightly louche', she said and his 'droll cynicism' intrigued her. She was rather bored by the young men she usually met, the preciously fastidious art historians and the priggish, over-earnest Christians. Appleby's worldliness aroused her curiosity. She never shared his political radicalism, but she admired his idealism.

A few weeks into their relationship Jenny went to see her younger sister Lucy.

'She asked me what I was doing sleeping with an atheist Trotskyite!' she told Appleby when she got back.

'So what did you say?' he asked.

'Well, if you really want to know, I said you like to act the godless cynic, but I can tell that underneath it all you want the best for your fellow man.' Appleby raised his eyebrows. 'Yeah,' Jenny grinned. 'She didn't buy that! So I told her how much you make me laugh.'

'And?'

'She said that would be the clincher!'

There were bumps in the road, of course, but Appleby and Jenny had made each other extremely happy for almost eight years before things started to go awry. He often wondered how different their lives might have been if they had not lost little Daniel.

It was during that spell in the Diocesan Archive that Appleby chanced on the first oblique references to the slaughter of Sir Nicholas Harker and his household in 1594.

Amsterdam

On the Saturday morning after his unexpected telephone call from Piet van Stumpe, Appleby and Iris were eating breakfast in the Hotel Admiral De Ruyter, a dowdy three-star establishment on the edge of central Amsterdam. They had been there since ten o'clock on Friday night, and he still hadn't phoned Jenny.

It had been months since he and Iris had made love quite so enthusiastically. For over an hour they had rediscovered the vigour of their first encounters, expanding their normal repertoire and manoeuvring each other into different positions like a couple in their twenties. Appleby had let many things slip in his life, but he had managed to keep reasonably trim, and thanks to regular swimming and cycling, his stamina wasn't bad either. He had woken with a hearty appetite and was tucking into stodgy bread-rolls with cold, slimy ham and tasteless, rubbery cheese from the breakfast buffet. Iris laughed at his greed and told him off for eating rubbish. She limited herself to strong black coffee and some kind of yogurt-based health drink she had brought from home.

'Give me one of those, then,' he joked.

'No way! You know they make you fart.' Sadly this was true – something about the 'bio-active' bacteria, he guessed.

They took a short stroll arm in arm, along the Herengracht, then prowled past the stalls in the Flower Market before Appleby hailed a taxi and went to his 10 o'clock appointment with van Stumpe in the modest office building that housed the Renaissance Institute. Iris headed for the Anne Frank House, popping into a coffee-shop to buy a small packet of grass on the way.

The Institute was a mile from the city centre in a characterless early 1950's block. Ever obsessed by historical contexts, van Stumpe had once explained that the building had been thrown up to replace a row of elegant seventeenth century town houses which had been accidentally demolished when an off-course Halifax bomber was brought down by

German night-fighters in 1943.

His office seemed to have been cryogenically frozen at the date the new building had been furnished. It had a peculiar, institutional smell which reminded Appleby of visiting his dying grandfather in hospital as a child. Perhaps it was the wax polish on the lino floor. The Tudor chest sat proudly in the middle of a large conference table. It was much bigger than Appleby had imagined, well over a metre wide, and it was already open.

'I am so delighted to renew our friendship, Doctor Appleby.' Van Stumpe's blend of obsequiousness and officiousness made him squirm. A passing whiff of halitosis didn't help either. 'I am afraid our secretary is not "on duty-call" as it is Saturday, so I cannot offer you some coffees, but I imagine you would like more to get straight to business!'

After the exchange of pleasantries, he produced a packet of protective gloves.

'I hope you are not objectionable to this latex,' he said. 'We do not use white cotton ones any more. We feel it may make as much damages to documents as nude fingers, or sometimes even more so.'

'That's all right,' said Appleby, wincing.

'Then we can begin without much ado!'

In fact Appleby hated the texture of the milky coloured latex. He thought it made the gloves feel like condoms, which he also loathed, unnatural synthetic barriers between his nerve-endings and the elemental contact of touch and texture. Van Stumpe carefully lifted the heavy chest towards them, struggling under its weight, as the two men sat down side by side.

'You will notice how fine the craftsmanship is here, brass-bound with beautifully regular carpentried dovetails joints.' He paused for Appleby's response.

'Yes,' he said. 'It's a nice box.'

'Now this is most gratifying. I sent this document to a laboratory for its chemicals analysis, and it was returned to here yesterday morning.' Van Stumpe picked a flat transparent plastic envelope from the top of the chest, containing a folded sheet. He handed it to Appleby. As he delicately slid the document from its sleeve, he felt a rush of reverent anticipation.

'The results give much satisfaction!' van Stumpe continued. 'The composition of the paper and the ink both give indication that it is pre-seventeenth century and of English manufacture. The ink could possibly be French, or even Danish as a matter of facts, but this is regarded as mostly not likely. As for the script, as you will notice for yourself, it is entirely consistent with the style that was a favourite to the southern English gentry of the late sixteenth century. Would you care to share with me your opinion?'

To an untrained modern reader, the irregular, sometimes bizarre spelling and florid writing would have made it almost indecipherable. The script was relatively open and large for a document of the period, but the letters were still small and oddly shaped by modern standards, and sometimes dwarfed by unfamiliar decorative flourishes. But by now Appleby could read Tudor handwriting almost as easily as his morning copy of *The Guardian*. He flipped it over to inspect the back.

The sheet had been folded over several times to form an envelope, concealing the contents before it was sealed. A small fragment of red sealing-wax still clung to the back. It bore the imprint of two stars. Appleby remembered that Harker's family crest displayed three stars at the top. On what would have become the front of the closed envelope were the words '*Sr Thos Cranham, Mill Ho.*'

Sir Thomas Cranham of Swively was known to be a neighbour and friend of Harker's who had disappeared after the destruction of Farthingwell Manor. Appleby had seen evidence that the agents, first of Lord Burghley and then of his son Sir Robert Cecil, had hunted him without success until the Queen's death in 1603. He also recognised the address with a jolt. He had actually stayed in what used to be Mill House, but without realising that it had once been Cranham's home. That meant that he and Jenny had almost certainly slept in this man's bedroom. Jenny, he recalled, had had a strange and disturbing dream that night. His scalp began to tingle. He turned the sheet over and read.

Dearest friende,

If it so please you, notwithstanding the late most unwelcome Inquisitions and the consequent Strictures imposed by Certayne Parties, we shalle resume once more our Solemnyties this Sat. morn. As ever the Lady Grace and self wold count it a grate Honor if you and your good Wif and all yr childern be in attendaunce, likewyse all those among your Householde who are of our Kindred, being yet mindful that more than heretofore, this must be dependaunt upon their most complete Discretion. I fear me that ere long, there may be little enough occasion for such Fellowshyppe. Please to make swifte reply by this bearer that we may know your inclination.

Your true and faithfull friende, N.H.

The note was dated 14th of May 1594. Van Stumpe had calculated that in the old Julian calendar that was a Tuesday, four days before the supposed date of the massacre.

'Incredible,' said Appleby. By now the small hairs on the back of his neck were actually bristling.

'Allow me to show you some more of the most interesting documents,' said van Stumpe.

*

Four hours later Appleby met Iris in a bar near the hotel. His head was spinning. 'I'm going to have to make some arrangements,' he said. 'I think I've just struck oil.'

'Let's go back to the hotel,' she said with a grin, showing him her small bag of grass. 'It sounds like this calls for a little herbal acknowledgment.'

Manhattan

Appleby was deeply shaken by the attempt on his life in Washington, and the FBI wanted to bundle him onto the first flight back to Heathrow. But it turned out he had supporters on Capitol Hill. Three Congressmen and two Senators had intervened, demanding he be allowed to complete his tour. The United States, they insisted, should never bow to acts of terrorism or religious intolerance. While the White House, various government departments and security agencies argued, these unknown friends invoked the constitution and demanded his official protection be reinforced.

And so he found himself in the studios of Wolff TV, half way up an art deco skyscraper in Manhattan. He was waiting in the comfortably appointed green-room of 'The Stote Longbaum Show', while his new minders, agents Keppler and Jones, two burly, taciturn men with 'preppy' hair-cuts, sat fiddling with their communication devices in the corner. He was caked in make-up and powder and sweating gently.

His fellow guests were to be New York controversialist, Diane Klauter, the leggy blonde scourge of America's bleeding-heart liberals, and a televangelist called the Reverend Ike Fawthorn from the Tennessee-based Ministry of Christ of the Talents. Appleby had once seen a documentary about him. His sect preached that it was the religious duty of all Christians to make themselves as rich as possible. He was also a vigorous proponent of 'intelligent design', and was funding campaigns in several states to make the teaching of Creationism compulsory in all publicly funded schools.

Longbaum had called Appleby personally to invite him on the show. 'People want to hear what this is really all about,' he said encouragingly. Appleby asked for an hour to think it over, then rang his agent Phyllida in London. He caught her on her mobile in a taxi with another client. Should he do it?

'It could certainly help sales,' Phyllida mused, 'but they'll give you a rough ride. I gather things get pretty raucous on those shows, and they won't spare you just because you're foreign or a serious scholar.'

'I couldn't care less about the sales. I just want a chance to explain things properly on national TV.'

'You can forget that,' she laughed. 'It'll be a bear-pit – an aggressively right-wing bear-pit.' He heard a soft sigh. 'Oh, give it a whirl if you feel up to it. At least no one's likely to try and kill you while you're in a TV studio.'

*

He had arrived a full hour early and been ushered straight into make-up. Now he was huddling in the corner of a green-room sofa, clutching a bottle of mineral water and hiding behind a copy of the previous day's *Guardian* he had found discarded in his hotel lobby. Diane Klauter walked in. She was an expensively coiffeured bottle-blonde, tall and elegant in a classic designer suit and black shoes with long, pointed toes.

'Hi,' she beamed, striding towards Appleby and extending a long, bony, immaculately manicured hand. 'You must be Jimmy Appleby, right? I'm Diane. It's *fascinating* to meet you. No, please don't get up. Well now, lookit! You're reading *The Guardian*. Do you write for them too?'

'Not really,' he mumbled, settling back into his seat. 'Just the occasional book review.'

'Well that's writing, isn't it? They have the best coverage of European cinema!' she gushed. 'Mind if I sneak a peek?'

As he passed her the paper, a tall, burly, flush-faced man strode in. He had short silver hair that stood up like a lavatory-brush. Appleby recognised him at once. He was beaming too.

'Hi there, good people! Hey! Diane! How's it hangin', darlin'? Looking as ravishing as ever, I see. And you must be our distinguished Professor from Olde England. We feel a special bond with your country over here, sir,' he said pumping Appleby's hand. 'America never had a stauncher ally.'

'Ike is such an old cornball!' Klauter chuckled confidentially to Appleby. 'That baloney won't cut any ice with you.' She turned to Fawthorn. 'Our guest writes for *The Guardian*, Ike. You patronise him at your peril!'

'Patronise? I mean every word of it!' protested Fawthorn. 'I'm delighted to make your acquaintance, sir. I'm the Reverend Fawthorn, by the way, but I hope you're gonna call me Ike.' (Did he just wink at me? Appleby wondered. I hate people who wink.) 'Now then, guys, are we hot to trot? I have a feeling in my bones about tonight's show. We're like family here, Professor. You just relax and enjoy the ride...'

In the studio two matching burgundy sofas had been placed on either side of the host's trademark desk. Klauter and Fawthorn sat on one; Appleby sat, angled towards them on the other. Informal but smartly dressed, also silver-haired and trim with a glossy perma-tan, Aristotle 'Stote' Longbaum, presided magisterially in the middle. Appleby could see the audience quite clearly beyond the glare of the studio lights and felt his nerves mounting as the moment approached to go live. He had hardly had time to take a deep breath when the floor manager cued Longbaum, and they were on air. The host launched into his intro:

'I just got back from my folks' place out West,' he said, his manner relaxed and chummy. 'Well my Mom keeps a few chickens and I can tell you those little guys know a thing or two, especially when they're young. I asked one fluffy little feller what he thought about our European allies' contribution to the NATO budget. Know what he said?' Longbaum stared meaningfully at the audience for a moment, then answered his own question. 'Cheap!' he said, to gales of laughter.

'Well I figured that might have been beginner's luck,' he continued as the hilarity subsided, 'so I threw him something a tad more specialised. "What do New York bell-hops think of British visitors' tipping habits?" Know what the little guy said?'

'*Cheap!*' shouted the audience in unison, amid more hoots of mirth.

Appleby was too nervous to take much of this in, beyond registering a vague sense of potential hostility. Longbaum was cruising.

'I was over in DC the other day, discussing the Democrats' health-care proposals with some guys up on Capitol Hill. Well, one of our distinguished legislators raised an interesting question. "Now tell me, Stote," he says. "Can you explain the difference between a hospital patient in a country with socialised medicine and a dead hog?" I don't know, says I, but I guess you're gonna to tell me! "Sure," says he. "... The dead hog has an even chance of getting cured!" '

As the laughter faded, Appleby heard himself being introduced.

'Our special guest tonight is Professor James Appleby from Cambridge,' said Longbaum. 'That's Cambridge University, England, not Cambridge Massachusetts, by the way! Welcome, friend.'

'Actually, it's just *Doctor* and I'm based at *York* University,' Appleby muttered awkwardly.

'Is that right? I apologise for that. That's not what it says on my card here!' Longbaum grinned at the camera. 'Someone's gonna get fired tonight! Anyhow, *Doctor* Appleby from *York* University is the man behind what folks are calling the "Harkerite" cult, which is sweeping America. If "cult" is the right word. Maybe the professor will put us straight on that one later. Now our other guests, the lovely Diane Klauter of *New Republican* magazine and my old pal Ike Fawthorn are well known to our regular viewers already. I guess you guys have some points to raise with our distinguished British guest?'

'Darn right we do!' said Fawthorn. His tone had switched completely from folksy bonhomie to aggressive hostility. 'I'd like to ask this so-called professor, what the hell business he thinks he's got worming his way into our country...' Fawthorn started jabbing his index finger at Appleby, '...to poison the minds of the weak and the spiritually vulnerable with this ant-eye-Christian...' (jab) '...ant-eye-American...' (jab) '...British bullshit!' (Big fat jab).

Appleby did not see the red 'APPLAUSE' lights flashing. But he saw the floor-managers turn to the audience, raise their hands above their heads and begin to clap vigorously. The audience responded feverishly. Appleby gulped. Did everyone in the studio hate him? 'I'm not sure I unders...' he mumbled. 'I'm sorry... is that actually a question?'

Fawthorn turned towards the audience, pulled a mocking face and assumed a grotesque, mincing parody of an English upper-class accent. 'Em so sawrry. Eez thet ekchewerly a questyin?' he drawled. Appleby thought he sounded like a drunken karaoke version of Marlon Brando playing Fletcher Christian in *Mutiny on the Bounty*. Fawthorn switched his accent back abruptly. 'You know what, buster? You should read your history books. I strongly recommend that. You Britishers have tried to lord it over plain honest god-fearing Americans before – when you aren't pleading for our greenback dollars to bail you out, that is!'

Fawthorn turned and winked at the audience, pausing to acknowledge more hoots and stomping. Had they packed the studio with isolationist neo-Cons and Bible-belt rednecks?

'Well you know what happened the last two times you guys tried *that*?' Fawthorn was on a roll. 'We kicked your snotty Limey asses the hell out of here, is what!'

The audience were ecstatic. Appleby was struggling to keep up. What on earth was the man on about? Presumably he meant the War of Independence. But twice? The War of 1812, perhaps? Surely that had ended in a draw! What the fuck had all that to do with Sir Nicholas Harker, anyway? This was not the level of debate Appleby had hoped for. Perhaps Diane Klauter would be more rational. She had a fearsome reputation, and he knew she had sometimes made ferocious personal attacks on opponents' sexuality, but at least she had said she enjoyed reading the European film coverage in *The Guardian*. She fixed Appleby with the stare of a buzzard that has just spotted a plump vole.

'You know what? I have it from the most authoritative scholarly sources that your precious Sir Nicholas Harker never even existed!' she said. 'Why don't you just come clean, *Mister Appleby* and admit right here, right now on the Stote Longbaum Show that this whole crock of BS…' She suddenly produced a copy of his new edition of Harker and waved it in the air. '…that this pancake-stack of cow-doo-doo is the product of your perverted little imagination?'

Appleby had heard this claim before. 'Why on *earth* would I make it up?' he protested.

'Why?' Klauter rolled her eyes towards the heavens. 'Where shall we start on that one!? Maybe it's because you're an attention-seeking loser, who never even made professor?' Monstrously irrelevant, he thought, but hurtful nonetheless. Was that just a lucky shot? 'Maybe it's because you're just another low-life, subsidy-parasite European academic ass-wipe who just hates true American values.' She turned theatrically towards the audience. 'But you know what my money's on, Stote?'

'Beats me,' said Longbaum, 'But your money's usually the smart money, Diane.'

Good to know the host was neutral, then.

'I believe we're dealing with a self-esteem issue here. I reckon this guy's got a tiny manhood!' She swivelled back to Appleby. 'I bet you've barely got four inches when fully erect, that's if you even get wood! You wrote this toxic trash to get revenge on God, didn't you, you cringing little creep?'

The audience howled with delight. Appleby's mouth did a passable imitation of a feeding goldfish.

'And you know what?' Klauter concluded with a triumphant flourish. 'You're obviously a commie who fell asleep and still hasn't noticed that the Cold War is over and America won! Stote, this guy just shamelessly *boasted* to me that he writes for *The Guardian*! For pity's sake! He might as well be reporting for *Pravda*!'

She turned back to Appleby: 'You're a Rip Van Communist Tiny Winkle who invented some bogus non-religion to bolster your limp British needle-dick loser ego. Why don't you just take your sorry English ass back home and slob around in that filthy litter-strewn garbage-dump of a country of yours, with its medieval plumbing and lousy socialist dentistry?'

The rest of the discussion became something of a blur to Appleby. When it was over he thought he might have managed to make one or two basic points explaining his perspective on the true nature of 'Harkerism' and his involvement with the movement's origins, but he really couldn't swear to it. He was still reeling from the torrent of deranged personal invective as the audience began to file out.

Stote Longbaum emerged from the protection of his desk as his guests stood up. 'Terrific show everyone! What a fire-cracker! Boy, the griddle was sizzling tonight!'

'You think maybe I went a tad too far with that "all Englishmen take it up the ass" thing, Stote?' asked Fawthorn reflectively. 'I hope folks'll realise that I was speaking metaphorically.'

'Doesn't matter one way or the other, Ike. The audience loved it! Your Super-Patriot schtick always goes down a storm.' He turned to Klauter. 'As for you, young lady, did your mother bottle-feed you on a milk-plus-strychnine baby-compound? That was pure poison. *Mag*-nificent!'

'Easy there, Stote!' simpered Klauter. 'It'll go to my head.'

Finally he strode over and almost crushed Appleby's hand in his. 'As for you, Professor, what can I say? Was this really your first time on a talk show? Tell me you're kidding me, please! You stood your ground like a true Redcoat, sir! You may be facing certain slaughter at the hands of those darned Yankees, but you ain't runnin' nowhere! Didn't he do well, guys?'

'Damn straight!' said Fawthorn. 'That was a mighty rumble, Professor. Well done, sir! What say, Diane?'

'You bet,' said Klauter with warm appreciation. 'It's so much more gratifying to tangle with someone who has the intellect – and the mighty cojones! – to fight back. You get this fella back on again, Stote, and make it soon!'

'It's a no-brainer, Diane! Professor, you have your agent call me the minute you know you're coming back over. I'm serious, now. Do it. Now what say we all hit the hospitality?'

Appleby wasn't in the mood to socialise. He was baffled by his companions sudden switches of attitude and wondering why some Americans think it's okay to say 'balls' in Spanish on network television, but not in English, especially as Klauter's language generally would not have been out of place in the locker-room of a boys' high school. He was also pondering his newly assigned mighty-testicles-plus-tiny-manhood combination when he noticed a short, dumpy middle-aged woman waddling down the central aisle between the seats as the rest of the audience filed out at the back.

'Looks like your fan club came, Professor,' said Klauter, as the woman walked up to him.

'Doctor Appleby?' the woman said, rummaging in a large, floppy shoulder-bag. 'I'm so fascinated by your teachings, I wonder if you'd be kind enough to sign my copy of your edition of the *Collected Works of Sir Nicholas Harker*?'

What a relief! A kindly voice! An admirer even! 'I'd be delighted,' said Appleby.

'Then suck on this, you Spawn of the Devil!' the woman hissed, producing from her bag, not a crisp, fresh paperback, but a can of Mace. She sprayed the contents right in his face. The pain was excruciating. As he doubled up, coughing and trying to protect his eyes, her hand plunged into the bag again. She grabbed his hair, pulled his head down to her own level and was poised to drive the sharpened end of a long-handled tortoiseshell comb right through his left ear-drum and into his brain, when Agent Keppler lurched out of the wings, caught her arm and wrestled her to the ground.

*

That night he lay on his back in his darkened hotel bedroom. The TV was tuned to a local news channel, but he wasn't watching.

He had just taken two strong pain-killers and a sleeping-pill. His eyes were covered by a cold damp flannel, but they were still smarting viciously, and his entire respiratory system felt as though it had been rubbed with sand-paper. He simply didn't understand what was going on. How could Harkerism have provoked such implacable rage? Such lethal hatred? And why did these people hold him personally responsible for it? All he had done was to edit some old documents.

He could hear Jones and Keppler talking in the corridor outside. At one point two new agents arrived to relieve them, the Night Watch as it were. He could just hear Keppler saying that he and Jones would be back at 7.00 the next morning. That was reassuring. Burbling away on the TV, news anchor Louis Fingler was winding up a wacky little item about the escapades of delinquent black bears in the Adirondack Mountains. 'Bears, eh?' Fingler chuckled, 'You can't live *with* 'em! You *can* live without 'em!'

Then Fingler assumed his serious voice. 'Police in New York have arrested an Idaho woman after what appears to have been a second attempt on the life of visiting British professor, James Appleby. Eye-witnesses say the woman, who has not yet been named, attacked Professor Appleby in the New York studio of Wolff TV's Stote Longbaum Show after he had appeared on tonight's edition. We'll be talking to the professor's fellow guests later in this bulletin. Meanwhile police in Washington have recovered the rifle used when Federal Agent Ashley O'Malley was shot to death, in what appears to have been an earlier assassination attempt. There is still no sign of the gunman, and sources close to the FBI suggest there is concern that the trail may have gone cold. Senator Karl H. Pelvey of Wyoming tonight called for Appleby to be deported from the United States immediately. Now we go over to Tamara Velcraux in San Francisco with more evidence of the growing popularity of America's latest cult. Tamara?'

'That's right, Louis.' Appleby imagined a leggy plastic-fleshed blonde with big hair and a sun-bed tan. 'At a press call this afternoon, Enrico

Morales, the self-styled Chief Mediator of the San Francisco branch of the Kindred of the Spirit has announced plans to build a huge new 'House of Association'. Morales claims his congregation has grown by a staggering six hundred per cent in the last three months, making it the largest Harkerite group anywhere outside of Great Britain.'

'And how do the other local faith-leaders feel about this, Tamara? I guess they're pretty sore.'

'If you'll excuse the expression, they're mad as hell, Louis! And to be brutally honest with you, it probably isn't helping any that this new cult is proving such a massive hit with the city's gay and lesbian communities. The problem for the objectors is that there seems to be no legal means of stopping this thing. So far nobody has been able to prove that anything these guys have said or done has broken any laws.'

'Thank you for that, Tamara,' said Fingler. 'Don't go away, now. We'll be back for more on that story real soon. That was Tamara Velcraux in San Francisco. And now the growing controversy over the British supermarket chain who want to take over Nevada's legalised brothels. It seems "the British are coming" in more senses than one, but the hookers just don't wanna play ball. Now where would you look for the "best before" date on a hooker, Wanda?' said Fingler turning to his co-anchor.

'Flip her over and check the bottom, I guess,' she quipped.

But Appleby was no longer listening. He had finally slipped into a fitful sleep.

Swively

Ten days after their first meeting in the Salisbury Cathedral gift shop, Appleby and Jenny slept together for the first time. The Dean who administered the Cathedral's various properties around the city was an old friend of Jenny's parents. For a peppercorn rent he had set her up in a pretty little guest apartment in an 18th Century terraced house near the Cathedral, which happened to be unoccupied over the summer. That night they went to the cinema, and she had asked Appleby in for coffee.

'You can help me set up this contraption,' she said, pulling a new filter coffee-maker from its box. 'Can you grind some beans? They're in a tin in that cupboard. There's a Moulinex thingy on the side.'

He noticed how slender and elegant her hands were, how neat and economical her movements.

'I'll have you know,' he said, imitating Michael Caine in *The Ipcress File*, 'that these beans were specially imported from a tiny plantation in Peru, where they were hand-roasted by Inca priests.'

'Tesco's own brand, actually,' she laughed. Her nose wrinkled slightly and her eyes sparkled. 'And you'll need the specs if you want to pass yourself off as Harry Palmer.'

'Well at least you got it,' he said, quietly gratified.

It was three hours before they got round to making love. Their relationship had got off to a promising start, he thought, but he still felt uncertain and cautious. Jenny was cautious too. She did not share her parents' stern disapproval of pre-marital sex, but she was uncertain of Appleby's true feelings. Both of them felt they were venturing into terra incognita, and both were anxiously unsure of the other's sexual expectations.

So they listened to Steeleye Span tapes on her new cassette recorder, talked about medieval history and listened to her early Dylan tapes, drank more coffee, talked about Carlos Castaneda and whether Michael Foot could ever win a general election, talked about their families and the Falklands War and illuminated Bibles and Third World charities and Bob Marley and trips abroad...

They were side by side on the sofa, both wilting with fatigue, when he finally risked putting his arm around her. She snuggled up happily, twining those elegant fingers around his and they started to kiss. He was wondering if he could safely put his hand on her breast when she pulled back slightly and looked into his eyes.

'I'm really tired,' she said simply. 'Shall we go to bed? I mean, that's if you want to...' He caught a nervous little gulp in her throat as she said it.

'Yeah. Yeah, I'd really like that,' he muttered. By then it was half past two.

'I've been on the pill for years, by the way,' she said, as they undressed shyly. 'So you...' She saw that he was startled. 'It's not because I sleep around!' she said quickly. 'My GP put me on when I was a teenager. I used to get these absolutely awful period pains. For some reason it stopped them. So you don't need to use anything, unless you think, there's a risk of, you know...You would tell me, wouldn't you?'

'No! No risk of anything like that!' he said, thrilled to discover that he did not need to wear a condom, even though he had taken the precaution of bringing a packet. As she slipped under the sheets he saw her naked breasts for the first time. They were full and shapely with large pale nipples. He was astonished by their beauty.

At 4.00 in the morning he heard the dawn chorus and realised he had fallen in love.

*

Back in the Cathedral Archive, Appleby asked to see the catalogue of the personal papers of John Cantwell, Bishop of Salisbury from 1591 to 1598. He had no idea what he might find. Anything relating to lapses of faith among his flock would be useful. He had barely started when a visiting trainee archivist arrived with a dusty old box.

'You can look through this lot if you like,' she said breezily in a New

Zealand accent. 'One of the maintenance guys found it last night, hidden at the back of an old store-room. We think they may be from your period. The Librarian will be cataloguing them properly next week, but he says I can let you have a quick shufty now, if you want – as long as you handle them carefully, of course!' As she set the box down, she stood a little too close, so that her thigh pressed gently against his side. Then she leaned forward, apparently to adjust the box, resting her other hand lightly on his shoulder. He could smell her scent and felt the warmth of her cheek beside his ear. Was she doing it on purpose? This privileged preview was extremely unorthodox, not to say improper. Was it, in fact, a form of flirting? If so, he was not complaining. He thanked her, and she sauntered off.

He pulled out a small bundle tied with a faded purple ribbon. It contained eight documents. Several turned out to be letters from the new parish priest in a small Wiltshire village called Swively. There were also copies of the Bishop's replies, a tedious job, no doubt, for one of his scribes. They all dated from the Spring of 1594.

The priest, one Jacob Mallaster, was reporting his disquiet over the conduct of a local landowner called Sir Nicholas Harker. In the first letter Mallaster complained that, although Sir Nicholas and his family attended church whenever duty demanded, the manner of his observance appeared perfunctory and insincere. Worse, Mallaster had heard disturbing rumours that, in the privacy of his own home, Sir Nicholas engaged in rites that were 'inimical to our true English faith'. As Sir Nicholas was greatly loved, nay venerated, and a most influential figure in the village, this matter was of the greatest concern to him as parish priest. Would the Bishop, perhaps, like to investigate the possibility that the Harkers were secret Papists? This was Mallaster's strongest suspicion, though some of the village rumours suggested it might be something even more abominable. His letter finished with a biblical reference which he had underlined twice: Deuteronomy 13: 12-19.

The bundle contained copies of a reply from the Bishop promising

to investigate and a letter, inviting Sir Nicholas to present himself
at the Bishop's Palace to discuss 'certain matters of the gravest
consequence'. There was also a brief reply from Sir Nicholas, agreeing
to come at the appointed date and time. This was the first document
written by Sir Nicholas Harker that Appleby ever saw, and the last
he was to see for another two decades.

Bishop Cantwell had then written two brief letters, both
meticulously copied. One was to his own boss, John Whitgift, the
Archbishop of Canterbury, a man noted for his rigidity and intolerance of dissent. The other was to Sir John Puckering, Lord Keeper
of the Great Seal of England. Appleby remembered that around that
time Puckering had rooted out a large gang of suspected atheists.
Cantwell sought guidance as to how he should proceed in this
matter. He made a point of informing each that he had also written
to the other. Covering his back with Church *and* State, thought
Appleby, a wise precaution, no doubt. But these were merely covering
letters. Cantwell wrote that he had enclosed transcripts of the
examination of Harker, together with with 'damning evidence of the
moste unspeakable and pernciouse Blasphemies'. These documents
were nowhere among the Bishop's papers. If either of the men had
replied, their letters were missing too.

The last document but one was barely literate. It was riddled with
obvious grammatical errors and the spelling was positively bizarre,
even by Elizabethan standards. It was a note from a man who signed
himself Captain Hugo de la Zouche.

There was no question of photocopying any of these fragile
documents. Appleby would need special permission to have them
professionally photographed, and that would be time-consuming
and expensive. So he had fallen into the habit of writing partially
modernised versions of documents for his own reference. In this case
the spelling and grammar were so erratic he decided to leave much of
it untouched:

Yore Grace

May it please you to know that we marcht yesternight to the Parish of Swyverly as Comandered by my Mastre on ye behoof of yore Grace, ariving close bye the villige soon after brake of day, and we did there attende to certain mischiefs at that place as reqyred by yore Grace. I took under my Comand twenty good men of Horse and fifty of Foote, ten baring yure Grace's new matchlockes, thirty of Bills and ten Halbardeers of youre Companie.

May yor Grace be holey assured that the Canker hath been chopp't from the sickerly tree and not a Trace remaining to plague youer Grace. I have give the Reckerning for thess service, which I pray your Grace will soon found has been exercuted Most Proper, to yore Tres'rer.

I remain yur Grace's Most Humble and Obedant Servent
Capt. Hugo d. l. Zouche

The final letter was from Mallaster, thanking the Bishop for his decisive and efficient response. The parish was greatly subdued in spirits, Mallaster observed, but this was a good thing for all were now in mighty fear of transgression against the true faith, even within the heart. And he trusted that their melancholy would pass soon enough, as 'the village is a safe haven once more for the saving of immortal souls'.

That night Appleby showed his transcriptions of the letters to Jenny.

'It sounds really sinister, doesn't it? I think I should look into this.'

Jenny pulled a battered old copy of the Authorised version of the Bible from her bookshelf and flicked through the pages. 'Here it is: Deuteronomy, Chapter 13, verses 12-19.' She began to read:

'If thou shalt hear say in one of thy cities, which the LORD thy GOD hath given thee to dwell there, saying, Certain men, the children of Belial, are gone out from among you, and have withdrawn the inhabitants of their city, saying, Let us go and serve other gods, which ye have not known...'

'Serve other gods?' said Appleby. 'Is that what this was all about?'

'Hold on,' said Jenny. 'Get this...

'...then shalt thou enquire, and make search, and ask diligently; and, behold, if it be truth, and the thing certain, that such abomination is wrought among you; thou shalt surely smite the inhabitants of that city with the edge of the sword, destroying it utterly, and all that is therein, and the cattle thereof with the edge of the sword...'

'Slice up the cattle too!' said Appleby. 'Bloody hell.'

'...And thou...shalt burn with fire the city...and it shall be an heap forever...I command thee this day, to do which is right in the eyes of the LORD thy GOD.'

'Jesus!' said Appleby. 'Reduce the place to a smouldering heap! It sounds like Lidice or Oradour-sur-Glane. Do you think they believed all that Old Testament stuff actually applied to them? That they were expected to act on it?'

'Generally, I think there was a certain diplomatic ambiguity...' Jenny mused.

'It might be worth taking a look in the parish registers, I suppose,' said Appleby. 'If they still exist.'

'I know Swively,' said Jenny. 'It's only about fifteen miles away. We used to go blackberrying round that way when I was little. You should check it out. It's lovely. I'll drive you up there if you like.'

'Would you?'

'Sure. There used to be a rather quaint old inn. Maybe we could stay over.'

*

The next Saturday Jenny arrived in her decrepit Morris Minor estate at the cheap boarding house where Appleby had taken a room.

A half-timbered car! How appropriate!' he said.

'Don't make fun of it. My mother gave it to me.'

As they drove north, she reached into the glove compartment and tossed a map into his lap. 'Have a look at that. See if you can sort us out an interesting walk.'

It was an old bright red Ordnance Survey map, one mile to an inch and well-worn. Swively was conveniently near the centre when he folded it in half.

'It's really out of the way,' he said.

'I know. I think that's why my parents liked it so much. We go through a place called Wolvington, which is the nearest small town, but even that isn't on the way from Salisbury to anywhere else. Then you sort of turn right and right again. If you didn't go looking for the place, you'd never know it existed.'

'It shows your inn. Are you sure they've got rooms?'

'I think so,' she said. 'I don't remember much about it, to be honest. Just that it's got a funny name.'

Jenny's underpowered period-piece poddled through the landscape at a stately twenty-five miles an hour, trapping impatient locals in its wake. It was a sunny day. They had the windows open and the country-side was gorgeous. After the open, gently rolling fields around Salisbury, they plunged into a labyrinth of narrow twisting lanes, some where the trees formed tunnels over the road. Occasionally they would surprise a juvenile pheasant in the road, which would scurry cluelessly to left and right, as Jenny slalomed around it. At one point they emerged onto a high ridge with sweeping views over fields of sheep and cattle. Then they passed through woods before dropping into a dell where a small stream cut through lush pastures surrounded by old thatched houses. He would have felt as if he'd slipped through a time-warp into some 1950s motoring idyll if it hadn't been for the Ford Escort and the grubby van which roared angrily past when they came to straight stretches of road. At one point they were overtaken by an impatient tractor.

Swively was not quite chocolate-box beautiful, but it was unpretentiously pretty. The inn sat at the sharp end of a narrow triangular green, opposite the village's dual-purpose shop, Swively Post Office & Household Supplies.

Jenny pulled up outside the square-towered church at the far end of the green. The Church of St Mary Magdalene lurked in a grove of huge old yew trees, behind a low wall with a mildewed lych-gate.

'Look at these tiny windows,' she said as they walked around the back. 'The apse is Norman. Quite early too, I'd say.' By the time they had worked their way back to the porch they had identified at least four architectural phases of enlargement or rebuilding.

'Drat. It's locked,' said Appleby, trying the door. 'I should have called ahead. We don't even know if they have a service every Sunday. It's probably one of these places where the vicar looks after about five parishes.'

'There's a service tomorrow,' said Jenny, pointing to a sheet on the notice-board. 'See.' She grinned at him again. As Appleby looked back at her he sensed her blossoming affection break over him like a puff of warm air. It felt like a kind of benediction.

They walked through the graveyard trying to read the names on the oldest, most eroded gravestones. He sat on the edge of a large rectangular tomb, badly worn and covered in yellow and blue-grey rings of lichen, but warm from the late morning sun. He gently brushed the dust and the dark, flat yew needles out of the carved inscriptions.

'Can you make this out?'

She rested her forearms on his shoulders and peered over at the lettering. He felt the soft pressure of her breasts on his back. He wasn't used to such easy intimacy. He liked it.

'Looks like it might be Crankam? Or Cranham?'

'Yes. I think it's Cranham.'

The inn was called 'The Kindred Spirit', and the sign showed a group of four laughing revellers, holding up foaming tankards. Inside it was a textbook country pub. A row of pewter tankards dangled over the bar, which was festooned with cardboard racks of salted peanuts and pork scratchings. There were hunting prints, horse-brasses and polished copper bedpans on the walls. The tables and chairs were of heavily varnished dark-brown oak. The deep burgundy carpet had a busy floral pattern, and there was an inglenook fireplace with a log-fire laid, but not lit. To complete the traditional rural image, a one-armed bandit bleeped quietly in the corner between a battered 1960s juke-box and a cigarette machine. The whole place reeked of stale fags.

There were three guest rooms, none of them occupied.

'I see you're not wearing a wedding ring, Miss,' said the landlord.

'So?' said Jenny, reddening.

'Sorry, I'm sure,' he muttered. 'There was a time when…' He looked up from the register and smiled. 'Meant no offence. Forget I spoke. I'll put you in Room 2 at the back. It's nice and quiet, with a nice view of the water-mill.'

'It's an unusual name for a pub,' said Appleby.

'That it is,' said the landlord. 'The only one in the country as far as I know. Dates back a long way, mind. I found an even older sign in the cellar with the same name on it. One chap told me he reckoned it was over three hundred year old. Wanted to buy it off me, but I said no. Me and the wife like to hang on to things of local interest. I'll find a space for it on the wall one of these days.'

'You've still got it then?'

'Oh aye. It's still down there where I found it.' He nodded towards the cellar door behind the bar.

'Do you think I could possibly take a look at it? My name's Appleby, by the way. James Appleby. I'm doing some research on the history of the area.'

'A historian, eh? You from one of they universities?'

''Fraid so.'

'Now there's a nice comfy billet at the tax payer's expense, I suppose.'

He noticed a flash of annoyance in Appleby's eyes. 'Oh, don't mind me. I don't mean nothin' by it. Someone's gotta keep they students out of mischief, and sooner you than me. I'm Bill, by the way. Bill Roachford.

I'll take you down the cellar now if you like. As you can see, we're not exactly busy.'

He lifted the flap over the gate in the bar. Appleby and Jenny followed him down a steep, narrow staircase, past the beer-barrels, crates of bottles and some half-empty wine-racks, though a narrow arch and into a small cellar full of junk.

'Here she is!' said Bill, lifting a large square of cracked wooden boards from a dusty shelf and holding it under the only source of light, a naked forty watt bulb. The sign was badly weathered and the picture faded. 'What do you make of that, then?'

'It looks like a family group,' said Jenny. 'Look. They're all wearing ruffs. Even the children! It's as if they'd posed for a photo in their Sunday best.'

'They're all wearing black too,' said Appleby. 'How strange. Do you think they were meant to be Puritans? That wouldn't make much sense on an inn sign, would it?'

'Dost thou think that because thou art virtuous, there shall be no more cakes and ale?' said Jenny.

'Eh?' said Bill.

'Shakespeare,' said Appleby. 'Twelfth Night.'

'I see,' said Bill. 'As a matter of fact you're not the first to ask about the way they're dressed, and my answer is always the same.' He left a slight pause for effect and lowered his voice to a confidential whisper. 'I haven't the foggiest idea!'

Appleby noticed that there were three small stars in an arc across the top of the picture. 'The lettering has survived remarkably well,' he said. 'Hang on. What's this? Do you mind if I ..?'

As he spoke he whipped out his hanky and spat on a corner. Before Bill could object, he rubbed it over a dark area in the middle of the picture. The faint words '*of the*' appeared.

'So it was "The Kindred *of the* Spirit",' said Jenny. 'They must have changed the name. I wonder what that meant.'

'You know I've never noticed that in all the thirty years I been coming down here!' said Bill. 'I'll have to be honest with you and admit I haven't got the foggiest idea about that either.'

As the nearest restaurant was ten miles back in Wolvington, they decided to stay and have dinner at the inn, which by now had acquired a few customers. Meals were served in a quiet dining-room at the back overlooking the garden. Bill introduced the waitress as his daughter Sue, and Appleby ordered the home-made steak and kidney pie. This turned out to be full of fat and gristle in a thick glutinous gravy, but at least it was a 'free house' and he enjoyed sampling three varieties of local ale. Jenny chewed her way through some leathery gammon with a slice of tinned pineapple, washed down with a glass of unchilled Liebfraumilch.

'You could play squash with these,' she laughed, the tines of her fork bouncing back from a roast potato. When Sue had cleared away their plates, Bill ambled over.

'Excuse me for interrupting, Prof, but seeing as you're interested in our local history you might like to take a look at this.' He handed Appleby an old leather-bound book. 'Have a look in the chapter on local myths and legends. I'm not saying it's relevant to any of your researches, mind you, but if you know a bit about the area, I'd be quite curious to hear what you make of it.'

Appleby read the title page aloud:

'A Short History of the Parish of Swively
by the Reverend Anthony Trott
Doctor of Divinity, Oxon.

Published by Parslew Brothers
Printers & Book-Binders
The Borough, Wolvington
Anno Domini MDCCXLII

1742, eh? What a beautiful book. This is probably worth a bob or two, you know.'

'Oh we wouldn't never part with it. It's the only copy left in all the world as far as we know. We see it as a sort of heirloom for the whole village, if you know what I mean.'

Appleby carefully turned the thick, well-worn pages, quickly finding a chapter entitled 'Lore and Legend in Old Swively'. There were tales of warlocks, strange black beasts on Salisbury Plain and a spectral highwayman. Then he came upon this. He started reading aloud to Jenny:

'Ghastly Occurrences in Farthingwell Meadows

It is commonly told around Swively that there was once a most hand-some timber-framed manor house standing in the fields now known as Farthingwell Meadows. These lie presently within the estates of Sir Charles Poulteney, and make fine pastures for the grazing of deer. The story has it that the house belonged to a well-respected old baronet of the parish who lived there with his numerous family, but that this baronet fell foul of the church authorities, incurring the particular displeasure of the Bishop of Salisbury.'

'Gosh,' said Jenny. 'This sounds promising.'

'On a fine spring day in the reign of Good Queen Bess, so the legend goes, a company of soldiers arrived numbering over one hundred and fifty of both foot and horse. They invested this house in which were gathered the baronet with all his family and servants and a fair few of his friends and neighbours too, perhaps forty or fifty souls in all, which must have numbered more than half the village in those far-off days. These unfortunate folk did the soldiers confine within a long gallery on the upper floor, the ground floor then being filled up with brushwood, faggots and loose timbers and put to the torch.

The fire soon raged furiously. In their desperation, several of the unfortunate occupants are said to have broken out through a side door or leapt from upper windows. All, it is said, were brought down by musket balls or cut in pieces by the halberds of the men at arms, their bodies being thrust back inside to burn with the living. By dawn the next day the house, and all contained therein, was reduced entirely to a pile of red-hot embers and smouldering ashes. All within had died a most cruel death. The old men of these parts take unseemly delight in describing how the victims' pitiful shrieks and screams could be heard more than a mile away in the village. It is said that a smell like that of hogs roasted on a spit was borne upon the wind for several miles...'

'Christ,' said Appleby. 'Is this what that De La Zouche fellow meant he'd done?'

'And it shall be an heap forever,' said Jenny. 'Carry on. Maybe he'll say what it was all about.'

'...Yet what these poor wretches' offences may have been, all have entirely forgot. There is much vain speculation and idle hypothesising that they may have been practitioners of some beastly vice or Devil-worshippers, or perhaps easier to credit, that they were heretics of some other fiendish sort, though none can say of what nature. I have made a most diligent search of both parish and county records, yet can find no mention of any such occurrence. I would not give any more weight to this legend than to the many tales of ghosts, werewolves and water-sprites and other fanciful fables recorded in the pages of this volume, were it not for certain peculiar circumstances. To wit:

Primo: there is a map of the parish in the town hall at Wolvington dated Anno Domini 1463 which marks a Farthingwell Manor in the place where the Meadows now lie.

Secundo: on the edge of the Meadows, close by a copse, there is a wide flat space of some fifty yards by twenty. Here the ground is perfectly even except for some long lines where the sward is raised by an inch or two, barely discernible to the passer-by. I observed these abnormalities by climbing a little way into the branches of a nearby oak tree and saw that they form a pattern of rectangles, as if marking out the foundations of a most commodious house.

Tertio: the early registers of our little church contain many references to the names of two particular families: the Harkers and the Cranhams. Both names appear most frequently from the very first volumes, begun in the reign of King Henry VIII, yet both suddenly disappear entirely from the records, the last entry marking the Christening of one Perdita Spirit Cranham in 1593. Poor little Perdita was a lost spirit indeed if the infant perished in so terrible a conflagration.'

'Good God!' said Jenny. 'That's horrible! When did you say this was published?'

'1742.'

'So it was still part of the local folklore a hundred and fifty years later.'

'It's hardly conclusive evidence, but I think this calls for liquid acknowledgment, don't you? Bill! Could I have a double whisky, please? In fact make it a treble! And make it a single malt! Have you got an Islay? Anything nice and peaty!'

'Lagavulin do you?' Bill called back from the bar.

'Perfect. On the rocks please.'

'My brother would burn you at the stake for that,' said Jenny. 'He says pouring single malt whisky over ice is a sacrilegious act.'

'I'm an atheist. What do I care?' Appleby grinned. 'Just look at this.' He swung the book round to show her a plate. 'It's a copy of the medieval map of the parish. See.'

The Reverend Trott's rendering of the Wolvington map was irregular and sketchy. There was no indication of scale, the place names were almost illegible, there were no compass bearings and the east seemed to be at the top of the page. Yet there were enough landmarks, like Swively church and the ruined Norman keep at a nearby hamlet called Sneckbridge, to line it up in a rough and ready way with Jenny's map. Using a bend in the River Swyve, an old clapper bridge and a fork in the road to Wolvington as references, they pinpointed the likely site of Farthingwell on Jenny's old Ordnance Survey map. It was on private land, but only a few yards from a public footpath.

This was the third night that they had slept together. They were both relaxed, enjoying being in a large comfortable double bed and they really found their rhythm. This time, rather to Appleby's relief, Jenny had an orgasm. It was a spasmodic, shuddery business, far too awkward to be fake, he thought. In fact the realisation that the great moment was en route, so to speak, seemed to take her completely by surprise.

'That's the first time that's happened to me,' she sighed, '…during sex.'

She lay with her arm across him, her head on his shoulder and her breasts pressed against his side. He decided not to spoil the moment by asking under what circumstances it had happened before. Such intimate conversations could wait. He drifted off to sleep feeling deeply pleased with himself.

The next morning they took a walk.

Cambridge

The budget flight from Amsterdam got in to Stansted at 1.45 am. Appleby had booked a mini-cab back to Cambridge, and the driver was waiting for them, holding up a piece of cardboard with 'APERBY' written on it in spidery felt-tip pen.

Iris came with him. 'I'll think of this as a DVD extra to our dirty weekend,' she said. 'Anyway I want to see this bastion of feudal privilege you've been hiding in all these weeks. How did you say you got this gig?'

'It's part of some convoluted scheme cooked up by the faculty at York and the Master of Despenser.'

'Oh? Remind me who that is. Isn't he famous?'

'J. D. Clovis?'

'Oh God! Not that right-wing economist?'

'The very same. Christ, that man's a shit! Talks to me like I'm one of the cleaners. He only invites me to college functions if he absolutely has to and then he refers to me as "our guest from the Railway Museum." Tries to pass it off as joke. Bastard!'

She gave his arm a reassuring squeeze.

'Whisky?' said Appleby when they got to his rooms.

'No thanks,' she said. 'This'll do me,' and she pulled a large made-up spliff from a box of tampons in her overnight bag.

'You can't smoke that in here!' he spluttered. 'You'll get me rusticated or something!'

'Do lighten up, dear,' she murmured, lighting up. 'I bet the students do it all the time. I'll open the window. The smell will be gone by morning.'

'Oh what the hell. After what I've just found, I won't have to worry about what these people think, anyway.'

She sat on a padded seat under the oriel window, gazing at the river in the moonlight. Her long straight black hair fell elegantly over the light olive skin of her shoulder. The tip of the spliff glowed intermittently as she drew, and the smoke wreathed past her face in lazy spirals.

He thought she was the most beautiful woman he had ever seen.

Towards the end of his second undergraduate year he had nursed an unrequited infatuation for a girl who looked very like her, an acoustic guitar-playing Anglo-Argentinian who reminded him of Joan Baez. They became very close, but it was over a year before he admitted to himself that, whatever else she wanted from their friendship, it would never be sexual love. He wondered what Iris would think if she realised that she was his consolation prize, deferred by thirty years. Slap his face and walk out probably.

But he really did love her, even though he knew it wouldn't last. It couldn't last. She was thirty, strong, independent, determined, her career set to blossom, at the peak of her powers in every way. He was old enough to be her father and had reached one of life's temporary plateaux. One, two, at the most three decades away, the slow descent into short-term memory loss and rheumatoid arthritis awaited.

In the meantime he'd be getting gradually less fit, less mentally agile and less attractive. It was only a matter of time. Then there was the question of Jenny...

'So tell me about this "convoluted scheme" then.'

'It's a sort of triangular swap,' he said. 'A bit like the slave-trade really. With me as the slave, probably. These rooms belong to a linguist from Despenser who wanted to take up an offer to spend six months at Harvard. It was meant to be a straight exchange, but nobody at Harvard wanted to come here, which is hardly surprising. The place makes Old Hall look like a powerhouse of cutting-edge innovation.'

'So how did you get involved?'

'One of their "professors" – they're all professors over there, of course, and paid like our vice-chancellors – wanted to go to the Institute of Demography in York to investigate some new theory about the ancestry of English immigrant groups in North America – something involving state-of-the-art technology analysing DNA, apparently. So the various registrars' offices leaned on Clovis to take someone from York for six months to keep things tidy and cost-efficient. Then someone in the Cambridge History faculty remembered that a batty old "Spenserian" called Toft had left his alma mater an enormous, but hopelessly disorganised collection of material on late medieval and Tudor agriculture. They needed a specialist to wade through it all with the librarians so they could work out what was rubbish and what was worth turning over to eager post-grads. Enter Muggins here – the Temporary Curator of The Toft Bequest.'

'That's not exactly glamorous, is it? Is that all you've been doing here, then? I thought you were teaching.'

'Oh, they've given me a few lectures and the history people have got me to keep an eye on a couple of PhD students, but Clovis treats me like a glorified filing clerk – which is pretty much what I am, if the truth be told. There are historians spread throughout the university doing wonderful work, people I would love to meet and collaborate with, even if I am just a loan player from a lower division, and I have to end up in this dump! At least it'll look classy on my "résumé", if I ever apply for a job in the States.'

Iris yawned. 'Let's turn in,' she said sweetly. 'How wide is your bed?'

'Let's just say it's cosy.'

*

She had slipped away when he woke up next morning. The kettle was still hot; there were an empty yogurt-drink carton and a herbal tea-bag in his bin and a recently washed mug upside-down on the drainer. She had left a note on the breadboard. 'Loved Amsterdam. Thanks so much. Call me. Love you. X.'

He passed his hand across his stomach to savour the lingering post-coital tautness, sighed happily and scratched his balls. 'Now,' he thought. 'How the hell am I going to play this?'

Harlem

Appleby had four hours to kill before he had to leave Manhattan for JFK. Keppler and Jones wanted him to extend his hotel booking and lurk in his room until it was time to set off. But by now he was recovering from the effects of the Mace spray, and his appetite had returned with a vengeance. As the hotel had no restaurant, they agreed, without too much persuasion, to accompany him to a nearby diner, snuggling under the base of the Empire State Building. They were hungry too and summoned a black unmarked SUV.

There didn't seem to be a standard protocol for accompanying vulnerable foreign academics who might be attacked by religious fanatics. Appleby got the impression they were making it up as they went along. This turned out to be useful. There was something he wanted to do.

Appleby loved American breakfasts. At the diner he ordered his favourite: French toast with maple syrup and chilled fresh orange juice. He watched with vicarious pleasure as Keppler demolished a heaped plateful of pancakes with syrup, thin strips of streaky bacon, small meaty sausage links, hash browns and eggs 'over-easy', sloshing back coffee and juice. Jones had a black coffee. As Keppler munched and slurped contentedly Appleby produced a crumpled letter from his jacket pocket and passed it over.

'I'd like to visit this place,' he said. 'We've got plenty of time. I don't mind going up there on my own if it makes it any easier.'

'I'm afraid we can't allow you to do that, sir,' said Keppler. He was the older and taller of the two, the one who had saved him from the comb-wielding Idaho housewife.

'We could take him, couldn't we?' said Jones. 'What's to lose?'

'Do you know these people?' asked Keppler. 'Are they expecting you?'

'No,' he said. 'They just wrote out of the blue before I left England and invited me to visit them. I never even got round to replying, I'm afraid. They'll have no idea where I am or what I'm doing.

Unless you guys have alerted the media, of course,' he added with a nervous laugh.

Keppler scowled. Anyone hunting Appleby would be just as likely to find him if they all went back to the hotel, although they had taken the precaution of switching his booking at the last minute. It certainly wouldn't occur to them to look for him at some random address in Harlem. It might even be safer.

'If no one knows he's going there, they won't be waiting for him,' said Keppler to Jones. 'I'll call Henry.'

He went over to the counter, murmuring into his radio and paid the check. Moments later the SUV returned. Keppler stepped outside, took a quick look up and down the street, then waved to Jones who ushered Appleby across the sidewalk and into the back seat.

Jones handed Appleby's letter to the driver. 'Take us here, willya, Henry?'

'What exactly do you propose to do when we get there, Professor?' asked Keppler. 'Do you intend to make yourself known to these people? I would strongly advise against that. In fact, we must insist that you do not reveal your identity to anyone while we're there.'

'That's fine by me,' said Appleby. 'I just want to take a look at the place and get some idea of what they're up to.'

The SUV made its way through the heavy traffic along Broadway to Columbus Circle, then continued north. Appleby looked wistfully out through the tinted windows. It was a bright sunny day and he would have loved to have been walking. With its skyscrapers, steaming underground air-vents and vast red fire tenders, the British often thought of New York as quintessentially American, but to Appleby, apart from The French Quarter of New Orleans perhaps, or parts of downtown Boston, it also seemed to be America's most European city. It was walkable; there was a street life; people sat at pavement cafes, drifted in and out of bars, grocery stores and bookshops or strolled through Central Park, just as they might in London, Paris or Barcelona.

When he first came over in the mid-seventies the place was a mess, full of litter, aggression and lurking menace, and most of the people he spoke to were surly or downright hostile. But over the decades there had been a sea-change. Now the city looked smart. It still felt energised but also friendly and safe. He felt safer here now, in fact, than he did in certain parts of London. He loved it. He wanted to be out there inspecting the shop windows and gazing up at the tops of the glass and concrete canyons, not cooped up in the darkened rear of some air-conditioned, gas-guzzling monstrosity.

The address was in the high 130s between Frederick Douglas and Malcolm X. He had read an article about the area the previous year, how what had once virtually been a black ghetto was being colonised by middle-class whites and was particularly popular with affluent liberals. Hadn't one of the Clintons had an office somewhere round here? In London they would have called it gentrification. Catching glimpses through the windows, the article seemed to be confirmed by the presence of delis with chi-chi names, bistros and coffee-shops.

They drove along Frederick Douglas, then Henry swung the SUV right into a street of smartened-up brick apartment blocks. They pulled up and double-parked outside an ugly Victorian chapel.

'This is it,' said Henry. 'You can have up to an hour if you need it.'

'Wait here,' said Keppler, as he and Jones got out and checked the street. They walked up the steps and opened the door. Keppler went inside for a moment, then came back down to the SUV.

'Looks pretty goddam weird in there to me, but I don't see any immediate danger if you wanna go in.'

The sun was blinding when Appleby stepped out. He looked up at the heavy brick façade. The original name appeared on a panel of moulded terracotta tiles, high over the entrance: 'West Harlem Baptist Mission. 1889'. But it was the hoarding beside the door that caught his attention, a large lurid sign behind a wire mesh: 'The Kindred of the Spirit. North Manhattan Convocation. Elder Celebrant: Jay Ophier.'

Convocation? Elder Celebrant? Where did these names come from?

They certainly weren't in Harker. The movement, if you could call it that, was barely five years old, yet everyone seemed to feel free to make up their own terminology. Harkerism had been splintering and mutating faster than a bird flu virus. Jones stood on the pavement looking uneasily to left and right. Appleby climbed the stairs to the heavy oak doors, Keppler following close behind. He opened the left-side door as quietly as he could and slipped inside. Keppler followed. A few people glanced round at them, apparently without recognition.

To Appleby's astonishment, the place was almost full. The heavy wooden pews had been rearranged to form a half-octagon, so that the congregation looked partly to the front and partly towards each other. This left a U-shaped space at the far end in which stood an empty prayer stool where one person could kneel, resting their arms on the top and facing back towards the crowd. A light-skinned African-American in his mid-thirties was standing in the old Baptist pulpit, though the congregation looked like a 'rainbow coalition', embracing the affluent and the down-at-heel, whites, blacks, East Asians and Hispanics. He even spotted a couple of Jewish men wearing black skull-caps.

Around the walls, seven or eight feet from the ground, were large flaming torches like those in a medieval castle. Then he saw the back wall. Beyond the altar where a Christian church would have displayed a large image of Christ, probably a crucifixion scene, hung a huge painted cloth. It depicted an old man in rich Elizabethan robes and a black, square-cornered cap, staring balefully forward. It was clearly based on the picture he had had on his study wall for over twenty years, the only known authenticated portrait of Sir Nicholas Harker. But in this rendition of the image Sir Nicholas was engulfed in flames. In vivid red, yellow and orange, they reached up towards his waist, then formed a frame around his body and above his head, as if the old man was cupped within giant hands of fire. It could have been an image of the Devil presiding over Hell. No wonder some people thought the cult was Satanic.

The picture also reminded him of a strange portrait he had once seen of an unknown Elizabethan aristocrat. It was thought to be by one of the great miniaturists, Nicholas Hilliard or Isaac Oliver and was called 'Man Against a Background of Flames'. Something about that image had filled him with a vague sense of dread. As he gazed at this extraordinary image of Harker, the feeling returned.

This ominous reverie was broken when everyone started singing, full and hearty from the depths of their bellies. Appleby stopped, rooted to the spot. He knew the song well, 'Let ever bright the spirit burn...' It was Harker's equivalent of a hymn, sung to a rousing tune by Gordon Fairview. Appleby had been involved in commissioning the setting for a Channel 4 programme, and Fairview had become something of a friend, a versatile composer who wrote church choral music, stage shows and television sitcom themes. Appleby still found the song stirring and he had never heard it sung with such uninhibited gusto.

As the last notes of the organ died away, the man in the pulpit – was this 'Elder Celebrant' Jay Ophier himself? – boomed into a microphone.

'Be the Spirit among you. Be the Spirit upon you. Be the Spirit within you, O my Brethren and Sistren! Now are we come to the time of Attestation, Redress and Redemption, O Kindred! Are we ready to Attest?'

'We are ready to Attest!' the congregation replied in ragged unison.

'Then let the Flame of the Spirit be lit!' said the Celebrant, pointing to an object approximately the size and shape of a font, positioned under his pulpit. A man in a cloak stepped forward and touched it with a burning torch. It lit up like the Olympic flame.

'Are we ready to Redress?' the Celebrant declaimed.

'We are ready to Redress!'

'Are we ready to Re-DEEM?'

'We are ready to Redeem!'

'Then who among us will come forward to Attest?' the Celebrant boomed. 'Now remember ye that what is spoke among the Kindred, stays among the Kindred, and only within the Realm of the Kindred.

Do we Pledge our Troth on this, O Kindred?'

'Yea, we Pledge our Troth!'

'Then whosoever will come forward, let them do so now.'

There was a long uncomfortable silence. Eventually a boy of about thirteen or fourteen stumbled out of a pew and shuffled towards the front, head bowed down, staring at the floorboards. He looked up at the Celebrant, as if seeking permission, then kneeled on the prayer stool facing the congregation. Appleby thought he looked Hispanic or possibly Italian-American.

'Welcome, child. What is your name?'

'Tony,' the boy muttered. He spoke quietly but there was a microphone on the prayer-stool too, and his voice filled the chapel.

'Then speak, Tony,' said the Celebrant. 'Know that your Kindred are ready to hearken unto you. To what do you wish to Attest?'

Tony cleared his throat. His voice was weak and nervous.

'It's 'bout my little sister,' he said. There was a long pause. Tony turned his head and looked up at the Celebrant who raised his eyebrows questioningly.

'Las' week she said she goan kill herself,' he said miserably. 'I guess it scared me. I think maybe she meant it…'

The congregation went silent.

'And why should this bring you to Attest, my child?'

'Cause it's all my fault,' he said, almost pleading.

'Why, son?'

Tony hesitated for what seemed an eternity, then blurted it out. 'Cause I done something bad – something real, real bad.'

There was another painful pause.

'Speak, child,' said the Celebrant. 'Be not afeard. You are safe among your Kindred here.'

The boy seemed to gulp as he found the courage to speak. 'I did something…when we was on our own in the 'partment.'

A subdued murmuring spread around the chapel.

'Attest to your Kindred of what you did, child,' said the Celebrant, 'so that we may purge your Spirit. Did you strike her?'

Tony shook his head.

'Then what did you do?'

'Sex,' he whispered.

Appleby heard a ripple of subdued gasps.

'How old is your sister, child?'

By now the boy could barely speak. 'She ten.'

There were more gasps, followed by angry mutterings. Now Tony seemed to feel an urge to explain himself.

'I only wanted to look at her.' He was mumbling again, but the microphone picked up his words with unforgiving clarity. 'None of my homies is virgins. But I ain't never even seen no pussy for real before. So I asked her to show me…and she did.'

Appleby leaned towards Keppler. 'He looks Latino, but isn't he talking like a black gangster?' he whispered.

'They all talk that way,' Keppler muttered under his breath. 'It's kind of *de rigueur*, I guess.'

'Did she do this willingly, child?' the Celebrant continued.

'Not so much. I didn't beat up on her or nothin', but I guess I shouted some. Anyways, when I saw it, I just wanted it so bad I thought I was gonna bust…' Tony stalled, unable to continue.

'Are you telling us that you forced yourself upon your sister, child?' The Celebrant sounded grave but calm.

Tony nodded and buried his face in his hands. His shoulders were heaving with sobs of shame. Appleby thought the lad was in the grip of some terrible catharsis. 'I'm sorry, Maria!' Tony gulped through his fingers. 'I'm so, so sorry! I'm sorry, I'm sorry, I'm sorry…'

The congregation was buzzing with shock and indignation. A middle-aged black woman stood up at the back, shook her fist and shouted something which Appleby didn't catch.

'Be collected, Brethren and Sistren,' said the Celebrant calmly. 'This is a brave young man!' he said emphatically, 'to come before his Kindred and attest to so grave a transgression. However heinous his offence, do we acknowledge this child's moral courage and respect it?'

'We acknowledge his courage and respect it,' came a few mumbled replies.

'Who is Aggrieved in this matter?'

'I am Aggrieved!' called a middle-aged woman after a brief silence. The boy had been sitting next to her. Appleby guessed she must be his mother. A young girl was gripping her side, her face thrust deep into the woman's chest.

'State your connection to this boy,' said the Celebrant gently.

'I am his mother,' said the woman in an anguished wail, '...and he just said he raped my little girl!'

'Then ye are indeed Aggrieved, Sister. You may pause to reflect if you so wish, as is our custom in matters of such gravity, but if you are ready to speak now, then tell your Kindred how ye would seek redress?'

'I don't know. It's such a terrible, terrible thing, he's just told us. I don't know what to say.' Raw anger was mounting inside her. 'Do you think he can ever make that right for my girl? Cause he cain't! Not never, ever, ever!'

'Is the victim here among us?' asked the Celebrant.

The woman turned to the little girl, who looked towards the pulpit.

The Celebrant's voice dropped to a new level of gentleness. 'Do you wish to speak of this matter to your Kindred, child? No blame will attach to you, if you do not.'

The girl looked up at her mother, then stood up shakily.

'Child, your brother has Attested before us all that he did you a most grievous wrong,' said the Celebrant softly. 'We will take counsel among the Elders of the Kindred on this matter, but in the meantime you are entitled by the practice of our Kindred to seek Redress of him. That means that if you can think of anything your brother can do that might make this better in any way, then you are entitled to ask it of him, here in front of everyone. Do you understand that, my child?'

The girl nodded.

'Is there anything your brother can say or do to make Redress for this grievous injury which he has inflicted upon you?'

The girl blinked, then looked at her mother. Finally she found her voice.

'He cain't give me what I want,' she said simply. ''Cause I know I ain't pure no more. He took that from me forever and he cain't give it back! I don't know what to ask for…'

The mother groaned. Suddenly the girl's suppressed rage and indignation erupted. '*He really hurt me!*' she cried. 'I'd like to git some big nasty man to hold him down and shove somethin' real big and hard right up his ass, even though he's shoutin' for him to stop, so he knows what that *feels like*!' she yelled.

Christ almighty, thought Appleby. These kids know far too much, far too young. Bloody internet.

'Tell him to cut off his own dick!' called a voice from the back.

'Make him brand his own forehead with a capital "R" for Rapist,' shouted another.

'I must prevail upon all Kindred to remain calm,' said the Celebrant solemnly. 'Has the boy not Attested of his own free will? Is his remorse not genuine? Girl, do you seek such violent Redress?'

Almost as quickly as the girl's rage had flared up, it seemed to ebb away.

'Them things'd just make him meaner, I guess,' she said. 'But he gotta show me respect! And he gotta respect *Momma*!'

'And how do you think that he might do that for you, my child?'

'Well I guess he could start by turning over the crack and that hard liquor he got hid in he old toy box! And he gotta stop lying to Momma and go to school every day, even if it means he gotta take a beating from he posse. That'd make a start, I guess.'

The girl paused as more waves of indignant murmuring spread round the room. 'I'm glad he said he's sorry,' she said quietly, 'like he really meant it.' And she sank back into her mother's arms.

The Celebrant turned to the boy. 'Child, do you pledge to begin by making this Redress as your wronged sister has asked of you?'

Tony looked shaken and drained, rocked by his sister's new revelations. Yet somehow, Appleby thought, he seemed suffused with relief, as though this bizarre procedure had opened a door for him to regain an innocence he had never really wanted to lose.

'Yessir. Yessir. I surely will. I most surely will.'

'And will you return to this place in a month to Attest that you have made Redress and, that Redress being confirmed by the Witness of others, to receive the Redemption of your Kindred?'

'Yessir, I surely will.'

'And will you then seal your Redemption, by submitting to the Purgation by Fire?'

'Yessir, I'll do that too.'

'Then go in the peace of the Spirit of your Kindred.'

The boy walked, head bowed, back to his seat beside his mother, who cradled his head against her shoulder. They were sitting towards the front, but Appleby thought he could see both the mother's and the boy's shoulders shaking violently.

Appleby was stunned. What on earth was 'the Purgation by Fire'?

'Let's go,' he said to Keppler. 'I've seen enough.'

'It's fucking Jerry Springer in there,' muttered Keppler as they stepped back into the blinding sunlight. 'I'm gonna have to report this to the NYPD…not to mention the Children's Services Administration…and the Fire Department. Did you know about this, Professor? Did you know what's been going on in there?'

'No,' said Appleby, taking a last look through the open doors at the burning figure of Sir Nicholas. 'All I know is that people call them "Flamers". I had no idea…this isn't how it was meant to be…'

York

'So you're pretty serious about your Christian art historian, then?' asked Pete Elyot. 'How long have you been seeing her now?'

'Nearly two years,' said Appleby, swirling the last of his scotch around the remains of the ice-cubes in the bottom of his glass.

It was a Sunday night. He had just waved Jenny off at York station, and they were sitting in a quiet corner of the Langwith College Senior Common Room. Pete was his closest friend on campus, a flamboyantly camp politics lecturer, specialising in something called 'Cultural Ideologies'. They had been friends since their undergraduate days.

Pete sipped his Campari-soda and gave a wicked little grin. 'Isn't she a bit wholesome for you? A bit of a – how can I put this? – a bit of a National Trust gift-shop tea-towel type?'

'Don't be so fucking patronising!' Appleby snorted. 'She's as sharp as you are, in her way, and, yes, I am serious about her. She's met my family, for God's sake.'

'Righty-ho,' said Pete, raising an eyebrow. 'It's just that I heard on the grapevine that you had a dalliance with a certain feminist literature lecturer at that symposium in Sussex.'

'Christ!' said Appleby. 'How did you hear about that? It was a stupid mistake. One night, and I don't know why I did it. I made a complete fool of myself, if you must know.'

'Oh?'

'Let's just say my heart wasn't in it. I think I really pissed her off, as a matter of fact.'

'So why did you do it?'

'I don't know. Habit, I suppose.' He threw his head back. 'To prove I can still pull...'

'I hate to say this, sweetie, but you heteros are just so boringly predictable. You're all unresolved conflicts on two legs.'

'Unresolved conflicts? That's rich coming from you! You're the only man I know who can make late Marxist theory sound like a sketch

73

from Round the Horn.' He assumed a Kenneth Williams voice. 'Ooooh, Mr Althusser! What a bona *contradiction* you've got there! You can analyse my *overdetermination* any time you like!'

'Touché,' Pete grinned, but he was not to be deflected. 'You know I'm right, though, don't you? You want the comforts of monogamy and the thrill of screwing around. You want to have your cake and eat it. And then have someone else's cake. And then eat that.'

'Not like you lot, then. All you want is to get married and settle down in a nice little semi with "Duncruisin" on the front gate.'

'We play by different rules, you know that. The difference is that we're honest about it...well, sometimes.'

'Well I won't be snaffling any more extra cake. Not while I'm with Jenny anyway.'

'While?' said Pete. 'Aye, there's the rub! She hasn't given you the ultimatum yet then?'

'Ultimatum? What on earth are you talking about?'

'Isn't that what happens? You rub along happily for a few years. You're genuinely fond of her. In fact you probably love her in your sad petit-bourgeois suburban kind of way. And you've got regular sex on tap without all that tedious getting-to-know-you palaver. But all the time there's this wicked little voice in the back of your head, saying "This is all very nice, old chap, but who knows? Maybe something even more exciting will come along one of these days." Then after a while she starts dropping little hints or probing you with questions about what you expect to be doing in the future. So you fob her off with vague non-committal answers, because you really don't want to have to think about all that. But gradually the pressure builds up. The ticking of her biological clock gets louder and louder until she can't stand it any more. Then BANG! You get the ultimatum...'

'My god!' said Appleby. 'Where did that come from? And how in hell would you know?'

'I'm a seasoned observer of human nature, my love, in case you hadn't noticed.'

'Well it's not like that. Not like that at all.'

A week later Appleby got the ultimatum.

*

After that summer in Salisbury, Jenny had gone back to the flat she shared with two friends in Muswell Hill and continued writing and giving lectures on medieval art. Appleby had returned to York, and they became what he called 'commuter-daters', alternating weekend trips up and down the East Coast mainline.

They developed a routine, grumbling about shabby, squalid Kings Cross station with its hideous modern forecourt while extolling the beauty of the curving Victorian station at York. They became aficionados of the refreshment facilities, taking a childish pleasure in comparing notes on the meat pies and slabs of cold bread-pudding available at each.

They planned expeditions around their research, trying to synchronise her visits to cathedrals and museums with his investigations in council record offices and local libraries. On one such trip they found themselves by the tomb of the Earl of Arundel and his wife in Chichester Cathedral. Someone had attached a copy of Philip Larkin's poem to a pillar by the reclining stone effigies. Jenny read it aloud.

'*What will survive of us is love.* That's so touching,' she said when she reached the end.

'Yeah, but look at that penultimate line,' Appleby said. '*Our ALMOST instinct, ALMOST true.* That's so typical of Larkin. He always undercuts sentimentality. It's brilliant.'

'That's because he's a knotted old cynic who can't bear to admit that he might actually have feelings,' Jenny retorted. 'It's the line of a man who's afraid of love.'

She sounded genuinely annoyed, so he left the issue hanging as they walked on, but it left him with a lingering unease.

At the time he hadn't wanted to think about the possible implications of this mild disagreement, but he remembered it after the conversation with Pete. Were their views of love and relationships really compatible?

He realised that they always enjoyed their time together without ever discussing such matters in any depth. They were easy together, warm and intimate, but were they just skating on the surface? Was that why he had found it so easy to lapse into infidelity?

The next day Jenny rang him excitedly. She had bought a new car, a third-hand Peugeot 304, and would drive up to see him that Friday night. On the Saturday morning she badgered him into going to the Minster. He realised he had not actually been inside since his first year as an undergraduate. He watched her sketching the grey grisaille glass in one of the five lancet windows in the north transept, entranced again by the elegance of her fingers and her nimble strokes with the charcoal. Then he wandered around on his own. After an hour Jenny found him gazing up at the intricately decorated vaulting of the ceiling under the central tower.

'I'd completely forgotten how fabulous this place is,' he said. 'Thanks for making me come. It's mind-blowing.'

'Now tell me it's all the accidental product of evolutionary mutation,' she said.

He looked for an ironical twinkle in her eyes, but they glowed with the quiet calm of absolute sincerity. He frowned. They had an unspoken pact never to argue about her religious beliefs, or his lack of them, and she had just broken it. But he really didn't want to get into a metaphysical debate, so he let it pass. They decided to drive out to Rievaulx Abbey for a picnic. After lunch they lay on a bank overlooking the absurdly picturesque ruins and slept in each other's arms in the glorious June heat.

Back in his flat they showered, made love, dozed for a while, made love again, then showered again. He cooked lasagne for the first time, using the recipe in his new copy of Delia Smith's *Complete Cookery Course*. Jenny was washing up while he watched the European Cup on his tiny new portable TV and drank Sainsbury's own label Chianti. It had been a perfect day. Then she called across to him from the kitchenette.

'Jimmy?'

'Uh-huh?'

'How do you see our future together?' There was a short pause. 'I mean, do you think we have a future together?'

Exactly as Pete had predicted, he fluffed and stumbled. He 'um-ed and ah-ed', and failed to give anything remotely resembling a straight answer. He realised what he was doing, but he couldn't help himself. He simply did not want to be put on the spot like that.

'Forget it,' said Jenny after a while. 'I get the picture.'

She turned her back on him in bed that night. The next morning she went straight back to Muswell Hill. She maintained a brisk, friendly manner, but it was plain enough that she was hurt, angry and deeply miserable. On the Tuesday he got a letter breaking it off.

*

For the rest of the day Appleby tried to unpack his feelings from the jumbled emotional holdall that passed for his mind. Finally he called Pete, who asked him over to his flat.

'Try this,' said Pete, pulling a bottle of Polish bison-grass vodka from his freezer. 'The spoils of a little conquest I made down in Soho. I think you'll admire its presumption. I certainly admired his.…Now what's on your mind, sweetie? Spill all.'

'You were absolutely right,' Appleby said, 'about the ultimatum, not that I realised it was an ultimatum. Not until it was too late, that is. Anyway, I completely fluffed it. She's chucked me.'

'And now you're heart-broken?'

'Yes…No…I don't know…'

'You can't not *know* if you're heart-broken, honey-bunch. For whatever reason you don't feel ready to breed mini-Appleby-ettes with this woman, let alone grow old and fat together. Just tell your Uncle Pete why not, and then maybe you'll understand it yourself.'

'I do love her. I realise just how much now. It's just that there's something I'd miss.'

'The thrill of the chase?'

'Not exactly. Do you remember that place I had on Bootham in the second year?'

'With those *dreary* Sealed Knotters? How could I forget that?'

'It had one of those old wall-mounted gas boilers. You turned on the hot tap and there was this deathly silence for a few seconds, and then it went WHOOMPH and ignited.'

'Ye-e-es?' said Pete.

'Well hasn't that ever happened to you? When you meet someone you really fancy, and there's this pause, and then something sparks inside you and you just go WHOOMPH! And it's absolutely the most fantastic feeling in the world. It's almost spiritual. Well I just can't face the thought of that never happening again…Or what if I settled down with Jenny and it happened anyway with someone else?'

'WHOOMPH, eh?' said Pete reflectively. 'I'm probably more of a PHWOOAR! man myself, to be honest.' He took another slug of vodka. 'Isn't this delicious? So fragrant.'

'It's too cold. It's giving me a headache,' said Appleby.

'Okay,' said Pete. 'I'll tell you what I think. I always thought you were rather in thrall to that incorrigible rogue Farnstable. Now he's definitely a PHWOOAR! man too, but he can get away with it. But you're not like that. You really aren't. Forget about those WHOOMPHs. How many of them actually worked out for you?'

Appleby shrugged.

'You need to work out who you are, Jimmy my sweet, and what you want out of life. And that's all I've got to say on the matter. Now let's get bladdered.'

The next day he spent his free time striding around the outer edges of the campus or lurking disconsolately in the topiaried yew garden behind the registry offices in Heslington Hall. Then he rang his sister. Kate was horrified. She and Jenny had hit it off rather well when they had met.

'She's too bloody good for you,' she told him sharply when he tried to explain his inner turmoil. 'If you feel like that you don't bloody deserve her.'

By Thursday night he had come to the conclusion that he was an immature fantasist and a complete mug who didn't know when he was well off. On Friday evening he caught a train to London. By the time he came back on Sunday night, though they were both considerably bruised emotionally, he and Jenny were reconciled.

*

So he was in an unfamiliar mood, both chastened and elated when he collected his mail from the staff pigeon-holes the following Monday morning.

He had been pursuing the business of what he now called the 'Swively Massacre', on and off since their weekend in the village. The Sunday morning after Jenny's breakthrough orgasm, they had walked out to the site of Farthingwell Meadows, and identified what they thought was the most likely location of the house. The patch of ground was overgrown now, covered with ferns and bracken so that, even in late summer, their feet and lower legs were damp and scratched by the time they left.

But Appleby convinced himself that he could make out the ridges of slightly higher ground described by the Reverend Trott, running under the vegetation, and that these formed a broken pattern of rect-angles. He made a rough sketch of the layout on a small spiral-bound note-pad. Meanwhile Jenny, who had brought a couple of old carrier bags 'just in case', was busy filling one with blackberries and another with wild mushrooms.

They got back to Swively in time to catch the end of Holy Communion. Jenny apologised to the vicar for missing the service. He nodded curtly and introduced himself as Julian Ferriby. He was a tall, sour-faced man in his mid-forties, but when Appleby explained his interest in the village he brightened up. Yes, he would be delighted to show them the parish registers. It would break the tedium of another routine Sunday. He kept them in a secure storage room in his vicarage in Wolvington these days, he said, and invited them over.

He could spare them half an hour before leaving for Evensong in another village.

'That was the Reverend Trott's house,' he told them as they walked to their cars past Swively's magnificent old Queen Anne vicarage. 'I'd have loved to live there.'

'So why don't you?' asked Appleby.

'It was sold off five years ago,' he said with ill-concealed resentment. 'A London insurance broker bought it as a weekend home. Never bloody there, of course.'

They followed his nippy little Volkswagen to Wolvington, the Morris Minor struggling to keep up. The new vicarage was detached and spacious, but modern and almost completely without character. Ferriby's wife Gloria was short, plump and nervy. She gave them her home-made sloe gin and shortbread, which they sipped and nibbled while her husband dug out the relevant volumes.

It did not take long to establish that the Reverend Trott's account of the disappearance of the Harkers and Cranhams from the parish records was correct. The only point of possible significance – and again none of them had any idea what to make of it – was that five Harker and three Cranham children, two children called Lovelock, and five called Wainwright, born between 1570 and 1595, all shared the same middle-name. They were all called 'Spirit.'

Both the Ferribys said they had seen the Reverend Trott's history, many years ago when they first came to the area. Gloria said she used to visit 'two old codgers', both in their nineties, who shared a cottage near Sneckbridge Castle. She was sure they had told her that the story of the soldiers coming and burning the manor house was true. She hadn't set much store by it at the time, though. The old men were permanently sloshed on foul-smelling home-made scrumpy. Their cottage was filthy and overrun with ferrets, and the other villagers all said they were barking mad.

And that was that. The village, the vicar and the parish records seemed to have no more information to yield. After that the research became a slow, frustrating process. He still had no clear understanding of what might really have happened or why.

A few months later he had discovered by pure chance that there was a portrait of Sir Nicholas Harker in a private collection in Berkshire, an exquisite miniature, showing a gaunt elderly man with haunted, limpid eyes and a long grey beard. He wore an elaborately embroidered gown, a simple white ruff and a black woollen cap with square corners. On the back were the words '*Sir Nickolas Harker, Bart. Mystickal schollar and Hereticke. Wyltshire, 1589*'. The owner had let him take a photograph which he enlarged and mounted in a clip-frame. It had been on his study wall ever since.

In the Public Records Office in London, he found legal documents confirming the granting of two adjoining Swively estates to Donald, the illegitimate son of William of Estrick, a favourite of King James VI and I. The grant included '*all the Faire Meades at Farthingweel.*' Yet he could find no trace of the Swively Harkers or Cranhams beyond 1594, nor any document explaining how the estates came into the possession of the King.

The archivists of the Church of England said that, apart from what he may have seen in Salisbury, they had no records of any kind relating to such an incident. He trawled through the archives of the various Wiltshire courts in case they yielded any clues, but bizarrely, there were no records of anyone from Swively standing trial for anything at all for the last four decades of the sixteenth century. 'Whatever dreadful heresy they were practising, it seems to have made them remarkably well behaved!' he told Jenny.

Then a researcher he met at a conference on Tudor history in Bristol directed him to a short memoir by a Yorkshire wool merchant called Amos Jowatt. The only copy was in the British Library, then still housed in the British Museum. Appleby read it in the vast circular reading-room, where his old inspiration Karl Marx once worked on '*Das Kapital.*' He wondered what the founder of international communism would have made of it all. Not much, probably.

In his memoir Jowatt boasted that, while waiting to take ship at Dover in 1598, he had been approached in a tavern by an agent of Sir Robert Cecil called Ephraim Jynes. Jynes haunted the port, looking for men who might do a little light espionage on behalf of the Crown when their business took them abroad. The Queen's Chancellor had 'intelligencers' in every important city in Europe, but merchants, Jynes explained, often came by useful information in the pursuit of their trade, and could innocently ask questions which might provoke suspicion in others. For a modest remuneration, Jowatt had provided titbits on a number of matters during his many trips to the continent.

On one journey, at Cecil's specific request, Jynes asked Jowatt to pose as a friend of one Thomas Cranham of Swively, Wiltshire and make enquiries as to his whereabouts in the markets of Flanders. He provided a brief biography of the man, so that Jowatt could appear convincing if challenged, but refused to explain why Cecil, and his father Lord Burghley before him, had been hunting him for four years. A Dutch cloth merchant Jowatt met in Ghent said he had been introduced to an Englishman called 'Krannem' in a tavern in Eindhoven two years previously. Otherwise, he had discovered nothing.

Jowatt's spying career ended abruptly when he learned that Ephraim Jynes had been run through in a drunken tavern brawl. He had been caught, literally, rolling loaded dice. After that Jowatt's journal became a tedious list of commercial transactions, interspersed with self-regarding reflections on his outstanding qualities as a husband and father.

A more intriguing lead had arrived four months before Appleby's near-rift with Jenny. A young lecturer at Lancaster University called Will Richardson was making a study of Roman Catholic recusancy, the refusal to attend the new Anglican church services, among the landed gentry of Elizabethan England, and had come upon the correspondence of a minor Devon aristocrat called Sir Richard Torville.

Torville was an enthusiastic huntsman, swordsman, a scholar and an extremely minor poet. (His sonnets in particular were quite spectacularly bad, said Richardson). Though never a mariner himself, Torville was fascinated by the sea and had invested heavily in several expeditions to Africa and the Americas. ('I guess the man was an early slave-trader,' wrote Richardson). He had met all the leading explorers and privateers of the day including Sir Francis Drake, Sir Richard Grenville (whom he detested as 'that lothesome braggart') and his own distant cousin by marriage, Sir Walter Raleigh.

Inconveniently Torville's letters had been bought in a job lot by Ohio State University. Apparently one of his descendants was an early grandee of the city of Columbus. But after a little horse-trading, an Ohio historian had agreed to make copies of a few potentially relevant letters and an envelope full of heavy grey Xerox sheets duly appeared in Appleby's in-tray in the History Department office.

Only one proved useful, but it was particularly tantalising. Torville had been in the habit of writing long, descriptive letters to his younger sister on the family estate, lacing them with moral observations and brotherly advice. He thought London was a moral cess-pit, 'a stew' as he called it, but seemed to take a salacious pleasure in his own graphic accounts of the city's many depravities. He had visited the capital in 1592, though he soon scurried home for fear of the plague that broke out that year. But not before attending a lavish feast given by Sir Walter Raleigh in Durham House, his showy London home on the Strand, which he described in detail in a letter home.

As the evening wore on, Torville wrote, some of the company became increasingly drunken and indiscreet. The playwright Christopher Marlowe was there, *'a venomous popinjay'*, according to Torville, complaining that Will Shakespeare *'was a sneak-thief and a pilferer, who "doth look upon my tragedies as his privy hunting-ground, like some cut-purse in a crowded fair".'* Whereupon some *'young whelp of a nephew'* of Sir Walter's declared that all the men of London's theatre companies were *'the most rambunctious pack of turd-nudgers and lick-rapiers a man could ever hope to fall among, in especial that upstart bumpkin Shakspere who, like the Lord of the Scriptures, both giveth and taketh, and does so without Consideration of Years, Sex or Station in the Order of the Kingdom of Beasts.'* Sir

Walter had replied that *'no prancing Player or snivelling Scratch-quill could surprise or discomfort a man who had passed a month or twain at sea. At this all had roared most heartily.'*

What had really bothered Torville, it turned out, was not all this scurrilous banter about sexual deviancy. It was the whiff of atheism. At least two among the company had openly vaunted the fact that they had *'no belief in the Divinity of Our Lord and Saviour or yet in the being of the One True God. One had raged that all religious doctrines were but the purest quackery. Sir Walter had moved quickly to steer his riotous young companions away from this theme, yet made no strong protest against such fiendish Blasphemies, treating all as mere jest.'* Only Torville himself had stood up to denounce the outrage, whereupon he was *'roundly mocked at, pelted with sweetmeats and told to be seated.'* Otherwise the entire company had acquiesced. Torville then listed all the names he could remember of those present, with a stern admonition to his sister to be most wary if she ever found herself in the company of any at some great house in Devon. Better still, to shun them altogether.

It occurred to Appleby that Torville was like some sixteenth century Mr Pooter, and he wondered if the rest of his letters were as naively pompous. At the end of his black-list, he wrote that he was seated beside an older man, *'most excellent courteious'*, a relative of Sir Walter's through his wife, who had sat quietly throughout the feasting, keeping his own counsel. His name was Sir Nicholas Harker.

Of course, Appleby had read the theories that Raleigh was a secret atheist and that he had a cabal of intimates, possibly including Marlowe, which had been assigned the suitably Hammer Horror title of 'The School of Night' from a line in Shakespeare's 'Love's Labours Lost'. One night spent in the company of a bunch of loud-mouthed drunks was hardly conclusive evidence of anything, of course, yet the letter at least raised the intriguing possibility that Harker too might have secretly entertained atheist ideas.

And yet. And yet, that certainly was not enough to explain the rumours of 'rites' or any horrendous decision, possibly taken on the advice of Archbishop Whitgift himself, to massacre his entire family, their servants and a good few friends and neighbours too. In the end, he thought, the Torville letter was just another straw in the wind.

On another occasion he was examining the Elizabethan portraits at the Victoria and Albert Museum when he came upon a miniature simply listed as 'A Man against A Background of Flames'. The unknown sitter was a handsome young aristocrat, standing thoughfully in front of a brilliant curtain of fire. There was no connection with Harker, of course, but something about this image sent a chill down Appleby's spine, as if it was a portrait of himself, and the flames somehow presaged his own fate.

Four months later, when he walked down to the porter's lodge the morning after his reconciliation with Jenny, there was another letter waiting for him. It was from the 'Librarian and Keeper of Muniments' at Salisbury Cathedral. Would Appleby like to come and see a most unusual book which had just been donated by the widow of an eccentric local collector? Nobody had even known this volume existed, and the author was anonymous, simply styling himself 'A Trew Man of God'. It was entitled 'On The Expurgation of Heresies in the See of Salisbury in the Raigne of Our Late Soveraigne.' It was dated 1622, so the 'Late Soveraigne' had to be Elizabeth I.

A third ingredient was stirred into Appleby's heady emotional cock-tail that morning. Not only was he chastened and elated over his reconciliation with Jenny; he was now burning with curiosity.

Amsterdam

TC: Methinks that any man that doth toy with others through deceit or knavish trickery, doth himself become the plaything of the Devil.

NH: Nay good Tom, he becometh the plaything of his own lies, and most speedily thereafter, their slave.

—*Sir Thomas Cranham & Sir Nicholas Harker,*
The Colloquies, Book 1, No 12

Before he left the Renaissance Institute offices on his 'dirty weekend' with Iris, Appleby had asked van Stumpe what he proposed to do with the chest of documents. He was most gratified to be given the first look, he explained, but what was to happen next?

Van Stumpe had evidently been giving this matter a great deal of thought. There were certain procedures to be followed and there could be legal complications of various kinds, he explained, but he believed that everything would eventually become the property of the Dutch state. That might seem like good news for van Stumpe and the Institute, but in practice they would have little control, if any, over what happened to the documents. If they were given to another institution, a museum or another library, they would be out in the public domain. Appleby would have to negotiate access anew, probably with dozens of other scholars clamouring to get a look.

If they were deemed to be the property of the owner of the farmhouse where they were found, the situation could be even more difficult. Once their financial value was appreciated, it might be decided to sell them on the open market. In that case they would almost certainly go to some institution in America or, worse, to a wealthy private collector, where scholars would have absolutely no guarantee of access. It was also quite possible that the collection would be broken up and sold off in job lots.

At the moment, he said, he was playing for time. His director knew that the chest contained documents in English and that it had been hidden away some time in the early seventeenth century. But van Stumpe, who had been given the job of assessing their importance, was being deliberately vague about what they were. He was implying that, as far as he could tell, they were all rather humdrum, mostly related to trade and agriculture, nothing they hadn't seen a thousand times before. He had asked for a few weeks to bring in an expert from England to help him sift through the mass of material, before any further action was taken. If Appleby wanted to fill this role, the job was his. The work would be unpaid, of course, but it would give him a head-start over the competition.

'Aren't you worried that your superiors will find out what you've really got? That you've been spinning them a line?' Appleby had asked.

'Not so much at all, my good friend. I am an archivist. My loyalty is to the documents, not the owner of the archive! That's why my hope is that you will be accepting this task. You have made some considerable personal investing in this subject, and I know out of my experience that you are an honest man, intellectually-speaking.'

Appleby suddenly discovered that he liked the elderly librarian a great deal more than he had realised.

'Thank you very much, Mijnheer van Stumpe.'

'Doctor Appleby, you may please to call me Piet if you so prefer it.'

'Certainly er – Piet.' He was so used to thinking of him as 'van Stumpe' that the forename seemed to stick awkwardly in his throat.

'And may I perhaps address you with James?'

'Of course, Piet,' said Appleby with new warmth. 'I'd love to do this. I have to go back to Cambridge tomorrow, but I'm sure I can sort something out.'

'My dear friend James, I cannot describe to you my delight that you are agreeable to be helping in this matter. Now I can have full assured that these most remarkable set of papers will be properly understood, catalogued and explained for the world by a scholar who is knowing their own business before it may become like some commodity of the international market for antiquities. I cannot tell you what a relief this is to me. But please, we must now begin most quickly!'

*

The morning after Iris left his rooms in Despenser, Appleby began to mull over the implications of this conversation. He realised he could be facing a rather difficult problem. And it wasn't just a matter of getting rid of the debris from Iris's spliff, with the cleaner due at any moment. He solved that one by scooping everything into an empty Sainsbury's carrier bag, rolling it up and stuffing it into his briefcase for future disposal.

Van Stumpe was offering him unlimited access to the documents, but within a strictly limited window. He had only had a brief taster of the contents of that chest, but what he had seen suggested they were so fascinating, so strange and so unexpected that they would cause a massive stir. If they were indeed genuine, they might provide an entirely new perspective on Elizabethan religious and social history. If, as he suspected, they would also confirm that the massacre had taken place and reveal the reason for it, there would be a dramatic human story in there too. At the very least it would make a subject for a remarkable scholarly study. If it was handled skilfully, perhaps he would have the raw material for a best-seller.

His quandary was this; he was committed to eight more weeks working on the confounded Toft Bequest. The simplest way to get a few weeks off to work on van Stumpe's treasure trove should have been to come clean and ask Despenser and York to agree between them to release him. He couldn't see Featherstone, the Dean of Humanities at York objecting, and Professor Howland, the Head of History couldn't care less what he did anyway. The faculty might not even expect him to take the time from his annual leave, if they thought the project might yield valuable points for the university's research score.

Despenser was another matter. He didn't trust J.D. Clovis any further than he could throw him, and J.D. Clovis was a very large man. If he gave him any real notion of what it was he wanted to work on, he had no doubt whatsoever that Clovis would try to find a way of sabotaging him and manoeuvring a Despenser man into his shoes. Van Stumpe might be on Appleby's side, but he had heard enough about the Master by now to know that when it came to promoting his college and its staff, he was devious, unscrupulous and frighteningly well-connected. Appleby could think of at least two Despenser historians, as well as an Elizabethan literature specialist and a theologian who would have sold their grannies to cannibals to get hold of this material.

A possible solution suggested itself that afternoon.

He was having one of his occasional supervisions with a clever and funny, if slightly fey post-graduate student called Claire Tenterden. Claire's father had risen to run a leading London publishing house, and when she wasn't out on the razzle with her friends, her parents had allowed her to attend their soirees and dinner parties in the family's Kensington home since she was fourteen. She seemed to have met everyone who had published a book of significance in the last ten years, though her anecdotes about London's literary elite tended to be on the lines of 'he had the most terrifying wart on his nose,' or 'she once tried to fondle my sister's breasts.' If she hadn't been so atten- tive to what he had to say, Appleby would have found her downright intimidating.

He had come across young women rather like her at York, girls from wealthy, influential families, attractive if not conventionally beautiful who had grown up surrounded by ultra-confident, sometimes neurotically high-achieving males. They seemed to develop a certain good-humoured detachment about life, a wry satirical distance. Though highly intelligent, they did not expect or seek to take centre-stage themselves, but they were gold-mines of shrewd, informed insights into the psychological quirks of the powerful.

In some ways, Claire's doctoral thesis seemed to parallel her own situation. She was working on a study of the wives of Elizabethan aristocrats and their role in the management of the great country houses. Appleby found it fascinating. Every household was different, and it was a far more complex and idiosyncratic business than he had ever imagined. She was uncovering wonderful material without needing anything but the most general guidance from him.

So their supervision sessions always seemed to veer off the subject into amusing conversations about anything and everything else. This time they found themselves talking about the ways academic historians could cash in on their subject with the general public, swapping anecdotes about famous biographers (Claire seemed to have met dozens of them) and popular TV historians. She had met most of them too.

'Or one could always write a bodice-ripper,' she said. 'That's what I'll probably do when I've got my fud.'

'Your fud?'

'Sorry,' she laughed. 'That's what I call my PhD. Or rather my putative PhD. Who knows, I may run off and marry a hedge-fund manager before it's finished and spend the rest of my life shopping for Jimmy Choos. I'm deadly serious about the novel, though. Just think of all the stories we historians come across. I've already got enough material for a complete Elizabethan soap opera. You could do it too, you know. You must come across fabulously entertaining stories all the time, what with all those poor starving peasants and things. Okay, well maybe not them, but didn't you say your first study was the navy? You could write swashbuckling Hornblower yarns only with Drake lurking in the wings instead of Nelson. Only you wouldn't. You'd write something frightfully clever like Patrick O'Brian. Did I tell you about the time my father drove us to his house in the South of France, and he wouldn't let us in?'

*

That night Appleby pushed a letter through the letterbox on the front door of the Master's Lodge. Then he emailed a slightly different version to the Dean of Humanities at York.

The gist of it was this. Appleby had just received a once-in-a-lifetime offer from an old friend to write a film-script set during the English intervention in the Dutch Revolt against Spain. The hero would be Sir Philip Sidney, and the story would culminate in the courtier-poet's heroic death: working title: 'A Greater Need'. Before he could start (and they were on a tight schedule) it was essential that he do some research in the Netherlands. He would like to suspend his work on the Toft Bequest for five weeks, confining his teaching duties at Despenser to Mondays or Fridays only. He pointed out that he could easily fit his two lectures and occasional supervisions into one day a week, and he would formally undertake to make up the lost twenty days working on the Toft archive during his summer vacation. As a token of his gratitude to the college he would ensure that the Master was prominently acknowledged in the credits of the finished film. Naturally he did not include that last ingratiating embellishment in the email to York.

It was an unorthodox proposal, and it wouldn't be easy for him if they agreed to it. Even when budget flights were available, the accumulated travel would be hideously expensive and it would mean he would never get more than one day a week back in York, which would make it even harder to spend time with Iris. On the other hand, it should give him just long enough to make full use of van Stumpe's generous offer without alerting any potential competition to his real purpose.

*

The next morning he was summoned across the quadrangle to the Master's Lodge.

When he arrived a plump housekeeper ushered him into the medieval hallway, a room of positively baronial splendour with an ancient carved staircase at the far end, leading up to a minstrels' gallery.

'Dr Appleby, is it?' she asked. 'The Master's in the library. They're expecting you.'

A door opened across the hall, and Clovis appeared. 'Come in, dear boy,' he said, waving Appleby towards him. He was a tall man and stooped over Appleby in a way that bordered on the overbearing. As for this tone of kindly avuncularity, Appleby found that downright sinister. The Master's library was furnished like an old-fashioned gentleman's club with deep green leather arm-chairs, padded seats in the box-windows; tall, highly polished bookcases and the portraits of previous Masters along the walls. There was a faint smell of stale tobacco smoke. It was curiously rich and pungent.

'Do take a seat, Appleton. You know Norman Skyne, of course,' said Clovis, indicating a trim man in his mid-forties.

Professor Skyne was wearing a black mohair polo-neck sweater, a dark suit (Italian, Appleby guessed) and the kind of narrow designer glasses he had seen worn by media executives who wanted to be thought of as razor sharp. They exchanged nods. Skyne was an expert on the late Ancien Regime in France and looked after History at Despenser. He had barely spoken two words to Appleby since his arrival at the college. What was he doing there now?

Clovis took a cigarette from a silver case, tapped the end and lit it. He must have caught the fleeting hint of disapproval on Appleby's face. 'I shan't ask if you mind if I smoke,' he said with a smile. 'Master's prerogative.'

Appleby recognised the smell. They were French, Gitanes presumably. He had read that Clovis had spent time at the École Normale Supérieure as a graduate student. Perhaps he had acquired the habit there, along with numerous influential contacts, no doubt.

'You seem to be in a remarkable hurry to leave us, young man,' said Clovis. By now he was standing by the hearth, with one elbow propped against the chimney-piece, gazing down at Appleby from a considerable height. 'Surely our fabled Despenser hospitality has not failed us?'

'You know the answer to that, you sly old shit,' thought Appleby.

'And you know that I now have to pretend that I haven't noticed how fucking rude you've all been, or I'll end up sounding like some bleating schoolboy.'

'Oh no, it's nothing like that, of course,' he said. 'Actually it's just as I explained in the letter. This is a unique opportunity.'

'Ye-es,' purred Clovis, 'but it's not really the sort of request we would expect from one of our own junior staff. Of course I realise chaps might follow rather different codes of, um, professional practice in the "new" universities, but if you'll allow an old hand to proffer a small word of advice, it's hard to see how writing for the *flicks* will advance your career as a serious historian. Still, that's not really Despenser's concern, is it?' he added with a kindly smile. 'If they're happy to indulge you back at the Railway Museum, I don't think we need to stand in your way.'

'Thank you,' said Appleby. That Railway Museum thing was really pissing him off by now. 'Did you see last week's THES, by the way?' he added testily. 'The university research league table? It was quite interesting. York came out ahead of Cambridge in several disciplines... including Economics.' Appleby was making this up. Pete Elyot had told him that York had done extremely well, but he hadn't actually checked the details. Fortunately neither had they.

'The Times Higher Ed., eh?' said Clovis, raising one eyebrow as if Appleby had just quoted *The News of the World* or *TV Quick*. 'I'm afraid we tend to avoid the Murdoch press here. Populism is all very well – if one is one of the populace.'

Skyne allowed himself a fleeting smirk.

'Now,' Clovis continued. 'Norman and I were intrigued to hear a little more about this "project" of yours. Curious that you've kept this passion for Sir Philip Sidney to yourself all this time. Complicated fellow, I gather. Has he been a hobby of yours for long?'

Appleby sensed that the conversation was about to take an awkward turn.

'Oh, I've always had an interest in the military matters of the era,' he said, trying to appear as complacently blasé as Clovis.

'My doctorate was on Elizabeth's navy, you know.'

'Well the Dutch intervention isn't exactly an under-researched area,' said Skyne. 'Tell me, what do you think of van der Valk's new theory about Sidney's deployment of artillery during the battle of Zutphen?'

'Oh shit!' thought Appleby. 'Who the fuck is van der Valk? The name seems familiar, but why?'

'Rather contentious, in some ways,' he mumbled, hoping to sound quietly sage. 'But I'm not entirely convinced. That's one area where I'd like to see further evidence, really.'

'Ah, wouldn't we all? If only it were there to be seen, eh!' Skyne gave him an indulgent smile. 'Well best of luck with your little venture.'

Skyne suddenly stood up, a clear signal for Appleby to leave. Was that it then? What a relief! It hadn't occurred to him that he might be cross-examined on his invented project. Thank god Skyne hadn't probed more deeply. He realised that all he knew about Sir Philip Sidney came from passing references in books on other subjects. It could be written on the back of a large postcard.

'One last thing, dear boy,' said Clovis. 'Would you do me a small favour?'

'Of course,' said Appleby.

'When this film thingummajig of yours comes to fruition, please don't put my name on the credits,' Clovis flashed him an unctuous half-smile, 'if it's all the same to you.'

Appleby had never been so happy to close a door behind him.

*

'So?' said Clovis after he left.

'He may know everything there is to know about Elizabethan hog-fattening procedures, but he knows about as much about Sir Philip Sidney's military career as my Colombian char-lady.'

'So he was bluffing about that chap's theory. I rather thought so.'

'Indeed he was. There's no historian called van der Valk as far as I know. I just plucked any old Dutch name from the air. And Sidney had nothing to do with deploying artillery. Are you still going to release him?'

'Why not?' said Clovis. 'It's no skin off our nose, as long as he finishes sorting out that dismal archive. But the fellow's clearly up to something – something he wants to conceal from us for some reason. I know we only have the privilege of his services temporarily, but technically he's still our responsibility while he's here. And of course there may be some kind of intellectual property issue, if he actually turns out to be doing anything interesting. We should check the fine print on that exchange agreement. Let's find out what he's really doing. Perhaps we can find a way to keep an eye on him.'

'I may be able to help you out there, J.D.'

'Excellent. In the meantime, I've organised a little "primary research" of my own.'

There was a knock on the door.

'Come!' said Clovis.

A fair-haired, fresh-faced graduate student called Chalmers came in.

'Well!' said Clovis.

'Not much I'm afraid. There were some boarding pass stubs on his desk. He spent the weekend in Amsterdam. He was with someone too. There was a hotel receipt for two people. I couldn't see anything particularly informative, though. Couldn't risk poking around his laptop in case he came back. The only odd thing was a scrap of notepaper by the phone with the name *Harker* scribbled on it followed by three exclamation marks.'

Clovis looked at Skyne. 'Mean anything to you, Norman?'

'Hmm,' said Skyne shrugging. 'The name's vaguely familiar. Can't think why, though.'

'I thought this might come in useful at some point.' Chalmers held up a scrunched up Sainsbury's carrier bag. 'He'd left his briefcase open and this was stuffed inside. I think you'll find it's the remains of a spliff.'

'A what?' said Clovis.

'A "joint", J.D.,' said Skyne helpfully, but Clovis was still non-plussed. 'A "reefer"? Cannabis? Indian hemp?'

'You could always claim it was handed in by a morally outraged cleaner,' said Chalmers.

'Ah!' said Clovis seizing the bag. 'Very astute of you.'

'I'll leave this here then,' said Chalmers, placing a skeleton-key on the chimney-piece.

'Well done, my boy,' said Clovis. 'Your father would be proud of you.'

Heathrow

Appleby had suffered two attempts on his life and lost a tiny piece of his ear in America, but if he thought his troubles would be over once he reached England, he was sorely mistaken.

He had stopped reading all but personal e-mails in the States and refused to respond to any communications from the media. As he left JFK, Keppler had told him to look out for his friend Iris at Heathrow. This puzzled Appleby greatly, but Keppler wouldn't, or couldn't explain why. He had been completely out of communication during the flight. As the plane landed, he knew there would be no escape. He just wanted to get home. Tomorrow he would ring Phyllida and they could work out some sort of strategy.

His story had been all over the American press, and the tabloid 'New York Today' had carried a detailed account of his disastrous appearance on Stote Longbaum, gloatingly recounting all the worst insults that had been thrown at him. Newshounds from their British counterparts were waiting in a pack when he arrived at Heathrow. They formed a scrum almost blocking the exit from Customs into the Arrivals hall. His immediate problem was simply getting through.

Between them his publishers and the Smithsonian Institute, who had organised his tour, had coughed up for a Business Class ticket, so the flight had been comfortable, and he'd been plied with champagne and good food. But he could never sleep on planes. He was always aware of the hum of the engines, and however smooth the flight, the constant sense of motion always made him queasy. Now he was jet-lagged, unshaven and faintly nauseous. He could do without this.

The shouting started as soon as he emerged from the green channel.

'Tell us about Washington, Jimmy!' (Why do journalists assume they can use people's most familiar names?)

'Do you think you're safe here?'

'How bad were your injuries?'

'Where are your bodyguards? Haven't you asked for police protection?'

Before he left the railed off entrance channel, he paused to scan the hall. Then he saw Iris. She was standing at the back, close to an exit, looking straight at him and muttering into a mobile phone. He fixed his gaze ahead and marched directly towards her, trailing his suitcase behind him wobbling on its silly, unstable little wheels. He tried to ignore the camera flashes and brush past the reporters who were pushing in front of him.

'Is it true you have a four-inch erection, Professor Appleby?' said an unshaven young man with spiky gelled black hair, waving a copy of 'New York Today' in his face.

'No!' he snapped. Damnation! He'd fallen for it. Trust a red-top hack to provoke a reaction!

'Have you any comment on the lashings in Saudi Arabia, Professor?' (That was two months ago, for heaven's sake!)

'What about the women who were burned alive in the Punjab yesterday?'

'What!?'

'Two young women who had your book? They were burned alive by a mob. Haven't you heard?'

'No.'

Without a flicker of recognition, Iris turned smartly on her heels as he approached, and he followed her out of the terminal. She led him straight over to the taxi bay, just as a large black BMW pulled up alongside the waiting cabs. The timing was immaculate.

She grabbed his suitcase and flung it in the front passenger seat. 'Get in,' she said striding to the far side of the car and jumping in the back.

'That was neat,' he said, as they drove off. 'Thank you so much.'

'Anything for you, my love,' she smiled.

'Where's little Eddie?'

'At home with the nanny. This is Giovanni, by the way.'

'Hi,' said Giovanni, catching Appleby's eye in the rear-view mirror.

'Thanks, Giovanni.' Appleby looked over his shoulder. All the photographers had given up the chase but one. He had dropped to one knee and pointed a massive zoom-lens at their rear windscreen as they sped away.

'Welcome home,' said Iris and she kissed him on the cheek.

'Where were the police?' he asked. 'I thought I was supposed to have protection. Actually it's a relief not to have two goons circling around me like pilot fish.'

'They're in the car behind us,' said Iris. 'And there was a team mingling with the hacks in the airport. You just didn't see them.'

Salisbury

A week after receiving the invitation, Appleby was back in Salisbury Cathedral library.

The Librarian was a softly spoken, but genial layman, a theology graduate in his early fifties called Hubert Entwistle. He was curious to know how Appleby's research was progressing and asked warmly after Jenny. Appleby read '*On the Expurgation of Heresies in the See of Salisbury in the Raigne of Our Late Soveraigne*' over two days. It was a priceless source, yet it only tantalised him the more.

True to his title, the anonymous author provided a painstaking, if somewhat erratic record of the campaign to impose Church of England uniformity in the reign of Elizabeth I. It was laced with colourful stories, and there was much useful material. Most of this confirmed the findings in his own book, which was almost ready to go to the publishers, but he would also need to make a few modifications. In particular the writer's complaint that most country people seemed 'as unknowing of the Principles of Christianitie as the red-skinned Indians of Americka' confirmed his long-held suspicion, that far from being saturated with religion, the rural poor had remained deeply ignorant and suggestible.

Inevitably the main focus was on the treatment of stubborn Roman Catholic recusants from the wealthier classes. Appleby was shocked by the way so many of them had been 'shopped' by their neighbours or betrayed by supposed friends. Were these snitches genuinely outraged by 'Popery' or just self-righteous hypocrites? How many acted out of jealousy, spite or lick-spittle favour-currying? He had often wondered what Britain would have been like if Hitler had invaded in 1940. The English liked to think that fascist behaviour was not in their nature, but he was sure there would have been as many collaborators, informers and Quislings as there had been in France, Holland or Norway.

The anonymous writer also recorded details of several trials for 'maleficent' witchcraft. Appleby knew about most of these, though not some of the more lurid details. Most of the accused had been acquitted and only two poor women had been hanged. Nobody had been burned alive. He did not know about the young Swindon man called Whittingdale who was accused of conducting illicit alchemical experiments in 1569. When his house was searched, the sheriff's men found a copy of John Dee's '*Monas Hieroglyphica*'. The hermetic philosopher was the Queen's personal astrologer, but his book was still deemed blasphemous. Whittingdale was sent to London to be 'put to the question'. There was no account of his fate.

After the defeat of the Spanish Armada and the various subsequent failed invasion attempts, the paranoia about the Catholic threat had subsided a little, and the local church turned its attention to Puritan separatists instead. Appleby had known about the two men who had been arrested, fined and put in the stocks in 1589 for distributing a Puritan tract, but not that the tract in question was by one '*Martin Marprelate*', and was a scurrilous satire on the role of the English bishops – or that the men had walked down from Warwickshire – or that one had a wooden leg.

In 1592 Archbishop Whitgift had sent Richard Hooker to serve as a canon at Salisbury while he wrote '*Of the Lawes of Ecclesiastical Politie*', the rule-book of the new Protestant church. Under Hooker's influence the pressure on local Presbyterians intensified, and the writer of the '*Expurgation*' included transcripts of some fierce debates between these Puritans and their accusers. This material was pure gold. These men were determined, stubborn and highly articulate, with fiercely held convictions and encyclopaedic knowledge of the Bible. To the author's clear annoyance, the clergy always seemed to come off second best in these encounters, resorting to bluster and bullying to assert their spiritual authority.

For Appleby these debates confirmed a crucial point. English language Bibles had been sent to the churches by Thomas Cromwell under Henry VIII, withdrawn by Henry's Catholic daughter Mary, then returned under Elizabeth. They had created a generation of avid new readers, independent-minded and quick to challenge authority.

Here, thought Appleby, lay the seeds of the English Civil War, the independent thinking that eventually fed into the Enlightenment and perhaps, in the distant future, spawned the American Revolution.

Near the end, he finally found what he was really looking for: a chapter entitled '*Dangerous Heretics in the Parish of Swively*'. During Hooker's residence in Wiltshire, wrote '*The Trew Man of God*', a zealous young priest called Jacob Mallaster was sent, on Hooker's urgent recommendation, to take over '*an obscure little parish of no great import*', after the death of an ancient incumbent called Elijah Wesson.

Appleby had brought his notes on the Cantwell correspondence with him, but he decided to ask if he could see the originals again. Entwistle looked puzzled as if he was not sure what he was talking about. Appleby explained that he had been shown them by a young trainee with a New Zealand accent.

'Oh, that would be Katie Bestwick,' said Entwistle. 'She was only with us for a few weeks. She shouldn't have been passing round newly discovered documents, though – very unprofessional.'

'She said you'd given her permission.'

'Did she now? I don't think I did!'

'She said you were about to catalogue them.'

'Really? I was on leave for a while around then, I recall. Perhaps someone else got hold of them. I'll ask the Dean.'

Two hours later he returned to say the Cathedral had no such documents. Whatever it was Appleby had seen, the material must have been passed on elsewhere. He suggested he apply to Lambeth Palace. But Appleby had already been told that the Church of England archives had no record of any such events. It was all very puzzling and slightly disturbing. He would have to rely on his old notes.

Yet '*On The Expurgation*' seemed to confirm almost everything Appleby had read. Soon after taking up his post in Swively, the author wrote, Mallaster had reported his unease about the activities of a prominent local landowner, 'Sir Niklas Harker'. A large number of villagers, including women and children, seemed to meet at Harker's house on

Saturday mornings, but none would say why they gathered there or what took place. Harker was held in the highest esteem, loved even, by the villagers, and Mallaster could find no one prepared to speak against him. He himself found Harker aloof and evasive. He was convinced that the Harkers, though attending his church, were either practising Roman Catholics or guilty of some '*even more terrible abomination*'.

Appleby was deeply sceptical about the first explanation. For one thing, the Pope had decreed that it was a sin for Catholics even to enter a Protestant Church. And they were obliged to hear mass on Sundays. As for an '*even more terrible abomination*', there was no indication of what that could possibly be.

Harker had been summoned to Salisbury by Bishop Cantwell, the chapter continued, who had questioned him closely and in secret over three days before allowing him to return home. Cantwell then wrote to Archbishop Whitgift (the writer didn't seem to know about the letter to Puckering). Whitgift's reply had arrived within a fortnight. Two days later a party of armed men had mustered on the green in front of the Cathedral and marched off into the night. Nothing was heard of Sir Nicholas again, and, as the Bishop had deemed it a matter of the utmost secrecy, no written records of these events were to be found.

Enquiries in the Parish had yielded no further information. The author had visited Swively and stayed at the inn, which, he noted, had an unusual name, The Kindred of the Spirit, having been known previously as The Swan. None of the villagers could explain this peculiar change. More strangely, all denied any knowledge of the events of 1594 and indeed, of Sir Nicholas Harker himself. Cantwell and Mallaster were both long dead.

'*If their actions in any way exceeded the strict Observance of the Lawes of the Realm,*' wrote the author, he believed it could only have been '*by urgent Imperative of the gravest Peril to the Godly.*'

It was all hideously frustrating. Here, apparently, was near-contemporary confirmation of the events implied in the bishop's correspondence and described so gruesomely to the Reverend Trott in the old village tales, but still there was no satisfactory explanation. What on earth were Sir Nicholas Harker and his coterie actually doing?

Appleby decided he had to 'go public' on the Harker affair. He returned to York and within a week he had written a 3,000 word article entitled '*A Massacre at Swively? The Strange Case of Sir Nicholas Harker*'. He sent it to the editor of '*History Today*'.

Then he hopped on a train to London, and took Jenny out for dinner in a French bistro.

'Jimmy,' she said as they sipped their digestifs, 'would you like me to move up to York? To live together?'

'Really?' he said. 'Is that what you want? I'd absolutely love that!'

'And how about children? Are you ready to start a family?'

'Actually…' he said, swirling his Armagnac around the glass. 'Actually …I'd love that too.'

'Great,' she said, wrinkling her nose mischievously. 'Then we're getting married.…That's not up for negotiation, by the way.'

Amsterdam

It was hardly an office, more of a walk-in cupboard. Not that Appleby minded. It had a decent sized desk, a phone and electric sockets. The door was secured with a mortise lock and a Yale, and it was hidden down a dark, unfrequented corridor on the top floor of the Renaissance Institute. By the door was an ugly modern cabinet secured with a chunky combination lock. The chest was inside. Van Stumpe had locked that too, attaching the largest, strongest padlock he could fit. Appleby found this reassuring. It would have taken determined professional burglars to find their way to the documents.

The small, dusty window was no more than fifteen feet from the opposite wall, at the top of a dingy shaft between buildings. It was hardly an inspiring vista, but he barely noticed. If there had been a picture-window overlooking the Victoria Falls or a grandstand view of the Rio carnival, he wouldn't have given them a second glance.

For five weeks he had agreed to spend Mondays fulfilling his teaching duties at Despenser. Late on Monday night he would take a ludicrously cheap budget flight from Stansted to Amsterdam. He would stay until Saturday afternoon, when there was a slightly dearer flight back to Leeds-Bradford where Jenny would pick him up and drive him home to York. Braving the inevitable engineering works, he would take trains back to Cambridge on Sunday nights, arriving at Despenser around 1.00 am. It was a punishing schedule. He had to spend the whole of Sunday at home, preparing his lectures, clearing his in-tray and answering emails. Seeing Iris became almost impossible.

Van Stumpe generously offered to put him up as a guest at his home in the outer suburbs. Two weeks before Appleby would have hacked his own leg off with a rusty pen-knife before accepting such an offer, but apart from the fact that staying in a hotel for so long would be prohibitively expensive, his feelings towards the idiosyncratic librarian were warming by the day.

Van Stumpe's house turned out to be a small detached two-storey villa with crenellations along the top of a gabled façade. It was approached over a small wooden bridge across a drainage ditch, with chains as handrails, which reminded Appleby of a little drawbridge. When he arrived on his first Monday night, van Stumpe ushered him into the living room and introduced him to an old man, who was sitting by the fireplace in a large wing-backed armchair.

'This,' said van Stumpe glowing with affection, 'is my father.'

Appleby's Dutch was minimal, but he got the gist of their conversation.

'Vaartje!' said van Stumpe. 'This is Doctor James Appleby from England. James will be staying with us for a few weeks.'

'Who?' said van Stumpe senior, turning to Appleby. 'He is a very good boy, my little Piet! A very good boy!' Then he subsided back into his chair with a grunt.

When he was nine or ten, Appleby's father had read him *Great Expectations* as a bedtime story, and Dickens's novel had powerful associations of family love for him. 'Wemmick!' he thought. 'Van Stumpe is Mr Wemmick.'

'You must be hungering,' said van Stumpe. 'Come to the kitchen and we will have some beers and perhaps you will like a broodje with some cheese?' He sat Appleby down at the table and put some bread rolls in the oven.

'Yesterday bread,' he said. 'Always tasting nicer if you make it warm.'

Then he produced a large bottle of Koningshoven Blond from the fridge and carefully filled two glasses. 'This is from Holland's only brewery for Trappist monks' beers,' he said. 'The other ones are all of Belgians. Let me have your opinion when you have tasted some. You see I have sampled from every year for twenty years!'

He pointed to what was evidently meant to be a decorative plate-rack high on the wall. Instead of blue and white Delft crockery, though, it bore dozens of empty Koningshoven bottles, one each for every type of beer for over twenty years and all sparklingly clean. Is there no limit to this man's anal retentiveness? Appleby wondered. But then perhaps it's not so surprising. He's still with his parents. He's never left home.

'I hope you like my little house?' van Stumpe asked. 'I was persuasive to my vaartje to come and live here by me after my mother died some three years gone.' He gave a heavy sigh. 'My own "better half" as you English are saying, has departed six years ago.'

Well we all get things wrong, thought Appleby. He decided not to ask about the 'better half'. He was too tired to listen to a tragic story. 'It's a very nice house,' he said, taking a deep draught of the ale. It looked like a pale lager, but it was much stronger than he expected, fruity, aromatic and intense. 'Hoo! That's good!' he said.

'Aha! We Dutch have our secret treasures too, you see, James,' he said, taking the warmed rolls from the oven. He split them, buttered them, inserted thick slices, cut from a large round orange cheese, put them on plates and handed one to Appleby. He was ravenous, and the ripe, tangy cheese began to soften in the warm, pillowy bread. The moment was ineffably comforting. He took another swig of beer and a wave of relaxed contentment broke over him. It would not be so bad here after all.

'Piet, have you ever read a Charles Dickens novel called *Great Expectations*?' he asked.

'No. I have not yet read that one. *Oliver Twist* yes, and *A Tale of Two Cities* also. Why?'

'I think you'd like it.'

It was only when he was unpacking in van Stumpe's spare bedroom that he realised that the bag containing the remains of Iris's spliff was missing from his briefcase. That was funny. He didn't remember disposing of it. He had planned to dump it in a litter-bin somewhere. But the last few days had been so hectic. Maybe he had…

The next morning van Stumpe took Appleby to the Institute on the bus. He gave him a set of keys to what Appleby had decided to call his 'closet', the combination of the lock on the cabinet and the key to the chest. They agreed to meet at 1.00 o'clock for lunch. Van Stumpe made it clear that he expected frequent verbal updates and regular written reports.

Appleby knew from his previous visit that his task would be daunting.

He plugged in his laptop, put on a pair of latex gloves and began to sort the books and documents by type. After twenty minutes the chest was empty. At one end of the desk was a pile of letters and other items consisting of loose pages. In the middle he had made a stack of manuscripts, tracts and pamphlets which were sewn, tied or at least folded together. At the far end he carefully placed the complete books.

He knew from the first trip that these books alone were worth a fortune. After he had noted down basic descriptions of each, he carefully replaced them in the chest. Everything he and van Stumpe had seen so far suggested that the chest had belonged to Sir Thomas Cranham. If these books were his, he must have been an exceptional scholar, extremely wealthy and with a most unusual range of contacts.

He must also have been prepared to take grave risks to acquire them. As far as Appleby knew, there was never anything subversive about owning copies of all the first three editions of The Book of Common Prayer from 1549, 1552 and 1559, although there were loose sheets inserted throughout each which appeared to offer some kind of notes and commentaries. Nor would an original Latin imprint of Erasmus's *In Praise of Folly* get him sent to the Bridewell prison for interrogation.

But the owner would almost certainly not have wanted it generally known that he possessed a copy of '*The Douai Bible*', the translation written and published in Flanders by exiled English Catholics. Or that he had a complete set of Giordano Bruno's Italian Dialogues, in which the individual tracts appeared to have been collated and loosely bound together in a book. Priceless today, these essays had aroused intense controversy when the freethinking young Italian had them published in London, not least among Bruno's own English associates. One of those English acquaintances, Appleby seemed to recall, was Sir Philip Sidney.

Perhaps most suspect of all would have been the holy texts of 'heathen' faiths. Van Stumpe had already told him that one was a German translation of the *Talmud*. There was also a copy of the *Qur'an* in Arabic, together with forty collated manuscript pages of a partial English translation. Whose handwriting was that? Hadn't he seen something like it before? Was it not like Sir Nicholas Harker's writing? Were these, in fact, Harker's books? Most exotic of all was a parallel text version of *The Bhagavad Gita*, one side in Sanskrit, the other in Portuguese. Van Stumpe and his colleagues would find out soon enough, but it was obvious that most of these volumes were exceptionally rare, and in some cases, possibly the only copies in existence.

When van Stumpe arrived to take him to lunch he made his apologies and said he would rather work straight through. Van Stumpe saw the piles on the desk and agreed.

Sorting the loose documents would take several days, so he decided to start by listing the tracts, pamphlets and apparently home-made booklets he had stacked in the middle of the table. Several looked like prayer books, some like collections of poetry. One was particularly intriguing. Ten pages of quarto had been folded in the middle and sewn to make a twenty-page octavo booklet. It was hand-written, yellowing and very well-thumbed. The title was '*The Common Rite*'.

Appleby rapidly scanned through the pages. It was laid out like the liturgy of a mass, with a script for someone called the '*Mediator*' and prescribed responses for '*The People*', a congregation presumably. There were allocated times for songs, readings and '*The Contemplation*', whatever that was. Most puzzling of all was a section near the end marked '*Attestations and Pleas for Consolation*'. What on earth was this? It certainly wasn't a church service. For one thing, he couldn't see a single reference to God. Two spidery initials appeared at the very end. '*N. H.*'.

It was 5.30, and he had barely started the job of listing and categorising the collection when van Stumpe appeared and asked if he was ready to go home. This turned out to be an instruction rather than an enquiry. He asked if he could stay longer on his own, but was told this was impossible. Unless there was some kind of evening event, the premises were locked up at 6.00 pm sharp.

This was a serious nuisance. Appleby simply couldn't afford not to use the evenings, especially as he would have to unpack and repack the chest at the beginning and end of every day. He knew van Stumpe could not possibly agree to let him take any of the precious material away with him. But time was short, and there was a mountain of work.

'Okay, then,' he sighed, when van Stumpe broke this bad news. 'Why don't I pack up here and join you in the lobby? I guess it'll take about twenty minutes.'

'Very good,' said van Stumpe. 'And then maybe we can be buying some interesting foreign sausage as our supper. There is a fine Polish delicatessen on just around the corner. Then perhaps you can compare our preliminary notes on our treasure box!'

As soon as van Stumpe left, Appleby picked up a thick bundle of papers which were tied together with string and placed it gently inside his briefcase. For the first time since Jenny had given it to him five birthdays ago, he used the combination locks. The code was still on a tag inside one of the document compartments. He took it out and slipped it in his pocket. He packed away the books and documents, just making it to the lobby by 6.00. Van Stumpe was looking at his watch, while a sour-faced janitor jangled his keys.

'Listen, I'm really sorry about this, Piet, but I'm going to have to pass on the interesting foreign sausage,' said Appleby. 'A friend from Germany is in Amsterdam and I promised to meet him for dinner tonight.'

'You were not telling this before, James.' Van Stumpe looked surprised and slightly hurt.

'He called me on my mobile this afternoon. Sorry. I forgot to mention it.'

'Is he a fellow historian? Might I know him?'

'No, no! Nothing like that.' As his recent interview with Clovis had reminded him, Appleby hated this sort of thing. Lying was bad enough; having to invent improvised elaborations was excruciating. 'We were pen-pals for a while at school. We kept in touch.'

'Oh, how very nice to keep friendship so long!' said van Stumpe. 'What is his name? Where is he from?'

'Um. He's called Fritz.' Appleby couldn't believe he had just said that.

'He's from Frankfurt. I suppose that makes him a Frankfurter,' he added with a silly little laugh.

'Well yes. If he is from Frankfurt of course he must be a Frankfurter. Where is he staying, your Frankfurter Fritz? Perhaps I can recommend some nice restaurant close by.'

Appleby groped in his memory for the name of a hotel. 'The De Ruyter,' he said.

'Oh! Where you stayed last week, was it not? How coincidence-making. Oh dear. That is not so very nice. But I know an excellent Indonesian restaurant by there. Please let me direct you. We can go there now if you like.'

'No. No. Please don't put yourself to the trouble, Piet. I won't hear of it! I'm sure we will find somewhere. I'll get a taxi back. I'll make sure I'm in by eleven.'

When he finally managed to shake van Stumpe off he set off towards the city centre carrying his laptop and briefcase. He knew exactly what he was looking for: a large anonymous tourist hotel with a restaurant which stayed open until at least 10.00 pm. He soon found one. It was called the 'Centraal Holiday', and the restaurant, as he hoped, was almost empty.

He set himself up at a table for four in the far corner, explaining to the waiter that he was here on business and needed to do a little work over dinner. He ordered the cheapest set menu, picking dishes that would generate the least possible mess. Even so, he was appalled by what he was about to do. It was staggeringly unprofessional. The waiter obligingly cleared the extra place settings so that he could open his laptop and briefcase and spread out the documents.

He put on a pair of latex gloves (heaven only knew what the waiter made of that), untied the bundle he had taken from the Institute and started reading. Neither he nor van Stumpe had looked closely at these particular papers on his first visit. He wasn't sure they had even untied them. That was a mistake. He realised within minutes that the sheets comprised Sir Thomas Cranham's private journal.

He had barely begun to look through them when the waiter arrived with his first course. He had ordered pate with toast, imagining it would be the least messy option, forgetting that he would have to spread the pate on the toast, then pick it up with his fingers.

'Could you possibly bring me a small bowl of warm water with a wedge of lemon and some paper napkins?' He asked the waiter.

'Very good, sir,' said the waiter, with a quizzical frown. He looked back at Appleby as he walked towards the kitchen and saw him trying to eat pate and toast with a knife and fork. Appleby smiled. The waiter whispered something to a colleague who laughed.

After he'd finished the pate, he washed and dried his fingertips and put the gloves back on. Parts of the journal had been written in small booklets, but many of the loose sheets were undated, and it wasn't even clear if they had been collated chronologically. He would simply have to read them all systematically and make detailed notes of their contents. He decided to follow his usual practice of writing up key passages in loosely modernised English, only this time he would type them directly into his laptop.

The first page was simply headed '*Sunday*'. He began reading:

'*Arose betimes. Watched young Piers a-milking. Methinks he is too fierce upon the teats. Griddled cakes, eggs and good broth for breakfast. Our walk to church marred by Anne mewling and whining over a hurte foot. Told Susannah that if she would not discipline the childe, then I needs must do so myself.*'

Appleby felt a powerful frisson. Susannah! Should he tell Jenny about that or would it freak her out?

'*Old Davie Wainwright missed Communion once more. He will be fined again and will on a surety come a-begging as he hath not the means to pay. I know not why he cannot yerk himself from his bed on a Sunday, when he must do so every other Day.*'

Cranham went on to describe the service at length, including Parson Wesson's sermon which he seemed to find baffling:

'For half its length did he rail against Sin and the works of the Devil, reminding us with many readings from Deuteronomy and Leviticus that the Lord our God is a jealous God, that vengeance is His and that He will repay. Then did he read from the Book of Ezekial how that the City of Tyrus was laid to waste and how they should know that He is the Lord when He lays his vengeance upon them with furious rebukes and that their daughters in the field should be slain by the sword...'

Appleby snorted. He recognised the passage from Ezekial. It provided a memorable moment in the film 'Pulp Fiction' when Samuel L. Jackson, playing the drug baron's eccentric enforcer, used it as the basis for a Biblical rant before casually shooting a sick student on a sofa. The waiter arrived with a plate of Wiener schnitzel and chips. Appleby put the sheet aside and removed his gloves again. He dispatched the meal quickly, washed the grease from his fingers with water and lemon juice, dried them on his napkin, put the gloves back on and returned to Cranham's account of the sermon. Half way through, it seemed, the parson had abruptly changed tack.

'...And yet,' quoth he. 'What do we find in the teachings of our Lorde and Saviour Jesus Christe but meekness, Charitie, gentil Mercy and Redemption for the penitent Sinner. Remember always the Storie of the Woman taken in Adulterie and how our Lorde laide bare for all to see the canting Hypocrisie of the Pharisees when he said unto them 'Let he among you who is without Sin, let Him cast the first Stone.'

Cranham wondered if Wesson had been at the mead again. He had rounded things off with the story of the Good Samaritan and some stuff about turning the other cheek before sinking back in one of the choir stalls, leaving his congregation with no idea how to square these apparent contradictions.

They were exhausted too, it seemed:

'He spake so long that many of the childeren could not hold their Water and the whole nave stank of piss e'er the good old Soule concluded.'

After the service most of the congregation lingered on the village green. Cranham complained that they only came to church *'to gossip or to gaze upon eeche other and prate without Cessation over Naughte.'* The young men and women clearly took the opportunity to chat each other up and were a prey to *'too much easy Lewdness'*.

Cranham had met his old friend 'Sir Nic', *'as is our wont eeche Sabbath'*. Harker had invited him to accompany him on a visit to an old lady, the Widow Wapshotte, who was sick in bed. On the way to her cottage Harker asked him what he had made of the sermon.

'I told him I knew not what to think. For are not Our Saviour and our Heavenly Father one and the Same? Yet could I hear but little Harmonie between these voices today.'

'I am of the same mind,' Harker had replied. *'Let us be thankfulle that the Holy Ghost hath not His own Testament also, for then might the Trinity give us three such Contrarie Dispositions to fathom.'*

Harker had said that he thought this troubled Wesson too. It was almost as if he *'lays suche Discrepancies before us'* hoping that someone would come forward *'and shewe him how the angry Godhead of the Old Testament may be reconciled to the gentil Savior of the Newe.'*

Harker then expressed the view that all people *'whose souls are not Malformed by Malice or ill-use'* have an inborn sense of what is good and what is evil, that they should listen to their own spirit and be guided by that. Such unorthodox musings worried Cranham:

'I wolde not quarrel with him, though I fear me such Speculations are too loose for some Ears and pray they visit no ill upon him.'

They had spent an hour at the old woman's cottage. Harker gave her a couple of coins to buy food while Cranham brought in wood. He rekindled her fire and warmed some ale, adding a pinch of cinnamon he had just bought from a man named Jack Randerson who had just returned from Salisbury.

Meanwhile '*Sir Nic read to her verses by the Earl of Surrie about a lovesick shepherd from Tottle's Miscellanie which he had left in her cot for such occasions. This did divert her grately and brought much Delight.*'

It was a sharp reminder of the vulnerability of the old and poor. '*I feare the Widow cannot last the Winter,*' wrote Cranham, '*though she says she cares but little to live since she ne'er had a son and all her five daughters are now dead.*'

Appleby also found the first indication that Cranham was remarkably frank about his personal life. He concluded the entry by complaining that he could not 'couple' with Susannah that night as she was suffering from '*a womanly Distemper*'. He had sat by the embers of the fire wondering which of his family snored the loudest.

The reference to 'Tottel's Miscellany' might prove useful. If Appleby remembered correctly it was an anthology of verse first published in the late 1550s, a first step in the dating, though it didn't narrow things down very much.

He decided that was enough for the night. The waiter cleared his empty plate and brought the creme caramel he had ordered for dessert. He asked for the bill and an espresso, and packed the papers away. He was eating the tiny square of chocolate that came with his coffee, a redundant flourish to a thoroughly indifferent meal, when his mobile phone rang. He didn't recognise the caller's number.

'Dr Appleby?' He recognised the voice, though. 'It's me, Claire. Claire Tenterden.'

'Claire! This is a surprise. What can I do for you?'

'I'm awfully sorry if I'm disturbing you. You must be frightfully busy researching your film script and things, but I'm in Amsterdam for a few days visiting an old schoolfriend. I wondered if you'd like to meet for a drink. Don't worry if you're tied up.'

'Gosh. What a nice thought. I'm sure I could spare an hour or two. Is tomorrow evening any good?'

'Tomorrow evening would be fab! About 7.00? I'll ask my friend to suggest a nice bar. Isn't it a coincidence us both being over here at the same time?'

Coincidence indeed, he thought. It seemed the city was full of old schoolfriends that week, imaginary or otherwise.

Holland Park

By the time Giovanni's BMW reached the elevated section of the M4 in west London, the traffic was almost at a standstill. It was dusk; there was a steady drizzle and the lights of the other vehicles seemed to form fantastical shapes which danced in the droplets of rain on the windows. After the stress and trauma of America and the interminable restless flight, Appleby felt insulated and comfortable, happy to sink into the deep leather seats.

'So are you going to tell me what is going on?' he asked Iris eventually. 'And why on earth have you come to pick me up?'

'Special Branch asked me to,' she said. 'Don't worry, They'll explain everything later.'

Appleby grunted, too tired to push the matter any further. 'How are you, anyway?'

'Not brilliant actually, since you ask.' She gave one of her sad little smiles.

'Oh? What's the matter?'

'Just some tummy trouble. It's probably just indigestion or an ulcer or something, but my GP thought I should have a few tests just to be safe. I'm going for the results tomorrow. I'm sure it's nothing really.'

'Well let's hope so.' He squeezed her hand. 'Do keep me posted, won't you?' He leaned forward towards the driver. 'Giovanni. Could you possibly drop me off somewhere where I can get a tube to Kings Cross?' he asked. 'Hammersmith would do. There should be a train to York in an hour. Do you think I could make that?'

Now Iris gave his hand a squeeze. 'That may not be such a good idea,' she said gently.

'But I must get back. Jenny's been worried sick. I just want to resume my normal life.'

'Jenny's not in York, Jimmy. She's here in London.'

'What? Why? I don't understand. Where is she?'

'We're taking you to her now.'

'Iris, please tell me what's going on.'

'We're going to Giovanni's house…for now. There have been some new developments.'

Eventually the car crawled round Shepherd's Bush Common and filtered away into the stately stuccoed avenues of Holland Park. Giovanni turned into a mews and pulled up in front of a garage with a new steel door. He pointed a remote-control at it, and the door rolled itself up and back. The unmarked police-car which had tailed them from Heathrow drew level. Giovanni turned and waved acknowledgement to the man in the front passenger seat. The officers watched the BMW drive into the garage, then sped away.

'Wait till the door's closed,' said Iris when they got inside. Giovanni stepped out of the driving-seat and Appleby heard a whirring sound and a heavy clunk. 'Okay, now,' she said.

'Welcome to my humble home,' said Giovanni with a warm grin. He spoke softly with a slight Italian accent. Appleby was no expert but guessed it was northern. Milan? Turin? He must be about forty, he thought, also noticing how handsome he was, tanned, with an athletic build. He was exquisitely dressed in what looked like an expensive designer suit and a silk shirt with hand-made casual shoes.

'Follow me please.' He led them through a door at the back of the garage, along a covered passage beside an ornate garden, illuminated by concealed lights. He opened a back door with three separate locks, one requiring a six-digit code, and they followed him up a flight of turning stairs into a magnificent tiled hallway. If this was his home he was also fabulously wealthy.

Appleby gave Iris a wan smile and bent down to whisper in her ear. 'It's just as well we broke up. First that rich Canadian Adonis, now this guy…I was done for.'

Iris smiled and squeezed his arm. 'You'll always be special to me, Jimmy. You know that. He is quite a catch though, isn't he? He's going to make some lucky young man very happy indeed.'

'Ah!' said Appleby.

'Anyway, don't worry about Giovanni. He's one of your biggest fans. He published the Italian translations.'

'What?' said Appleby startled.

The man turned round and offered his hand. 'Please allow me to introduce myself. I am Giovanni Angelini. You wrote to me once...'

'Fuck me!' said Appleby. 'So it was you! I knew it!'

'There will be time enough to discuss all this later,' said Angelini. 'Follow me, please.'

He turned into a huge sitting-room, with wide French doors onto the garden which seemed to glow magically in the darkness beyond.

As Appleby entered the room Jenny sprang up from a sofa and flung her arms around him. She didn't say anything, just hugged him tightly for what seemed like an eternity. She was sobbing gently.

'It's all right,' he murmured, kissing the top of her hair. 'I'm safe home now.'

'But that's just it,' Jenny was looking up into his face, her eyes wet and blotchy. 'It's not all right, and we're not safe.'

Appleby was only half listening. He was wondering who the two men in dark weather-proof jackets at the back of the room were. The shorter of the two strode towards him.

'Allow me to introduce myself, Doctor Appleby. Detective Inspector Kot. Metropolitan Police Special Branch. And this is my colleague Detective Sergeant Handley. May I suggest you take a seat for a moment, sir?'

Appleby did so, and the two detectives sat down again.

'So?'

'Now I wouldn't want you to get too alarmed, sir,' said Kot, 'but I'm afraid we've had some worrying information about the man who tried to shoot you in Washington.'

'What? Have they caught him? He's a Christian fundamentalist nutter, right?'

'That's just it, sir. Our FBI contacts don't think he is. You're probably aware of the fact that these Harkerites have been recruiting rather briskly among the more westernised Arab communities in Europe and America. One group tried to take some literature into Saudi Arabia and were promptly arrested. They claim it's a "philosophy" and not incompatible with Islam, but that's not how the Saudi authorities see it. Or the Mullahs.'

'Yes, yes. I'd heard about that. They were flogged.'

'Then perhaps you also know that this, er, development has gone down particularly badly with several militant Islamic groups. They see it as the latest decadent western attack on their faith. The FBI think they've identified your attacker as a member of the Wahabi sect, a Jihadist, travelling on a Lebanese passport. We still don't know his real name. He seems to use four or five aliases. They think he managed to get out of the United States, on the night of the shooting. All this biometric malarkey is proving much easier to circumvent than anyone realised. It would have been extremely helpful if they had been able to tell us this sooner, because we now fear he may have slipped through the net.'

'Slipped through the net?'

'We have reason to believe he's in England, sir. Hoping for a second bite at the cherry, as it were.'

Appleby didn't know what to say. He was scared, depressed and suddenly felt crushingly weary.

'We think it advisable to take you and your wife to a safe house, sir,' Kot continued. 'Tonight.'

'A safe house? Where?'

'Giovanni has a place on the edge of Exmoor,' said Iris. 'It's very remote. No neighbours for miles. These gentlemen think they can guard you as effectively there as in one of their own places, don't you?'

Kot nodded. 'We've checked it out, sir. It's eminently suitable.'

'Not to say extremely luxurious,' Iris added.

'That is an advantage' said Kot. 'To be brutally honest, most police safe-houses are pretty much arm-pits.'

Appleby looked at Angelini. 'Are you sure about this?'

'Absolutely. For me it will be a very great privilege to help you.'

'But what about Jenny and my work? And all our things?'

'If you give us a list of what you need we can get it down to you in due course,' said Kot. 'But I cannot stress strongly enough that, for the time being at least, there must be no contact with the outside world of any kind whatsoever.'

Appleby sighed and shook his head.

'There's something else I have to tell you,' said Jenny.

Something in her tone made Appleby shudder.

'Yesterday, someone fire-bombed the Renaissance Institute in Amsterdam. They managed to put the fire out eventually, but they've lost tens of thousands of documents.'

'Including the archive?'

'Including the archive.'

'Oh, God!' Appleby groaned. 'And what about Piet? Is Piet okay? He wasn't in there, was he?'

Jenny's voice dropped to a near whisper. 'Piet is missing, Jimmy. He was definitely in the building earlier in the day, but no one saw him come out. They think...they think he's dead, Jimmy...I'm so sorry.'

Appleby went white. He stared at the carpet, utterly lost for words.

'This is ghastly,' he said eventually. 'The poor man. And it's all my fault. Sometimes I wish I'd never set eyes on that bloody chest...I can't bear it.'

Jenny put her arms around him.

'Why did they do it, Jenny? Why bomb the Institute?'

'MI6 think we may be looking at some kind of co-ordinated international campaign,' said Kot, 'to wipe out Harkerism. Apparently GCHQ have been picking up chatter.'

'I suppose they think that destroying the archive will somehow undermine the movement,' said Angelini. 'It is a tragic loss.'

'How did it come to this?' Appleby groaned. He looked up at Jenny, miserable, almost defeated. 'Did I ever tell you what my old headmaster said about me, Jenny?'

'Something about you being harmless?'

'That's right – harmless, trivial and flippant. Now people are dying because of what I've done. Things like this aren't meant to happen because of people like me…'

Norwich

The response to Appleby's article in '*History Today*' was disappointing. He had deliberately chosen a popular rather than a specialist academic journal to reach a wider audience. He had systematically set out all the evidence he had uncovered, hoping that someone, somewhere would hold the key to the mystery. It was not to be.

There were three enquiries about Amos Jowatt's chronicle. An authority from Oxford on Queen Elizabeth's first great spymaster, Sir Francis Walsingham sent him some mildly entertaining titbits about Ephraim Jynes. Jynes turned out to have been a professional con-man and extortionist as well as a spy, and an associate of the shadowy Robert Skeres who had been in the room in Deptford when Christopher Marlowe was stabbed through the eye. But none of it was remotely connected to Harker or Cranham.

An antiques dealer in Herefordshire wrote to say he had acquired a wooden panel-portrait, probably of Sir Nicholas Harker as a young man. But when Appleby travelled up to see it, he found the man had only the most tendentious circumstantial evidence for the identification, and the young man in the picture looked nothing like the elderly man in the authenticated portrait. Appleby concluded that the dealer was simply trying to invent a connection in the hope of hiking up the price on an item he was finding difficult to sell.

Several Anglican clergymen wrote indignant responses. The very idea that the Bishop of Salisbury and the Archbishop of Canterbury might have ordered a massacre, they protested, was absurd and outrageous. In truth, Appleby was finding this hard to swallow himself. However cruel some of the punishments of the era may seem to the modern mind, they were rarely arbitrary. On the whole the Elizabethans had a fierce respect for the law and for due process. Even when suspected heretics like the playwright Thomas Kyd were brutally tortured, it was done following established procedures. But as he pointed out to the clergymen in his unfailingly courteous replies, he was merely presenting the available evidence.

Three readers offered the names of possible authors for *On the Expurgation of Heresies*, though none proved convincing. Then he was invited to join a discussion of the issue on Wilts FM. He took himself down to the BBC studios at Leeds for his first ever appearance on radio. He was led into a cramped soundproof room, which was almost filled by a large round table and set up with headphones, a microphone, a small glass and a jug of tepid water.

A technician told him to put on the earphones, tested Appleby's sound levels and told him that when he heard the presenter's voice, he would be live on air himself. The presenter of 'About Wilts Tonight' turned out to be a man in his late thirties called Dave Runacles. Or rather 'Wunacles': he had a mild speech impediment.

'Now you may have wed the article in the local paper yesterday about the discovewy of a fascinating old book fwom the time of King James I,' he said. 'It's called *On the Expurg*...What's that word? Sounds like something you take to make you thwow up! Well it's all about the howible things that were done to hewetics in these parts in those dim dark days. Only twouble is, the book's anonymous, which means we don't know who wote it! Now we're gonna be joined on the line fwom Leeds in a moment by Pwofessor James Appuwby who weckons he's got evidence for some kind of *massacre* taking place at Swively, which is mentioned in this book. Well I've been to Swively a few times myself and I certainly wouldn't put it past that lot. No! I'm only kidding, you Swivelovians. Just because you'w' all in-bwed, that doesn't make you mass-murdewers...'

Appleby winced. Evidently the rapidly spreading spirit of political correctness had not yet reached this particular broadcaster.

'...but first we're going to hear from Swindon accountant Hector Sneasby who thinks he knows who wote the *Ex-pur-gation*– there! I said it! Give us the low-down, Hector.'

'Well, Dave,' said Hector Sneasby, 'I should explain first that I have developed a sophisticated computer programme which subjects any written text to a complex semantic and syntactical analysis and uses this to establish, *beyond peradventure*, the identity of the true author of any given work.'

'Beyond perwadventure, eh? Isn't that out in the South Pacific some-where? Sounds pwetty exotic to me! Sewiously though, you mean like the way people are always saying other fellas wote Shakespeare's plays? You can pwove or dispwove stuff like that scientifically, can you?'

'Exactly.'

'Have you wun any of Shakespeare's plays thwough your pwogramme yet, then?'

'I have indeed. All of them, in fact.'

'So who wote them, then? Wemember you heard it here first, folks!'

'Shakespeare.'

'Wight. Shakespeare wote all of Shakespeare's plays?'

'Yup.'

'Well there's a turn up for the books! Blow me down with a feather! But what about the claims that all those other guys like Fwancis Bacon or Chwistopher Marlowe or the Earl of Whatsit wote them?'

'They are totally incorrect. In fact the evidence from my programme all points overwhelmingly in the other direction. What it shows us is crystal-clear – that Shakespeare wrote their plays and treatises as well.'

'What? You're actually saying Shakespeare wote – what's it called? *Doctor Faustus* and *The Jew of Malta* and all that lot as well as his own stuff?'

'Yes he did. All of them. I'm afraid the evidence of my Lexico-Syntactic Frequency-Tracking Matrix is simply incontrovertible.'

'Wow. It's a bit like you're saying he wote evewything that was witten back in the days of Good Queen Bess. I mean what about all that poetwy? Like that weally long one by Edmund Whojumaflip? *The Faiwy Queen* is it? Isn't that title a bit of a tautology, by the way, folks, like calling it the *The Poovey Gay*? Does your computer pwogwamme have a theowy about who wote that one, Hector?'

'Shakespeare. It's quite conclusive.'

'Okay. Well that must be a bit of a scoop for you among the litewati. So who wote *On the Expurgation of Hewesies* then? No don't tell me…'

'Shakespeare.'

'Wight. So Pwofessor Applebuwy. Shakespeare wote your *Expurgation*. What do you say to Hector's wemarkable wevelation?'

'It's an intriguing hypothesis,' said Appleby, 'except that Shakespeare had been dead for eight years when the book was published, so it doesn't really seem terribly likely.'

'And he wrote the authorised version of *The Bible*,' said Hector Sneasby. 'I can prove that too.'

'I learned two interesting lessons tonight,' Appleby told Jenny when he got home. 'Firstly, that there are some complete raving loonies out there, and secondly that they find it surprisingly easy to get access to the mass media.'

*

He and Jenny had set their wedding for the following July, after the university exams were over and before their friends began to drift away on holiday. Her parents insisted on a church service, but Jenny wanted one too. At first he resisted, but it didn't take him long to decide that the affront to his principles would be much less bitter than the disappointment Jenny and her family would suffer if they ended up in some municipal registry office.

Jenny wanted to marry in her childhood parish church, a 15th Century gem in a village on the other side of Salisbury from Swively. They travelled down to meet the vicar, who was wearily resigned to marrying the non-observant, the lapsed, the agnostic and even sometimes the adamantly atheist. He was delighted to marry Jenny, though. He remembered her well, and after subjecting Appleby to the lightest of grillings about the seriousness of his intentions, they fixed a date and time.

Appleby felt the need to explain this apparently reactionary decision to his more radical friends. Pete Elyot just shrugged. 'Whatever floats your boat, sweetie.' On an impulse Appleby asked him to be his best man, and to his surprise, Pete readily agreed.

Secretly, he was beginning to find the whole idea rather romantic, and thought he might actually enjoy the traditional religious theatricals. This feeling was confirmed for him with unexpected force that Christmas.

*

In fact it was the first Christmas they had spent together. Early in their relationship Appleby had discovered that, although Jenny had a wide range of friends, there were few, if any, with whom she was still in close contact. One reason for this was that her parents had moved from Salisbury to Norwich during her gap-year, before she went up to read Art History at Durham. It had become quite tricky to see her old schoolfriends in the holidays, and her friends from Durham were scattered, literally around the world.

Her parents had bought a large detached double-fronted Victorian house in a leafy avenue about a mile from the city centre. Appleby had been brought up in a compact three-bedroom inter-war semi in the Birmingham suburb of Handsworth Wood. It was neat and homely and remorselessly humdrum. With its gravel drive, looming bay windows and yellow-brick façade, the Webbs' house seemed dauntingly grand.

As the couple were effectively engaged, and had been sleeping together for over two years anyway, Jenny's parents broke with their lifelong principles and allowed them to sleep in the same bed. There would be no midnight corridor-creeping, or 2.00 am rendezvous on the living-room sofa. It was a massive concession on their part, but it had the effect of putting Appleby off sex completely. It was embarrassing enough going to bed with their precious daughter, without 'doing it' while they were in the house. They cuddled up at night, but they did not make love once during his four-night stay.

Jenny's whole family were at home: her parents, her older brother Toby and her younger sister Lucy. Even her grandmother Edith, who had been installed in a nearby care home, was fetched over before lunch on most days and taken back after dinner. Jenny's mother Zeta had a cut-glass accent, had never had a job and ran the home as a 'tight ship'. She was completely certain about her views on every conceivable subject and unnervingly direct. On his first night in the house, she asked him what he was likely to be earning in five years' time, by when, she announced, he and Jenny should have started a family. When he gave her a rough, but realistic figure, she suggested crisply that he should start thinking about ways of supplementing his salary.

Her father was easier going. Ralph Webb was a retired solicitor on an extremely generous pension, but his origins had been relatively humble and he disliked pretension. He insisted, for instance, that his name was to be pronounced 'Ralf'. He couldn't stand the upper-class 'Rafe', he said. He had served in the Fleet Air Arm during the war and turned out to be a naval history buff, who was genuinely fascinated by Appleby's store of knowledge about the revolutionary design of late Elizabethan galleons and the calibre of the artillery-pieces deployed at the battle of Gravelines. He had ended as a partner in a large firm which specialised in representing professional criminals. Appleby in turn was riveted by his lurid accounts of cases involving violent sociopaths.

Lucy was fun. She was reading Drama at Bristol, had a breezy cynicism and a veneer of worldly sophistication, which Appleby suspected masked considerable vulnerability. She subjected him to a kind of gentle mockery that constantly teetered on the edge of flirtation. Appleby was secretly flattered.

Toby was the problem. Whereas the girls had gone to a good local grammar school, Toby had been sent away to a minor boarding school near Gloucester. Jenny had already given Appleby her 'take' on her older brother. The experience of being sent away, she said, had made him feel both privileged within the family and excluded from it. After a couple of evenings in his company Appleby was building on this psychoanalytical platform for himself. The underlying sense that he was special (combined with the usual excessive and often wholly unmerited self-confidence of public schoolboys) seemed to have made Toby insufferably arrogant and elitist. The underlying sense of rejection and exclusion, Appleby guessed, accounted for a tendency to hostility and aggression.

After completing a law degree at Kings' College London, Toby had landed a plum job in the legal department of a multinational drinks corporation. He assumed, not wholly inaccurately, that his middle sister's boyfriend was a) a 'leftie cretin', b) a free-loader, living on his tax-money and c) a holier-than-thou do-gooder who would have all sorts of wet, liberal reasons for disapproving of the corporate activities he was paid so generously to protect.

In the course of three days they managed to argue through gritted teeth about the Falklands War, Michael Foot's fitness as a political leader and the miners' strike. Appleby was constantly goaded by mocking propositions beginning 'I suppose you think that...' or 'I expect you're the kind of person who...'

At first Appleby tried not to let himself be provoked. If it got too bad, Jenny or Lucy would come to his defence. 'Oh do shut up, Toby!' or 'Stop being such a pompous ass!' Appleby began to wonder if they might achieve an uneasy truce until Toby produced a bottle of a hideously expensive twenty-year old malt whisky from a tiny distillery owned by his employers.

When Appleby asked to have his glass 'on the rocks', Ralph happily obliged. Toby almost exploded, berating him contemptuously as an uncivilised ignoramus on whom such priceless nectar was wasted. Appleby tried to laugh it off, but he felt hurt and humiliated. To Jenny's annoyance, he started looking for opportunities to needle Toby on the sly, casually suggesting that Margaret Thatcher should be impeached for lying to parliament, for instance, or that Arthur Scargill should be given a life peerage.

This last point infuriated Jenny because she knew Appleby had no time for Scargill. 'That man can't find a patch of moral high ground without abandoning it,' he had said. 'Don't play childish mind games with Toby,' she snapped. 'He may act like a pompous buffoon, but this is my family, and I really don't appreciate you stirring it like that!'

*

After dinner on Christmas Eve, Jenny asked him if he wanted to go with the family to Midnight Mass. At first he was taken aback. Wasn't it enough that he had already agreed to a church wedding without this further breach in their pact not to inflict their beliefs on each other? Apart from a few weddings, three funerals and a christening, he hadn't been to a church service since he was thirteen.

When he was a boy, his mother used to take him and Kate to the local Anglican church occasionally, though she had never tried to get them confirmed. He hated it. St Augustine's was a gloomy Victorian pile blackened by many decades of coal smoke. The mere sight of it depressed him, and he found the services excruciatingly dull. He loathed being expected to confess to being a 'wretch' and a 'sinner'. It was so unfair, especially as his junior school classmates were always making fun of him for being such a 'goody-goody'. The dirge-like Psalms were simply baffling, and as for the long, rambling, barely intelligible sermons, to a restless child they were a refined form of purgatory.

The only element of the services he actually enjoyed was singing hymns. He didn't mind the jolly ones like 'All things bright and beautiful' or 'At the name of Jesus' but for some reason he didn't even try to understand, the slow, solemn, melancholy ones touched his soul. The vicar could elaborate for hours on the sacrifice of 'our Saviour Jesus Christ, who died for us upon the cross' and make not the slightest dent in his juvenile consciousness, but one verse of 'There is a green hill far away' and young Appleby was flooded with empathetic awe.

His mother abruptly stopped taking them when Kate reached fourteen and refused point blank to go again. When Appleby was home for Christmas during his first year at York, she admitted that she herself had ceased to believe in God when she was at university. She had dragged them to church all those years because Christianity provided a sound 'moral education'. Appleby was indignant on behalf of his childhood self: all that time when he could have been playing with toy soldiers or building model Spitfires, wasted!

His 'moral education' continued at Archbishop Cranmer's. There was a full Anglican assembly every morning complete with prayers, lessons from the Bible and a sermon from the Chief Master, an ordained Anglican priest. And there were plenty of those spine-tingling hymns: 'Disposer supreme, and judge of the earth', 'I lift mine eyes unto the hills', 'O come, O come, Emmanuel'. He had a particular relish for the more sombre Christmas carols like 'In the Bleak Midwinter' and 'Once in Royal David's City'.

But he still detested those prayers and sermons, and as for the boys who took religion seriously, who joined the Young Christian Society or the Bible Reading Group, they were simply incomprehensible. How could anyone believe in anything so completely irrational? So patently historically unreliable? They were not just deluded, but wilfully deluded, willing slaves, who had deliberately forfeited their intellectual independence because of some craven need to placate their parents or teachers. He and his friends regarded them as terminally 'uncool' and rarely spoke to any of them.

So his affair with Jenny had involved overriding, or at least suspending, long-standing and tightly held prejudices. He guessed she was making an equivalent accommodation for him. She normally didn't bother with church on their weekends together anyway and if she did, he simply had a lie-in or read the papers before starting to get the lunch ready. So when she invited him to come to Midnight Mass his first instinct was to refuse.

Then he contemplated the alternatives. He would be alone in the house with Toby, now in a permanent sulk, who was monopolising the only television set. And after a boozy dinner, Appleby wasn't in the mood to read. At least this special service would be a new experience. He might even enjoy the carols. Zeta had been listening to the *Festival of*

Nine Lessons and Carols on the radio that afternoon. He had caught most of 'O little town of Bethlehem' on the radio earlier in the day, and it had given him goose-pimples.

'Okay,' he said. 'Why not? I'll look on it as a form of immersion anthropology.'

'Don't be so bloody patronising,' Jenny snorted.

There was a brief debate over the venue. Jenny wanted Appleby to experience the service at the Cathedral and described it in rapturous terms. It would be at its most magnificent, she said, the teams of clergy in their full regalia, the interior illuminated with countless candles. The singing was always wonderful, ethereal. The voices of the choir seemed to hang magically in the vast, elegant vaulting of the nave. He was almost getting enthusiastic, but Ralph and Zeta put their feet down. They preferred their regular place of worship, a large handsome late medieval church near the city centre. It was much nearer the house, the service was high Anglican and utterly traditional, and the vicar, who was such a decent young chap, might notice their absence and be hurt.

Outside the night air was crisp and clear. It was refreshing to be out in the cold after a large dinner, a treble whisky and several glasses of Ralph's best Burgundy. He enjoyed the brisk walk, following Jenny's parents, both couples arm-in-arm.

As they approached the churchyard gate, the Webbs started to meet old friends, and Appleby found himself hovering on the fringes of convivial conversations about children, elderly relatives and church events. So it wasn't entirely about blind faith and following centuries of convention, he thought. The church provided membership of a community, not a particularly stimulating community admittedly, at least to Appleby's taste, but a community nonetheless.

There were forests of candles here too, and the interior was bathed in their soft warm light. A faintly perfumed odour hung in the air. Women helpers with benign smiles handed out copies of the order of service and thin white lighted candles, each in a round paper collar. Appleby felt awkward carrying his, as if he had been lumbered with someone else's wine-glass at a party and couldn't find anywhere to put it down. A sweet touch, perhaps, but it was a relief when the moment came to put it out and hand it back.

He gazed around the congregation which was swelling rapidly, trying to get a fix on these practising Christians. But it was difficult. The menswear departments of Marks and Spencer and C & A seemed heavily over-represented, and there was a super-abundance of women in 'sensible shoes', but they were far more varied in age, dress and demeanour than he had expected. Very few looked like the young prigs he remembered from school.

When the service began he found the liturgy no longer seemed oppressively dull. Rather it aroused his curiosity. He didn't join in the prayers and he didn't kneel, but he stood or sat with his head bowed respectfully and contemplated the implicit moral messages, trying to match them against his own view of the world. At other times he gazed around, absorbing the details of the architecture, the intricate wooden beams in the roof, the elaborate ribbing of the columns. Or he tried to read the inscriptions on the stone plaques on the walls, the faded, discoloured flags and heraldic boards. When the clergy passed down the aisle waving their censers he breathed the perfumed smoke in deeply, as if he thought it might get him high.

Halfway through the service everyone was told to turn and shake hands with their neighbours in a sign of peace. Appleby expected to find this ritual excruciatingly embarrassing. In the event he didn't mind at all. He was simply saying 'Happy Christmas' to a few strangers. It was quite agreeable.

The first carol was 'The first Noel', another of his childhood favourites. The congregation had some difficulty coming in on time. Appleby had even more difficulty finding his own voice, hobbled by his self-consciousness. But the choir sang clear and true and seemed to draw everyone else along with them. Suddenly he became aware of Zeta. She had a wonderful voice which trilled into the air like liquid crystal. Ralph sang in a resonant baritone, soaring off into descants which almost threw Appleby completely. Neither hit a wrong note. He looked round at Jenny, flashing her a little 'Gor blimey!' grin. She smiled and raised her eyebrows. Her own voice was almost drowned out.

Whether it was the heady, incense-laden atmosphere, the lingering effects of the evening's food and wine or an unfamiliar sense of general well-being he could not say, but Appleby found himself slipping into a trance-like state. It was time for the Eucharist. As the congregation lined up to take communion he stayed in his pew and gazed dreamily around the church. He thought he was hallucinating. He was seeing the place as it would have looked before the Reformation. The pillars were coated in gaudy painted patterns and the walls with scenes from the Bible. Every free space was cluttered with statues and carvings. There were no pews, and the nave was heaving with worshippers, including tiny children clinging to their mothers' knees or sleeping in their arms. There was a strange, pungent smell: incense mixed with a faint aroma of pee from those who had not been able to hold on in the interminable service. He was part of a large huddled crowd of humanity, sharing an overwhelming communal experience. It was partly spiritual, but there was also something else which he couldn't quite define. It was as if he was feeling a pulse... a pulse which had run through the veins of history for fifteen hundred years.

The vision passed in moments, leaving him confused and slightly shaken, but also curiously energised. With every carol he sang louder and clearer. From somewhere deep inside a voice emerged he had never heard before, forced out by his diaphragm, unexpectedly tuneful, reverberating through his body. He almost lost his concentration during 'O Come All Ye Faithful' when they hit the line 'Lo, he abhors not the Virgin's womb'. Wasn't this one of the most awkward, badly phrased lines of verse he had ever read, let alone belted out at full volume? He suddenly remembered Hector Sneasby, who would surely claim it was written by Shakespeare, and he almost got the giggles. But his confidence in his singing grew with every verse, and with it came an overwhelming sense of delight in becoming a part of something so beautiful, so majestic. The feeling reached a crescendo during the last carol, 'Hark! The herald angels sing', and he opened his voice to full throttle during the ecstatic final chorus.

The vicar stood by the door as they filed out, wishing everyone a Merry Christmas. Appleby shook his hand and thanked him warmly. A light dusting of snow was falling. Ralph and Zeta said goodbye to their friends, and they set off home. Jenny pulled tightly against his arm and looked up at him. How terribly pretty she looked.

'You really got into that, didn't you?' she said with a gratified little grin.

'Yes,' he said. 'Yes I genuinely enjoyed it.' They walked on in silence through the softly whitening streets. 'I still don't believe in God, though.'

A few minutes further down the road Appleby noticed that caps of snow had formed on the front of his shoes. He stamped his feet to dislodge them.

'You know what I think?' said Jenny, gripping his arm a little tighter. 'I think you had a religious experience in there.'

'No,' he said. 'It wasn't religious exactly.' There was a long pause. 'It was...I can't really explain it...It was something else...'

Amsterdam

As soon as Appleby snapped his phone shut he regretted agreeing to meet Claire. She was bound to ask him about the film, about his script and his research. Worse, she had been reading voraciously about anything connected to Elizabeth's court. In her study of the domestic economy of the great aristocratic houses she had probably come upon all sorts of titbits about Sir Philip Sidney. If she started to question him closely, he put the percentage chances of his getting rumbled somewhere in the high nineties.

Back at van Stumpe's he spent an hour chatting inanely with Piet and 'Vaartje' in the sitting room, for the sake of politeness. Conversation mainly involved shouting phatic pleasantries at the old man, who was virtually deaf and didn't understand English anyway. When he finally reached his bedroom, he plugged his laptop into an adaptor, which he plugged into a wall-socket. Then he hooked it up to his mobile phone and plugged that into the wall with another adaptor to save the battery. He sat up till three in the morning surfing the internet for anything he could find about the warrior-poet.

The connection was painfully slow, and he wasted a good thirty minutes searching for references to a historian called van der Valk. Skyne had implied that this man was at the cutting edge of research on the war, but he could find nothing, even though he scoured the websites of every relevant historical journal he could think of, including several Dutch ones and tried a dozen possible spellings. He might have misheard of course, or Skyne might have misremembered the name. It was strange all the same.

Back in his claustrophobic little office the next morning, he finished logging the booklets, pamphlets and tracts. Some of this material was printed: religious or philosophical essays, many imported. There were texts in Latin, Dutch, German, French, Spanish and Italian. Appleby recognised some as Lutheran or Calvinist; a few were Zwinglian. Two or three were full of esoteric symbols and calculations. He assumed these were alchemical treatises: arcane mysticism and superstition dressed up as science. It would be easy enough to check. This was the kind of paranormal rubbish craved by the gullible and the deluded today, in fact. It was less bonkers than Scientology anyway.

The owner of this collection must have been a true 'Renaissance man', with an apparently insatiable and omnivorous appetite for any kind of religious, philosophical or scientific theory. As with the books, the mere possession of some of these works would have been enough to attract an extremely unpleasant investigation. One pamphlet seemed to concern the centuries-old heresy of Arianism, exactly the kind of tract that got Thomas Kyd into trouble when it was found in the rooms he shared with Marlowe. Despite the fact that it was a critique of the heresy written by an Anglican clergyman, Kyd had been hauled off to be racked in the Bridewell. Could this even be a copy of the same one?

Many of the documents were hand-written, with neat, obviously home-made binding. A lot of the material looked like poetry, though when he skip-read the texts they seemed more like prayers, psalms or meditations. Appleby imagined nimble female fingers, pressing needle and thread through folded parchments on kitchen tables by candlelight. Several booklets were marked as '*Colloquies*' and seemed to consist of transcriptions of conversations with a religious or philosophical theme. They were written in a hand he did not recognise, but the participants were labelled as '*T.C.*' and '*N.H.*' presumably Cranham and Harker.

Some were marked '*Contemplations*' and looked like short meditative essays. Others resembled services devised for specific occasions: '*On the Eve of Nuptials*', '*For those Afflicted by Great Loss*', '*In Celebration of a New Birth*', '*On the Death of a Mother at Childbirth*', '*On the Death of a Newborn Infant*'. He paused at that last one, remembering little Daniel with a sharp pang. It seemed to be a kind of litany, with scripted responses. At a quick glance, the sentiments seemed unexceptional, kindly, but trite, the sort of thing you might find in a greetings card today. Again, there was no mention of God.

Finally he turned to the pile of loose pages. Much of this material was commercial: orders, invoices, receipts, promissory notes. There were legal documents too, and correspondence with lawyers in England and the Low Countries. Some papers related to Cranham's family. He had kept pages of his children's earliest writing and scribbled drawings, just as a modern parent would have. There were dozens of letters, many of them from Sir Nicholas Harker. These he would read with particular attention.

The process of cataloguing was arduous and often dull, and his mind kept returning to Cranham's journal. After two hours he could bear it no longer and picked it up again. He decided to work back from the end of the pile.

The last quarter of the journal dealt with Cranham's life as an exile in the Netherlands. Evidently he had escaped with one of his children, his infant daughter Perdita. Had she too been ill on the day of the massacre and stayed at home with him? He seemed to have bought himself a small farm, learned to speak Dutch, attended the local church, married a Dutch wife eventually, despite his advancing years, and started a second family. He appeared, in short, to have done everything he could to disappear into the flat Dutch landscape, a tiny windmill turning to face the prevailing wind. It was as if his previous life in England had never existed.

Then Appleby found the entries written during the first few years after his escape. These told a different story – a story of constant flight from city to town and from town to city, of bribed officials, of hiding in lofts and hair's breadth escapes, of fear in the night and mounting paranoia. Eventually on a torn sheet slipped between the pages, he found this:

'Antwerp, Tuesday 16th July 1594

I fear my Hearte is crack't in twain. Young Luke Wainwrightte hath found his way to my Lodgyng here at grate Perill of Discoverie to us bothe. The Tidings from Home are a thousandfold worse than I could e'er have dreamt. My sweete sweete Susannah, the Sun of all my days, and all our darling Children save my beloved little Perdita, good Piers and all the others of our Household, all murdered by the most cruellest means. Likewise my Dearest Friend, good noble Sir Nic, the Lady Grace and all their Family, even half the good Folke of the Village, all burned to death and their fine House to a heap of Ashes. I knowe not how I shall find the Hearte to live. Yet fain must I, if only to protect that which has beene entrusted to me, by the Grace of a Spirit far greater than mine owne.'

The writing was smudged and spattered. Had Cranham been weeping as he wrote? Appleby could almost feel his hot tears splashing the sheet. Then he came to the last entry written before Cranham had left England:

'Mill House, Thursday

I am still sore afflicted by the ague, though I trust now that the tide of its wrath is turned and the fever doth begin to ebb. Susannah did cool my head with a wetted cloth through day and night. The nightmarish spectres and dread premonitions that assailed me for three days and nights are passed, for which I most heartily thank the mercy of kind Dame Nature. Yet am I still weak and shake as a leaf in the Winter wind if I essay but to walk across my chamber.

Good Sir Nicholas came to attende upon me this afternoone. I admonished him for such a foolish hazard to his own good health. He had learned of my sickness by my reply to his last summons to our Rite and was most urgent to see me.'

Appleby paused for a moment. Surely that was a reference to the letter which van Stumpe had first shown him when he came over eleven days ago? He read on.

'I bid him return on the instant to Farthingwelle, but he would hear none of it and bid me most earnestly that we should talk privvily.

When that Susannah had left us, he spake once more of his interlocutionnes as the most especial guest of his Grace the Bishop. His mind had returned to these discourses each and every day the while, and at every time his disquiet grew the greater. 'I could be in no wise mistook,' quoth he, 'The Bishop knows of our Ceremonies and doth condemn them, in their very esssence, as Heretickal. I am likewise persuaded that he took my feeble Protestations of enduring Faithe to be but mere dissembling, for I laid before him that which hath moved our heartes.'

I told him again, that nigh on three weeks had passed since his return, and that surely the time was passed when the Bishop would move against him.

'Nay, good Tom,' quoth Sir Nick. 'I have an honest intelligencer at the Cathedral who hath sent word that His Grace hath writ to London and to Canterbury to be advised upon my case. He awaits but for Guidaunce from above. And I know in my heart that what passed between us cannot go without Consequence. They will come to me e'er long,' says he, 'and I fear this Saturday's solemnities needs must be our last.' It was his greatest sorrow that I was too sick to attend, saith he, though he hoped the Lady Susannah, the children and all would come 'as welcome Ambassadors of the House of Cranham.'

'Now dear Tom. There is another matter of yet greater moment. I have brought with me my sturdiest cart, piled high with logs and sacks of I know not what, and left it in your great barn. Underneath this motley cargo, there is a chest within which are my most precious books and mine own scribblings and all that might call Destructionne down upon us. I implore you to add thereto any correspondences you have of me and every account you have kept of our intimacies and exchanges these many years of our true Fellowshippe, in special those musings, our Colloquies, recorded with such pains by your good wife. Likewise I implore you fervently to take especiall means to conceal that Booke of whiche we may not speak.'

By this I knew he spake of that which was writ by the Brother of the Murdered Man. I enquired of his owne moste peculiar treasure, but he bid me give no further thought to the matter, for 'twas putte away where none should find it.

If, as one day soon you surely must, you hear that I am beset by unwelcome callers,' saith he, 'then do you take this chest away and hide it wheresoe'er you may, else, upon extremity to save your very life, cast it into the deepest waters or down some bottomless chasm.'

With that he leaned towards me, pressed a great key, most wondrously ingenious, into my hand, and kissed me upon my brow. 'Farewell, sweet Tom,' quoth he, and he was gone. Enfeebled as I was, I wept as I were a tiny child, for I knew it in my heart that I would never see him more.'

The entry was dated 16th May 1594.

It was now overwhelmingly clear to Appleby that within this journal lay the key to the whole mystery. Everything else that he found in the chest would, he was certain, be explained within its pages. Cranham, it seemed, was Harker's chronicler and his sounding-board, his Boswell and his Doctor Watson. Appleby was startled by his candour. Everything he had read previously about Catholics, alchemists and any other kind of recusant, heretic or dissenter had been wreathed in secrecy, in a shadow world of opaque allusions and veiled hints, of secret codes and cryptic ciphers.

Cranham's references to what were clearly illegal activities were often oblique, it was true, but only partially so. An inquisitor who came upon them would have taken them as open evidence of guilt, and could simply have demanded to be told, on pain of torture, what it was that they actually referred to. In places Cranham had recorded conversations verbatim in which he, Sir Nicholas and others openly doubted the teachings of the church, as if these discussions were of no greater moment than the weather or the proverbial price of eggs. Appleby began to form a picture of a small, enclosed rural community that had gradually become a law unto itself, a community with a confused or acquiescent parish priest, which had, under the guidance of a charismatic and beloved leader, begun to follow its own spiritual destiny.

Harker must have been extremely well educated. Appleby quickly found a reference to his time at Winchester and several to his time at New College, Oxford, which is where he seemed to have developed an interest, not only in classical philosophy, but in the theologies of non-Christian religions. From a young age, it seemed, Harker's curiosity had been racing down tracks his fellow scholars would have considered dark and dangerous. It might also begin to explain the extraordinary book collection.

He was puzzled by the reference to a special book, 'by the brother of the murdered man'. He guessed he would discover what this was in due course. As to Harker's 'owne moste peculiar treasure', presumably that was lost to history. He locked the closet and went down to see van Stumpe, taking the journal with him.

It took him over an hour and every argument and emotional manoeuvre in his repertoire to persuade the librarian to yield. Eventually, though, against his every instinct and principle of good practice, van Stumpe agreed that Appleby could take the journal out at night, but only on the strict condition that the papers would always be protected, that they never be exposed to potentially damaging atmospheric or environmental conditions and that they would be locked in Appleby's briefcase, which would never be out of his sight.

Appleby set off for his rendezvous, happily unaware that van Stumpe was sitting at his desk with his head in hands. He sensed this Englishman was leading him into territory which was far more risky and unpredictable than he had imagined. He felt he had let slip control of the situation, and that scared him.

*

The journal was safe inside Appleby's briefcase when he arrived at the quiet, smoky bar where he had arranged to meet Claire. It was not as secure as he had promised van Stumpe, though. Old habits, after all, die hard. He had forgotten to lock it.

'James! Over here!' Claire's voice rang out. She was sitting at the far end in a wooden booth with a young man Appleby didn't recognise.

'This is my old school-friend, Hans! The one I was telling you about,' she burbled. 'Hans, this is James, my supervisor from Cambridge, though only for the rest of this term, worst luck! Isn't it funny us both becoming historians – and the same period too! Hans is doing his thesis at Hamburg on the Eighty Years War – that's what they call the Dutch Revolt over here – but why am I telling you that, like you don't already know? Anyway, he's approaching it from a kind of Teutonic angle, aren't you, Liebster.'

'Goodness!' said Appleby. 'I thought you were joking! You see I made up this imaginary friend, a Frankfurter called Fritz. And I thought you'd made one up too – a Hamburger called Hans! Oh never mind.' He thrust a hand towards the young German, a slight figure with spiky hair carefully gelled into stylish faux-chaos, and a five o'clock shadow. 'Nice to meet you, Hans,' he said. 'It's good to know you really exist.'

'I'm quite pleased about that myself,' said Hans dryly, 'especially if the alternative is being some poor quality meat product you Anglo-Saxons put in a nasty little bread-roll and cover with tomato sauce. But aren't we getting a little existential already? It's only seven-thirty, and we're not even high yet.'

'So tell us all about your research,' said Claire. 'We're dying to hear everything. Hans is an expert on all this, you know. Actually he says the English intervention in the war was almost completely ineffectual, mainly because the Earl of Leicester was a total toss-pot. Not like 1944, eh? Oh, sorry, Hans. *Don't mention the war*, and all that!'

This was an alarming development. Appleby decided to stonewall.

'It's very much in the early stages of development, I'm afraid,' he said. 'I'm not really supposed to discuss it, if you don't mind.'

'Well, at least tell me where you are researching now,' protested Hans. 'I may very well be able to give you some useful indications. I can tell you where to find the best source materials on any aspect of the war you could mention.'

'I'm based at the Renaissance Institute at the moment,' Appleby mumbled.

'Oh!' said Hans. 'With old van Stumpe, I suppose! He's such a *weirdo*, as the Americans like to say. And such a big fairy, too.'

'What?'

'Van Stumpe. He's so gay, it's not true! Don't tell me you hadn't noticed! I'm surprised you are starting there though. They have got nothing interesting! I went right through their catalogue last year. There was masses of wonderful source material on art and trade and religion and the legal system, but almost nothing military. And copies of what they do have can be requested through their website anyway. I expect they have a reciprocal arrangement with your library. You could probably have read it all back in Cambridge!'

'Don't worry,' said Appleby. 'I've found plenty to keep me occupied.'

'Okay then. If you say so. But in that case you must have found something that was not there last year!' Hans started to pull on his jacket. 'Listen Claire, my darling, I am off to have some fun now. Call me if you want to come and join in later. Goodbye, Professor, and good luck. I think you're going to need it. Just tell Claire when you're ready for some information that is actually useful. I'll be delighted to help a friend of my Little Dumpling.'

He stood up, leaned over and planted a big wet kiss on Claire's cheek.

'There is one thing,' said Appleby. 'I'd be curious to know what you think of van der Valk's theory about the English use of artillery at Zutphen? Can it be substantiated?'

Hans looked non-plussed. 'Van der Valk? The only van der Valk I ever heard of was a television detective with pretty blond curls who my mother had the hots for when we were living in England. Is this some mad American? Sidney was wounded in a small cavalry engagement. There was no artillery! Don't you know that?'

'You're right, of course,' mumbled Appleby. 'I must have been confusing it with some other paper. I've been reading so many...' But Hans was already sweeping out of the bar, giving Claire a cheeky wave and blowing her another kiss.

This was even worse than Appleby had feared. Van der Valk was Skyne's elephant trap, and he had fallen right in and impaled himself on the stakes. What would Skyne have said if Appleby had had the knowledge and confidence to call his bluff? *He'd* have claimed he was confusing van der Valk with someone else presumably. Either way he clearly couldn't care less what Appleby thought of him. He didn't even care if Appleby *knew* that he couldn't care less. The level of professional contempt was breath-taking.

'You look like you just swallowed a live toad,' said Claire. 'You mustn't mind Hans, you know. He's such a poser. But isn't he delicious? For a Hamburger I mean. I'm absolutely famished. Let's get something to eat. They do the most scrummy mussels here.'

'Sure,' said Appleby. 'Listen, I just...' He nodded towards the toilets and got up.

He looked back as he reached the door. Claire was watching him. She smiled. He had left his briefcase on the table. Had he locked it? He wasn't sure if he had. Did it really matter? Maybe Sir Thomas Cranham's paranoia was infectious.

'Isn't this place cosy?' she said when he got back. 'I'm afraid I went ahead and ordered. I hope you don't mind. It's run by a couple of Belgians, and the *moules-frites* are to die for. We can get something else if you like.'

The briefcase looked undisturbed. Appleby finally relaxed.

'*Moules-frites* is great.'

Claire gazed into his eyes. Her expression was amused, but affectionate. Could she possibly be flirting with him too? 'You are the man of mystery aren't you?' she said. 'It's terribly attractive you know.' She was.

The waiter arrived with a huge steaming bowl of mussels in wine and garlic sauce, an even larger bowl of chips, a pot of home-made mayonnaise and a basket of fresh, crusty bread.

'Mmmmh!' said Claire, helping herself to the plump, fleshy molluscs. 'Perfection! Use the bread to mop up the sauce.' For the first time, he noticed how small and delicate her fingers were, like shorter versions of Jenny's in fact, though the nails were bitten. Less at ease with herself than she seemed, then.

'This is good,' he said. And it was good, eating simple delicious food in a homely Belgian bar in Amsterdam, opposite a beautiful, funny young woman, only half his age, who seemed to hang on his every word.

They had been eating in contented silence for a couple of minutes when she looked at him with a mischievous little grin.

'James,' she said. 'I don't suppose you're going to tell me what you're really up to?'

'What do you mean?'

'I thought not,' she sighed. 'You're such a sweetie when you're being secretive.'

Appleby briefly wondered what it would be like to make love to her, but quickly dismissed the thought as a lecherous middle-aged fantasy. Anyway, girls like Claire used such mild flirtation as a form of social lubrication. They probably taught it at finishing school.

'Hans is off tomorrow,' she said casually as they finished their meal, 'but I'm staying on one more night'. She stretched her hand across the table and laid it on his. 'Why don't you take me to dinner tomorrow?'

'Yeah,' he said. 'Okay.' Well it was only a meal. What harm could it do? 'How do you fancy Indonesian?'

'That sounds fab.'

He had an uneasy feeling that he was getting out of his depth.

*

At ten o'clock the following morning J.D. Clovis took a call from Norman Skyne.

'Our friend in Amsterdam has got hold of some kind of journal, apparently. It seems to be Elizabethan. And it's very long.'

Exmoor, Archway

'How is our apprehension of our own fortune in this world shattered all in pieces, when we but glimpse how others live?'

—*Sir Nicolas Harker, The Colloquies, Vol II, No 23*

The party left Holland Park in the late evening, when the worst of the rush hour traffic had subsided. Angelini drove with DI Kot in the front passenger seat. Appleby and Jenny sat in the back. DS Handley followed alone in an unmarked black Land Rover Discovery. West London was still congested, and they crawled along the M4.

'Don't you hate driving in all this?' asked Kot. 'Don't you have a driver?'

'I love to drive,' said Angelini. 'Besides, my driver becomes uncomfortable if I sit next to him up front, and I get so bored in the back.'

'You're very quiet, back there,' said Kot looking round. 'Are you okay?'

'He's dozing,' said Jenny.

Appleby's eyes were closed but he couldn't sleep. His mind was in a sort of anxiety-lock, stunned by the terrible news from Amsterdam, the knowledge that a trained assassin was somewhere out there looking for him and a growing dread that he might never return to his normal life again.

As the BMW nudged its way into the multiple lanes of the M25, he finally drifted into sleep. He saw Piet van Stumpe in some ghastly dumb-show, leaning out of the window of a burning Elizabethan manor house, shouting silently for help. Then van Stumpe had morphed into the boy from Harlem who had confessed to raping his sister. He was engulfed in flames, writhing in agony while the Elder Celebrant stood over him laughing. Now in an obscure corridor in the Renaissance Institute, Appleby was searching desperately for a fire-extinguisher. Agent Ashley O'Malley appeared and handed him a bucket of water. Half her head was missing. He thanked her and woke with a start.

He was drenched in sweat. He saw a road-sign. They were passing Basingstoke.

'We will leave the motorway now,' said Angelini. 'There will be less traffic.'

Kot radioed back to Handley, telling him to follow them down the A303. Appleby knew this road well. He associated it with mid-term breaks and long weekends with friends of Jenny's near Exmouth. They swept past the ghostly silhouette of Stonehenge, passing signs, first to Salisbury, then to Wolvington. They were within a few miles of Swively. Every time they crested a ridge a new vista of rolling hills appeared. He remembered the keen anticipation of gentle pleasures, of pints outside pubs in lovely fishing villages, seafood lunches at quaint, old-fashioned seaside resorts, of bracing walks on Dartmoor and cream teas. Now the pale night sky signified uncertainty and fear. When they finally crossed into Devon, his exhaustion overtook him again.

*

'Wake up, sir. We're there.'

Kot leaned round and gently touched his knee, and Appleby surfaced again. Angelini was using another electronic device to open a pair of tall iron gates. He heard the thin mechanical whine of a turning security camera. It followed them as they drove onto a long gravel drive, which snaked through a garden of mature rhododendron bushes. Appleby climbed groggily out of the car onto the forecourt and found himself gazing at the side of what looked like a small, squat industrial unit. It was hardly inviting, especially in the dark.

Handley's Discovery pulled up behind them a moment later, and Angelini led the party inside the house. Appleby wondered if he had stumbled into the pages of some futuristic design magazine.

'Gosh!' said Jenny. 'It's like entering the Tardis!'

'Yes,' said Angelini. 'It was designed by the Fentons. You have heard of them perhaps? The husband and wife team? Their homes are very special.'

The living area was dominated by a large glass-sided indoor swimming-pool, lit from above by solar-powered lamps which used low-energy lights by night and channelled sunlight through fibre-optic cables during the day.

'Like a giant fish-tank, isn't it?' said Kot. 'For human fish!'

'I hope I don't have to see your beer belly wobbling about while I'm eating my lunch,' said Handley.

As the group moved into the first reception area, Angelini placed his hand lightly against a panel of sensors near the front door, and the house sprang to life. Ambient lighting suddenly illuminated a sitting area and a huge plasma TV screen came on at low volume, pre-tuned to the BBC's 24 hour news service.

As Appleby and Jenny followed him into the open-plan kitchen, concealed spots lit up the polished concrete work-surfaces, and a set of surround-sound speakers began playing soothing classical music. Appleby thought he recognised it. Wasn't it something by Boccherini he recognised from a film score? It was suddenly overlaid by a loud hum.

'What's that?' he asked.

'Oh,' said Angelini walking into the kitchen area. 'That is the *forno* - the oven. I asked my housekeeper to prepare a casserole and a *risotto*. His *osso bucco* is exquisite. It will be ready in half an hour. He should have left some salad in the fridge to accompany it.'

'Your cook?' said Appleby, suddenly alarmed. 'Who is he? Has he got keys?'

'Don't worry,' said Angelini. 'These officers know all about him. He has handed his keys into the local police, and he has been given strict instructions to keep away from the place until further notice. He knows I have guests but he has no idea who you are or why you are here. I sometimes have discreet private parties.'

'Could I get a glass of cold water?' asked Jenny.

'Please,' said Angelini, handing her a glass. 'Here is the drinking water tap. It is ice-cold and filtered.'

'Where's the handle?' asked Jenny, moving the glass towards the spout.

'Oh!' she jumped back as a hidden sensor turned it on automatically, splashing her wrist. 'Is there anything in this house which is operated by a normal switch or tap?'

Angelini thought for a moment. 'No,' he said eventually. 'I don't think there is. But don't worry, you'll soon get used to it. And the security is second to none.'

At that moment a light beeping noise began.

'Aha!' said Angelini, pointing across to a panel of twenty small TV monitors. A red light was flashing over one screen. 'We have a visitor.'

An automatic floodlight had illuminated part of the ten foot high perimeter fence. Angelini picked up yet another remote-control unit from the worktop and zoomed in on a startled fox, sniffing at the fence from the outside, unable to find a way in.

'Sometimes we get curious local children or even poachers,' said Angelini, 'but when the floodlights come on, I can tell you they can't get away fast enough. They know we will have them on film. Also the compound has been designed so that the house, the terraces and the inner gardens are not visible from anywhere outside the perimeter. I think there is only one place a mile away where you can just see the top of part of the roof. So nobody will be able to take a shot at you so long as you don't go wandering through the woods towards the fence.'

The group ate their supper in front of the television.

Jenny swallowed a mouthful of the veal and risotto. 'This is a bit like our host,' she whispered to Appleby, when Angelini went to get wine.

'What do you mean?'

'Extremely rich, slightly glutinous and strangely comforting.'

'Let us watch the headlines,' said Angelini returning with the wine and turning up the volume.

The first three items were routine enough: another disappointing performance by the England football team; a collision in the English Channel and the efforts to rescue the missing skipper of a small yacht and the Chancellor of the Exchequer reacting to yet more worrying inflation figures.

'Elsewhere,' said a strangely nondescript newsreader called Phil Whitegrove, 'it has been another day of controversy surrounding the ever-growing Harkerite movement. Police in Leeds have scuffled with the congregation of a Harkerite rite after receiving a call claiming that a woman had just confessed to poisoning her husband. Worshippers forcefully prevented officers from entering the hall where the rite was being held, on the grounds that anything which occurs during a Harkerite ceremony is confidential. Police reinforcements arrived, but by the time they managed to get into the hall, the woman had gone. Thirteen people have been charged with public order offences and are being held at different police stations around West Yorkshire.

'International protests are mounting over the burning alive of two young women found distributing Harkerite texts at a remote village in the Punjab,' said Fiona Twelfe, Whitegrove's equally nondescript female partner. 'When a petition with over 50,000 signatures was presented at the Indian Embassy in London this afternoon, staff refused to accept it. In a brief statement, a spokesman said this was a purely internal matter and that his government would not be pressurised by foreign religious groups.

'The new cult is also causing further dissension within the international Anglican Church,' Whitegrove resumed. 'A bishop from South Africa has denounced it as "modern witchcraft, invented by the Devil", reacting angrily to a statement issued by leading Massachusetts Episcopalians that Harkerism and Christianity are not incompatible, and that there is nothing wrong with Anglicans attending Harkerite ceremonies. The Archbishop of Canterbury has announced that he intends to convene an international commission to investigate the movement and its impact on the Anglican Communion.'

'So you had no idea what you were unleashing when we published these books, James?' said Angelini.

'None whatsoever,' said Appleby. 'Did you?'

'I expected controversy,' said Angelini, 'but not perhaps on this scale.'

'The irony is that if it hadn't been for you, I would never have got to publish them at all. It would have been those bastards from Despenser dodging the assassins' bullets.'

'Whatever do you mean?' said Jenny.

'Shh!' said Appleby. 'I want to hear this.'

A sun-burnt correspondent in Beirut was delivering a live report.

'…well actually it's quite unprecedented,' he said. 'They call themselves the Tribes of Abraham after the Biblical figure considered a founding patriarch by Jews, Muslims and Christians alike, and the group consists of representatives of different branches of all three religions. They met in a conference suite of this city centre hotel here, surrounded by heavily armed guards. It's all shrouded in secrecy. They have refused to allow any media access whatsoever. Nobody outside the group seems to know why they were meeting or what was on their agenda.'

'But given the level of hatred and violence in the middle-east,' said Whitegrove, 'especially the unresolved disputes between Israel and the Palestinians just over the border, isn't such a meeting a good thing, a hopeful sign that the more moderate factions are beginning to talk to each other?'

'You would think so,' said the correspondent, 'but what is puzzling observers is that the representatives who have been seen coming in and out of the hotel – and this has just been confirmed to me by a senior intelligence officer in the Lebanese police – have all been associated with the most fundamentalist or militant organisations within each religion. They may not actually belong to terrorist groups themselves, but the Lebanese authorities are extremely uncomfortable about their presence in the city. These are not people who believe in compromise.'

'So what could they possibly have to say to each other?'

'Well that's just it. Nobody seems to have the slightest idea, and unless they decide to issue some sort of communiqué, then I doubt if anyone will. The only point I can add is that there may be a lot of money behind this organisation, whatever it is. My source in the police says they have identified several business tycoons, bankers and billionaire princes from the Gulf states among the delegates.'

'Intriguing,' said the anchor.

'Just so,' said Angelini, flipping the television off. 'But surely that is enough discord for one evening. Can I tempt anyone to a nightcap?'

'Not for us,' said Kot. 'Young Handley and myself will take shifts patrolling the property and keeping an eye on the security monitors.'

'Then please, James, Jenny, why don't we sit for a while on the terrace?'

They followed him onto a high, wide deck of polished teak boards with a sweeping view over the sea towards Wales. In the distance they could make out the lights of passing ships. The trees rustled slightly in the breeze and an owl hooted away in the woods. Otherwise it was perfectly calm.

'It's warmer than I thought it would be,' said Jenny.

'Is it too hot?' asked Angelini, gesturing towards a pair of outdoor heating units. 'I can turn it down. At the moment they are set to maintain a consistent twenty degrees.'

'I might have guessed,' laughed Jenny. 'Please leave it as it is. It's lovely.'

'Cognac?' Angelini walked over to a bar built into the side of the deck, produced a bottle from a concealed shelf and poured three generous glasses.

'Christ! This is nice!' said Appleby. 'What is it?'

Angelini passed him the bottle and he read the label to Jenny. 'Louis Royer Grande Champagne, 32 years old. Where do you get stuff like this?'

'I have a dealer. It's not really that fancy, actually. I get it for about £120 a bottle. I keep it for everyday drinking. It's beautifully smooth, don't you think? A touch fruity with a hint of spice. Perfect for a late summer evening, would you not agree, Mrs Appleby?'

'I'm afraid it's wasted on me,' said Jenny. 'We could be drinking a ten quid bottle of Asda's own-label and as long as it wasn't actually like paint-stripper, I probably wouldn't notice the difference.'

'You are absolutely right!' Angelini laughed. 'I am foolish to waste my money in this way! The principle is really extremely simple, you see. The price of luxury goods expands to meet the pockets of the ludicrously wealthy. As soon as there are millionaires someone will make a cognac so expensive that only millionaires can buy it. Then along comes a multi-millionaire so they market a brandy ten times more expensive than that. Then for a billionaire there is a cognac so old and exclusive that the price must quintuple once more. The trick is that only they and the billionaires themselves, along with a tiny number of specialist dealers and perhaps the occasional journalist, will even know these drinks exist. So even possessing a bottle marks your membership of one of the world's most exclusive clubs and only your fellow members will know.'

'Yes, but even so,' said Jenny.

'That's how it's always been,' said Appleby. 'I bet there were guys selling exclusive luxury mud pies in Ur of the Chaldes.'

'Of course!' Angelini was warming to his theme. 'Look at my shoes! Do you know how much I paid for them? 18,000 Euros! They were hand-made to a personal fitting by the finest bespoke shoe-maker in Milan. Nothing about them is ordinary. This supple, but otherwise ordinary looking brown leather is from a rare breed of calf reared at only one farm in the Dolomite Mountains. I could tell you the name, but it would mean nothing to you. The tanning process also is unique. These laces are spun in a tiny workshop near Genoa using specially imported Japanese silk and what look like ordinary brass eyelets are made of solid gold. Do they need to cost so much? Of course not. Even given the exclusivity of the product the profit margins are outrageous. They are a device by which the shoe-maker can help himself to as much of my fortune as possible. Would my feet be as comfortable in shoes from your Clarks or a pair of trainers from Marks and Spencer? Of course, my feet would probably be every bit as comfortable. The reward for me is that I know I am wearing the finest shoes that money can buy and that only a tiny number of people around the world could ever afford such an extravagance. And believe me, I know men and women who will pay far more than this for more ostentatious footwear!'

'Well you're remarkably open about it,' said Jenny, 'yet you still buy all this stuff.'

'Ah, well,' he sighed, 'I may understand how ridiculous it is, but it is still delightful to have these things. I suppose it is a kind of drug. The richer we become, the more we want to hold onto what comes with it, to the cognac and the shoes, the more we like to keep our wealth subtly hidden from the jealous or indignant gaze of the masses, and the more we will fight against anything that threatens to diminish the appalling inequalities of wealth that underpin our status. You should realise that we live in an age of infinite selfishness, that western democracy has been completely and utterly corrupted by it. At least the old aristocracies of Europe occasionally had some sense of social responsibility, of what you British liked to describe in the French term, *Noblesse oblige*.'

'Hasn't it always been that way?' said Jenny.

'No, I really don't think so. This is something much harder and colder. It has crept into the soul, first of America, then of Western Europe. Now it infects Eastern Europe, especially Russia, China, India, Latin America. You hear people complaining about the dictators of sub-Saharan Africa and their Swiss bank accounts. I tell you they are amateurs compared to the corporate moguls and the high financiers who control the developed world. These people are utterly amoral, they have no commitments to nation, to community or, despite some hypocritical posturing, to religion. They have cut free from any sense of responsibility to their fellow men. Sure, they manipulate these concepts when they need to, but only so they can corrupt them, to bend them to serve the ends of their own insatiable desire for wealth and power. Now *that* is a drug, more powerful than any narcotic or aphrodisiac. They are high on the ecstasy of their power'.

'I don't understand,' said Jenny. 'If you feel like that, why don't you do something about it?'

'Oh but he has done something, about it,' said Appleby. 'Unless I am very much mistaken, Signor Angelini here is not just my Italian publisher. He was the anonymous purchaser of the Harker-Cranham archive.'

'Ah!' said Jenny. 'So that's what you meant...'

By now Appleby had got his second wind. He was wide awake again, excited by the extraordinary surroundings, and the cognac was loosening his inhibitions.

'I'm sorry if this sounds ungrateful,' he said with sudden gusto, 'but you can't have it bloody both ways! You come on like an anti-globalisation demonstrator outside a meeting of the World Trade Organisation! I know you own that collection of subversive literature and all that, but you still run a multi-national publishing corporation, peddling heaven knows what rubbishy tat all over Europe. I don't get it.'

'For heaven's sake, Jimmy!' said Jenny. 'Giovanni is trying to help us.'

'No, no,' said Angelini. 'James is right to make this point, Jenny, but I hope you will allow me to explain. It is true, I am a very rich man, but perhaps I am not entirely the man you think I am. I believe James once read an article I wrote several years ago about my family. We Angelinis have a long history as trouble-makers in Italy. One of my ancestors was boiled alive in a vat of oil in front of the duomo in Perugia for insisting on his right to question the doctrines of the Papacy. There were Angelinis secretly selling Protestant texts in the bookshops of Venice when the Roman Inquisition closed them all down. You see perhaps I have more in common with men like Harker than you suppose. Several prominent Angelinis fought with Garibaldi and others were outspoken opponents of Mussolini who paid dearly for their anti-fascism. My great uncle was murdered by the S.S. for helping Jews escape from Firenze.'

'I know,' said Appleby. 'Your radical credentials are impeccable. But that still doesn't explain...'

'Let the man finish,' said Jenny.

'I made my fortune extremely quickly,' Angelini continued, 'more than I could ever want or need. My empire was secure. I could have gone on expanding, devouring my rivals, but I saw what this was doing to men like Berlusconi and Murdoch. A kind of insanity. So I stopped. Oh I do what I must to protect the interests of my corporation, I will not deny that. And I am still capable of extreme ruthlessness if I sense that part of my domain is under attack. But I became interested in my own family's history, and it began to change my view of the world. I began collecting books and documents about them. Very soon I had a small library. Then I began to buy anything that was subversive, heretical, revolutionary. Now I have the finest such collection in Europe. Then someone sent me some information about a certain archive in Amsterdam...'

Jenny turned to Appleby. 'Was that you?'

He nodded.

'You never said anything.'

'All I did was tip him off. Until today I never knew if he was actually the owner. That was a closely guarded secret.' Appleby tilted his empty glass to his mouth and ostentatiously drained the last drop.

'Pardon me,' said Angelini. 'I forget I am your host. More cognac? Mrs Appleby?'

'Not for me, thanks!' said Jenny. 'I'm done.'

'Yes please!' said Appleby. 'It's absolutely delicious.'

'Do you want to know what got to me?' Angelini resumed. 'It was the idea that all altruism in public policy is a delusion. This is the belief of all those free-market fanatics, especially the laissez-faire fundamentalists, the compulsive deregulators. They have convinced themselves that all forms of socialism and communism are simply disguised and inefficient forms of selfishness. But people like that are the secret champions of a dark principle. They are evil. They speak to the worst in human nature and proclaim it is the best. Theirs is a cruel, desiccated vision of humanity. The philosophies of these evangelical capitalists have brought disease to the soul of the modern world.'

By now Appleby was reeling. Having let his own socialist ardour atrophy over the decades, it was bizarre to be lectured in left-wing principles by a reformed plutocrat.

'And you were looking for a cure in the works of Harker...?' Jenny mused.

A look of infinite sadness passed over Angelini's face, and he let out a long slow noise, somewhere between a sigh and a faint wail. It reminded Appleby of recordings of whale-song he had heard on nature films.

'And now it's gone,' said Jenny gently. 'And you are grieving as if you had lost a child.'

At that moment a helicopter passed close overhead. They all fell silent. 'We should go to bed now,' said Angelini.

When Jenny and Appleby reached their bedroom, he was exhausted again and tipsy. He took his shoes off, threw his jacket over a chair and stumbled into the en-suite wet-room to brush his teeth. Fumbling for a light switch he brushed against a sensor which turned on the power-shower and was instantly soaked to the skin.

*

The next morning Iris walked out onto the smart new concourse in front of the Whittington Hospital in North London. It was a lovely day, warm and sunny with a pleasant breeze. Maybe she would take Eddy up Parliament Hill later. They could try out his new kite. It would give her some time to think. She took her mobile out and called home.

'Hi, it's me. How's he been?…Good…No, that's all right. I should be home in half an hour…Yeah, I saw the big boss man…I'll explain when I get back, but it's not good…No, it's as bad as it could be, actually… For God's sake don't say anything to Eddy.'

She stared down at the phone. She would have to tell James at some point. That would have to wait, though. She couldn't face it yet.

Wiltshire

'Mum and Dad are really upset, Jimmy. They'd never dream of saying anything to you, but they feel completely excluded from the preparations.'

'Oh God,' Appleby groaned down the phone. 'I know, I know, but it's all been taken out of my hands, Kate. Jenny's mum is a steamroller in a Harvey Nichols twin-set.'

Appleby's life was punctuated by episodes when he felt he had lost control of his fate, and his wedding to Jenny was one of them. From their arrival at church in an early 19th Century open landau to the classical quartet hired to play during the service, the release of hundreds of white butterflies as he and Jenny left the church and the tiniest details of the reception at Hanbury Hall 'Country House Hotel and Conference Centre', Zeta Webb was planning everything. Never mind Appleby: she barely even consulted Jenny.

In truth he was trying not to think about it. His book had finally come out to quietly appreciative reviews and he was working on a proposal for a sequel on rural life before the Civil War. He had been bitterly disappointed by the feeble response to the '*History Today*' article and was also desperately trying to think of ways of unearthing more information about Sir Nicholas Harker.

The phone-call from Kate about his parents simply intensified his discomfort about the whole business. It was bad enough that so many of his friends and colleagues disapproved of this ostentatious patriarchal pantomime. Hurting his own parents like this made him feel wretched.

In the end Jenny applied a little discreet diplomatic pressure and persuaded Zeta to let Tom and Barbara Appleby pay for the late night disco. They hired Kate's brother-in-law (a superannuated hippy called Kevin) to DJ. Appleby, Kate and Kevin spent a happy weekend in Handsworth Wood sorting through boxes of old vinyl albums for a night of 1960s and 70s nostalgia. He did put his foot down over the wedding list. He was not prepared to require his family and friends to buy their presents at Harrods. In the end Zeta agreed, extremely reluctantly, to the greater economy and convenience of John Lewis.

*

When the day arrived Appleby felt like an extra in a film about his own life. To his relief his parents got on fairly well with Ralph and Zeta. Zeta bossed Barbara around, but she laughed it off. Ralph whisked Tom off to the hotel bar for a pint, and they quickly discovered a mutual interest in the Second World War. Appleby found them deep in a comparative analysis of the relative merits of Generals Montgomery and Alexander. By the time he joined them they had agreed that neither was a patch on Bill Slim.

The service itself proved unexpectedly enjoyable. Jenny looked gorgeous as she walked down the aisle, trailing five impossibly cute bridesmaids in her wake, each done up like something from Botticelli's 'Primavera'. But it was only when he saw Ralph's eyes fill as he gave Jenny away that he felt a real connection to the proceedings. With it came a new and somewhat ominous sense of responsibility.

Zeta, of course, had no control over Appleby's choice of best man. As Pete Elyot stood up to give his speech at the remorselessly tasteful wedding breakfast, Appleby realised that the unresolved contradictions in the situation were about to hit the proverbial fan. Pete's pale grey morning suit was embellished by the loudest orange waistcoat Appleby had ever seen and a huge floppy red velvet bow-tie with tiny gold hammer-and-sickle motifs embroidered on each wing. He was swaying gently as he tapped the side of an empty champagne flute with a butter-knife.

'Lay-diz an' gen'lemen! I would like to call thiz meeting to order, if you please.' His voice was slightly slurred; his manner more than slightly camp. 'Comrades! Comradettes and those of as yet indeterminate gen'er orientation! I would like to open these proceedin's by sayin' what'n extraord'nary turn up for th' books it is to see my old *tovarish* from the barricades of Academe marryin' into what can only be described –

an' please don' take offence at this – as the *Oat Bourgeoisie*. You see, I've known Comrade Jimmy for fourteen years now, and I've come to think of 'im as a *lov'ble little mole…*'

At this point Pete paused to burp. A few guests tittered uneasily.

'Scuse me…as a *lov'ble little mole*, tunnelin' his way into the innermost recesses of our nation'l hist'ry. An' I have it on exc'llent authority that the lovely Jenny, can testify *in graphic detail* to Jimmy's excepshn'l talents when it comes to tunnelin' into innermost recesses…'

Pete paused for a fortifying slurp of champagne.

'…If only I' had that priv'lege m'self…' Another slurp. '…the tunnelin' I mean…'

There was another short pause in which the guests absorbed the purport of this off-colour remark.

'…but 'nfort'nately Jimmy dances at the *wrong en' of the ball-room*, as the sayin' goes…at least as far as I'm concerned.'

By now some guests' nervous laughter was mixing with the disapproving rumbles of others. For the stuffier members of the 'oat bourgeoisie', the speech went steadily downhill from there on. Appleby spent the rest of the evening apologising for Pete to Jenny's contingent and agreeing with his own about how funny he'd been.

At about half past one in the morning a ferocious argument erupted. Kevin was playing slow, soulful Motown classics for the few dancers left at the disco, when Toby's voice roared above the dance-floor from the bar.

'You can't actually believe that, you stupid leftie wanker!' he bellowed.

'Don't you call me a wanker, you arrogant monetarist cunt!' Pete flounced back.

'Have you seen the figures on the French economy, you ignorant twat!? They're a fucking shambles! Mitterrand's a useless compromising loser just like those useless fuck-faces Wilson and Callaghan.'

'That's a fucking Thatcherite lie, darling, and if you'd pull that hideous little excuse for a head of yours out of your over-stretched public-school arsehole, you would realise why.'

'Thanks to Maggie, this country is turning into the most efficient, lean, competitive economy in Europe, able to hold its own in the global market and pay the bloated salaries of useless, waste-of-space twats like you, you ungrateful moron. The French are backward, uncompetitive, subsidy-junky, socialist shits with feudal agriculture propped up by my taxes. They'll be dead in the water in five years!'

'Then how come they've still got their own car industry, a ship-building industry and their aircraft industry is second only to the United States, you arrogant pillock! And how come they have better roads, faster cleaner trains, a better health service, far better education and a much lower crime rate? The only reason Thatcher is killing off our heavy industry is to destroy organised labour. She's deliberately and cynically killing the very industries that made this country great because she wants to destroy the working-classes as a political force. She wants us living in a Third World economy where she has turned the entire workforce into "Have a nice day" minimum-wage-slaves who bend over and say "Missing you already" while her City friends fuck them up the arse!'

'Bollocks! Crap, shit and bollocks!'

'Ooh! Eat your heart out, Oscar Wilde!'

They were still at it when Appleby and Jenny finally staggered up to the bridal suite.

Over breakfast he caught up with Tim Farnstable who had come with a well-bred, leggy blonde called Amanda, the latest in his string of increasingly elegant conquests. Farnstable flirted outrageously with Jenny, as if to demonstrate that, even on the first day of Appleby's married life, he could have swept her off her feet if he had wanted to. Jenny kept her good humour, gently implying that she would rather poke her eye out with a burnt stick than succumb to his charms. Appleby was deeply gratified.

Farnstable had left a safe job as an assistant producer in the BBC's News and Current Affairs division to join a friend who had set up an independent production company called simply, 'Burst'. They existed to make documentaries for the infant Channel 4, and Tim had undreamed of freedom to devise and produce one-off documentaries, possibly even whole series of his own. He had just returned from filming in India and was now editing his documentary about the Mogul palaces of Rajasthan. Amanda, it turned out, was his personal assistant.

Appleby felt a twinge of envy over his friend's glamorous career. He slipped up to his room, dug out a spare copy of his article in '*History Today*' and passed it to Farnstable. It wasn't much of an achievement, but it was an intriguing story, and at least it showed that his own working life was not entirely mired in ecclesiastical courts and crop rotation systems. Farnstable made politely interested noises and tucked it into a pocket. Appleby wondered if he would ever actually read it.

*

The honeymoon was like some lazy fantasy which evaporated as soon as it was over. Jenny's grandmother had paid for them to stay in a Kenyan beach hotel. Their chalet looked like an African grass hut, though it had an en-suite bathroom and a telephone. They crossed a lawn to the fine sands of the beach. By mid-morning the sea was as warm as bath-water, and they could walk the hundred yards to the reef, beyond which fishermen in long narrow boats stood silhouetted against the burning blue sky.

In the morning they made love, showered, swam, ate breakfast, sat on their veranda reading, swam again, ate lunch, went for a nap, made love again, read again, went for another swim, showered again and changed, drank cocktails on the hotel terrace, ate supper, read, went to bed and made love. The pleasure almost got boring.

They only made two trips outside the hotel. One was to Gedi, the ruins of a deserted Swahili town hidden in a tropical grove between the Mombasa-Malindi road and the sea. It was a haunting place which had been abandoned some time in the seventeenth century, no one knew why. There were the remains of carved tombs, a mosque, a palace, drainage channels in the paved streets and houses with water closets. Archaeologists had dug up expensive trade goods from Europe, Arabia,

India and China. Appleby was pulled up short. This was his era, but compared to his Elizabethan country-folk, even the gentry, these people had been living in hygienic cosmopolitan luxury.

The second outing was spent wandering around the streets of Mombasa, still safe for foreigners then, and with a fine selection of gleaming temples, churches and mosques, including a fabulously decorated Jain temple in brilliant white marble. In a dungeon in Fort Jesus, the old Portuguese bastion, a captured English sailor had scratched a picture of an Elizabethan galleon into the plaster. The crude drawing was still there, four hundred years later, an outrider from a nascent empire and a delayed signal from the world of Appleby's own research.

*

Two weeks after their return, they moved into their new home. It was an early Victorian three-storey terraced house in a small irregularly shaped 'square' behind York station. The area had once been rather grand, but had run to seed.

'You've got your work cut out here, son,' his father said when they showed him round. 'Look at these fireplaces. They've never been touched. Will you be taking them out?'

'No way,' said Jenny. 'We're going to restore the whole place to its original state.'

'Apart from putting in central heating,' Appleby added quickly.

'Sooner you than me,' said Tom, though he did all he could to help them.

They bought books on original features, found specialist merchants and craftsmen and spent the next year stripping paint off pine doors and banister rails, restoring plaster cornices and ceiling roses, sanding the floors, replacing missing dado-rails and buffing the cast-iron fireplaces with blacking. It wasn't a hobby; it was a way of life.

Appleby found an unexpected joy in watching Jenny at work in the garden. She was filling out slightly, he noticed as she bent over the plants, her bottom a little more rounded. In her long loose skirt and headscarf she looked like a Breugel peasant woman. It aroused a warm, homely lust and made him think about children. The nimble craft in those elegant fingers found a new creative fruition when her artfully chaotic flowerbeds burst into life the following spring.

He had never been so happy. As they cuddled up at night, they could hear the muted rattle of the trains from the railway line in the quiet of the night, but he found even that curiously soothing. Life was going to be good in that house. He knew it.

*

In early October '*History Today*' forwarded a letter from a man called Guy Charlton. He was the new owner of the Swively estate which included Farthingwell Meadows. He explained that he had made a great deal of money as a City banker but had decided to quit the rat-race before he was burnt out. He had bought the site of what he now knew was once Sir Nicholas Harker's domain.

He enclosed a publicity leaflet outlining his ambitious plans for the place. He and his wife were going to plant traditional English apple varieties in organic orchards, 'grow' rare breeds of cattle, sheep and even wild boar, to run a stable of shire-horses and open a visitors' centre and a shop selling the work of local artists and craftsmen.

It struck Appleby as a painful irony that this wholesome, nostalgic vision of a rural Eden should be financed by the profits of the same giant capitalist maw which was turning the rest of the landscape into a vast, homogenised, characterless, open-plan ocean of cash-crops, cultivated by overworked, underpaid tenants. Not that there was anything Olde Englishe about the Charltons' plan to keep llamas and a herd of American bison.

Appleby had tried repeatedly to get access to the presumed site of Farthingwell Manor, and had been hoping to organise a dig there, but the previous owners had refused to answer his letters or respond to telephone messages left with the agency who organised the estate's management. Guy Charlton, on the other hand, was only too keen to talk to him. A friend had sent him a copy of Appleby's article, and his letter concluded with an open invitation to visit. Would Appleby care to come and stay one weekend? He would be welcome to bring his wife or partner.

Jenny was delighted by the idea, and they were looking at possible dates for a visit when their plans were unexpectedly pre-empted. Appleby was marking essays in his campus office, under the austere gaze of his portrait of Harker when the phone rang.

'Ellow,' said a man in a grotesque fake Birmingham accent. 'Is that Appleboy's Awthentic Brummagen Toik-Away Ristront and Massawge Pawler? Oi'd loik a Number Therty-Throy please with lots uv Extras! Yow dow provoid extras Oi troost!'

'Farnstable! This is a surprise.' Fake Brummy had been one of their favourite student comedy voices. 'To what do I owe this unexpected pleasure?'

'Aha, well now.' Farnstable switched back to his familiar clipped public school tones. 'I've just been reading an extraordinary article by someone called Dr James Appleby of York University. You wouldn't happen to know the fellow by any chance?'

'Ah, so you finally got round to…'

'No. No. I should have said "re-reading". I read it on the train home from that splendid wedding of yours. I would have got back to you more promptly, but I wanted to discuss it with people here at Burst. The consensus seems to be that there might be something in this, and we've had a preliminary chat about it with the Factual people at Channel 4. Now the thing is, they think it could make a rather interesting documentary, but it's a bit thin on hard facts at the moment. If it was possible to organise a dig on the site, on the other hand that would be another matter altogether. Channel 4 love wallowing in the mud-baths of archaeology. Listen. I'm going to be up in York this weekend for the races. Why don't I take you and the lovely Jennifer out for Sunday lunch and we can talk about it then?'

'I wouldn't hear of it! You must come for lunch with us and see the new house.'

'That would be delightful! So long you promise not to do any of the cooking yourself, that is.'

'My cooking isn't bad these days, as it happens, but don't worry, Jenny rarely lets me in the kitchen. It's a sort of territorial, scent-marking thing.'

'Boy boy then,' said Farnstable, reverting to mock Brummy. 'Oy'll be round for thows ixtras in due course. Yow better not furgit them or thu'll be hell to poy!'

'Bye bye, Tim. See you on Sunday.'

Amsterdam

When Appleby got back to van Stumpe's house after his Belgian supper with Claire, he was surprised to find his host waiting up for him.

'Let us be seated in my kitchen,' he said excitedly. 'We can be seeing this most important of documents together for some time. I have most carefully cleaned and dried the table.'

Appleby followed him through, and the two men sat down, put on protective gloves and began to look through Cranham's journal together.

'I am wondering why we did not notice the significances of these documents before,' said van Stumpe. 'Perhaps they looked not quite meaningful enough because so much of the sheets are loose and some binding on the other sections is so obvious to be amateur.'

'It's a wonderful discovery,' said Appleby, 'just as a record of Elizabethan village life. But I'm sure we'll find clues about what led to the massacre. Cranham was obviously Harker's best friend.'

'Read this one, James,' said van Stumpe, passing over a sheet dated September 1568.

'*Passed the evening at the Swan, with Sir Nic,*' Appleby read aloud.

'Was this the village's tavern?' asked van Stumpe.

'Yes,' said Appleby. 'It's called The Kindred Spirit now, and has been for over three hundred years. I'm not sure when they changed the name exactly. Or why.' He continued:

'*He spoke most kindly of my affection to the olde ways. I have never made a Secret of my Convictions with him, for he is a most trusted friend who puts good fellowshippe above all Lawes.*'

'Old ways? What might this be meaning?' asked van Stumpe.

'It means our friend Cranham was still a Roman Catholic, Piet, at this point, anyway. This part of Wiltshire wasn't a particular stronghold, but there were plenty of them in the west of the county where the Arundells held sway. You can't change the official religion and expect everyone to follow like sheep. Perhaps Parson Mallaster had grounds for his suspicions.'

'*He advised me most earnestly to keep these matters close to myself, if only for the sake of Susannah and my children. There were desperate men abroad whose Plots and Machinations would lead to nought but Cruelties and Destruction. Was it so great a Privation to do my duties as set out in Law, even if in the privy places of my heart I was but performing a part upon a Stage. Why he did so himself every week and found but littel Evil in it.*

I asked him what he would have me apprehende by that, but he would not be drawn further. He said only that the best in man is to be found within his innermost Spirit, and that the Spirit of good men doth burn as a beacon in the thickest fog, and that this Spirit may burn in any man, be he Papist, Lutheran, Mohammedan Turk or a black-skinned Heathen of Africk.

I protested that true Goodnesse came only from submitting ourselves in obediance to the Truth of God.

'Perhaps,' quoth he, 'yet must we find it first within ourselves not in some form assigned to it, by the Mighty and the Vain. Trust in the Goodness within,' saith he. 'Believe what your own Eyes have seen to be true, what your own Ears have heard Aright and what your own Heart doth know to be Just.'

'This sounds to me almost like the basis for some form of humanism,' said van Stumpe.

'It does, doesn't it? And exceptionally pragmatic and tolerant for the time.'

Van Stumpe got up and poured them a glass of cold wheat beer each.

'Tell me about your "better half", Piet,' said Appleby.

'He died of pneumonia,' said van Stumpe simply. 'Six years ago. But he was very sick for some years before that because he was suffering with AIDS. I am a homosexual gay man, you see.'

'I had sort of guessed that,' Appleby fibbed.

'He was called Ruud. He was fifteen years younger than I. He was very beautiful, to me at least, and not so shy and inhibited like some of us older gay men. He liked to go to some special clubs. I did not want to go to those places myself – they frighten me – but I did not mind that he was going. I have never been a jealous guy. I had become more like a father to him by then besides. At first we had no ideas of how he was exposing himself to such terrible dangers. Then when we realised these dangers, it was already too late. I became a nurse for him for three years before he died.' Van Stumpe took a long meditative draught from his glass. 'I can tell you, James, that I did not know such sorrows were possible.'

'My God,' said Appleby. 'All those times I met you at conferences and things, I had no idea you were going through all that.' It seemed that every day something happened which made him see van Stumpe in a new light.

'You are a good man, Piet,' he said. He wanted to add 'I badly misjudged you in the past,' but why insult the man with the knowledge of his earlier impatient disdain?

'Now you are sounding very kind and tolerating,' said van Stumpe, half laughing, half sniffing. 'Like our friend Sir Nicholas, perhaps.'

'I'm beginning to think that would be quite a compliment,' said Appleby, and he meant it. The more he read, the more he admired Harker. A benevolent charisma seemed to emanate from the pages of his writing. In some ways he reminded him of his own father. He was almost beginning to love the man.

'So are you now deducing what was the nature of this man's heretical activity, James?'

'Yes, I think I have, but it's quite unexpected. I'll explain everything soon, I promise.'

*

The next evening he met Claire at an Indonesian restaurant near the Flower Market, recommended by van Stumpe. Neither of them had any idea what to order so they followed the waiter's suggestion and had a *rijstaffel* for two. This turned out to be rice, with an enormous selection of small dishes, meat, fish and vegetables ranging from mild coconutty things to ferociously hot concoctions exploding with chilli peppers.

Appleby found the business of ordering and the unfamiliarity of the menu useful because it gave them something to talk about for the first twenty minutes. In truth he was not sure what to say to Claire because he was not really sure why they were having dinner together. Her flirtatiousness the night before had been rather flattering, but he didn't suppose for a minute that she actually meant anything by it. And even if she did, there were a thousand reasons why he shouldn't even think about taking matters any further.

Having sex with a student whose work you were supervising, even temporarily, broke every rule in the book. He hadn't checked for a while, but suspected it could even lead to dismissal. Anyway, he had no desire to make his love life more complicated than it was already. Cheating on his wife made him feel guilty enough, without cheating on his mistress. And even if the heady intimacy of the moment led his lust and ego to ignore all that, there was the question of performance. She must be used to strapping young twenty-somethings. He would only embarrass himself. With any luck she just wanted a cosier version of one of their tutorial chats…

'Gosh! What a banquet!' she said as the waiters placed the dishes of food around them.

'Just standard tourist fare, I fear,' said Appleby, 'but it does look good.'

'Ouch! This one's hot,' she spluttered, pointing at a bowl of bright red chilli sauce. She grabbed for her glass of water.

'Don't drink that! It'll make it worse. Have some beer.'

'My eyes are streaming,' she laughed. 'This is torture! Why didn't you warn me?'

'If Hans has gone back to Germany, where are you staying?' he asked after she had recovered a bit.

'In his flat,' she said, wiping away the tears. 'I have to push the key back though the letterbox when I leave.' She flashed him a smile. 'Now why would you want to know a thing like that?'

'No reason. Just idle curiosity.'

'I make a point of never paying hotel bills,' she said. 'I've crashed with friends in Paris, New York, L.A., here of course, Geneva, Rome, Cape Town. I'm a shameless intercontinental ligger, I'm afraid.'

They munched their way through the meal talking about Amsterdam and her 'fud' and what she might do afterwards. She told him all about Hans's bisexuality and his omnivorous sexual appetites. Without Appleby asking she volunteered all sorts of information about her own past. How at school she had dated boys whose parents had endowed them with suggestive names like Pierce and Lance which they did not necessarily live up to, and how she had suffered the unwelcome attentions of louche friends of her parents. When she was seventeen an elderly celebrity chef, she said, had chased her around his hotel room. She had had several relationships at university, but none of them had worked out. She delivered this information with her usual wry wit, but he began to suspect that underneath her poise and humour she was lonely and vulnerable.

Why was she sharing so much? She hadn't asked about his own personal life, and he wouldn't have wanted to discuss it with her. He was pondering this when the coffee arrived, and Claire broke his contemplation.

'James,' she said gently. 'I wish you'd tell me what you're really doing here.'

'What do you mean? You know what I'm doing. I'm researching a film-script.'

'Oh yes, I forgot.' She gave him a wicked little grin. 'You're working on Sir Philip Sidney and the Dutch Revolt…And I'm the reincarnation of the Duke of Parma waiting to invade England and reclaim it for the Pope.'

Appleby laughed. 'So what do you think I'm doing?'

'Well whatever it is, it clearly has nothing to do with poor old Sir Philip. I'm afraid Hans rumbled you there, not that I didn't have my own suspicions.'

'Just presuming you were right about that – and I'm not saying you are, mind – why is it so important for you to find out?'

'I love mysteries,' she said gazing into his eyes. 'And you're my man of mystery.'

'Why do you bite your nails?' he asked.

She frowned. 'Okay, you've rumbled me. I'm not nearly as confident and self-possessed as I try to make out. Now don't change the subject. Shall I tell you what I think?'

'Could I stop you?'

'No. I think you've stumbled on something amazingly interesting, something of great historical significance, and you want to keep it all to yourself for as long as you possibly can without anyone else finding out about it.'

Appleby looked down at the table.

'There! I'm right, aren't I?' she said triumphantly. 'I can see it in your face!'

Appleby gazed out of the window and bit his lip.

'It's all right,' she said. 'You don't have to tell me if you don't want to. Let's go. I'll get this. Daddy has just sent me an obscene amount of money on some pretext or other. Then you can walk me home.'

The route took them close to the red light district.

'I can't figure it,' he said. 'Generally the Dutch seem so enlightened, but this…Look at that miserable-looking woman with the sunken cheeks. She's not even trying to look sexy. How old do you think she is? It's like she just left a hospital ward, put on some tacky lingerie and wandered into a butcher's window. How can they do it?'

'Come on,' said Claire, gripping his arm. 'All these stag-party drunks are creeping me out. You must come and see Hans's flat. It's really something.'

So she was asking him in then. The flat was a huge open-plan loft conversion at the top of a five-storey town house, an Aladdin's cave of kitsch ornamentation where every nook and cranny was illuminated by arty lighting.

'It doesn't have rooms, it has zones,' said Claire. 'This is the sleep zone.' She pointed to a large circular bed on a dais. 'Let me get you a drink… from the hospitality zone.'

Before he could answer she walked over to him and started to take his coat off.

'I want you to make love to me tonight,' she said quietly. 'Nothing heavy, mind. I don't want an affair. I know you have other commitments anyway. Have you heard that actors' expression DCOL?'

'What?'

'DCOL. It means "Doesn't Count On Location". I think academics should have their own version: DCAC. "Doesn't Count At Conferences" or in this case, on research trips, so that's a DCORT.'

Before he could respond she put her arms around him and kissed him on the mouth. Her lips were soft and yielding, warm damp cushions of sensuality. It was intoxicating. He was lost.

Half an hour later as their love-making reached a climax she gave a series of short, muffled exclamations.

'What was that?' he said. 'You said something.'

'Oh dear,' she said. 'I was probably gasping. I do rather tend to do that.'

But he knew what he had heard. Masked in her rhythmic panting were the words 'Daddy. Daddy. Daddy.'

He was ruminating uneasily about this as he drifted off to sleep. It tainted the serenity of the moment. They lay naked side by side, her face against his shoulder and her arm resting on his chest. A pleasant physical exhaustion mingled with vague, anxious guilt.

'Is it some kind of diary?' she whispered.

'Yeah,' he said drowsily. 'But it's more than that…much more.'

'Tell me. You can trust me, you know.'

'It was some sort of cult, in a Wiltshire village, towards the end of Elizabeth I's reign,' he yawned, 'and they all got wiped out. The Dutch have found records of the whole thing.'

'My God! That's amazing! So who were they?'

'I'm all in, Claire. Sorry. We'll talk in the morning.'

York

There was so much post behind the Applebys' front door that Iris could hardly push it open. Detective Sergeant Jenvey of the Metropolitan Police Special Branch hovered uneasily behind her on the garden path, while DC Eckersley of the York CID surveyed the square for suspicious activity. The trapezoidal patch of lawn in the centre was screened by iron railings and an irregular line of trees and shrubs, so that it was almost impossible to see cars parked on the far side anyway. There were no pedestrians about.

'It's nearly all junk,' said Iris impatiently, as she scooped up the snow-drift of free newspapers, polythene-wrapped mail-order catalogues and unsolicited offers of insurance, loans and credit cards. 'What a criminal waste of trees!'

'How long did you say the Applebys have been away, Miss Tulliver?' asked Jenvey, a trim, smartly dressed black man in his late thirties, brushing down the lapels on his dark grey linen jacket.

'Jimmy's been away about a month, but Jenny only went down to London a few days ago. I still can't see why I needed to come all the way up here for this,' she said.

Iris quickly rifled through the pile of letters, discarding the circulars and retaining what looked personal including a few bills and credit card statements. A few were addressed to Jenny in her maiden name of Webb, which she had kept for her work. These included a letter from her publisher, a bank statement and a couple of circulars relating to her various charitable activities. Iris noticed several of Appleby's letters had return addresses suggesting they were from Harkerite organisations. One was from Australia and another from India. 'Here,' she said handing them to Eckersley. 'You'd better see they get this lot.'

'We'll hang on to the other stuff anyway,' said Jenvey, 'just in case it's not exactly what it seems.'

'Take a look at this!' called Eckersley from the front garden. 'This is where they tried to force the bay window!'

'The local plods had a report of an attempted break-in two days ago,' Jenvey explained to Iris. 'A neighbour disturbed them, and they waved a gun at him, jumped into a car and zoomed off.'

'Probably just an attempted burglary by some local junky,' said Eckersley.

'Three of them? In black balaclavas? With a gun? In a Lexus? I don't think so,' said Jenvey wearily.

As Iris walked into the kitchen-diner a stray cat panicked, yelped and bolted out through a gaping hole in the window onto the small back yard.

'Oh my God!' she called back to Jenvey. 'Someone did get in! The kitchen window's been smashed.'

Yet apart from the broken glass the disruption downstairs seemed minimal. In the sitting-room the standby lights on the Hi-Fi system, TV, video, DVD player and Freeview box gleamed happily undisturbed.

'I'll switch all those off,' said Iris crossly. 'They're haemorrhaging electricity.'

Upstairs the Applebys' bedroom was undisturbed too, with no sign of the usual frantic search for hidden jewellery or secret stashes of banknotes. Appleby's study, on the other hand, looked like an Oklahoma trailer-park after a visit from a tornado. The floor was strewn with books and papers. Every drawer had been ransacked. The contents of his filing cabinet had been flung on the floor, the folders thrown onto a chair in piles as if discarded by someone who was looking for something specific. On a bookshelf near his desk Appleby kept box-files of notes on a career's worth of research and boxes of the floppy discs he had used for years before changing to USB memory sticks. Almost three feet of shelving was now completely empty. The last two boxes standing next to the empty space were marked 'Toft 1' and 'Toft 2'.

'They've taken all his notes,' said Iris.

'What? On that cult?' asked Eckersley.

'It isn't actually a cult, you know.'

'Aye. Whatever,' said Eckersley. 'Still at least they've left him his PC.'

'That's just the monitor, you muppet,' said Jenvey. 'Where's the control unit? They've got his bloody hard-drive. Now make yourself useful and get some SOCOs over will you? Tell them we want DNA tests on every single stray hair and flake of skin in the house! And organise someone to secure the premises while you're at it.'

'Shall I?' asked Iris, indicating the combined fax and answering machine on Appleby's desk.

'Be my guest,' said Jenvey, taking out a small voice-recorder and a notepad. 'We'll leave it in place for now in case anything interesting turns up later.' He began to record as Iris pressed the blinking green button, jotting down the details of each call on his pad.

The first message was from Appleby himself, telling Jenny he'd just had another nasty scrape and would she call him back on his mobile. 'That must have been the evening the mad woman maced him,' said Iris. There was a call from Pete Elyot, sounding very worried. He had just heard about two assassination attempts on the news and wanted to know if Jimmy was all right. Would Jenny ring him back? Then there was a call from Lucy Webb saying Jenny's mother was sick with worry. 'Please, please, please give her a call before she completely loses it!' Appleby's head of department, Professor Howland had left a sarcastic message wondering if he 'thought he might be ready to get back in harness at some point'. He appeared to be completely oblivious to recent events.

They could hardly make out the last message. It appeared to come from a mobile with very poor reception: 'James? Are... there?... south... England... can't say... it with me...'s safe...Cranham...'s on...age 1- 3 – 3... call back...'

'What the 'ell was that?' asked Eckersley.

'I'm not certain,' said Iris, 'but I think it might be someone called van Stumpe. Jimmy really needs to know about this. That man's supposed to be dead.'

Jenvey and Iris left Eckersley in the house to await the forensics team and supervise the boarding up of the broken window.

'Thank you for doing that, Miss Tulliver,' said Jenvey as they walked to his car. 'You've been a great help.'

'Anything for Jimmy,' she said with a tired smile.

'Are you all right, Miss?' asked Jenvey. 'You seem a bit under the weather if you don't mind my saying so.'

'I'm fine,' she said. 'When will I be able to see him, do you think? There's something I really need to discuss with him.'

'I really couldn't say, Miss. I can put in a request to my superiors on your behalf, but I suspect it may be quite a while before it's safe for him to have any contact with the outside world. You could always write him a note.'

'No,' she said. 'I'll wait till I can see him in person.'

'As you wish, Miss. But as I say, that may be quite some time.'

They set off back to London in Jenvey's new Audi. Neither of them noticed the small grey hatchback pulling out after them from the far side of the square.

Swively

Two weeks after the unexpected phone call from Farnstable, Appleby and Jenny found themselves sitting around a large scrubbed pine table in Guy Charlton's kitchen. They had arrived after dark, and Guy's wife Izzy was heating home-made lentil and bacon soup on her newly installed Aga.

'So you've never been in this house, then?' said Guy. 'Mind you, it's not so surprising. The last owners were a rum lot.'

'The place has been terribly neglected, which is a frightful shame,' said Izzy. 'It's a real architectural hotch-potch, but it's got tremendous character. The oldest wing is late fourteenth century. We've put you in the main bedroom over there, if that's all right. Everything's a bit higgledy-piggledy, I'm afraid, but it's the most interesting part of the house for a historian like yourself.'

'You'll have to mind your heads, though,' said Guy, 'especially in the dark!'

'You said in your article that some favourite of James I got hold of it,' said Izzy.

'That's right,' said Appleby. 'Donald, the bastard son of William of Estrick. It was a grant from the King. The documents are at Kew.'

'Well he built what was effectively a complete new house on the side of the old one,' said Izzy. 'The central section of the house as it is now is Jacobean – all very dark and heavy. As you said in your piece, they amalgamated this place with the big estate at Farthingwell. The site of the old Farthingwell Manor is on our land, but it's a mile away across the fields. The bit we're sitting in now was a third wing added by a railway magnate who bought the place in 1864. As you see it's Gothic Revival. He seems to have added it to balance the original medieval house on the far side. The whole thing forms a three-sided court around a lovely garden designed by a pupil of Gertude Jekyll.'

'It's wonderful,' said Jenny. 'Did you say you'd changed the name?'

'Yes,' said Guy. 'Thanks to your hubby here, actually. When we bought it, it was called Swively Grange, but the deeds show several name changes as the owners got progressively grander ideas about themselves. The first name was plain old Mill House.'

'So what have you changed it to?' asked Appleby.

'Farthingwell,' said Izzy. 'Farthingwell House. We thought it was rather pretty.'

'And it's also sort of in honour of the house that may or may not have stood in our meadows,' said Guy.

That night Appleby and Jenny slept in a four-poster bed in the master bedroom of the original Cranham house. The floor was of highly polished oak, so dark it was almost black. The boards were worn and uneven. Some were disconcertingly loose underfoot. The bed was badly sprung and creaky, and the mattress sank in the middle. They spent most of the night hunched together in an awkward tangle in the middle.

Izzy had thoughtfully left out a bottle of chilled mineral water and two glasses. Even more thoughtfully, Guy had added a decanter of decent scotch. After Appleby had banged his head twice negotiating the steps to and from the tiny guest bathroom, the second time really hard, he poured himself a generous treble. Minutes later he was snoring loudly as Jenny struggled to get comfortable.

'Got any paracetemol?' asked Appleby the next morning, draining a large glass of water.

'In my bag,' Jenny groaned.

'How did you sleep?'

'Awful. You were snoring like a pig with catarrh. I couldn't get comfy and when I finally did drop off, I had a really creepy dream. At least I assume it was a dream. It felt spookily real as a matter of fact.'

'Oh? What was that?'

'I'd rather not say. It sounds silly.'

'Oh go on. You know you want to.'

'Well…The door opened and this elderly woman with long straggly hair came in, wearing a sort of full length nightie. I said "Hello. Can I help you?" thinking there must be another guest we hadn't met or a mad old granny or something, and she'd wandered in by mistake.'

Appleby put on his most ominously sinister voice. 'Oh no! You have seen the White Lady of Farthingwell! All who set eyes on her grizzled spectre die within the year!'

'Oh do shut up. I knew you'd react like this! I told you I was asleep and I was.'

'Did she answer you then, this nightmare vision?'

'Yes. She said, "I am Susannah." Then she just said, "Tell them." In my dream I said, "Tell who? Tell them what?" She said, "Tell them what befell us." That was all. "Tell them what befell us." Then she turned round and walked out again. Then I woke up.'

Appleby switched to his Viennese psychologist impression. 'In ziss case zer diagnosis is quite zimple, yoong lady. You are suffering from a clear caze of a bedly oferective imachination!'

'Yes, I'm sure you're right, Herr Doktor, but it was really spooky all the same. I'm still quite upset actually. A bit of sympathy would be nice.'

Appleby gave her a cuddle. 'Do you think we should mention it to the Charltons?'

'No!' she said. 'It's embarrassing. Besides they'll think I'm claiming I saw a ghost, when it was just a bad dream.'

'They'd be absolutely delighted if it was a ghost. They'd put it in their next brochure.'

'Well, don't say anything. They'll think I'm potty.'

*

After breakfast the Charltons gave them a tour of the estate. It was a bright, crisp morning. The leaves were beginning to turn, and there was a chill in the air. Guy strode ahead with Appleby while Jenny and Izzy followed at a more leisurely pace. In one large paddock lurked a dozen wild boar.

'You need really strong fences,' Guy explained, 'and we've got an electric wire as back-up, see. They can be pretty fierce, especially the males, so we don't want them escaping.'

'I had some on holiday in France once,' said Jenny. 'It was rather good.'

'Sanglier,' said Izzy. 'Like in the Asterix books, Obelix's favourite dinner. It's delicious, like a cross between pork and venison, very lean, so it's frightfully good for you. I've got some chops out of the freezer for our supper tonight. We'll gather some mushrooms in a moment for the sauce.'

'You're a girl after my own heart,' said Jenny. 'We used to come mushrooming out this way when I was little. And blackberrying.'

'Oh golly! Did you? We've got tons of the damn things in the freezer. You must take some when you go.'

'Izzy? Has anyone ever said anything to you about a…' Jenny let her voice tail off.

'About a what?'

'Oh no, it's too silly for words.'

'Come on you two! You're falling behind!' shouted Guy. 'These girls are my real pride and joy,' he said to Appleby, 'and Sultan over there.'

They had reached a large field containing six North American bison, five cows and one bull. 'You see the gates in the corner of the fences? If you open them up there are four big fields which connect into one bloody great circuit, so they can have a jolly good stampede. I got that tip off the old cove who sold them to me. They love it! Last time I chased them round on my quad-bike, shouting "Yippee aye-oh!" Fantastic!'

Then they took a path across an old clapper bridge and into Farthingwell Meadows.

'So you still don't know what was going on here, James?' said Guy.

'No,' said Appleby. 'It's incredibly frustrating, actually.'

'Well you were right about those ridges, anyway,' said Guy. 'They really do look like they could be foundations.'

'Have you got plans for this field?'

'Not as yet. I want to leave it as a wild meadow for a while – see what grows here and if we get any rare butterflies and what have you.'

'Would you consider giving permission for a dig?'

'What sort of dig? A real dig, with beardy-weirdy archaeologists and young girls with hairy armpits? That kind of dig?'

'Yes.'

'Let's discuss it over a pint and a bite of lunch.'

They cut through to the same footpath which Appleby and Jenny had used to get to the meadows just over three years previously and set off towards the village. Appleby remembered their night in the inn. Jenny had explained later how she had been getting her orgasms. He had never looked at an electric toothbrush in quite the same way.

The Kindred Spirit had been transformed since their last visit. The hideous old carpeting had gone, revealing old floorboards which had been lovingly sanded and waxed. There was a real log fire burning in the hearth. The place smelled fresh, and the one-armed bandit and juke-box had been banished. They evidently had a new cook too. A large chalk-board now hung by the bar, listing bistro type dishes with pretentious descriptions. In pride of place over the fireplace stood the old inn sign from the cellar, cleaned and somewhat garishly restored. It now clearly read *The Kindred of the Spirit*.

'Interested in the old sign?' the barmaid called out from behind the bar.

Appleby recognised her. It was the landlord's daughter who had served them their dinner.

'Yes,' he said. 'Your father showed it to me three years ago as a matter of fact, down in the cellar.'

'I thought I reco'nised you. You're that historian, aren't yer? Take a look over there.' She nodded towards a notice-board in the far corner where they had pinned up a copy of his article. 'That's caused a fair bit of interest, I don't mind telling you. We've had a few people sniffing around asking questions since that came out.'

'How is Bill? Is he around today?'

'Sadly, no. Dad passed on over a year ago, I'm sorry to say.'

'I'm so sorry. What happened?'

'Heart attack, rest his soul. Too many pork scratchings and "have one yerselfs", the doctor said. Mum and I run the place now. We're trying to make it smarter, a bit more upmarket. The day-trippers seem to like that.'

They ate their lunch in a bay by the fireplace. Appleby explained what a dig would involve and how the disruption could be kept to a minimum. Izzy wanted to know what would happen if they found something important. Would that mean they could no longer use the field for their own purposes? Guy said that even if it did, they could turn it into an asset. Appleby mentioned the possible documentary. By the time their slices of 'hand-baked New York cheesecake with coulis of dew-picked forest fruits' arrived the Charltons had decided it would be wonderful publicity and they should go ahead.

*

They made the documentary the following spring. Farnstable's researchers assembled a team of volunteers from Oxford and South-ampton universities for the two week dig. Several of the Southampton contingent turned out to be theology students. This reminded Appleby of a conversation he'd had with Pete Elyot. A few years previously Pete had spent a term on secondment advising Southampton's Sociologists on post-structuralist theory. 'Theology's absolutely huge down there!' he had said. 'You can't move for Christians. Just think! A whole university devoted to the study of something that doesn't exist!'

'You could probably say the same thing about post-structuralism,' Appleby had said dryly, causing Pete to guffaw loudly. By now Appleby was thoroughly disaffected with the wilder shores of left-wing theorising. On reflection, he decided not to share the happy memory of this conversation with the Southampton diggers.

The Charltons put mattresses down for the volunteers in the corners of barns and haylofts and kept them supplied with cider, hot soup and cheese sandwiches. Appleby, Farnstable, the young director Barnaby Crouch and the rest of the crew all got rooms in the house. Farnstable was the producer, but he would disappear mysteriously for hours at a time.

'He's off "on business" again,' Barnaby said one afternoon, adjusting the elastic band on his pony-tail. 'You know what that means?'

'What?' said Appleby innocently.

'Notice how it always happens when we've seen the Lord of the Manor's Range Rover disappearing down the drive?'

'What? You mean he's...with Izzy?'

'Never misses a trick, that one. You've known him for a while, haven't you? Has he always been like that?'

'Actually, yes.'

The archaeologists began by cutting a trench three feet wide and twenty feet long, diagonally across the walls of what looked like the main hall and into a side-building. It yielded results immediately. First stone foundations appeared, together with a post-hole for one of the upright beams which would have supported the original timber framework. About thirty centimetres down they came upon a layer of softish black material mixed with small fragments of debris, the first evidence of a massive fire.

By day two they had uncovered blackened pellets of melted glass and lead, so they knew the place had had leaded glass windows. In the remains of the side-chamber, which they concluded was the kitchen, they found a badly rusted iron latch, the crushed and partly melted remains of a pewter tankard, a sheep's shoulder-blade and numerous pieces of pottery, all badly charred. On day three they found a piece of human jaw-bone with five teeth still attached (it belonged to a small child), along with several deformed musket-balls and the snapped-off axe-head from a halberd. Next to that was a large skull with a deep slice through the forehead.

Appleby was profoundly moved by these finds. The Reverend Trott's folk-tale and that sinister note from Captain de la Zouche now took on a savage human reality. On one level he was delighted to be vindicated; on another he was horrified.

'They're digging up the site of a mass-murder,' he told Jenny. 'It's absolutely chilling. Somewhere under there, I expect, are the mortal remains of Sir Nicholas and his family.'

The Charltons were so impressed by the finds that they asked them to excavate the entire site. They would even subsidise the dig themselves if necessary, as an investment in the estate. Izzy told Farnstable that Burst could stay and film the whole process. The longer they stayed the better as far as she was concerned. Guy didn't notice the knowing smirk as Farnstable thanked her, but Appleby and Barnaby did. Barnaby started singing 'Lock Up Your Daughters' under his breath.

*

After some cursory screen-tests, Farnstable asked Appleby to present the programme himself, rather than lurk in the wings as the 'historical consultant'. As the dig progressed, they returned at regular intervals with the film crew to talk to the archaeologists and film Appleby's pieces on camera.

'You're like a dog with two tails,' Jenny said when he got back to York after his first shoot in front of the camera. 'You're all the same, you historians. One glimpse of a lens and you all think you're film stars.'

'And art historians don't, I suppose! Sir Kenneth Clark? John Berger? I rest my case.'

Not least Appleby was delighted by the prospect of the fee which seemed extremely generous at the time, though he later discovered it most definitely wasn't. He began fantasising that this documentary could prove the first of many, the beginning of a steady progress to fame and fortune.

They celebrated that first shoot with a bottle of Moet left over from the wedding. They were already 'trying for a baby', but that weekend he took to the task with joyous, exuberant enthusiasm.

*

By the time the dig was completed in late May, they had found human remains from at least forty-two separate individuals. That must have been almost half the village. Years later DNA testing would prove that over fifty people had died in the flames. Analysis of charcoal pieces suggested that the centre of the house had been full of bundles of wood of different types, which were certainly not part of the furniture or the fabric of the building. A fire-brigade expert was brought in to comment on the likely cause and progress of the conflagration.

They supplemented the footage of the dig with shots of the area around Swively and visits to Salisbury Cathedral and the armoury at the Tower of London, where Appleby was shown how to wield a halberd and fire a matchlock musket. They visited Sir Walter Raleigh's birthplace at Hayes Barton in Devon to illustrate the Torville connection and located the ruins of Torville's old house near Bovey Tracey. Then they filmed at the Weald and Downland Museum in Sussex where a similar, if much smaller house had been rebuilt. They even spent a happy weekend wandering around the markets of Bruges like Amos Jowatt.

Appleby had warned Farnstable that the documents he had seen in Salisbury Cathedral Archive had gone missing, but Farnstable's researchers put in a request to see them anyway. As expected, they were told that the Archive was unaware of any such documentation. If Appleby had seen anything of that description, it was no longer in their possession. It was exasperating. Appleby would have to rely on his own transcriptions, knowing that people could, and would, accuse him of inventing the whole thing.

He was granted a brief interview with a Church of England archivist called Canon Dexter, who denied categorically that the church had any record whatsoever of any such events. He was adamant that the idea that the Bishop of Salisbury or the then Archbishop would have instigated such a massacre was quite simply incredible, even in an age of religious violence when the English church felt besieged by hostile forces.

Appleby was allowed to write his own commentary, although Farnstable had it heavily edited before recording, ruthlessly pruning out scholarly caveats and qualifying clauses. Farnstable also insisted on including a series of appallingly unconvincing silent dramatisations by re-enactors in ridiculously clean period costumes. Appleby tried to talk him out of this, but the commissioning editors at Channel 4 were adamant: they were essential to make the whole thing 'sexy'. Appleby couldn't watch them without wincing.

They were in the middle of the final edit when Farnstable took an anonymous call from a woman with an antipodean accent. If they came to an address on the edge of Salisbury at 10.00 pm that night they could photograph the Mallaster correspondence. The address turned out to be the bedsit of a visiting librarian.

'Its' you!' said Appleby when they arrived. 'Tim, this is Katie. She's the nice young woman who showed me the letters in the first place! What are you doing here? I thought you'd gone back to New Zealand.'

'I have. This is just a six-week placement,' she explained, 'more of a sort of working holiday really. But I heard the Librarian discussing your request with the Dean. The Dean got really heavy about it, and I knew they were going to tell you all this stuff had vanished. I was so disgusted I found out where they keep it. I'm afraid I've "borrowed" it for the night. You can film it if you swear on your mothers' graves you won't say it was me. Not till I'm safely back home at least!'

'But why on earth is the Church so bent on hiding this stuff?' asked Appleby.

'Well I don't think Lambeth Palace has a clue about any of this,' she said. 'And as far as this place is concerned, it's just this Dean. He seems to hate anything that might upset the established view of church history.'

'It still seems a pretty extreme reaction,' said Farnstable. 'Isn't the Church all touchy-feely and tolerant these days?'

'Well, that's just it,' said Katie. 'If what these documents suggest really happened it doesn't help that image much, does it? To be honest I think he finds the thought of it so shocking and repellent that – well – he just wishes you'd shut up and go away basically. But I hate that, covering things up, especially when they happened so long ago. Apart from everything else it breaks the 9th Commandment – bearing false witness and all that!'

'I really don't know how to thank you,' said Appleby.

'No worries. How've you been keeping, anyway? Are you still seeing that pretty little art historian you were so keen on?'

'Jenny? Yes, we're married actually.'

'Aah, sweet! Lucky her,' Katie simpered. 'The one that got away, eh?'

'You see, Jimmy, personal charm can be an extremely valuable professional asset,' said Farnstable crisply as they left.

They edited in the documents and tweaked the commentary of the final programme, in a way which did not reflect particularly well on the church authorities. Farnstable was delighted by the hint of cloak-and-dagger mystery. Appleby was just relieved.

*

He was relieved, too, when he saw the finished programme. Farnstable and Barnaby had managed to thread the few tantalising fragments of hard historical evidence into a series of questions which were confirmed or deepened by the unfolding of the dig. As a final flourish Farnstable had commissioned a series of primitive computer generated images of the layout and likely appearance of the house, and the probable progress of the fire. There was much debate about the final title. In the end they settled for 'A Very English Massacre: The Strange Case of Sir Nicholas Harker.'

Channel 4 appointed an eager young publicist to market the programme and Appleby spent much of the summer fielding calls from television journalists who seemed to know absolutely nothing about history and were mainly interested in gore.

On the night of the broadcast, Appleby and Jenny invited a small party of close friends round, recording it on their new VHS player, bought specially for the occasion. He could hardly bear to see himself on television, made an excuse to get something from the kitchen, and ended up watching most of it from behind the half-closed sitting-room door.

'*So what has this excavation taught us?*' he concluded, as the programme ended, staring thoughtfully at a CGI image of the house. '*A great deal in some ways and tantalisingly little in others. We now know definitely that there was a fine medieval manor house here and that it was destroyed in a terrible fire. Tragically we know too that it was packed at the time with at least forty men, women and children who, unless they were lucky enough to suffocate first, must have died hideously painful deaths. We have seen evidence of military action and the marks of lethal injuries caused by the weaponry of the period, and we know that the names of at least two prominent local families disappeared from local records, more or less overnight.*'

'*But for the time being at least, the biggest questions must remain open. Exactly what were Sir Nicholas Harker and his companions up to? What was so outrageous, so threatening to the Elizabethan church and establishment that it provoked a large party of heavily armed men to come to this house one bright May morning in 1594 and slaughter the lot of them? And were those men really acting on the instructions of the church? Perhaps we will never know...*'

'Well it's screamingly obvious, darlings,' said Pete Elyot. Everyone was fairly merry by now. 'They were prototype Althusserian Marxists! That's enough to get anybody slaughtered in any age!'

'Or Foucauldian poly-sexual orgiasts!' said Pete's latest boyfriend, Zack. 'I bet there were a few of them hiding in Elizabethan closets.'

'Never mind the Gay Liberation Front here,' growled Ivor Gruffudd. 'Of course it was religious. What else could it be? Bloody religion! It's the curse of civilisation, if you ask me! But I won't bore you with my views on that matter yet again.'

'Oh go on, Ivor,' trilled Pete. 'You know we love it when you bore us!'

As they were leaving, Ivor took Appleby warmly by the hand. 'Well done, m'boy! It was a tour de force. Maybe it'll present a new opening for you.' Then his tone turned ominously grave. 'I do worry about your career, you know, Jimmy. You're a smashing teacher – all your students say that – but you need to publish more and keep up with the latest developments. I'm due to retire next year. They ought to bring in an outsider, of course, but Andrew Howland will probably end up getting the chair. And, well, you know he's not your biggest fan, is he? If you're not careful this place could turn into a bit of a trap for you. I'd hate to see that happen.'

It was a sobering end to an exciting evening.

*

The next morning Appleby rang Farnstable.

'Absolutely splendid!' he said. 'Channel 4 are thrilled to bits, and everyone here at Burst thinks you're the bees' knees.'

'Have you seen much press? There was a nice paragraph at the end of the Guardian TV review.'

'Ah, yes, dear old Nancy! Always ready with an appreciative drollery.'

'Have you seen anything else?'

'Not that much, I'm afraid, and mostly pretty neutral. I think because it was so open-ended, people found it hard to know what to make of it. Anyway, we were up against a new cop show and some drivel starring David Jason. Some fool in The Times said you looked like a polytechnic lecturer who buys his clothes in an Oxfam shop, which is true actually. That's my fault, though. We should at least have bought you a decent jacket.'

'Oh,' said Appleby, disappointed. 'Is that it then?'

'Well the Channel 4 switchboard have been fielding lots of calls from head-cases, if that's what you mean. Religious conspiracies are all the rage since that thing about Jesus founding a dynasty in the south of France.'

'You mean "The Holy Blood and the Holy Grail"? But that's complete rubbish!'

'I expect it is, but lots of people believe it. Or want to. You'd better brace yourself for some peculiar letters.'

Farnstable wasn't wrong. It turned out that Appleby had tapped into something.

The first trickle arrived the next morning, followed within a day or two by a steady stream. When Channel 4 repeated the programme in a late night slot a week later, word had spread through the thousands of individuals and communities with an interest in fringe religions, mysticism and the occult. The stream became a flood. The history department office installed an old cardboard fruit-box just for Appleby's mail. Bags of letters sent on by Channel 4 and Burst were delivered to his home. Appleby tried to read them all, hoping that someone might have something helpful to say, but he found himself opening them with increasing trepidation. He began skipping to the end first. If they finished with 'Burn in hell, you evil bastard!' or some such he threw them straight in the bin, and an average of four pages of densely packed green ink went completely unread. Gentle Jesus may have been meek and mild, but it was amazing how vicious some of his supposedly devout followers could be.

What amused, and eventually disturbed Appleby most, however, were the scores of letters from people who were absolutely convinced that they alone knew what Sir Nicholas Harker 'was up to'. Every fringe religious group in the country, it seemed, wanted to claim him as their own. Sometimes the logical leaps required to achieve this were breathtaking.

One of the first he opened was from a man calling himself Taranis ap Brythonic, 'Arch-Druid of All the Britons'. He declared that the fact that Farthingwell Manor had been built near a grove of oak trees was '*incontrovertible proof*' that Harker and his followers were Druids because oak trees harboured mistletoe, and mistletoe was the sacred plant of the Druidic Rite. He invited Appleby to attend their next 'Sacramental Rite' which would be held outside a scout hut in Croydon. A small gold address label had been stuck on the top of the letter. It read 'Darren H. Bullock, 73a, Wellington Crescent, Croydon.'

He showed the letter to Jenny. 'In what sense does Darren H. Bullcock imagine he actually is a "druid"?' he asked. 'Apart from a few scraps of Roman propaganda we know sod all about the real druids! We know next to nothing about what they believed or how they worshipped,

apart from the odd human sacrifice. If you want to hug trees and do weird things at the solstices, go ahead, but don't pretend you're a druid! The guy's obviously a sad fantasist who likes dressing up in white robes and talking gibberish.'

'Some people would say that was a description of the Anglican clergy,' said Jenny dryly, 'and even more so of the Catholics. I can think of all sorts of reasons why people do these things. I know it's not dreamt of in your philosophy, Horatio, but I really believe people have a kind of spiritual hunger, a craving to believe in something beyond what we understand rationally. These people just want to feel they are discovering religion for themselves or getting back in touch with some ancient way of finding spirituality. My own faith isn't "rational" either but for some reason it feels right to me. I can't criticise people for wanting something to put their faith in too.'

'By standing around outside a scout hut dressed in an old sheet with a bunch of mistletoe on his head?'

'Hmm…' said Jenny. They both exploded with laughter.

But there were so many Taranis ap Brythonics out there. According to 'Freya Watersprite' of Berwick on Tweed, the proximity of the oak grove was '*compelling evidence*' that Harker was a Norse pagan. The use of the term 'Kindred' was the clincher, she said, as this was the term for a gathering of adherents of *Asatru*, the modern revival of Norse religion. 'How,' she asked, 'could Harker possibly have come to use this term if he was not in touch with this ancient Nordic lore?' It didn't seem to occur to Ms Watersprite that Harker would know the word 'kindred' because it had been in everyday use for centuries and just meant your relatives or your clan.

The adherents of another Germanic pagan group enclosed a letter written in indecipherable runic script. That one went straight in the waste-bin too. Three groups wrote to claim Harker for the Wicca folk. One modern witch claimed Harker *must* have been a woman. Everything in the programme, she argued, '*pointed overwhelmingly*' to the influence of the Great She-Spirit. 'It is *transparently obvious* from

the picture of Harker you showed on the programme, that the beard was false. It is only your imbecilic patriarchal conditioning that makes you fail to see this yourself.' she added kindly.

There were letters about Devil-worship, picking up on Parson Mallaster's reference to Deuteronomy. One group even called themselves 'The Children of Belial'. Creepiest of all was an envelope full of sheets of pentangles and other Satanist symbols drawn in what looked like dried blood. One bore the legend "Sir Nicholas Harker – 666 – Prophet of the Anti-Christ, Herald of Armageddon and Harbinger of Your Own Death, O Unbeliever!" Appleby decided that one might constitute some kind of threat and handed it over to the police. A week later they rang to say the blood had once belonged to a gerbil.

Appleby had letters arguing that Harker must have been a Jewish convert, a Gnostic, a Cathar, a devotee of the Roman cult of Mithras, an anarchist, a British Celtic Christian, a forerunner of the Woodcraft Folk, a Rosicrucian, an Eastern Orthodox Christian, a Freemason, a Grand Master of the 'Priory of Sion', a follower of the Arian heresy and most bizarrely of all, a 'proto-Mormon', whatever that might be.

The Reverend Trott's reference to '*beastly vice*' inspired another cohort of vivid theorisers. Kenneth and Bridie MacTeagle from Aberdeen had even worked their fevered visions of rampant wife-swapping, incest, bestiality and paedophilia into a pornographic pamphlet entitled 'The Swively Orgies: Great Britain's First Swingers' Parties?' It was lavishly illustrated with line-drawings by Bridie, in whose over-heated imagination Sir Nicholas was hung like an African elephant. Ludicrous hedonist explanations, probably written by drunk students, included mud-wrestling tournaments, nude Morris dar ing and marathon sheep-shagging contests.

Appleby was quite taken by one correspondent who sent him a copy of his book hypothesising that Jesus had spent the 'missing years' of his youth training as a Buddhist monk in northern India, that he had survived the crucifixion and lived out his days back in India where his tomb could still be visited. If Harker had somehow stumbled

expectation of her departure, but that didn't justify him cheating on her while she was still kind enough to stick with him. He lay back in bed, staring dejectedly at the skylight.

'Good morning,' Claire chirped. She sat up beside him, exposing her small, shapely breasts and kissed him lightly on the cheek. 'Don't look so miserable, James. You're so sweet. You've no need to feel guilty, you know. I asked you to stay with me, didn't I? I won't get pregnant, if that's what's worrying you. I'm not going to fall in love with you, stalk you or boil your family pets. And I'm not going to tell anyone, I promise. I'm not the kind of girl who talks.'

Appleby wondered if he could believe that last comment. He had never known anyone with a more colourful collection of anecdotes or who enjoyed sharing them more.

'Anyway, you weren't that bad,' she said teasingly, as if reassuring a small child. 'A safe 2:1 at least,' she laughed as she got up and walked naked across the 'sleep zone' to the bathroom, or 'wet zone'. He may have been in reasonable shape for his age, but Appleby was far too self-conscious about his body to display himself so casually. Even Iris would probably have pulled something around her. He envied the young their lack of inhibition.

Finally he began to relax. They got up and went for breakfast together in a nearby café.

'Are you going to tell me anything more about the fascinating things you've found?' she said. 'You don't have to if you don't want to.'

He decided to trust her.

'The trouble is that I'm only just beginning to get an idea of what it all adds up to,' he said. He outlined the story of the massacre and the frustrating hunt for clues and the unexpected call from van Stumpe. And he gave her a rough idea of the kind of things they had found in the chest. 'It's quite mind-blowing actually. But it's a bit of race against time.'

'Before what?'

'Before…It's just that I don't know how much longer I'll have access.

Listen, Claire, you won't tell anybody about any of this will you? Not until I say it's okay. Do you promise?'

'Of course, I won't,' she said with a fleeting smile. She did not hold eye-contact when she said it, and her brows were momentarily furrowed. As they waited for the bill she became abstracted and started biting the nail of her right index finger.

He wondered what the etiquette was when saying goodbye to a graduate student half your age, with whom you have just had a one-night stand, and who might be using you to satisfy an unconscious desire to fuck her own father. Claire gave him a little hug and a light kiss on the mouth, as if to say, 'That was nice, but it's over.' So that was it.

*

A new anxiety assailed him as he set off for the Institute. Claire had told him over dinner the night before that she'd had several lovers in the last year or so, and he suspected she might have been up to something with the rampantly promiscuous, poly-sexualist Hamburger Hans. They had not used a condom. The thought of getting an STD himself or worse, of passing something on to Iris made his blood run cold. He would have to get himself checked out, but when could he possibly make time? And where could he go?

Then he remembered van Stumpe and his dead lover. Piet might know somewhere.

Why did love and sex have to be so unpleasantly complicated? So difficult and messy? His sister Kate had a weakness for romantic fiction, but he couldn't bear it. How did it help to immerse yourself in escapist twaddle? It bored him rigid. Life was only rewarding if you learned to enjoy it for what it really was. You had to face its grimmer realities with honesty and good humour. Suddenly he felt an overwhelming urge to talk to Iris.

'Why are you calling now?' she asked. 'You normally wait till the evening.'

'No reason really. I just wanted to hear your voice.'

'Why? Is something wrong?'

'No. Nothing.'

'It's a bit awkward at the moment. I'm half way through the door. Are you sure you're all right?'

'Yes, I'm fine. I'll catch you later... I love you, Iris.'

*

'Good girl!' said J.D. Clovis. 'That was splendid work! Wouldn't you say so, Norman?'

Clovis was in his preferred position, half-standing, half-leaning, a Gitane between his fingers, with one elbow propped casually against the chimney-piece in his library. Norman Skyne was sitting back expansively in one of the big leather armchairs. Claire was perching uneasily on the front of another, contemplating her bitten nails.

'This is all very intriguing,' said Skyne. 'Something like that might provide an excellent launch-pad for Nicholson, or better still young Dilke. Far too juicy to waste on a nonentity like Appleby, anyway. No wonder he's kept it so close to his chest. Why don't you make an excuse to pop over again in a couple of days and see if you can get a bit more detail, Claire. We'll take care of the tickets and so on.'

Claire coughed. 'Would you mind awfully if I didn't?'

'Oh really? Why would that be?'

'Because I feel like an absolute heel, Professor Skyne, if you really want to know. I don't actually enjoy betraying people's confidences. Especially if...'

'Especially if what, my dear?' Skyne fixed her with his most penetrating stare.

Claire reddened slightly. 'He's just such a decent sort of chap, that's all,' she mumbled.

'Well, well,' said Skyne raising one eyebrow knowingly. 'Has our little Mata Hari fallen for her prey?'

Claire transferred her gaze to her shoes.

'You have, haven't you? You surprise me, Claire. I thought your taste would be more…upmarket. Not to mention younger.'

'I trust your friendship has not become *too* close,' said Clovis. 'As a supervisor who could be responsible for assessing your work, that would constitute gross misconduct on Dr Appleton's part. *If* we were to choose to act on it, that is. Have matters strayed into what could be called *professionally inappropriate territory*, dear girl?'

'Don't be silly!' she said, trying to laugh it of. 'He's old enough to be my... to be my uncle or something! He's just such a nice little chap, that's all.'

'I don't want to sound too cynical, Claire,' said Skyne gently, 'but one shouldn't lose sight of who is in a position to help one in life. And who isn't. If the study of history teaches us anything it is that advancement inevitably involves a certain amount of personal betrayal. Only this morning you were talking to me most perceptively about Francis Bacon and the Earl of Essex. A rather apposite example, don't you think?' Skyne noticed that she was on the point of tears. His voice lowered and softened. 'Never mind, my dear. You've already done enough for us. More than enough.'

'Do you mind if I go now?' she muttered.

'Of course,' said Clovis. 'And thank you. Despenser is in your debt.'

Claire strode out of the Master's Lodge, scurried across the quad to the nearest ladies' lavatories and locked herself in a cubicle. Two minutes later a cleaner, imagining she had entered an empty cloakroom, was startled by a loud honk.

*

'Do you not think we should have pushed her just a little bit further?' said Clovis when Claire had left. 'It might have been useful to get her to admit to sleeping with him – given us a bit more leverage. We've still got that "spliff" thing I suppose, if we need to apply a little pressure. Possession is still a criminal offence, is it not? And we now know he lied to us about his reason for requesting leave, which is another disciplinary matter. Do you think she did, by the way?... Fuck him, I mean?'

'Until this morning I'd have said the idea was utterly absurd. Now I'm not so sure.'

'If that's how she got her information, I'd say that was going a considerable distance beyond the call of duty.'

'Perhaps he has hidden depths,' said Skyne with a sarcastic little smirk. 'Either way, she clearly feels some kind of loyalty to him. I doubt if she'll be much use to us any more.'

'Time to pass on the baton then?' said Clovis.

'Quite,' said Skyne. 'Do you happen to have any pull with anyone at the Renaissance Institute by the way, J.D.?'

'Funny that should come up today. I was lunching with an old school friend at Black's on Friday. I've a feeling he chairs the EU committee which subsidises the funding for several of those places. And he owes me a favour. But let's find out if this is really worth pursuing.'

*

'If I can be saying so, you look more happy this night,' said van Stumpe. He and Appleby were sitting over another Koningshoeven in the kitchen. 'May I be knowing why?'

'I got the all-clear from the clinic this morning,' said Appleby with a sigh. 'Thanks for recommending them. They were brilliant: no fuss, friendly, quick, efficient... Oh yes, and I've finished the preliminary catalogue.' He reached into his brief-case, pulled out a set of stapled sheets and slid them across the table. 'Here you go.'

Van Stumpe snapped up the sheets and started flicking through them eagerly. 'Excellent, James! Such fulsome note-making! This is most excellent.'

'Can I ask you something, Piet? Was anything removed from the chest before I came over?'

'Certainly no! I only have the custodianship. Why are you asking?'

'Cranham makes a couple of references to something he calls '*the book by the brother of the murdered man*'. He and Harker seem to consult it occasionally, but I haven't come across anything that matches that description.'

'I regret I cannot be helping here.'

'Never mind. I'll take another look. It's probably not important anyway. I really must read as much of the stuff that is there as I possibly can before my time runs out.'

'Ah, yes,' said van Stumpe. 'I must be revealing all these findings to my Director very soon. He has been becoming most impatient. Then who knows what will be transpiring.' He opened another bottle and topped up Appleby's glass. 'So,' he said, 'can you tell me now the solution to this most perplexing mystery of ours?'

By now Appleby had a very clear picture of what had been going on in Swively. He just wasn't quite ready to share it with van Stumpe yet.

'It's probably best if I write you a report,' he said. 'I'll do that tomorrow, I promise.'

*

The next day he carefully re-read the longer hand-written documents, concentrating on the ones which most resembled the liturgies of religious services. The last pieces of the jigsaw had fallen into place. He had cracked it. He opened his laptop and drafted the report for van Stumpe, but he was bursting to tell Iris about it. He glanced at his watch. It was four o'clock.

The mobile reception in his office was lousy, but he had discovered that if he went out onto the corridor and halfway up a little turning staircase that led up to the roof, it wasn't too bad. He had become increasingly lax about security, leaving the door unlocked when he slipped out to the loo or to get a cup of coffee from a vending machine two floors down. There was never anyone around. So he didn't lock up when he went to make the call. It would only take a few minutes. He squatted on a step and took out his phone.

'What are you up to?' he said, when Iris answered.

'Marking.'

'Have you got a moment?'

'Not really. Why?'

'Because I now know why Harker and his family were killed.'

'Really?'

'They were...'

But Iris cut him off. 'I'm terribly sorry, Jimmy. I'm dying to hear all about it, but I've simply got to get this marking done before I go out. You can tell me all about it when we get some proper time together.'

'Sure.'

'And when do you think that might be?'

'I don't know. It's still difficult...'

Appleby heard a resigned little sigh. 'Okay,' she murmured. 'Love you.'

'Me too.'

He flipped the phone shut and tucked it back in his pocket.

He felt a terrible wave of loneliness. This was such an important moment, not just in terms of his stalled career, but in the whole narrative of his unfulfilled life. He desperately wished he could share it with Jenny, as he would have done thirteen years ago. She was the one person who had been there from the beginning, who might understand the full significance of it all. But Jenny had long since lost more than a cursory interest in his work, just as she had lost interest in him as a human being. Now she lived only for her research, her writing and her endless voluntary projects. Their relationship was a husk. It had been for years.

His mind drifted back to that terrible October evening when he had stood in the corridor outside the operating theatre, exhausted and nauseous with anxiety. Then the surgeon had come out, his gown soaked in Jenny's blood, and broken the devastating news. He felt his eyes begin to fill. He slipped down to the gents to wash his face.

*

'Who the hell are you? What are you doing here?'

Returning to his office, Appleby was astonished to find a fair-haired, fresh-faced young man leaning over his desk. He was holding something over the documents. Was it a small camera? When Appleby appeared in the doorway, he looked round with a start.

'Oh. Dr Appleby? There you are!' He slipped the small black object into his jacket pocket. 'The porter chappie told me I'd find you up here. I hope you don't mind me letting myself in. The door was open, so I thought I'd come in and wait for you. I'm Giles, by the way. Giles Chalmers.'

He turned towards Appleby proffering his hand. Appleby did not take it.

'What were you doing? What did you just put in your pocket?'

'Oh that? Just my mobile. I was texting.'

'Really?' said Appleby. 'Who are you? What are you doing here?'

'I'm from Despenser. The Master asked me to look in on you, as a matter of fact. I'm one of J.D.'s doctoral students, you see. He knew I was coming over, and he was wondering how you were getting on, so he asked me to pop in and say hello. Just a courtesy call really. Listen, I don't want to pry or anything, but this stuff looks rather fascinating. Is it to do with your project on Sir Walter Raleigh?'

'Sir Philip Sidney. Indirectly.'

'Right, Sir Philip Sidney. Some of these books must be unique. Would you mind if I took a quick look?'

'Yes.'

'Gosh, thanks.'

'Yes, I would mind.'

'Ah.' Chalmers paused for thought, taking a good look around the small room. 'Look, Appleby old man, I can see I'm interrupting you, so why don't I just scuttle along and let you get on with it? J.D. sends his warmest regards, by the way.'

He flicked a shock of straight blonde hair from his eyes and headed past Appleby to the door.

Appleby called after him, 'How did you know I was here?'

'J.D. told me,' said Chalmers innocently. 'Why?' He looked Appleby straight in the eye. 'Is that an issue? Is this all meant to be frightfully hush-hush for some reason?'

'Not really,' said Appleby. 'I just don't recall mentioning it, that's all.'

'Oh well, you know what old J.D.'s like.' Chalmers gave him a knowing little smile. 'Not much gets past a fellow like that now, does it?'

Appleby felt a sudden chill. How much exactly had Clovis discovered and how?

'Bye then,' said Chalmers breezily. 'Oh, by the way. Where would you recommend I go to get some decent skunk?' He lingered in the doorway just long enough to register the reaction on Appleby's face, then wheeled away without waiting for an answer.

Appleby realised that his laptop was still open on his desk, the draft of his report to van Stumpe lurking behind the screen-saver.

Swively and Exmoor

'The greatest Virtues of men are like unto their most diligent and ingenious labours. Suche Enterprise doth rarely go to waste, e'en though its usage fit not the Laborer's intended purpose. Let enough time pass and Providence will surely furnish some other use for the Issue of such toils. Likewise doth Goodenesse always bring forth fruit.'

—*Sir Thomas Cranham, The Colloquies, Vol III, No 16*

Izzy Charlton woke with a start.

'Guy! Wake up! Did you hear that?'

Guy surfaced beside her and peered at the clock-radio.

'For fuck's sake, Izzy! It's 3.00 am. I've got to be up at 5.30. I need to sleep.'

'There it is again!'

This time the sound was unmistakeable. Someone was throwing gravel at the upper windows of the façade. Guy pulled his dressing gown around him, scurried across the corridor from their bedroom in the Victorian wing, round the landing and into the small bedroom over the grand Jacobean porch at the front of the house. He flung open the central leaded window.

A grey figure looked up at him from the drive, indistinct in the pale moonlight, standing in front of a small hatchback.

'Who the devil are you? What do you want? How dare you throw stones at my house!'

'Please excuse me. I would not have thrown the gravels, except that your front doorbell does not appear to be functioning, and the matter is of the most great urgency.'

'Who the fuck are you!?'

'I am a friend of Doctor James Appleby. Please help me. I can explain everything if you will only let me inside.'

'Ah,' said Guy testily. 'Wait there.'

By now Izzy was standing behind him. 'You're never going to let him in!' she said. 'He could be anybody. I'm calling the police!'

'No don't. I think I know who it is.'

Izzy followed Guy downstairs and stood nervously behind him, clutching her mobile. He opened one side of the heavy oak double door in the porch. A shortish man of late middle-age in a grey-green raincoat stood squinting towards the bright light of the hall.

'Please let me introduce myself,' he said. 'My name is van Stumpe. I am...'

'I know who you are,' said Guy. 'Please come in.'

'Oh, thank you!' Van Stumpe almost groaned with relief. 'Thank you so very much! But first please can you help me bring out something substantial from here.'

'Don't!' said Izzy. 'It could be a trick.'

'For God's sake, Izzy, put a sock in it,' said Guy, following van Stumpe to the car.

'It was too high to fit in the – do you English say "trunk" or "boot"? I can never recall which words are the British and which Americans – it was too tall to go in, so I have it on the back seats. It is most important that we put this in the house without any delay.'

Loosely covered by a cheap travel-rug, the object in question was a large and extremely heavy wooden chest with brass bindings and the biggest padlock Guy had ever seen dangling off the front. The two men carried it awkwardly through the front door.

'Take it through to the kitchen,' said Izzy, whose fear that they were going to be robbed at gunpoint, or worse, had now subsided. 'I suppose I should put the kettle on.'

All things considered it was a minor miracle that Guy and Izzy Charlton were still living together at Farthingwell House, over twenty years after Appleby had filmed his documentary on their land. After her fling with the irrepressible Farnstable, so swiftly noted by Barnaby Crouch, Izzy had developed a late taste for extra-marital entertainments. By the time she did a course on Agricultural Management with the

Open University a few years later she was getting careless. Perhaps, subconsciously, she even wanted to get caught. Either way, Guy discovered an incriminating note from her tutor. Under his fierce cross-examination, she confessed to a string of such adventures, due, she explained exasperatedly, to sheer sexual boredom.

By then they had had the first of their three children (the youngest was away at university on the night of van Stumpe's arrival), and they decided to try and patch things up, though Guy proceeded to repair his own sexual *amour propre* by shagging a succession of au pairs and stable girls. Izzy pretended not to notice. There was still genuine affection lurking in their marriage, and even occasional moments of passion. But over the intervening years they had settled into a tetchy equilibrium of mutual mistrust, and neither of them had the slightest patience for the other's foibles or neuroses. Now in their mid-fifties, they were growing old gracelessly.

The estate too had had a bumpy ride, but after innumerable near-death experiences, the business had finally thrived. They now sold rare meats to the finest shops and restaurants in England and abroad. They pressed their own apple juices and made fine ciders in a range of styles from traditional English varieties. The stables were booming and the Shire Horse Centre and craft shop complex attracted a steady stream of visitors. All that had happened before the surge of interest in anything connected to Sir Nicholas Harker brought a new kind of activity altogether.

'Be careful, Guy. Don't scratch the wood!' said Izzy. 'Those corners look lethal!'

'Is this what I think it is?' said Guy in a hushed tone, as they heaved the chest into the kitchen table. 'This is the Cranham chest, right?'

'Yes,' said van Stumpe. 'Please forgive me, but I have brought it here for security, until it can be safely retrieved. There are many people who want to destroy it.'

'Why?' said Izzy. 'That's plain crazy.'

'Because they hate what it stands for, Mrs Charlton. They are fearing the effect the writings in here are having among followers in their own faiths, now they are in public international circulation. When our mutual friend Doctor Appleby was publishing these materials, nobody was expecting they could be having so great an effect, and all around the world. Now they want to say everything was all made up by him, and indeed by me myself also, if I may say so. They want to say that it is all – what do the Americans like to say? - *phoney baloney*. If they are destroying this chest, they think they will also be destroying the evidence that gives the proof that it is real! That is why they burned my Institute in Amsterdam. Such shameful destruction – it makes me weep to think it.'

'Who exactly are they?' said Guy.

'Have you been hearing reportage of an organisation called *The Tribes of Abraham*?'

'I think I heard something on the news about a conference some-where,' said Guy. 'Who are they?'

'Ah yes. That meeting in Beirut where they are making some kind of "unholy alliance". They are fanatics, fundamentalist religious zealots. Some are Christians, some Jews and some Muslims. They are thinking of Harkerism as a "common enemy" and they have come together to destroy it.'

'What makes you think it's them?' said Izzy.

'Before the attack I was given briefing of this by an officer of the Royal Netherlands secret intelligence service. He said they have in-formation from the Israeli's Mossad and the CIA and also your MI6. The French *Direction Centrale* for intelligence are also hearing things.'

'I'm sorry, Mr van Stumpe,' Guy spluttered, 'but doesn't that make this the worst possible place to bring these documents? This estate is a shrine to Harkerism. You know that. The replica of Farthingwell Manor is virtually finished, and the Visitors' Centre and the rest. We assumed you'd be coming to the launch! Didn't you get your invitation? You must have spoken to Dr Appleby about it. You must know he's going to perform for us? We're expecting several thousand visitors.'

'Of course I was expecting to be here,' said van Stumpe, 'before all these most traumatising events. But you see this makes the very reason why nobody will think to be looking here! You would have to be a crazy man to bring these things here to hide them.'

'Quite...' said Izzy.

'But you see I am thinking you have the most perfect place to conceal this chest.'

'We do?' Guy looked baffled. 'And where would that be?'

'You know the most old wing of this house was once the homestead of Harker's confidential friend, Sir Thomas Cranham?'

'Of course,' Izzy snapped. 'What of it?'

'Do you have a copy of Cranham's journal to your hand? Could I please point to you something in it?'

Guy went to the room he used as his study and returned a few moments later with a well-thumbed edition of Cranham.

'Turn to page 133, please,' said van Stumpe. 'Now please to read the third paragraph from the top of that page.'

Guy cleared his throat:

'"*LTWZ arrived this morn bearing letters from certain gentlemen of the west praysing his craftsmanship and requesting I grant him leave to attend to certayne works. Asked him to survey the great staircase. There was much damage to the slabbe to the right in the back corner, which he did replace most artfully. Truly he was well commended. He is by thrice as careful about his work as any other artisan and can turn a cracked seat better than any man I knowe.*" What's so mysterious about that? A builder arrived with letters of recommendation, so Cranham got him to replace a broken paving stone in the hall floor and repair a broken chair! So what?'

'Have you read these journals Mr Charlton?'

'Of course.'

'Then you know that in the more early years to be covered within these entries, Thomas Cranham was a Roman Catholic Papist, a "recusant", and that, even though he was devoted to Harker and shared many of his philosophical outlooks, he never in entirity abandoned the faith that he was brought up in since it was his boyhood?'

'Sure.'

'Mr Charlton, *LTWZ* are unusual initials. If you make referral to Dr Appleby's end-note you will read that this may probably have been a man called Luke Tanner of Weston Zoyland. This was a builder and joiner of the Shire of Somerset, who undertook work for many big Roman Catholic households of the west of England.'

'What sort of work?'

'He was an artificer of priest holes, Mr Charlton. They were so skilful in concealment that the queen's pursuivants rarely found them. Some people say he was even better skilled at doing this than the legendary Nicholas Owen. And, unlike Owen he was never caught. They still are discovering them sometimes in old houses all these four centuries later. The last was uncovered during renovations to a house in Lancashire in 1983. I think he was surely coming here to build one somewhere in the old Mill House. Perhaps this entry is giving informations and it is to be discovered under the floor in your hall. What is more, I believe that it will be still there.'

*

It took them almost an hour to find it.

Guy fetched his toolkit from the cellar, and they went round to the medieval hallway. The stone slabs on the floor seemed undisturbed for centuries, the gaps between them wedged fast by ancient mortar and impacted dirt. Izzy pointed out that the slab in the right-hand corner at the back was partially covered by a section of the base of the staircase anyway. Then Guy noticed a faint line, dividing this section from the rest of the staircase. He crouched down and gave it a series of vigorous tugs. It seemed to move a little. He took out a hammer and started tapping it. Eventually it came away completely, leaving the corner slab fully exposed.

'Well now!' said van Stumpe, and before the Charltons could stop him he stamped on the edge several times. It suddenly gave way, pivoting downwards to reveal a cavity roughly two feet square by two feet deep.

'Voila!' he said triumphantly. 'Such a concealment place would be most perfect for storing Latin missals and other such paraphernalias for performing the Catholic mass!'

'You couldn't get a priest in there, though,' said Izzy. 'Unless he was a contortionist...and a midget.'

Guy shone a torch into the hole and peered inside. It was lined with wood.

'Hang on,' he said, 'There's a sort of panel at the top here. I think I can just... there!' He pulled out a small board and passed it to Izzy. 'There's another hole behind it. It seems to run back under the next slab. It's very narrow. What to you make of that?'

'Allow me, please!' said van Stumpe.

The two men swapped places, and van Stumpe thrust his arm into this new space.

'I can feel something in here that is hard and cold, like a stick of iron.' He began pushing and pulling. 'Aha! This moves. It is like some lever!'

As the little Dutchman panted and strained, there was a loud scraping sound. A large section of the wooden panelling in the wall behind them slowly began to open.

'Brilliance!' said van Stumpe. 'Like many most inventive priest-holes of Nicholas Owen, it must be accessed via another, smaller hiding place first. So the royal pursuivants will not be thinking this is the hiding-place for a whole man and will be "off the scent"! And before entering, the priest could be replacing this small wooden board, the paving slab and this staircase bit all on himself, before he steps inside. So ingenious!'

Guy pulled the panel door fully open, and they took it in turns to inspect the interior. The space was about two metres high, but it was less than a metre wide and less than a metre long. On one side Tanner had thoughtfully attached a sort of misericord to the wood that lined the inner wall. It was like a plainer version of the ones found on medieval choir-stalls, a small sloped shelf that jutted out, so that the concealed priest could lean back and take some of the weight off his feet as he waited for the coast to clear. It was split vertically down the middle, though it still looked fairly sturdy.

'Amazing!' said Guy.

'Incredible!' said Izzy. 'I wouldn't want to spend long in there myself, mind.'

'I hate to poop the party, Mr van Stumpe,' said Guy, 'but I'm not sure your clever plan is going to work. We might be able to get that chest inside, but only if we turn it on end. And then I'm really not sure we'd be able to close it up again.'

'You are right,' said van Stumpe. 'It is so much satisfying to find this place, and yet such disappointment that we may not use it…But excuse me, some moments, please…'

Van Stumpe stepped back inside. The back of the hall panel had a simple latch mechanism, so that a priest could shut himself in and let himself out again unaided. He pulled the panel shut, perched against the misericord and pondered in the darkness. Something about this wasn't quite right. The cramped space would quickly become cripplingly uncomfortable, and the priest would only be separated from the outside world by the thickness of the panelling. The slightest cough or sneeze, and certainly snoring, would be clearly audible in the hall outside.

Van Stumpe kept turning this over in his mind. On reflection, some of the phrasing used in Cranham's journal seemed decidedly odd: '*by thrice as careful*' …Thrice? Why thrice? If Nicholas Owen sometimes concealed a second hiding place behind his first, might not Luke Tanner have taken this principle one stage further and concealed a third behind his second? What was that other phrase? '*can turn a crack'd seat*'? Van Stumpe stood up, opened the door a little to get some light and looked down at the misericord. The split made a clean break, right through it. He gripped the larger section and turned it. It was a door handle. He pushed it open.

'Gross God!' he shouted. 'Come to see this.'

Artfully concealed between the house's internal walls, was a tiny room, apparently undisturbed since it was installed over 400 years ago, still ready to receive a fugitive. Against the wall was a thin, narrow straw mattress. Beside it stood a stool and a small table where they found a Latin Bible printed in Queen Mary's reign, a drinking mug, two tallow candles in pewter holders and a tinderbox. In the far corner stood a wooden pale with a rope handle and a lid, a small pile of rags and a large earthenware jug, presumably for water, but now home only to a few dead spiders.

Guy rushed off for his camcorder and filmed the scene exactly as they found it. Then they fetched the chest. The two men manoeuvred it inside and put it on the mattress. Over the centuries the dry straw stuffing had turned to dust which burst through the sacking cover in a small cloud as they put the chest down. Then they left, carefully replacing each false surface behind them. After a cursory dusting, it looked as if nothing had been disturbed.

When they got back to the kitchen the exultant van Stumpe quizzed the Charltons closely about the house's security arrangements. They had a horrendously expensive alarm system linked to a 24 hour monitoring service, Guy explained. Every door and window in the place had sensors, though they could all be disabled individually if you wanted to open a bedroom window at night, for instance.

'Except that door into the medieval cellar,' said Izzy. 'He completely forgot that one.'

'I know, I know, but they're coming to do it next week. Anyway, you're the one who keeps forgetting to lock it.'

Van Stumpe did not find this entirely reassuring. Even so, he could not imagine a safer hiding place for his treasure. There was no time to make other arrangements, anyway.

'So nobody except us knows you've brought this chest here?' Izzy asked.

'No,' said van Stumpe. I tried to be contacting Dr Appleby but he is not to be found after those terrible attacks he had in America. I was leaving a message on his answering device, though. It was some kind of clue, but he is the only one who could know that.'

The Charltons offered him a bed, but he refused. He was desperate to get home.

*

'Sorry to bother you again, Signor Angelini, but how the hell do I open the front gates?'

Angelini was leaving a meeting in Canary Wharf, and Kot could hardly hear his reply above the howling wind that swept across the bleak concourse between the skyscrapers. 'Did I not show you?' Angelini shouted. 'Please forgive me. You must pull down the small framed David Hockney print near the front door. It will reveal a control-panel. Turn the blue switch to the left, then press the small yellow button two times. Press the red button to operate the intercom at the gate. The doors will close automatically after the vehicle has entered. You can watch this on the little monitor screen.'

'Thanks.'

'*Fa niente*. Please do not hesitate to call if you have any more problems.'

Kot watched the monitor anxiously as the gates swung open and Jenvey drove in. This time he was in an unmarked Ford Galaxy, chosen because it looked like an ordinary family car. He had left the Audi at his home in north London.

'That idiot Howland has sent me next term's teaching schedule,' said Appleby as he and Jenny rifled through their post, 'with all my classes highlighted in yellow! Has he no idea what's going on? Could one of your people explain the situation to my head of department?' he asked Jenvey.

'I believe my boss spoke to him yesterday.'

'Oh, dear. This one's from Guy Charlton. They're going ahead with the grand opening of their centre in two weeks. Am I still up for doing my performance of Harker's Rite?'

'Well that's out, under the circumstances,' said Jenny.

'I hate to let him down. Maybe someone else could do it. Have I any means of contacting the outside world?' he asked Kot.

'We can pass things on for you, but you can forget making personal appearances.'

By now Appleby was tearing open the next letter. 'That's more like it! There's an invitation to Australia: a three week tour of the major universities, all expenses paid.'

'You're not the only one in demand,' said Jenny. 'My publishers want me to do a guide to French stained glass windows. What a fabulous job. Still, fat chance of that at the moment,' she sighed stuffing five letters and a bank statement into her handbag.

Appleby wasn't really listening. 'Bloody hell! This one's from India. Chap called Kabir has set up something called the All India Harkerite Kindred. He says Harker was obviously a spiritual brother to the Mughal Emperor Akbar the Great who tried to unite the world's religions in a tolerant all-embracing faith called the Din-i-llahi. He wants to hold an international Harkerite convention in Akbar's deserted palace at Fatehpur Sikri. Would I give the keynote speech?'

'So you really had no idea things would kick off like this when you started all this shenanigans?' asked Jenvey.

'How many times do I have to say it?' said Appleby wearily. 'It never even occurred to me. If I'd known I'd end up cowering in a safe house under police protection, I probably wouldn't have got involved at all.'

'He doesn't mean that,' said Jenny.

'Don't I?'

'It's the most important spiritual movement since the Reformation!' she persisted. 'When all this vile nonsense dies down, people will realise that it's a huge force for good.'

'There was a time when she hated it, you know,' said Appleby wistfully.

'Yes, but I saw the light, my love.'

'Well, that's as maybe,' said Jenvey. 'But in the meantime, would you mind listening while I play back your voicemail messages. If you want to write replies to people we can make sure they get them…Maybe not the last one, mind.'

He played the recording through to the end.

'My God!' said Appleby. 'It's Piet. He's alive. And he's in England. Did you trace the number?'

'We're working on it. Why is he so desperate to contact you?'

'He wants me to know that he is trying to protect something…He's in as much danger as I am and he knows it.'

'Have you any idea where he might be?'

'Possibly,' said Appleby.

He fetched his copy of Cranham's journal from his suitcase and turned to page 133.

Soho

NH: What caprice of God is this that shapes men's lives, blessing one with boundless benisons and the joys of all affections, while another must abide the winter storms all naked and unloved? As a boy doth trap a spider for his idle diversion and pulls the hapless creature's legs off one by one, so doth He toy with many a poor wretch, and in His 'Infinite Mercy' besets them with woe on fearful woe. And to what end? For His wanton sport?

TC: Nay, are we not instructed that we may not know His innermost purposes? That howsoever we may suffer in this earthly Realm, if we yet remain true to His word, we shall find joy in the Life hereafter?

NH: In truth, good Thomas, I find but little conviction in this promissory note, and still less consolation.

—Sir Thomas Cranham & Sir Nicholas Harker,
The Colloquies, Vol 1, No 32

Delighted with the success of the Swively programme, Farnstable asked Appleby to suggest ideas for more possible documentaries and invited him down to London for a working lunch. They met in a fashionable Hungarian restaurant in Soho. Appleby spent several days drafting and polishing his best idea and took a five page treatment with him.

It was the outline of an ambitious new series to be called 'The Tudor Farm'. Burst Films would furnish and equip a real farmhouse exactly as it would have been in the late sixteenth century. A team of historically minded volunteers would undertake to spend a year there, living exactly as their ancestors would have done, with the same clothes, food, agricultural tools and methods, right down to the sanitation and personal hygiene arrangements. A series of six shows would follow them through the seasons, including the feast days, high days and holidays.

When Appleby passed his small A4 folder across, Farnstable took a long meditative swig of the fruity Romanian Pinot Noir he had ordered and furrowed his brow.

'It all seems a bit brown rice and lentils, if you know what I mean,' he said eventually. 'Rather complicated and expensive to set up too. I'm not sure it's quite sexy enough for Channel 4. I think I'm going to have to pass on that one.'

Years later when historically based reality shows became fashionable, Appleby felt a bitter pang. That pang became even sharper when he saw a show following more or less exactly the same idea as his. Why hadn't Farnstable seen the potential?

Farnstable had asked to see a sample of the loonier letters which Appleby had received after the Harker documentary and sat chortling over them all the way through dessert. When he got to the bit about the false beard in the 'Harker was a woman' letter, it made him laugh so violently he snorted a mouthful of ludicrously expensive vintage Tokay all over Appleby's creamy lemon pancakes.

'Why don't we pick a few of the dottier cults and tell them you'd like to spend a couple of weeks with them, filming how they live, finding out what it's all about and so on. We could see who bites, then select the best four or so. You could be terribly sweet and charming and empathetic and all that. Get them to relax and really open up and get lots of candid footage. We'd only need an AP, one camera and a sound man. Then you can write what the hell you want on the final commentary and we can edit it to include all their looniest moments!'

'Mockery masquerading as empathy?' said Appleby. 'I'm not sure that's really me. It sounds a bit sneaky, to be honest. And wouldn't viewers object? I mean watching people get stitched up like that, wouldn't that be a turn-off? Besides, that sort of thing would be completely unethical for a serious historian. And it would be a lot of time to take off work for something that wasn't in any way related to my day job.'

'You're much too nice for this business,' said Farnstable, 'and far too honest.'

He wasn't joking, either, Appleby realised with a shudder. The conversation maundered on, as they both made increasingly desultory suggestions, knowing the other wouldn't like them. They parted amicably enough, agreeing to get in touch if either had a brain-wave, but Appleby sensed that the engine of his new career had just veered down a siding and hit the buffers.

The following year, something caught Appleby's eye as he scanned the Guardian TV guide: '*Eugene Leclerc's Bizarre Believers*: Channel 4, Sunday 9.00 pm.' 'Eugene Leclerc is a gentle, friendly, slightly gawky young man, but be very wary if he tries to invite himself into your home. In the first of what promises to be an unmissable new series on Britain's more eccentric religious cults, he spends a long weekend with a family of "druids" in Croydon. Who would have thought a solstice ceremony outside a scout-hut could be so hilarious? If you're going out, be sure to set your video!'

He watched the programme, if only to see what Darren Bullcock was actually like. Eugene Leclerc was very engaging and quietly funny, without being unkind or patronising. So Appleby also had to swallow the realisation that, even if he had thought it a worthy project, he could not have done it half as well.

Years later he realised that the lunch with Farnstable had marked a watershed in his life, a Great Divide between a period of optimism and happiness and the long slide into what Pete Elyot liked to describe as his permanent state of 'good-humoured dyspepsia'.

Farnstable's rejection of his big idea was only the first blow. When he returned to York that evening he found Jenny in bed complaining of painful abdominal cramps. Later that night she had a miscarriage.

*

They spent Christmas at his parents' house in Birmingham that year. Kate and her family lived round the corner from their parents, but on Boxing Day evening she stayed behind to help Appleby clear up after the others had gone to bed.

'That'll do for now,' she said after a while. 'The rest can wait till morning. Come and sit down. Let's have another glass of that Bailey's.'

He joined her at the dining table, sipping his drink in silence.

'You're not yourself, Jimmy,' she said. 'I don't think I've ever seen you look so down. Is something the matter?'

'Nothing really...' he sighed.

'Come on,' she said.

'Nothing...well, everything actually...'

'Jenny told me about the miscarriage,' said Kate softly. 'Why didn't you tell us she was pregnant?'

'We were waiting till the second trimester, just in case...'

Kate put her hand on his, 'I know it's awful,' she said, 'but it happens to loads of women, you know. I had a couple myself along the way. You get over it, and it doesn't mean you won't have lovely children. Look at us.' She topped his glass up. 'Don't you remember those little fantasies of yours? You had it all mapped out: the home in a leafy Victorian suburb near good state schools with nice liberal parents to make friends with...'

Appleby smiled wistfully. 'I know, I know. God, you make it sound so complacent!'

'It sounds great to me! The holidays in the Dordogne or wherever, working on your latest magnum opus while the kids splash about in the pool...'

'You've left out the exciting new jobs,' he smiled, 'and the secondments in the States.'

'...the books, the TV series presented by the distinguished Professor James Appleby...'

Appleby sighed. 'Yeah, well, I'm not sure any of that will happen now.'

'Why not? You're still young, for heaven's sake.'

Then it all came tumbling out. He talked for several hours while she listened. The miscarriage itself had been bad enough, he said, but Jenny's reaction to it had completely thrown him.

'She's always been quite self-contained,' he said. 'You know that. It's one of the things I love about her – no fuss, no histrionics, no compulsion to justify everything or verbalise her every emotion or analyse it to death.'

'I know,' said Kate. 'She's the antidote to Cosmo Woman. It's great.'

'But this – this was different. It was like she just retreated into herself. Her misery was so *powerful*. It left me floundering. And she wouldn't let me help her. I called her parents at one point, but that just made her angry.'

'Maybe she just had to come to terms with it in her own way.'

'That's what her sister said. Lucy just showed up unannounced one weekend, otherwise Jenny would have told her not to come. It seemed to help for a bit, but as soon as she went home the shutters came down again. I felt completely shut out. We still ate together, but that was about it. She spent longer and longer in her study working. I began to think it must be because she didn't love me any more, but couldn't bring herself to say so.'

'I don't understand,' said Kate. 'She seems fine now.'

'It was weird,' he said. 'One Saturday I came back from the market with a bunch of flowers. It was nothing special, just a pretty little bouquet. I can see it now: blue irises, white carnations and some of that white feathery stuff. When I gave them to her she burst into tears, thanked me, hugged me, kissed me and asked if I'd like to go for dinner in my favourite Indian restaurant. After that it was like nothing had happened.'

'Maybe the cloud just lifted,' said Kate. 'It can happen like that.'

'No,' he said. 'It felt heavier than that. It was as though she'd been locked in some miserable, dark dungeon where she had to stay until the demon that had kidnapped her got bored and let her go.'

'Actually, it sounds to me like she might have been clinically depressed,' said Kate. 'Couldn't she see her GP?'

'Oh, I suggested that several times. She refused point blank.'

'Well at least she's okay now,' said Kate. 'She's obviously over it. So you can cheer up.'

'Trouble is, that's not the only problem. Things haven't been going well at work either.'

'I'll make us a coffee,' said Kate. 'Sounds like we're in for a bit of a session.'

He followed her into the kitchen. 'Do you remember a few years ago I mentioned I had a new colleague called Andrew Howland?'

'The Oxford bloke? Bit of an elitist? The one who said he only wanted to write about people he'd be amused to have dinner with?

'Yeah, him.'

'I thought you quite liked him, though?'

'I did at first. He was a bit patronising, but he clung to me like a limpet for the first few weeks. He'd been teaching in New Zealand, and he was desperate to know what we were all reading – all the new Marxist theory and the post-structuralist stuff. He kept badgering me about it, so in the end I offered to set up a cross-departmental reading group for staff and post-grads. He was dead keen and said he'd help. So I drew up reading lists, put notices up and everything. Anyway, we're in this staff meeting and he announces it as if it was his own initiative.'

'What a cheek. Surely everyone knew it was you, though?'

Kate poured the coffee, and they went back to the dining room table.

'That was the thing. He managed to convince everyone it all came from him. I even caught him boasting about it to an external examiner. Even Ivor Gruffudd was taken in. The group was a great success, by the way, but Howland hardly bothered coming to the sessions. He wasn't really interested in it at all. It was just a way of sucking up to Ivor.'

'He sounds like a classic office politician to me.'

'Yeah, well I'd never encountered one before, and he's done a real number on me. I was always seen as Ivor's protégé, his heir apparent. But Howland could sense Ivor was slowing down and kept quietly offering to take various responsibilities off him. He never actually did the donkey work himself, mind. He always farmed it out to some minion or other, and I'd never find out what was going on until it was done and dusted. By the time Ivor retired Howland was virtually running the department.'

'And then he got Ivor's job…'

'Well he had all the administrative experience, on paper at least, and it looks like he's published way more than me, even if it is all editing collections of other people's work. I needn't have bothered applying. I never stood a chance.'

'Well, I'm sure there'll be other opportunities.'

'But he's taken all my administrative responsibilities away, and I'm sure he undermines my applications for research funding. He treats me with open contempt at meetings. He's behaving like some alpha male wildebeest, driving a rival away from the herd.'

'He can't stop you doing your own research though, can he? What about Sir Nicholas Harker? That documentary was brilliant. Didn't you get some new leads after that?'

'Nope. All dead-ends – ravings from loonies. To be honest I don't see where I can go with that anymore.'

'Oh dear, poor Jimmy. I'm sure things'll pick up. And at least you've still got Jenny.'

'Yeah. I guess so.'

Cambridge

'*Agnostics*!?'

J. D. Clovis drained his glass of Glenturret as if he was throwing down an unpleasant medicine.

'Did you say *agnostics*!? I've never heard anything so preposterous in my life! Whoever heard of a secret sect of *agnostics*!?'

He took a Gitane from his silver cigarette case and lit up. His study began to fill with the smell of French tobacco, his head fading behind a cloud of smoke. Norman Skyne thought his scorn was majestic. He resembled an angry dragon breathing fire.

'It sounds so *wishy-washy* - so bloody liberal!' Clovis fumed. 'You'll be telling me next they were running a – a vegetarian bear-pit – or a Fairtrade bordello!'

'Are you sure you've got this right, Giles?' said Skyne, trying to muffle a cough. 'There doesn't seem to be anything particularly conclusive in your photographs.'

'Oh, I'm sure,' said Chalmers. 'Appleby was writing a report on his laptop, and I managed to read most of it before he caught me snooping. And when I got to his office I overheard him talking to someone about it on his mobile. It sounded as if he'd only just managed to work it out for himself, but he's obviously completely convinced.'

'He is a bit slow on the uptake,' said Skyne. 'Do you remember that Dutch historian I invented, J.D.? Van der Valk or whatever? According to the fragrant Miss Tenterden he was still trying to work out who that was a week later.'

'Hm!' Clovis gave a contemptuous little snort. 'Do you think he may have simply got all this wrong, Giles?'

'No.' said Chalmers. 'Not from what I saw on his desk. I said "agnostics" because his report suggested they were keeping their options open as far as belief in God went. I'd say they were Humanists really, in the modern sense that is, not the way they used the term in the Renaissance. And it looks as if Harker had converted half the village.'

'But how the devil could they get away with it?' Clovis spluttered. 'They'd have had the lot of them tied to stakes before you could say "Consubstantiation"!'

'It looks as though the villagers were all covering for each other,' said Chalmers. 'This guy was seriously charismatic and hugely respected. And the report mentioned a drunken old vicar who used to attend their little ceremonies himself. It wasn't until the old cove finally popped his clogs and a new one appeared that Harker got shopped.'

'Well!' said Skyne. 'I really can't remember the last time such a juicy haul of significant new primary source material turned up, from this period – or any other period before the last century, come to that.' He turned to an intense young man with large, bulging black eyes sitting in a window seat across the study. 'What do you think, Jeremy?'

Jeremy Dilke was Skyne's star post-graduate, a brilliant Wykehamist. Skyne was lining him up to take over Appleby's project if it appeared to be worthwhile.

'It certainly sounds intriguing,' he said, his face turned abstractedly towards the open window. 'If this is all kosher, it might overturn some basic assumptions about the history of religious belief.'

'Quite.' Clovis frowned.

'It sounds as if there might be enough material to keep a small team busy for a year or two.' Skyne gently swirled the remaining half inch of Clovis's third best cognac around the deep bowl of his glass. 'It could be quite a coup for History at Despenser. It would need someone senior to shepherd the project along, of course, but I'd be willing to take on that role myself. What about access, Giles?'

'That could be a little delicate,' said Chalmers. By now he too was gently wafting his hand in front of his face. 'It seems Appleby's in there courtesy of his friendship with one of the senior archivists.'

'Who's that?'

'Some ghastly old queen called van Stumpe. Still, I believe you already have at least two possible transgressions you can blackmail our friend with. Or is it three by now? It shouldn't be too hard to persuade him to withdraw from the field, should it?'

Clovis took a deep drag and exhaled with a pained sigh. 'I do wish you would choose your words with more delicacy, Giles. One lesson you have not yet learned from your dear father is discretion. He was a master of the oblique hint and the coded allusion. You really should try to emulate his lightness of touch.'

Chalmers shrugged and flicked his hair back.

'Anyway, that issue is no longer relevant,' said Clovis crisply. 'Such vulgar measures won't be necessary. The matter is already in hand. I am happy to say that our little train-spotter's feelings on the subject are immaterial. Now if you would finish your drinks, gentlemen...'

*

When his visitors had left the study, Clovis topped up his Scotch and sat down in an armchair. He was deep in thought for several minutes. Eventually he stubbed out his Gitane, went to his desk and picked up the phone.

'Freddy? It's Jack. I need to ask a small favour. Something has come up which could prove somewhat — unhelpful...Yes, exactly, to that... Could you possibly do a search?... A man called Harker – Sir Nicholas Harker – late sixteenth century... Anything. Anything you can find... No, don't bother with that. Go straight to the Black Room.'

*

Appleby made a determined effort to forget about his night with Claire. Even so the episode began to haunt him. It was as if he had been transported back thirty years to his undergraduate days, when sexual encounters had seemed to appear almost magically out of nowhere, when they had felt mysterious and beautiful, but also baffling.

He remembered a poem by Sir Thomas Wyatt, which a flatmate had shown him. At the time it had seemed to capture the exquisite, dreamlike moment of fulfilment, and the chilly bewilderment of being dumped. He was so affected by it that he memorised it:

They fle from me that sometime did me seke
With naked fote stalking in my chamber
I have sene theim gentill tame and meke
That nowe are wyld and do not remember
That sometyme they put theimself in daunger
To take bred at my hand; and now they raunge
Besely seeking with continuell chaunge.

Thancked be fortune, it hath been otherwise
Twenty times better; but ons in speciall,
In thyn array after a pleaunt gyse,
When her lose gowne from her shoulders did fall,
And she me caught in her armes long and small;
Therewithall sweetly did me kysse,
And softely saide, "dere hert, howe like you this?"

It was no dreme; I lay brode waking.
But all is torned thorough my gentilnes
Into a straunge fasshion of forsaking;
And I have leve to goo of her goodness,
And she also to use new fangilnes,
But syns that I so kyndely am served,
I would fain knowe what she hath deserved.

Wyatt seemed to think that it was his very 'gentleness' that had turned his 'special' lover off. Appleby had once been told that his own tentativeness, or rather excessive attentiveness, had had the same effect. He didn't much like the bitter sarcasm in the final couplet, but he recognised the stab of helpless anger that came with rejection. It was not, on reflection, a particularly good poem. The scansion was diabolical, but it had captured his mood at the time, and he found it strangely comforting to think that Henry VIII's one-time ambassador to the

Pope might have shared his romantic difficulties, and that the poem might possibly have referred to a one-night stand with Anne Boleyn.

As for Claire, she could 'range' and 'besely seek' with as much 'continual change' as she wanted (Did 'besely' mean 'basely' or 'busily'? He had never checked that out.) and if she wanted to 'use new fangledness', well, good luck to her. The trouble was, that for all his misgivings about what he had done, about her motives and his resolutions that it would never happen, Claire had got under his skin.

He confided his feelings to van Stumpe. They were sitting over a beer round the living-room hearth with van Stumpe's father. 'The Aged V', as Appleby now called him (the name was Appleby's Dutch version of Mr. Wemmick's dad, 'The Aged P'). The old man listened to their English conversation with benign incomprehension.

'What can I say to you, James?' sighed van Stumpe. 'For we homosexual gay men, such feelings are all too often a part of our life. Especially with the younger ones, they often expect their encounters to be short and have little meaning in the heart. Yet we cannot help but to fall in love just as any straight man or woman. I think it must be true to say that all sexual relationships have some more powerfulness of feeling on one side than on the other. The scales of love are never balanced even to both sides. I do not wish to be the one who makes critique of the acts of another, but your sleeping with this Claire was – do you say opportunistical? And now you find she has affected your heart. Well that is part of the risk of this sport, my friend. Sometimes these things will happen, and the best choice for you now is probably to forget you ever made love with her.'

Appleby felt a little deflated by this unexpected dose of common sense from the world of casual same-sex encounters. 'Thanks, Piet,' he said flatly. 'I expect you're right.'

The Aged V held up his glass of beer and beamed silently at Appleby from his armchair.

'Cheers,' said Appleby, returning the gesture and smiling back broadly.

*

The next morning he returned to his work with manic energy. His time in Amsterdam was short, the fate of the archive still uncertain. The more he could learn, the better his chance of keeping the project after the question of ownership was settled.

And there were still so many unanswered questions. How had the whole thing started? How had a series of informal Saturday morning gatherings evolved into formalised ceremonies? What were the villagers' attitudes to religion? Were they not deeply superstitious? If so, how had Harker dealt with that in his teachings? How had they survived for so long without being betrayed or discovered in some other way? And what about the vicar? How had he reached a state where he was not only tolerant of Harker's activities, but a willing participant himself?

One of the 'Colloquies' dealt with the issue of superstition. Both well educated, Harker and Cranham regarded some of their neighbours' stranger beliefs as a form of rustic idiocy, a phenomenon they referred to as the 'Magpie's Curse'. Yet they were equally scornful of more urban obsessions like astrology and the widespread sale of 'Almanacks' purporting to predict the future. These, they agreed, were pure 'quackery'. Neither could understand why the Queen had any time for her astrologer, 'that Mountebank', John Dee. Their scornful comments reminded Appleby of Edmund's speech, contemptuously dismissing that pseudo-science in *King Lear*.

He also discovered several passages in Cranham's journal which directly addressed the vicar's mental state. Probably in his early fifties when the journal opened, Wesson was already considered to be at a ripe age. In various entries he told Cranham about his education in the reign of Henry VIII. He once confided that, as a young man, he had been horrified by the break with Rome in 1534 and had contemplated fleeing to France to join a Catholic seminary. It was only loyalty to his family that had kept him in England.

Eventually, and with much soul-searching, he had reconciled himself to the new order and continued his career as a junior cleric. Appleby knew that for many at that time, little seemed to have changed, once they had accepted that their titular head was now their King rather than an ageing Italian or Spaniard over a thousand miles away.

A series of unsettling disputes over doctrine had followed, as Lutheran ideas and practices spread through the English church, but the real challenge came with the accession of the young Edward VI. Under Archbishop Cranmer's influence, the boy king's increasing Protestant zealotry, forced young Wesson to face the fact that something fundamental had changed. The denunciation of the papacy in Edward VI's version of *The Book of Common Prayer* had really stuck in his throat. But yet again, after much agonising, he had adjusted to the new order.

To the now middle-aged cleric, the accession of Queen Mary and the official return to Roman Catholicism should have come as a relief. But Cranham described a drunken conversation with Wesson when the old man admitted that this brought its own form of spiritual torture because it confronted him with the full extent of his own betrayal. This was complicated by the fact that the queen's marriage to the Spanish king aroused a visceral xenophobic disgust. Wesson had only just come to Swively as a re-conditioned Catholic priest when Queen Mary died. Elizabeth ascended the throne and, by the Act of Uniformity he was obliged to change back yet again, this time to a more moderate and inclusive version of Protestantism.

That was four fundamental changes in the nature of the official religion in less than thirty years, each to suit the predilections of the next Tudor monarch. For every self-satisfied, time-serving 'Vicar of Bray', Appleby reflected, there must have been a dozen poor souls for whom these changes had been a source of bemused anguish. In one entry Cranham described Wesson's predicament in homely countryman's terms:

'If you do bend a hazel switch first one way, then the other, then back again, then back once more, be it never so wet with sap, in time the bark must fray and the heartwood tear and it will surely splinter apart and break in twain. Thus hath our old priest's Faith been broke apart by the many contrary wrenchings of a line of sovereigns, and with it, I fear, the poor soul's wits.'

Increasingly Wesson had sought relief from his spiritual torment in the bottle. In the end he was more or less permanently befuddled by ale, cider or mead. Yet he was a kindly soul, much loved by the villagers, including the churchwardens who were at pains to cover for him during inspections by the archdeacons from Salisbury. If that poor old man hadn't taken to the bottle, Appleby reflected later, none of this could have happened, including the changes the rediscovery of Harker's writings might bring to his own life.

He was still buzzing with all this when Saturday came. He would put the finishing touches to his report over the weekend and present it to van Stumpe with a flourish when he returned on Monday night. He set off for York, desperate to get through the weekend and back to the documents. He was due to see Claire at Despenser on Monday. He had decidedly mixed feelings about that.

*

Appleby and Jenny had finished Sunday lunch and were reading the papers at their old pine table. It was ten years since they had had the kitchen and breakfast room knocked through and fitted with 'Shaker' style units from a budget chain. The room was bigger, but still got little natural light. By now the units looked dated and shabby.

He was trying to read the review section, but he couldn't concentrate. He looked across at Jenny. She wore reading glasses these days, which she kept on a cord around her neck. Apart from the merest hint of wrinkling, those slim, delicate fingers were as beautiful as ever. She had aged well. Her cheeks, though slightly fuller, were soft and smooth. Her light brown hair, recently re-styled in a bob, was full and lustrous. It was the eyes that were different. That old warm glow had gone, replaced by a persistent dullness which seemed to mask fathomless depths of unspoken hurt.

Suddenly he felt a surge of anguish. It was a toxic brew: guilt over his betrayals; fear that she could see through his pretences; indignation that she didn't seem to care enough to suspect or challenge him; resentment that she didn't seem to care how he felt at all; above all a deep, miserable yearning for what he had lost. Eventually he broke the silence:

'I really must find a way of letting you read Cranham's journal, Jenny. There's so much about life in Swively. The places we visited from Salisbury – and when we stayed with the Charltons – they're all in there. Do you remember that book about that Cathar village, Montaillou? It's like that really. It's the day-to-day stuff that's so fascinating.'

She looked up briefly 'Uh-huh.'

'If you came to Amsterdam, I could show you. I'm sure van Stumpe wouldn't mind.'

'It's a nice thought, Jimmy,' she said getting up, 'but I really don't see how I could spare the time.' She began clearing the table.

'Well that's a pity.' He decided to try another tack. 'How are you fixed this afternoon? I could easily take a few hours off this week. Why don't we take a drive out into the country and go for a walk like we used to? We haven't done that for years.'

'What a nice idea,' she said, 'but I promised I'd see the new canon, I'm afraid. He wants me to take an art class for a group of children at the local care home. Some of them are very disturbed, apparently. He thinks they might respond to painting and making things. I assumed you'd be working as usual.'

'Can't you put him off?'

'Not really.'

'Never mind,' he sighed. 'It was just a thought. I'll see if Pete's about.'

'Do you mind washing up? I have to be off.'

As she left the room he realised that she had hardly made eye-contact for the entire conversation. He had been wondering for a long time if there was any point in continuing with this pretence of a marriage. It was as if their relationship was in a vegetative coma. He was like some anxious loved one, visiting regularly, talking to it, occasionally playing a favourite song, unable to move on until the patient either woke up or died.

Ah well, he had done his best. The weekly bedside vigil was over. It was time to return to the temporary arrangements of the outside world. He had no intention of seeing Pete Elyot, who, he happened to know, was giving a paper at a symposium in Berlin. As soon as he had washed up he would pay a surprise visit to Iris.

*

Iris lived in a neat little terraced cottage about twenty minutes' walk away. He climbed the steep stairs onto the old city walls at Micklegate Bar and swung round to the south, taking the last set of steps down before Iris's street. It was a crisp clear day and the jumble of slate roofs and mottled redbrick walls seemed warm and vibrant. They were interspersed with pale stone church towers and half-timbered façades. York was a pretty little city, he thought, unpretentious and workmanlike. It was not quite as quaintly picturesque as Canterbury, or as crowded with medieval architecture as Oxford or Cambridge. It was just quietly characterful. He had fallen in love with the place when he came up for his first year, and the feeling had never gone away.

He knew Iris usually stayed in on Sunday afternoons, preparing for the week ahead. When she didn't answer the door, he thought she must be out and kicked himself for not ringing ahead. Unannounced visits are always problematic, he reflected. They can seem spontaneous and romantic, or it can look like you're checking up. You risk the disappointment of finding your lover out, or worse, of finding them in, but with someone else. They are the ultimate gesture of trust or of mistrust, of complacency or paranoia.

The house had a tiny porch, but he could see that the inner door was open, so she must be in. After ringing the bell, repeatedly banging the brass knocker and shouting through the letter-box, he was on the point of doing what he should have done to begin with and phoning her on her mobile, when she finally appeared. She had been reading in the back garden and had fallen asleep.

'What a lovely surprise!' she said, ushering him inside, throwing her arms around him and kissing him languidly. The warmth of the sun seemed to radiate from her bare arms.

'*And she me caught in her armes long and small,*' he murmured. '*Therewithall sweetly did me kysse, And softely saide, "dere hert, howe like you this?".*'

'What?' said Iris, looking at him as if he had gone amusingly potty.

'Sorry,' he said. 'It's a poem.'

'*Dear heart, how like you this?*' she repeated, kissing him again, even more softly.

'*Besely!*' he said.

'Beezely?'

'It's got to be "busily". It stands to reason.'

'Now you've really lost me.'

'It's nothing. Never mind.'

The hurt and frustration melted away in the warmth of Iris's relaxed sensuality. He was suffused with desire and hugged her to him, luxuriating in the contours of her body. He slid his right hand over her left buttock and squeezed gently.

'Sorry,' she said, grinning and gently flicking the end of his nose with the tip of her index finger. '*Pas ce soir, Jamesephine.* Time of the month. Come and sit in the garden, I'll make a fresh pot of tea. You can finally tell me what your heretics were up to.'

He looked around the room, cluttered with trophies and mementos of her life. There were wood-carvings from a gap year as a volunteer in Zambia; a brilliant throw over the sofa had come back from a conference in Mexico, along with a primitive painting on beaten tree-bark which she had mounted over the fireplace. A large poster from a David Hockney exhibition she had seen with her parents as a teenager in New York was mounted in a clip-frame, as was a poster for a Joan Armatrading concert which had particular associations with the start of their affair. There were framed group-shots from a holiday spent with her mother's family in Ravenna and a charming little print of a mosaic duck from one of the city's Byzantine basilicas, along with fading boozy snaps of a post-A level holiday with her school-friends at a camp-site in Cornwall.

Under a lamp on a small side-table he noticed the inlaid Moroccan cigarette box where she liked to keep her made-up spliffs. She would usually treat herself to one when she was winding down for the evening, about the same time he'd have a stiff scotch. The tiny mantelpiece was cluttered with scented candles which she had always lit on the rare occasions they had spent the evening together in her home. Propped behind them were postcards sent from abroad, a couple of old invitations and some shots from a party she had thrown last summer for the trainee teachers from her tutor group. Finally he noticed a new addition: a photo of himself, leaning over the parapet of a canal bridge in Amsterdam. He had forgotten she'd taken it. He was touched to see it there.

Iris always made proper leaf tea in an elegant Victorian china pot inherited from her grandmother. They sat in the garden sipping some fragrant blend from the matching cups, enjoying the late afternoon sun.

'So,' she said. 'What about these Wiltshire heathens of yours? Were they sacrificing goats or burning the local constables in giant wicker baskets?'

Appleby finally had the conversation he had so badly wanted earlier in the week, or indeed with Jenny that morning. He explained that Sir Nicholas Harker was an agnostic and a Humanist two hundred years before the Enlightenment; that he had created a community of followers in his obscure rural backwater who called themselves 'The Kindred of the Spirit'; that they practised communal rites and ceremonies in which the human spirit was venerated rather than a deity.

Iris was astonished, and not a little sceptical. She asked all the same questions which had tormented him since he first began to realise what had been going on in Swively. And she pushed him hard for explanations.

'How could a thing like that even get started?' she said incredulously.

He explained how it began after Holy Communion one Sunday when a group of villagers stopped Harker on the village green and asked if he could explain one of Parson Wesson's loopier sermons. They barraged him with so many questions that he invited them to his house the next Saturday morning. Two dozen villagers had turned up, including Harker's best friend, Sir Thomas Cranham, who described the meeting in detail in his journal. Harker had travelled extensively and was exceptionally well read, and the discussion branched off onto all sorts of tangents. Several villagers asked if they could come again the following week, and Harker agreed. The Saturday gatherings had quickly become a fixture.

Some villagers wanted to discuss their personal problems, said Appleby. Others started asking Harker if he could help them settle their disputes. Harker encouraged them to discuss such matters openly in front of the group, asking their neighbours to suggest how the situation could be justly resolved. Over the years this became formalised in a process like a public confession called an 'Attestation'. This was followed by a communal discussion where the villagers agreed on appropriate 'Redress'. When 'Redress' had been accomplished the wrong-doer was granted 'Redemption'.

'They must have found it rather therapeutic,' said Appleby. 'The whole village seems to have become incredibly well-behaved!'

'Okay,' said Iris. 'But that still doesn't explain how a bunch of ignorant, deeply superstitious peasants whose lives were dominated by religion, could end up thinking that there might not be a God!'

'They were ignorant,' said Appleby, 'but I don't think they were stupid – no more than your average Joe, anyway. They were certainly full of questions, and Harker seems to have been an inspired teacher. He started introducing little talks, which he called "Contemplations". I haven't had time to read them all yet, but I think he was gradually introducing ideas that had them subtly questioning religious dogma.'

'So it all came from him?'

'Yes, initially, and he was very good at gently leading people to see things his way. It's funny, though. Harker and Cranham used to have these long philosophical conversations and at some point Cranham's wife started writing them down. She called them "Colloquies". Looking through them I get the impression that Harker was an unbeliever from the off. Something had turned him into a Humanist when he was quite young. There are several references to a book which seems to have something to do with it, but I haven't found it yet. Anyway, over the years the meetings acquired a structure, echoing the format of an Anglican liturgy – all written by Harker.'

'I know you said the vicar was a confused old sot, but didn't he twig what was going on?'

'Yes, he asked Harker about it quite early on, and Harker invited him along. According to Cranham's journal he really enjoyed it.'

'I don't know,' said Iris. 'I thought everyone was absolutely ruled by religion at that time. It wasn't so different from the Middle Ages, really.'

'Yes, but poor people were far more ignorant of Christian teaching than is commonly supposed,' he said, 'and it was often mixed up with ancient superstitions and traditional lore that dated back to pagan times. Besides, I've always suspected there was a lot more doubt and scepticism about than people think,' said Appleby. 'You get whiffs of it in Shakespeare sometimes, and Chaucer for that matter. It's just that you couldn't express it openly. The punishments for any kind of heresy were so draconian.'

'Well,' she said. 'It all sounds extraordinary. You might find it's a bit of a hornets' nest, though. So what happens next?'

'Well, I've finished the preliminary cataloguing. What I really want is permission to edit the documents properly... and then publish

– hopefully.'

'Hopefully? Is that a problem?'

'I don't know. Did I tell you I caught one of Clovis's minions snooping in my office in the Institute after I phoned you last week? I'll swear he was photographing the stuff on my desk.'

'Why would they do that? That's weird. What does it matter to Despenser?'

'I think they've sussed that I've turned up something really unusual, and they don't see why some hick from the sticks should get the benefit.'

'You mean you think they might try to hijack your project?'

'Yeah,' he sighed. 'Basically. Or at least elbow me aside. It's been done before, believe me. That's why I lied to them when I was getting permission to take time off, but I guess they've rumbled me now, which makes me look like a complete tit. Still, as long as Piet van Stumpe stays onside, it should be okay.'

There was a short silence while Iris poured more tea.

'I met your woman from Harvard at a party last week,' she said.

'What? The American side of my slave-trade triangle?'

'That's her. The demographer. Carla. Did you know she was gay? Or a least bi.'

'No. I don't know anything about her. How did you find that out?'

'Because she tried to hit on me. It was quite flattering, actually,' she laughed, widening her eyes at him. 'She's very striking looking...and seriously fit!'

'It sounds like you were tempted,' said Appleby, trying to conceal his sudden discomfort.

'Don't worry, dear. My days of experimenting with that sort of thing are long gone.'

'So you mean you...'

'Sure,' she said. 'Why not? For the generation that ushered in the sexual revolution, you baby-boomers can be surprisingly priggish.'

'There's an awful lot I still don't know about you,' he said.

'Oh, you're so sweet, Jimmy.' She leaned over and put her hand on his knee confidentially. 'Every girl has her secrets, you know. Even your buttoned-up wife, I expect,' she added as she sat back. That last remark wasn't really meant hurtfully, but it still gave him a painful twinge. It was not as if it was something he hadn't thought about.

'Listen, Jimmy,' she said after another pause. 'There's something I need to tell you.'

'Oh?' Her tone had become ominously serious.

'I'm leaving York in a few weeks.'

'What? Why?'

'I've been sort of head-hunted really. Or at least I was invited to apply for a lectureship. It's at the Institute of Education in London. Do you remember that research project I completed last year?'

'The one on teaching History to trainee gangstas?'

'At Key Stage 3, in inner-city comprehensives. Yes, that one.'

'All right. Your foray into the underclass of the West Riding conurbation. You did a superb job.'

'Well they thought so too apparently. I had the interview last week and they offered me the post. I'm sorry. I would have told you earlier, but it seemed wrong to do it over the phone, and I haven't seen you for so long.'

'But I thought you said you could never afford to live in London.'

'Ah, well, that's the other thing. I've got a free flat! My dad inherited it from his sister. It's in Crouch End. He was going to sell it, but house prices are going up so fast down there he thought he might as well keep it. He says I can live there as long as I like.'

'What about the death duties and things?'

'He paid them out of his savings. It's gorgeous, all grand and Victorian with its own garden and five minutes' walk from all the trendy shops. Apparently the area is absolutely crawling with actors and media types, so you can rubber-neck in the queue at the post office. I'm not sure if that's a recommendation or not.'

'Well congratulations,' he said. 'I'm really happy for you. When do you start?'

'I'll be moving down in late July, and starting at the Institute in September. I was supposed to serve a term's notice at St John's, but they've been really nice about it and got temporary cover so I can start next term.'

'Right,' said Appleby. 'That's terrific. Absolutely brilliant. Well done!' He felt completely crest-fallen and hoped he could disguise it by getting up to go. 'Listen. I really need to get back now. I have to leave for Cambridge in a couple of hours.'

She gave him a big hug by the front door. 'Come and see me again soon,' she said tenderly. 'I hate it when you leave it so long. I know things are complicated, but I do miss you, you know.'

Her affectionate words only made his sense of imminent loss the keener. As he made his way back home, he reflected that the long-feared moment when he lost her could not be far away. When it finally came it was bound to catch him off-guard and it would hurt far more than he had ever thought.

Jenny would be home by now, probably waiting with a pot of tea and a home-made cake. They would make polite, meaningless conversation before she drove him to the station.

After he had gone, Iris went upstairs to her study and Googled 'Dear heart, how like you this?' It only took a minute to find the Wyatt poem in the original early Tudor English, and another five to read it. Of course '*besely*' was 'busily'! What else could it be? Then it sank in. He thinks I'm going to leave him, she thought. He thinks it's inevitable.

She printed off a copy of the poem, went back into the kitchen, poured herself a glass of chilled Australian Gewürztraminer and lit a spliff. Then she pulled out a note-pad and started writing.

*

Next morning Appleby was back in his rooms at Despenser, trying to sort out his thoughts. He had already seen Chalmers on the far side of the quadrangle and wondered what he had reported to Clovis. Had he seen the draft report on the laptop? Either way the Master now knew for certain that he had been lying about his research, and that the film about Sir Philip Sidney was a clumsy fabrication.

He had no lectures that week, and his other PhD student, a rather earnest Canadian lad, was back home in Vancouver for a family funeral. So he was bracing himself for his next meeting with Claire who was due to see him in an hour, his mind a jumble of guilt, embarrassment and lustful memories. Then the landline rang. The last person to ring him on that number had been van Stumpe nearly five weeks ago. He picked up.

'Hilloo? Is that you, James?' It was him again. He sounded extremely agitated.

'Piet?'

'James! I have some terrible news! Have you said anything to any staffs or collegues of your college about my chest?'

My chest? Van Stumpe had never spoken of it so proprietorially before.

'No. Why? Has something happened?'

'Awful things! This morning I was summoned to see the Director. Someone has told him something about what is in the chest! He demanded me that I take him upstairs and show him the contents immediately. He was absolutely most furious with me that I had misled him over their importance. Of course he knew you were cataloguing them because he had himself agreed for this to happen, but he was demanding to know exactly who you are, and are you really qualified to be doing such works. I tried to explain about your early research, but he said that was not of importance.'

A chill ran through Appleby's body. 'I don't understand,' he said. 'How did he find out?'

'There is a European Union cultural heritage sub-committee which is funding our work at the Institute. Not all of it, but it is of a most significant contribution to what we can be undertaking. The Director was invited to lunch with the chairman of this committee on Saturday – he is an Englishman – and this Englishman told him all about my chest! He also knew about you. He said you were not an important and significant enough historian and that the Director should consider using some scholars he knew from Cambridge. If he handed the project over to the right team, he said he would find him substantially more special fundings!'

'Clovis!' said Appleby. 'Bloody Clovis! I knew it!'

'And he knew many things about what was in the chest and of Harker's story – things you have not even yet told to me, James! Have you spoken to people of all this? If so, that was against our agreements! I still do not have the report you have promised to me!'

'I've only just finished it, Piet. You'll get it tomorrow!'

'Not so. James, I am very sorry, but my Director has instructed me not to give you any more of access to the documents. He is saying that I have already made a serious breaking of Institute discipline, and I may be receiving a formal reprimand! I am so distraught I cannot tell you.'

'No more access to the documents at all? Please say that's not true!'

'The Director was most emphatical. You may not to come back in the Institute. I am sorry, James. That is absolute.'

After the call Appleby sat in stunned silence for several minutes, his anger against Clovis mounting all the time. Part of him wanted to burst into the Master's Lodge and strangle him in his own library. He was sure he could do it. His sheer rage would overcome the difference in size. Mainly, however, he felt an icy sense of defeat.

There was a knock on the door. One of the porters handed him a scribbled telephone message. 'Miss Tenterden sends her apologies, but she is unwell and will not be attending her supervision.'

Why had she not rung him in person? Was she genuinely ill? Did she now feel awkward about meeting him again? Was she standing up a casual lover with whom she did not want a second date? Did she feel ashamed of their one-night stand? Had he ruined their teacher-tutee relationship, such as it was? Whatever the explanation, it was galling. If he had known she wasn't coming he could have stayed in York another day. Or flown straight to Amsterdam on Sunday night…except there was no point in going there any more apparently. Clovis had seen to that.

Chalmers had been spying for Clovis, that much was obvious, but how had they known he was at the Institute at all? Then the obvious truth hit him with the awful, disabling force of a punch in the solar plexus.

'Claire!' he wailed. 'Claire, you total bitch!'

*

The following morning Appleby got a letter from York. It contained a single sheet, unsigned, on which was written, in a neat italic hand, the following:

She flees thee not that sometime ye still seek
With naked foot stalking within her chamber
And still for thee she's gentle, if not meek
But wild at heart, yet e'er she will remember
How sometimes we have put ourselves in danger
To take bread at our hands. Nor doth she range
Busily seeking with continual change.

Thanked be fortune, 'twill yet be otherwise
Twenty times better, and often special,
In thin array, after a loving guise
When our loose clothes shall from our shoulders fall
And she shall catch you in her arms long and small
And therewithal most sweetly will you kiss
And softly say 'Dear heart, how like you this?'

It is no dream, for she lies broad awaking,
Her world is turned through your gentleness,
'Tis she who fears a fashion of forsaking,
You have no leave to go of her goodness,

She doth not wish to use new fangledness,
But since by her, you are so kindly served,
She would fain know, what she hath now deserved.

Shortly after he had read it the cleaner arrived and was surprised by the sight of a middle-aged lecturer, wiping his eyes with his hanky and blowing his nose loudly. It was the same woman who had entered the ladies' toilets and heard Claire sobbing in a cubicle.

'I dunno,' she told the other cleaners at tea-break. 'I can't seem to go anywhere in this place without finding someone blubbing.'

Suffolk

Second Lieutenant Driberg, the duty officer at the main entrance to RAF Hallingham, was out of his skull with boredom when the car drew up. Hallingham, an RAF base in name only, had been run by the United States Air Force since 1943. It housed one squadron of long-rangebombers and one of multi-role interceptors. Driberg had been on duty at the gate for three hours that night, accompanied by three black bereted men from the Air Force Security Force, carrying automatic rifles. Conversation had been desultory. As the car stopped in front of the barrier between two sets of electronic gates, Driberg stepped forward.

'Hi there,' said the driver, lowering his window. 'Name of Davidson. You wanna check these?'

He handed Driberg a small bundle of documents including his United States passport, his driver's licence, the rental agreement from the Hertz office at Heathrow and a letter of introduction to a senior aircraft engineer on the base.

'Wait there, please sir,' said Driberg, stepping back into his booth.

Davidson could see the black-and-white image of his Japanese four-by-four on a small monitor as Driberg methodically logged his paperwork. Looking up, he noticed the security camera pointing towards his windscreen. Driberg made a brief telephone call, then returned to the car.

'Would you step out of the vehicle please, sir?'

Davidson climbed out and stood to the side while one of the security officers frisked him. Driberg noted that the man was probably in his mid-forties, stocky and powerfully built. He had a thick, but neatly trimmed beard, but no moustache. Driberg thought this made him look like a goat. The other two SFs rooted through the car.

'Your suitcase key, please, sir,' said the man who had frisked him.

Davidson handed it over, and the man rummaged through his spare shirts, underwear and toiletries, while his colleagues lifted seats, opened glove compartments and inspected the underside of the chassis with a mirror on a little trolley.

'She's clean,' said one eventually.

'Your friend is expecting you,' said Driberg. 'Take the first left, the second right, then left again. 55 Eaker Drive is in the block at the end. Enjoy your visit, now, Pastor Davidson.'

Eaker Drive was dimly lit and deserted when Davidson pulled up. He walked round to the back of the SUV and lifted the tailgate. He opened a small toolcase and took out a box-cutter. Then he unzipped his suitcase, ran it around the false base and pulled out a wide flat bag.

'Come in, buddy,' said the engineer when he rang the bell. 'I been expectin' ya.'

The exchange was over in minutes. Davidson passed over his package. The engineer opened it, counted the money and opened a small case of similar size and shape to the one he had just been given.

'You got all you'll ever need here,' he said. 'Have you used one of these before?'

Davidson nodded.

'You attach the stock to the rifle like so to use it as a shoulder-weapon,' said the engineer. 'This model is pin-point accurate up to fifteen hundred metres. But you'll need to to adjust the scope first. There's extra ammunition in this box, including exploding rounds. They'll pretty much demolish anything they hit. The pistol is a Glock. It's rugged and reliable but don't believe that old myth about metal detectors. It'll set them off. The other items you requested are in the compartment at the side here.'

Back at the SUV, Davidson slotted the case into the cavity in his suitcase, carefully replacing the false base before re-closing it. He needn't have bothered. When he got back to the gate Driberg simply made a note of the time of his exit and waved him through. Ten minutes later he was on the A11, speeding towards London.

He was fiddling with the earpiece of a new Bluetooth hands-free set when it started to beep. A voice he did not recognise gave him a man's name, the description and registration number of a car and an address and postcode in Enfield, north London.

'Enfield? Like the rifles?' said Davidson as he keyed the address into the sat-nav on the dashboard. There was no reply. The line went dead.

*

Four men climbed the narrow staircase at the back of The Magic Tandoor restaurant in Brick Lane. A bearded middle-aged man of South Asian descent in a crumpled brown jacket opened a door on the landing and went into a small, cluttered office. He was followed by two young men, also South Asians, both in black waiters' suits, and a fourth man wearing a dark weatherproof jacket who carried a large holdall. The fourth man was in his thirties, with lighter skin. The waiters took up positions behind their boss. One leaned against a filing cabinet, the other against a stack of bags marked 'Gram Flour'.

'Take a seat,' said the older man. 'Put your bag on the table.'

The visitor obeyed, silently taking in his surroundings.

'So,' said the host. 'First let's confirm some details. What is the name on your passport?'

'Kyriakou – Andros.'

'And how did you come here today?'

'From Canterbury, by train.'

'How did you enter the UK?'

'On a shoppers' coach from Calais.'

'How did you get to Calais?'

'On the Eurostar from Paris.'

'How did you get to Paris?'

'What is this? You don't need to know all this...'

'Just answer the questions. How did you get to Paris?'

'By air from Reykjavik – via Oslo.'

'Which carrier?'

'Enough. I'm tired. You should know all this. You should have been briefed.'

'Which carrier?'

'SAS.'

'How did you get to Iceland?'

'On a freighter – from Quebec.'

'And how did you get into Canada?'

'In the back of a beer truck.'

The middle-aged man turned to one of the waiters.

'It's okay. It checks.'

He clicked his fingers and pointed to the filing cabinet. The waiter opened the middle drawer, pulled out a transparent A4 plastic folder and handed it to his boss.

'Give me your papers,' he said to the guest. 'All of them.'

The man unzipped a side-compartment in his case and carefully removed a wad of documents.

'Wallet too.'

He reached into his jacket pocket, took out his wallet and pushed it across the table with the other documents.

The older man passed them to the other waiter.

'Burn all this.' He pushed the plastic folder across to his guest. 'This is your new identity: your passport, registration documents, credit cards – and some cash. You are now Kerim Mehmet, a mature Turkish student on an Accountancy course at De Montfort University in Leicester. Tonight the boys will take you somewhere safe. We will send food round. Tomorrow morning you will be collected and driven to a friend in Leicester. Be ready to leave by 6.00 am. You will access your instructions in the usual way after you arrive.'

The guest began rifling through his new papers. 'Do you know…'

'You missed in Washington. We were told that would never happen.'

'The target was lucky. He moved his head. That won't happen again.'

'It won't be him this time. Someone else is looking after that.'

Five minutes later the two young men escorted the man down Brick Lane. Waiters stood under gaudy signs in the doorways of other restaurants, hassling the crowds of late-night diners with offers of discounts and free bottles of wine. He had been surprised to be summoned here. The local Bangladeshi community did not have a reputation for fundamentalism or militancy. Perhaps that was the point.

His soul recoiled from this bizarre mis-begotten offspring of cultural miscegenation: a neon-lit oriental bazaar, grafted onto an austere 19th Century London street where young Muslim men openly sold alcohol, cheerfully mingling with westerners, including immodestly dressed young women.

None of this would happen after the return of the Caliphate.

York

'How many times has this happened, then?' said Kate. 'You really should have said something.'

She cast her eyes around her brother's kitchen, noting how gloomy it looked in the fading dusk light. It was surprising that they still hadn't got round to installing fitted units. Everyone else she knew had them.

'Five, I think,' said Appleby. He was sitting opposite her at the table. He buried his face in his hands. 'I'm losing count to be honest. I'm pretty sure this was the fifth.'

'What do the doctors say?'

'Not a lot. They don't seem to have an explanation really. She's had various tests, but they can't find anything abnormal. They seem to think it's just bad luck.'

'She did seem very low,' said Kate. 'I've never seen her like that before. I remember you telling me about the first time. Is this how she was then?'

Appleby nodded.

'And the others?'

'They weren't quite so bad,' he said. 'They all came in the first few weeks.' He gave a sad little smile. 'We were almost getting used to it in an awful sort of way. It's become a sort of routine.'

'Tell me about it…I've been there, remember.'

'She got me to look once, just to be sure.' He shuddered at the memory.

'I did that to Rob,' said Kate with a sheepish grin. 'It put him off sex for a month.'

'Nobody talks about this sort of thing when you start trying.'

'Well you don't want to think about it, do you? Especially once it's behind you.'

'This time it was different, though. Nineteen weeks! We really thought we were home and dry. Honestly, Kate, it was awful! Just horrible. She was in so much pain.…They said it was a little girl…' His eyes filled.

'Oh, Jimmy…' Kate put her hand on his.

'I just don't know how she's going to be when she comes home…

I'm scared, Kate.'

'She's very robust, you know, your wife. She's got over it before, and I'm sure she will again.' She came and stood behind him, leaning down and gently putting her hands on his shoulders. 'Listen, I'm going to ring Rob and tell him I'm staying over. He won't mind. Then I'll take you to the hospital tomorrow. You both need a bit of moral support.'

'Oh, you don't have to do that. It was so kind of you to come up today...'

'No arguments.' She squeezed his shoulders. 'Didn't I see a leaflet for a Chinese takeaway somewhere? Let's order some dinner. You've got to eat, Jimmy.'

The next afternoon they brought Jenny home. She was fragile, but seemed to be recovering her spirits a little.

'See,' said Kate, when Jenny went up to rest. 'She'll be fine.'

After Kate had gone home he went up and sat beside Jenny on the bed. She took his hand.

'I'm so sorry,' she said tearfully. 'We're never going to have a baby. I'm so sorry. I've let you down.'

'Don't be stupid,' he murmured.

He leaned over to hug her, buried his head in the pillow by her head and sobbed silently.

The next morning he was woken by the sound of the doorbell. Jenny was already out of bed. As he pulled on his dressing-gown he heard the front door shutting. He went to the window and pulled back the curtain just in time to see her climb into the back of a taxi.

*

For most of his adult life Appleby had been conscious that, unlike his father and his grandfather before him, he had never had to go to war. For this he could thank, in roughly chronological order, the Treaty of Rome, the dismantling of the British Empire, the abolition of National Service, the apocalyptic equilibrium of the Cold War and the good sense of Harold Wilson in resisting L.B.J.'s pressure to join the

Americans in Vietnam.

But when he first came across Dr Johnson's remark, faithfully recorded by Boswell, that 'Every man thinks meanly of himself for not having been a soldier', it hit a deep nerve. Life in the tepid comfort of post-war England meant that he had never been tested by extreme danger or stress and probably never would be. He knew his father's deep moral convictions, fearsome work-ethic and generosity of spirit had been forged during his struggle from extreme boyhood poverty, but they had then been tempered in the furnaces of North Africa, Sicily and Italy.

Appleby had never yearned for adrenal adventure. He did not want to free-fall parachute out of aeroplanes, scale dangerous peaks or drive dog-sleds alone across the frozen wastes of Siberia. In fact he suspected that the people who did seek such experiences were suffering from a sort of neurological deficiency, an existential numbness, as if they could only convince themselves that they had fingers by hitting them with hammers.

To his mind enduring dangers you had engineered for your own entertainment didn't actually count as a test of moral mettle, anyway. It was the unexpected, the unlooked-for peril that taught people who they really were. That was what had made the experiences of conscripted men in war so unpredictable. You could never tell. When the artillery shells burst overhead and the Hun stormed your trench, the mousy little chap from Accounts Payable might be the one with bayonet fixed, roaring like a lion, while the school rugby captain was curled up in a jibbering heap in his dugout.

Finally, he sensed, his own moral fibre was being put to the test, but in a way he could never have predicted, which offered no heroics, and which he would have sawn off his right arm to avoid.

He went into his study to check his diary and saw the picture of Sir Nicholas Harker looking down at him. Those limpid eyes seemed to be searching him out – and yet they were strangely reassuring too. 'So what would you have had to say?' he muttered to himself. 'What secret wisdom would you have to offer?'

Jenny had left a note on the kitchen table: 'Gone to Norwich. Sorry. Will call later.'

She's like an injured animal, he thought, crawling away to lick her wounds.

*

He spoke to her on the phone every night, short inconsequential conversations. She had been for a walk round the campus at the university and seen an exhibition in the Sainsbury Centre or sat for an hour in the Cathedral. She had gone to the market with Zeta and helped her choose a cardigan at Jarrold's. She had done a few sketches in St Peter Mancroft. Lucy had been over with her toddlers. They were a terrible handful.

Then after four weeks, he cycled home from campus one evening and she was there, sitting at the kitchen table with a fresh pot of tea, surrounded by flowers.

'Pretty aren't they?' she said as she got up to greet him. 'Mummy bought them in town before they went back home. We thought it would be nice to surprise you.'

'It is,' he said, grabbing her in a huge shuddering hug. 'It's wonderful.'

Suddenly her light tone turned grave. 'Jimmy, I'd like to try again... For a baby I mean.'

'Are you sure?'

'Yes, but only once. If we lose another, that will be it. I simply couldn't bear to go through all that...not again.'

*

Within three months she was pregnant.

Cambridge

'Tell me, Norman, how is young Dilke getting on in Amsterdam?'

The two men were strolling along the Backs near Kings College. When Clovis had rung to suggest this little constitutional, Skyne knew that it could only mean one thing. The Master was troubled and wanted to discuss something confidential.

'Pretty well, I think, J.D.. He's been through most of the archive by now. The train-spotter had done a sort of preliminary catalogue, anyway. The archivist chappie didn't want to hand it over for some reason, but the director ordered him to. Appleby did a pretty good job, apparently – saved Dilke a lot of time.'

'I called on Freddy yesterday.'

'What? You went all the way to...? Why?'

'As I suspected, there's a file on that man Harker.'

'Aha.'

'Has Dilke mentioned finding anything particularly – unusual?'

'Well the whole thing's pretty bizarre, if you ask me. And there are several extremely rare books, I gather.'

'It would be a book, but I mean something really extraordinary – something that would be a complete game-changer.'

'Such as?'

'Believe me, Dilke would know if he had found it.'

'Well he hasn't mentioned anything, but I'll ask him.'

'Listen, Norman. We need to find a way of making this damned nonsense disappear.'

'The archive?'

'The whole shooting-match.'

'You can't mean destroy it, J.D.?'

'If only we could! No, it needs to fizzle out – to evaporate. Encourage Dilke to find a way of discrediting it. Find some evidence indicating it's all the work of a lunatic or a big hoax of some sort. Concoct something if you have to.'

'Dilke won't like that. This is supposed to be his big break.'

'Then we must make it worth his while, mustn't we? You can find some other plum project for him afterwards. And I want you to lean on Appleyard as well.'

'Oh?'

'Point out that we have evidence of his consuming illegal drugs on college premises, lying to his superiors to take unauthorised leave and seducing a tutee. Tell him that if he so much as mutters in his sleep about Sir Nicholas Harker, we'll start by reporting the drug thing to the police, then we'll make damned sure that he gets a dishonourable discharge from his own university and loses his bloody pension!'

'Very well. Dilke will have to look sharp, though. There could be a complication.'

'Oh?'

'Access. The owner of the farm where they found all this stuff has been trying to establish that it is all his property. Apparently the place has been in his family for centuries, and he claims it's all his rightful inheritance. Dilke says the Director thinks he has a pretty good case, and the court is due to rule in a couple of weeks. If he wins, he'll be able to do what he likes with it.'

'Then tell him to get his bloody skates on…and make sure Appleton understands that we mean business.'

Skyne carried out both these orders the same afternoon.

*

Appleby was still fuming about it as he sat at his desk in Despenser a fortnight later. The most exciting project he had ever encountered and the prospect of an unprecedented resurgence in his moribund career had been snatched away through the arrogant machinations of men who treated him with undisguised contempt.

The day after van Stumpe's call he had written an impassioned plea to the Director of the Renaissance Institute, explaining his involvement with Sir Nicholas Harker over the decades, how he was the first scholar to discover the man's existence and had been on the case ever since. There was no reply. He tried phoning him in person. His P.A. took messages but the calls were never returned. Eventually van Stumpe rang again and asked him to desist. Appleby was only making things worse for both of them.

Then Norman Skyne passed on Clovis's threats. He was completely boxed in.

In the absence of a film-script on Sir Philip Sidney, he had no choice but to return full-time to the Toft Bequest. If Cranham's chest had contained a rich banquet of human drama, historical insights and philosophical revelations, this was the historian's equivalent of chewing though a bucket of dry bran.

The rest of his work was going just as badly. By now his lectures on rural life in Tudor England were embarrassingly poorly attended. After the family funeral, his Canadian post-grad had arranged to remain in Vancouver until the following October, though nobody at Despenser bothered to tell Appleby this. Claire seemed to have disappeared too, but under the circumstances, that was just as well. If he met her, he might not have been answerable for his actions. If he encountered Skyne or Chalmers about the college, they simply blanked him.

Things were little better back in York. Jenny was as politely indifferent as ever. Iris was busy all the time, letting out her house and preparing for her move to London. He was drinking too, a lot more whisky, not the delicious malts he so loved, but the cheapest blended rubbish he could find in the supermarkets.

As he told Pete Elyot one evening, 'I haven't been so down since… since, you know…the night when…'

Then came a tiny, bitter crumb of consolation. Back in his rooms at Despenser that morning he had noticed a small paragraph in the News section of the Renaissance Institute's website. The Dutch courts had decreed that a large collection of English documents, in the temporary care of senior archivist Piet van Stumpe, were the legal property of the farmer in whose house they had been discovered. They were now to be sold at auction. All access to these items had been suspended, pending the sale.

Appleby couldn't resist sending an email: 'Dear Professor Skyne, so sorry to learn of your little disappointment in Amsterdam. Kind regards. JA.'

He had just pressed 'SEND' when there was a knock at the door. It was the porter.

'This came for you, sir, by courier.' He handed Appleby a thick A4 envelope.

It contained an old issue of a journal called The International Book Connoisseur. He had never heard of it. There was no covering letter, but someone had circled a strap-line on the cover and dog-eared the corner of the corresponding page. It was an article entitled 'The Subversive Billionaire' by one Francesco Angelini. The stand-first said he was an Italian publishing tycoon. Appleby began to read the article.

'I am a wealthy man, but perhaps I am not entirely the man you think I am,' it began. 'I don't think you're anything,' Appleby thought. 'I've never bloody heard of you!'

There followed a detailed history of the Angelini family and their formidable track-record of heretical and politically subversive activities. They seemed to have been mixed up in every important event in Italian history, and always on the side of free-thinking, free-speech and democracy.

After establishing these impeccable radical credentials, Angelini went on to describe his extensive and fascinating collection of rare historical volumes. He specialised in any kind of book or tract which had been banned or suppressed in the author's lifetime. Someone had marked the last paragraph with a highlighter:

'My fortune from the publication of books and magazines across Europe has been a blessing in that I am able to acquire and preserve these threatened voices from the past, regardless of cost, and I welcome applications from serious scholars who may study them free of charge at my private archive. It is my privilege to serve as the custodian of the heretical, the librarian of liberty, the archivist of taboo!'

There was a contact address in Milan at the end.

Appleby spent the next few hours writing, printing and photo-copying. He reached the post office just before it closed for the day, carrying a fat envelope marked 'Strictly Confidential'. It was a risk, but a risk he was prepared to take if it meant he could undermine Skyne or Clovis's plans in any way. And if they did find out? Well, fuck 'em!

Back at his desk, he fished the A4 envelope out of his waste-paper basket and checked the despatch label. It had been sent from Amsterdam.

*

By 8.30 that evening he was ensconced in a cosy wood-panelled room in a Victorian pub ten minutes' walk from the college. He was on his second double scotch, idly reading a discarded copy of *The Independent*. It was an article about the burgeoning 9/11 conspiracy theories and how they got started. Wasn't there something quasi-religious about the way people yearned to believe these stories, no matter how far-fetched or improbable? It was as if nothing had changed since the Elizabethan era.

A sallow young man with large bulging eyes came over, put his pint on Appleby's table and sat down.

'You're Doctor Appleby, aren't you?'

'Am I? And who the fuck might you be?'

'I'm Jeremy. Jeremy Dilke.'

'My God! You're the little shit who stole my research project! You've got a nerve...'

'Yes, I'm sorry about that, believe me. I know it was viciously unfair.'

'But you've lost it too now, haven't you?' Appleby said with a forced grin. 'Please excuse me while I gloat!'

'I can't blame you,' said Dilke. 'Old van Stumpe told me all about you, and I saw for myself how Clovis and Skyne stitched you up. But I had to take the chance when it was offered. It was a once in a lifetime opportunity, and they'd only have given it to someone else...'

Appleby grunted.

'...The director made van Stumpe show me your draft catalogue, by the way, and all those annotations. You did a terrific job. I was going to try to persuade Skyne to get you back on board when the dust had settled a bit. You obviously know far more about these people than anyone else. Van Stumpe gave me a copy of your old History Today article and a video of that documentary you made. What a saga! He's a sweet old stick, isn't he? He thinks you're the bee's knees, you know. He'd do anything to help you.'

Appleby grunted again. Why was this man being so nice? It was disconcerting.

'Anyway, as you clearly know, I'm off the project too now. They're putting everything up for auction at Christie's in Amsterdam next month. It's been broken up into separate lots, so it'll probably get dispersed all over the world. In the meantime nobody's allowed to touch a thing.'

'Maybe some of it'll come to England. It bloody well should. It's our history.'

'You can forget that. Do you realise that the Metropolitan Museum in New York has sixty times as much cash to spend on acquisitions every year as the British Museum? We're not in the game anymore. Let me get you another. What are you drinking?'

They sat and talked for hours, swapping anecdotes and insights, like two boys who had loved and lost the same girlfriend. The conversation came round to the murderously violent reaction to Harker's activities.

'They were obviously afraid of it spreading,' said Dilke taking a meditative swig on his beer. 'Then again...maybe they decided to wipe them out just because they could.'

'How d'you mean?' said Appleby, stifling a hiccup.

'Well the whole thing seems to have been neatly contained within that one little village, right? My guess is that they calculated that if they could get rid of everyone infected by this plague in one blow, they could eradicate a new and dangerous heresy before it could spread anywhere else – and the rest of the country would be none the wiser. The other villagers would be too damned terrified to make a fuss – and, as we know, the one hardcore survivor, Cranham, scuttled off to Flanders with his baby daughter.'

'In which case they've been proved right, haven't they?' said Appleby. 'Apart from the chap who wrote "On the Expurgation..." and the Reverend Trott, nobody heard a peep about it until I found that bundle of letters four hundred years later.'

'Quite,' said Dilke.

'I have another theory,' said Appleby after a pause. 'I think they found Harker's very reasonableness made him more of a threat than if he had been a fanatical Catholic or a Presbyterian – or even a full-blown atheist. I think they couldn't handle the idea of living with the possibility of doubt.'

'Maybe,' said Dilke ruminatively. 'Isn't it strange? Everything's so different now we've passed through the Enlightenment and come out the other side. I've lost count of the number of people I know who are agnostics of one kind or another. No one feels the need to commit to anything anymore. In this country agnosticism has supplanted Anglicanism as the national faith – or rather lack of faith. In fact, I would venture to suggest that the historic role of the Anglican church has been to pave the way for agnosticism! The Queen should change her Latin tag to 'I D': *Infides Defensor!* ...Another scotch?'

'My round,' said Appleby, swaying gently as he rose to his feet.

'I'll tell you something really odd,' said Dilke when Appleby tottered back from the bar. 'Skyne and Clovis wanted me to say it was all a hoax. Don't tell any bugger I told you that, will you, or they'll do me. But they were really leaning on me – offering all sorts of inducements. They were absolutely desperate to discredit it.'

'Why?' said Appleby, perplexed. 'Why would they want to do that?'

'Search me,' said Dilke. 'They kept going on about some book – asking if I'd found anything earth-shattering. God only knows what that was all about. Clovis is deeply weird, you know. "He moves in mysterious ways his blunders to perform". Anyway, it's all out of their hands now…so fuck 'em!'

'Funny you should say that,' said Appleby. 'I was saying the very same thing only this afternoon – fuck 'em!'

By the end of the night Appleby and Dilke had decided that they were best friends. They staggered off, each promising to tell the other if he heard of any developments.

*

A month later Appleby had wrapped up his work on the Toft Bequest and was back in York, gloomily preparing for the new academic year.

He was cycling home after a departmental planning meeting in which Andrew Howland had managed to fit in three sarcastic remarks about his status as 'a Cambridge don' and two jibes about his research trips to 'the city of legalised hemp and whoring.'

'God, how I loathe and despise that man!' he shouted as he came through the front door.'

'Jimmy!' Jenny called from the kitchen. 'You have a visitor!'

'Oh?'

'Mr van Stumpe is here.'

And there he was, sitting at their kitchen table, as Appleby told Pete Elyot later that night, 'bright-eyed and bushy-tailed, like some Puckish old satyr'.

'Please to excuse such intrusion,' van Stumpe gushed, 'but I have such wonderful news to tell, I had to come all the way here to say it in person!'

'You'd better sit down, Jimmy,' said Jenny. 'This may take a while.'

Van Stumpe's words came in a torrent. 'I am so sorry I could not telephone to you about that disastrous auctioning,' he gabbled, 'but my director expressly forbade me to do it. But the auction has not proceeded ahead! A private buyer has come forward. He has made the legal owners of our chest an offer of an amount far in advance of the expected auction prices of all the lots, to buy the entire collection. And they accepted this!'

'Gosh,' said Appleby. 'I don't see how that helps, though. Well, me anyway.'

'Oh, but it does! So very much! This buyer has sent his representatives to meet with us at the Institute. They have asked most detailed questionings about the documents and the books and taken away a copy of your cataloguings and notings and I also gave to them a tape of your programme about the mystery burning of the house – I hope you do not object to that. Yesterday I have received a letter from them on the behalves of this new owner, requesting to the Institute to continue to house the collection for his safe-keeping, and making specific recommendation that you be offered without delay the job of editing and preparing the most significant of the documentation for publication! This owner wants you to come back, James! He wants you to do this job! If you can arrange some sabbatical leaves, the owner is even willing to pay for your expenses! You can come back, James! And please, you will be most welcome again in my house – if you so wish.'

'But who is this person?' said Appleby.

'Ah,' said van Stumpe, suddenly rather quiet, 'this I cannot say. In facts, I am not knowing myself. For this moment he wishes to be secretly anonymous.'

'It's just that I got a package from Amsterdam a few weeks ago. You wouldn't happen to know anything about that would you, Piet?'

'Package?' Van Stumpe stiffened visibly. 'I know nothing of any package. Please, James, do not speak of a package. Can you not just be happy that you may return?'

'Of course,' said Appleby. 'I'm bloody ecstatic, actually. I don't know what else to say.' He finally pulled off his bicycle clips. 'Jenny, I love this man!'

Van Stumpe blushed.

'That's right. I love you, Piet van Stumpe.'

Enfield

'This the practised Inquisitor knoweth right well: that the mere sight of the Instruments of Torment will oft loosen the Resolution as readily as their use. Yet there is naught upon this Earth that will prise apart the most obdurate jaws more certainly than the threat of hurte to those their owner loveth.'

—*Sir Nicholas Harker: The Colloquies, Vol III, No 22*

'Honey, I'm ho-o-me!'

DS Trevor Jenvey was hugely relieved to be off duty. Long round trips, first to York, then to north Devon had been followed by a tedious day at the office trawling through Appleby's email and phone records. He let himself in through the little glassed-in porch of his semi, hung up his coat and, after making sure both doors were closed behind him, strode down the narrow hallway towards the kitchen. From the gardens beyond he could hear the reassuring muffled chug of his neighbour's old lawn-mower.

'Why's it so dark?' he called. 'Have you drawn the blinds? Something smells good!'

'It surely does,' said the stranger as Jenvey entered the kitchen. 'Nothing beats good old home-cooking now, does it, Sergeant Jenvey?'

'Who the fuck are you!?'

It took Jenvey several seconds to comprehend the scene in front of him. A short, thick-set man with a beard and no moustache was standing in the middle of the room, pointing an automatic pistol straight at him. Jenvey recognised it as a Glock. The kitchen table had been pushed to the far side of the room. Jenvey's wife Louise, his twelve-year-old daughter, Lisa and his nine year old son Craig were sitting facing him on a row of chairs. Their hands and legs had been secured tightly to the chairs with sturdy plastic cable-ties, and they all had big strips of silver duct-tape over their mouths. Craig had been crying and was breathing in short, panicky drafts through his nose. To the side was a plastic bowl of water containing their three mobile phones. Jenvey realised instantly that he had to remain as calm as possible. He took a deep breath.

'Now I'd like to keep this little transaction as straightforward and painless as possible,' said the stranger. 'I think you'll agree that would be to the benefit of all concerned.'

'You're American,' he said. 'Who are you? What are you doing? What do you want?'

'How very observant of you, Sergeant. I expect my accent has betrayed me. Before we go any further I need you to tell me if you are carrying a sidearm. Would that be the case?'

'No.'

'That's good news. Let's all hope it's true because I would surely hate to have to put a slug or two into your wife's head. Now I need you to take out your cell phone, and your police radio if you have one, and drop them in this bucket of water. You think you can do that? Nice and slow, now.'

Slowly and very cautiously, Jenvey obeyed the stranger's instructions. 'What's this about? If this is a robbery, you can take whatever you want.'

'There's no need to worry about your hard-earned property. All I want is one small piece of information. As soon as you give me that, we can all relax and go home... Or in your case, stay home,' he added with a grin.

'What?'

'I merely require the location.'

'What location?'

'I believe you know exactly what I mean now, Sergeant. Please don't make this unnecessarily difficult.' He moved his face disconcertingly close to Jenvey's and smiled. 'Now where precisely is he?'

'Where is who? Who do you mean?'

'Trevor, my friend, this could get real vexatious, real quick. You are going to tell me exactly what I need to know. Let me explain why.

I'm sure you are a very brave police officer, a true British hero, with a powerful sense of duty. I would not insult your professional honour by threatening your person with any kind of violence because I do not doubt that you would endure to the last drop of blood. But you see, that's not what I'm gonna do, because, when we cut to the chase, I don't believe I need to. Right now I'm trying to decide which item from which member of your family's anatomies I need to amputate first to persuade you of the advantages of co-operation…'

The stranger continued to hold Jenvey's gaze, searching his eyes for signs of weakness and uncertainty. There was something icily mesmeric about his oddly mannered speech. His gun remained pointed at Jenvey's heart.

'… I could start with something they wouldn't miss too much, like the tip of your wife's little finger, just to show I mean business. Or I could go straight to a more dramatic gesture. Your daughter, I notice, is about to enter those sensitive teen years. How do you think she would enjoy the transition into womanhood if the end of her nose had been clipped off? Do you think that might adversely affect her psychological development? I have a feeling it might. Then again perhaps we should go for something totally life-changing. How do you figure your son would enjoy his adult life without his genitalia?'

'You're sick,' said Jenvey. 'You wouldn't …'

The stranger pulled a pair of garden secateurs from his pocket with his free hand and squeezed them open and shut a few times.

'Oh that really is too bad. I was afraid it might come to this. I can see I am going to have to give a demonstration. You know what? I think we'll skip the fingertip and go right to that nose.'

As the three captives squirmed in their seats, the man moved across to Lisa and pressed the open blades of the secaturs around the fleshy tip of her nose. Lisa's body tensed in a spasm of fear and she gave a muffled squeal.

'Stop! I'll tell you!'

'Well?' The man squeezed the blades together. The tip of Lisa's nose turned pale under the pressure.

'It's a place in Devon. At the edge of the Exmoor National Park. The exact location doesn't appear on the maps. I'll have to draw it for you. Now let her go!'

'Whoa there, cowboy! One thing at a time now. Just take that little note-pad from the counter there and draw your little map for me. Nice and clear, now. Be sure to mark the route from the nearest road with a number. Then slide it along here.'

Jenvey obeyed, using the pad the family used for shopping lists. The top of the sheet read 'ketchup, avocados, loo-rolls'. He tore it off, picked up the ball-point pen they kept by the pad and carefully drew the map. He slid the pad towards the man, who moved away from Lisa and put down the secaturs. Still holding the gun towards Jenvey, he pulled out a smartphone and photographed the map. He put the phone down on the counter, barely glancing at Jenvey as he methodically pressed the keys with one hand.

'There's gonna be a brief delay now,' he said, 'while my associates check this out. If these instructions are designed to mislead, I suggest you let me know that right away – to avoid unfortunate consequences.'

'They're accurate,' said Jenvey. 'What do you want him for anyway? He's just a historian. He's completely harmless. What's he done to you?'

'Just a historian.' The man gave a sarcastic snort. 'That's just the kind of response I would expect from an Englishman. You are a weak, decadent nation who turned your backs on God many, many years ago, including those of you who still pretend to be Christians. Even your clergy rarely accept the literal truth of the Bible. You tolerate or actively encourage the abomination of homosexuality which is expressly prohibited by the laws of God, along with abortion and every other form of sin and depravity. Your historian, sir, is an enemy of Christ.'

'So you want to kill him for being English and tolerating gays? Is that what you're saying?'

The man gave a sigh of frustration. 'I have no desire to get involved in some pointless theological debate with you, Sergeant. Nor do I propose to do so. But I will say this: The twin viruses of atheism and agnosticism have been spreading across the United Sates for many decades now, polluting the spiritual waters and placing the immortal souls of the weak and gullible in peril of eternal damnation and the fires of Hell. But this creature, whom you and your colleagues are currently protecting, is the source of something much more deadly than the sickness of so-called "honest doubt". The belief-system he has introduced is an aggressive, metastasising cancer spreading through the tissues of my country, destroying healthy flesh and organs. And it does so by the most treacherous possible means, by mimicking the joy and bliss of worship, which is mankind's route to know his Saviour, and turning it into a hollow parody. Your "harmless historian", Sergeant Jenvey, is a malignant tumour – and I am God's scalpel.'

'You're a fucking nutter,' muttered Jenvey.

The smartphone beeped, and the man read his new message.

'Isn't modern electronic technology a wonderful thing? You can track down almost any kind of information in seconds if you only know who to ask. It's a real gift of the Almighty. You will be gratified to hear that your story checks out. It seems he's holed up with that publisher. Now he's what we call back home a Guido faggot, a man of the lowest possible character.'

The distraction was momentary, but Jenvey calculated it was the only chance he would get. He launched himself across the kitchen, throwing his shoulders towards the man's midriff, hoping to send him crashing to the floor.

Unfortunately the man had made exactly the same calculation. He raised the Glock almost casually as soon as Jenvey began to move and fired two shots into his chest.

*

When the next door neighbour switched off the motor of his noisy old lawn-mower, he heard three muffled bangs. He assumed the Jenveys had their TV on loud or that Trevor was doing a spot of DIY.

At eight o'clock Louise's friend Vicky arrived to take her to their weekly salsa class. She rang the doorbell repeatedly, knocked and shouted. The inner door of the porch had been left open, and she peered through the letter-box. She could see a man's foot on the floor behind the half-open kitchen door.

An hour later Jenvey's colleagues broke in and found the bodies. Wisps of smoke were escaping from the oven, where Louise's chicken casserole was slowly burning itself to the inside of the Le Creuset.

York

This time they were sure they had made it. Jenny had gone over seven and a half months, well within the limit of viability for a premature baby. The ultrasound showed a healthy, well-developed baby boy.

'It does rather take over your life, doesn't it?' said Kate.

'You could say that…' said Appleby.

Kate had arrived from Birmingham with a car-load of her children's cast-off baby clothes, miscellaneous equipment and the old wooden high-chair she and Appleby had been fed in themselves. He had just finished decorating the nursery, and they took her upstairs to show it off.

'You should have seen him trying to hang the wallpaper,' said Jenny. 'Do you remember Mr Pastry? It was like that – absolute chaos!'

'But what a lovely room,' said Kate. 'Ooh, teddy bears! I'd have expected little aeroplanes or toy soldiers from you, Jimmy. I don't suppose they do mobiles with Elizabethan peasants at Mothercare, do they? Have you chosen a name yet?'

'We're thinking about Daniel,' said Appleby.

'I believe that's quite fashionable at the moment,' said Kate. 'What a fabulous cot! Wherever did you get that?'

'Jenny's mum bought it. She picked it up in some village market in Provence.'

'She made Daddy drive all the way back with it strapped to the roof of the car,' said Jenny laughing. 'She claims it's 18th Century. And she's given us that new Moses basket; and Daddy's given Jimmy an expensive little video camera. He seems to expect him to film the birth. I've told him that's right out!'

'Now Zeta really is taking over our lives,' said Appleby.

'Oh just indulge her,' said Kate. 'It's special having grandkids. Mum was like that with mine. Now have you been doing your homework, Jimmy?'

'He's been to every single pre~antenatal class,' said Jenny.

'Oorgh. The National Childbirth Trust,' Appleby groaned.

'You should see him lying on the floor, panting. The tutor makes the dads pretend they're having contractions. It's hilarious. Some of the blokes are so self-conscious. Jimmy got a bit carried away last week and this other dad said, "I'll have what he's having!".'

'Jenny wants a natural delivery,' said Appleby. 'A home-birth's out of the question, of course...'

'You go for it, my love,' said Kate, 'but if you're like me, you'll be screaming for the Pethidine in minutes! That rocking-horse is a bit moth-eaten.'

'Jenny's great-great-grandmother's,' said Appleby. 'A family heirloom.'

'Oops,' said Kate. 'Sorry.'

'No, I don't like it either,' Jenny laughed. 'It looks really malevolent actually. We'll discreetly remove it at some point.'

'Is he kicking yet?'

'Kicking?' said Jenny. 'Sometimes it feels like a rugby scrum in there.'

'Well don't forget to pack your bag well in advance,' said Kate. 'You'll need lots of little luxuries. It's your first, so it could take bloody hours.'

'He's been working on my compilation tape for weeks,' said Jenny.

'Soothing classics,' said Appleby.

'Soothing's good,' Kate laughed. 'You'll need soothing. Believe me, nothing will be the same afterwards.'

*

But no words of jovial common sense from Kate, earnest NCT classes or expert advice books could have prepared them for what ensued five weeks later.

Jenny had been in the delivery room for sixteen hours, alternately asking Appeby to comfort her with little luxuries and biting his head off. An hour earlier she had given in and asked for Pethidine. She was fully dilated, and had been pushing hard for twenty minutes when the nurse noticed that the foetal heart-beat had disappeared.

The midwife was a tiny Sri Lankan woman, built like a sparrow.

Appleby looked away as she felt for the baby's head.

'I think it's the cord!' she said to the nurse. 'It may be stuck! Press the alarm!'

The midwife was desperately trying to release the child, staring at the monitor which was now bleeping furiously.

'What's going on?' Jenny shouted. Despite the injection she was clearly in agony. Her face had turned puce. 'What's she *doing*?'

Appleby grabbed her hand. 'Just keep calm,' he said. 'The consultant's on his way.'

A surgical team burst into the room.

'You'll have to wait outside now, Dr Appleby,' said the midwife. 'Baby's in severe distress. Doctor is going to do an emergency C section.'

It was the longest thirty minutes of his life, standing in that corridor, listening to Jenny's anguished cries and the urgent voices from inside the delivery room.

Things went briefly quiet. Then a team of nurses and auxiliaries arrived at a trot. Moments later they rushed past with Jenny unconscious on the trolley.

'What's happening?' he yelled. 'Where are you taking her?'

'Intensive Care,' called a porter over his shoulder. 'Don't worry. She's in good hands.'

Eventually the surgeon came out. He was a tall man in his early forties with tufts of blonde hair protruding beneath his hairnet. There was a lot of blood on his gown. He was wearing white clogs. They were spattered with blood too.

'What's going on?' Appleby was quivering with fear and alarm. 'Where's our baby?'

'Maybe we should sit down,' said the surgeon, guiding him towards a row of chairs lined up against the corridor wall.

Appleby felt the blood draining from his face. 'What's happened?' he said. 'What's gone wrong?'

'I'm very sorry, Dr Appleby. I'm afraid your son didn't make it.'

'What? You don't mean…you don't mean he's…I don't understand.'

'Somehow the umbilical cord got twisted around your son's neck before he left your wife's womb. As he moved down into the birth canal it seems it became constricted. His blood supply was cut off. The midwife tried to release him, but the cord was too tightly coiled. I performed a C section to get him out, but I'm afraid we were too late.'

Appleby had gone numb. 'What about Jenny?' he mumbled. 'Will she be all right?'

'She has lost a great deal of blood, but she should pull through. They'll be giving her a transfusion as we speak.'

'She'll be devastated,' he said miserably. 'She wanted this baby so badly. We both did.'

'There's something else you need to know, I'm afraid. There was a complication.'

'What?'

'There was a problem with the placenta. When it finally came away, the uterus began to haemorrhage severely. I'm afraid I had to remove it or she might have bled to death.'

'You've removed her womb?'

'I'm sorry, Dr Appleby, we had no other option. It was the only way to save her life. A few more minutes and we'd have lost her. I was able to save the cervix. Her gynaecologist will explain why that's important. I'm so sorry, Dr Appleby.'

There was so much information, all of it unspeakably horrible, that Appleby could barely take it in. He hardly noticed as the surgeon said goodbye and disappeared up the corridor. The midwife came out and took him by the arm.

'You should come and see your son,' she said softly. 'It will help you later.'

The child looked perfect in every way. He weighed seven pounds eleven ounces, the midwife said. They had cleaned him up, and his face had that new-born baby's look of a plump, wrinkled old man. The fingers of one hand protruded from the blanket, soft and tiny with perfectly formed nails. He might have been asleep. But his flesh was tinged, a washed-out bluish grey, and when Appleby laid the outside of the fingers of his right hand gently against the baby's cheek it was cold and motionless.

He bent down and kissed the lifeless form. Then he swept him up in his arms and cradled him to his chest, turning from side to side, as if that might somehow bring him back to life. Eventually he laid the child back down and wiped his tears with his sleeve.

'Did you bring a camera?' asked the midwife.

'Yes,' he said. 'But I couldn't bear to take a picture…'

'Then let me do it for you,' she said. 'Your wife should see him, later. It will help her to grieve. She never got to hold him, you see…not even for a moment.'

*

Appleby rang Kate who passed the news on to his parents. He couldn't face speaking to them himself. Their sympathy would be profound and heart-felt. It would crush him.

A few days later he was slowly clearing the furniture from the nursery, when he heard the post drop through the front door. There was a condolence card from his parents. Inside Tom had written a message:

Dear Jimmy

I can only guess at the way you and Jenny must be suffering at this time. It is such a cruel blow after all the two of you have been through over the years. Fate can be so unjust. I cannot think of two people who would have made better or kinder parents or who better deserved to have a family.

You once told me that you thought your generation had had it easy, not having been to war like myself or my dad, but life can maul us savagely however comfortable our circumstances may seem.

I just wanted you to know that I appreciate that the kind of suffering that you and Jenny have endured is, in its way, as hard to bear as anything my father and I ever went through and that I am full of admiration for the steadfastness and courage you have shown throughout.

I am proud of you, son, and my heart goes out to you both,
Your loving Dad.

At first he couldn't bring himself to tell Jenny about the letter. It unleashed a torrent of pent-up grief, but it also brought a sense of overwhelming relief. It was like a laying-on of hands, a blessing which had finally released him from the sense of moral inadequacy that went right back to his early childhood.

They postponed the funeral for a fortnight until Jenny was home. Zeta insisted on a proper church service. She said it would bring Jenny spiritual comfort. Jenny was still physically frail and emotionally drained, so they let Zeta make the arrangements.

When everyone had gone home, he told Jenny about his father's letter and tried to explain the effect it had had on him.

'So what did you do?' she asked.

'I drank half a bottle of scotch and fell asleep on the sofa.'

*

Appleby's fear that Jenny would be plunged into a catastrophic depression proved unfounded. In the event she appeared quietly resigned, as if the removal of her womb had wiped a whole landscape of worry and potential misery from her life. Rather she seemed perpetually numb. She was with him; she was responsive in her way, but at some deeper level her spirit seemed broken.

While she was still in hospital he gave her the photograph of little Daniel. She stared at it for several minutes without saying anything. Then she thanked him, made a wistful comment and put it away in the bedside drawer. Weeks later he came home one evening to find her sobbing inconsolably on the bed, the bent and crumpled picture clutched in her hand. But the moment brought no catharsis, and she quickly returned to her former state. Appleby sensed that she had somehow detached herself from life, and he soon began to wonder if this was to be permanent.

One afternoon she returned from a visit to her gynaecologist and announced, almost casually, that it would be safe for them to make love again – if Appleby wanted to. 'She told me I'm lucky they left my cervix in. Apparently it's not the same without it. At least I can still get some form of fulfilment, I suppose. Apart from my work...'

And for a while their love-life revived again, even though Jenny was beset by the symptoms of a premature menopause. Yet somehow each of them felt that they were making love to comfort the other, as if they needed to convince themselves that everything was still all right between them. And with each coupling came an unwelcome reminder of what they had lost and now could never share.

She had rarely initiated these encounters. Eventually she stopped altogether. When Appleby stopped bothering too, she didn't even seem to notice.

*

'Happy families are all alike;' wrote Tolstoy in his much-quoted opening to *Anna Karenina*, 'every unhappy family is unhappy in its own way.' And so, thought Appleby when he re-read the book one holiday, is every unhappy childless couple.

His and Jenny's unhappiness came in the form of a long, slow process of atrophy. As the months passed their sex-life became increasingly spasmodic and lacklustre. Jenny retreated ever more deeply into her research, her writing and ever more demanding voluntary projects. They spent less and less time together. She went to the services at the Minster as regularly as ever, but always seemed to return tetchy and depressed.

At one point he began to wonder if she was having an affair. Occasionally he thought he caught a low, intimate tone in her voice when she was talking to an associate on the phone, a tone he recognised from their own courtship, and wondered if she could have met someone on a research trip or at some charitable event. Yet none of the tell-tale signs were there: no sudden spring in her step, revived interest in her appearance, or mysterious calls to her mobile phone – just a remorseless slither into polite indifference.

From time to time, but with decreasing frequency, he tried to get her to open up emotionally. He suggested counselling again, but she would have none of it. Did she want to consider adoption? She rejected that out of hand too. She would always know that the child was not hers, she said, that it wasn't Daniel.

He began to feel excluded from the lives of his friends as they shared tales of first words and first steps, of pre-school play-groups and catchment areas, birthday parties, theme parks, music tutors, sex education, public exams and eventually gap years. Almost unconsciously, they began to avoid socialising with friends who had children. Jenny didn't seem to mind particularly. Appleby felt isolated and lonely.

*

Meanwhile his university work plodded along dully. The Swively investigation and even the documentary were fading from memory, though he still kept the portrait of Harker in his study, a reminder of more exciting times...and of unfinished business.

By now he had become terminally disillusioned with the Marxist theory which had once fired his imagination. His trendier colleagues, especially among the English staff, seemed to be moving on from post-structuralism, and had started embracing the various forms of 'postmodernism'. He was secretly appalled. To Appleby the development represented a repugnant lurch into vapid, soulless poseurism, a triumph of empty, self-regarding style over intellectual substance. Leftwing intellectuals had virtually disappeared from the mainstream media anyway, or any other forum where they might usefully influence public opinion. The academic left, so vigorous in his youth, was a spent force in the new monetarist climate, occasionally mounting a rearguard action over some specific issue, but constantly in retreat and ever easier to ignore. He yearned for a return to the uncomplicated, pragmatic idealism that had fired his father's generation.

He published two more books on rural history, the one about the decades before the Civil War and a follow-up on the late Stuart era. And he started attending conferences again, for the companionship as much as anything.

*

One summer he was invited to give a paper entitled 'Why Rural History Matters' at a conference on 'History in Education' held at Leeds University. As he wrote, he felt an overwhelming urge to get everything off his chest. The lecture became an angry plea to retrieve the values which had motivated the pioneers of British social history and to make the subject relevant, accessible and exciting to modern students. In the process he took carefully-aimed sideswipes at every movement and approach he had ever found pretentious, deluded, self-serving or downright reactionary.

His performance was impassioned, highly personal, laced with witty asides and telling anecdotes. The audience of young teachers loved it. For the first time in his life, he was greeted with prolonged, enthusiastic applause. That felt very good.

A young woman in her late twenties came up to him afterwards.

'Doctor Appleby? I hope you don't mind...' she hesitated for a moment, searching his face for a reaction. 'I just wanted to say that was absolutely brilliant! Really inspiring! I'd love to talk to you about it? Can I buy you a drink?'

'Sure,' he said. 'Why not? I'm sorry – have we met?'

She was extremely beautiful, slim, with long black hair and olive skin.

'I'm Iris,' she said with a warm smile. 'Iris Tulliver. I teach at St John's in York.'

Quite unexpectedly, something deep inside him went, 'WHOOMPH!'

York

'Feasting is the herald only of cholic and distemper, and the joys of the marriage bed, however sweet in the performance, are quite forgot by noonday. I tell thee there is nought in a man's life that bringeth him greater delight and ease of spirit than the Completion of a worthy Enterprise, when right-well wrought.'

—Sir Thomas Cranham, The Colloquies, Vol II, No 43

Appleby's request for a sabbatical year was granted with surprising speed. Normally these matters had to be arranged months in advance, but Howland was only too happy to see the back of him again; the Faculty sensed a major research coup for the university, and he was long overdue for this privilege anyway. By December he was free to leave.

That year they spent Christmas with his increasingly frail parents in Birmingham. They were in their mid-eighties now, and their health had been deteriorating for some time. His mother was almost deaf. His father's memory was becoming increasingly unreliable, and he had trouble walking any distance.

Tom Appleby had become pleasantly mellow and good humoured as he became more confused and dependent, but the fire had gone from his belly, and Appleby missed it. He was in the middle of the most exciting breakthrough in his career. The little boy inside him still wanted to shout, 'Look, Daddy! Look what I'm doing! Aren't you proud of me?', but old Tom could barely take it in. A light was fading from Appleby's life too.

*

The sabbatical seemed to pass in a flash.

Van Stumpe was now using the Aged V's pension to employ a live-in nurse, a young gay friend called Freek. It was a semi-formal arrangement. A short, slight figure with ash-blonde highlights in his mousy hair and artfully torn jeans, Freek got board, lodging and a modest wage, and was free to go out most evenings and at weekends. He was also an accomplished cook, and there was usually a tasty supper waiting when van Stumpe and Appleby got home from the Institute.

A certain melancholy had lifted from the house too, Appleby noticed, partly, as he discovered later, because Freek was ministering to van Stumpe's sexual needs from time to time. Appleby was not sure if this was part of his terms of employment or an act of general goodwill. He did not like to ask, but it was clear his host was deeply attached to the young man, who seemed perfectly happy to indulge him.

The Harker-Cranham Archive was now stored in a suite of atmospherically controlled rooms on the top floor. An expensive conversion had been paid for by the anonymous owner, the cramped, gloomy closet replaced by a spacious modern office space.

The owner expected Appleby to prepare the most important material for publication and let it be known that, although he would retain the copyright of all documents, Appleby would be entitled to any advances or royalties. He would, however expect regular written progress reports. The pace of work was brisk, but every day brought extraordinary new revelations about Harker, his followers and the life of the village.

*

The preceding summer, Jeremy Dilke had emailed him to say that he had become disillusioned with Despenser and had accepted an assistant lectureship at Birkbeck College in London. Appleby asked if he would be willing to help with his research, cross-checking background material in the relevant archives in England. Dilke readily agreed.

Appleby frequently stopped in London to see him on his journeys between Amsterdam and York. He usually tried to see Iris too. He still had no rival, apparently, though he sensed that her social life was blossoming. Sometimes he met her near her work at the ziggurat-like Institute of Education in Bloomsbury; occasionally he went to her flat in Crouch End. On these occasions she would continue to probe him about Harker.

'I still don't understand how he could have survived so long without getting rumbled,' she said one evening as they walked back from Farfalli's, her favourite Italian restaurant in Crouch End. 'Surely somebody would have let the cat out of the bag...'

'They knew which side their bread was buttered on,' said Appleby. 'Harker wasn't just charismatic, he was canny. And so was Cranham. It turns out that between them they'd made sure that none of the common land around Swively was enclosed. Their villagers were among the most prosperous and best fed in the county, and the most independent financially. They knew who to thank.'

'But whatever turned Harker into an agnostic in the first place?' she asked as they reached her flat.

As they got ready for bed, he told her about Harker's fascination with comparative religion and his amazing collection of holy books from different faiths.

'Maybe,' he said, his mouth frothing with toothpaste, 'maybe he thought – well here are all these religions, each convinced that they are the only ones who have got it right...' Iris had to wait while he gargled, '...which means the others have got it wrong. Maybe he thought – well what if they've *all* got it wrong?'

'Well, it's a theory,' she laughed. 'I bet there was something else behind it, though.'

He was still explaining how he had traced the evolving use of the terms 'Spirit' and 'Kindred' and how Harker had kept the churchwardens onside as they climbed into bed. After twenty minutes she yawned and said she had to get up early in the morning. If they were going to have sex, would he mind getting on with it?

As a post-coital treat he told her about how Harker and Cranham had taken their wives to London where they had marvelled at the treasures and curiosities on display in the Long Gallery in Whitehall Palace. They had even been to see a performance of Henry VI by Lord Strange's Men at The Theatre in Shoreditch, though it was not clear which part.

'Cranham says they went to a tavern afterwards and met some of the actors. Do you know, I think they might possibly have met Shakes... Iris?'

She was fast asleep.

He lay there thinking. Something else behind it, eh? It's funny. I've read every single item in that archive now, and I still haven't found that book Cranham mentions...

*

By the autumn he had finished editing Cranham's journal and the first draft of a collected edition of Harker's writings. These included the *Colloquies*, which would have made a small volume in themselves, the various *Rites* (or *Solemnities* as he sometimes called them), along with the *Contemplations*, which read like sermons, and numerous poems and the lyrics of songs which, he assumed, were used like hymns, anthems or even psalms. He also included the more significant letters.

Friends had advised him to get a literary agent, and a circuitous relay of recommendations brought him to the formidable Phyllida Trask. Phyllida said that they should try to get two volumes published separately. A complete edition of 'Swively papers' could always be published to renew interest a few years later. While she began the artful process of ensnaring a publisher, Appleby got on with tying up the innumerable loose ends in his annotations and bibliography.

By late October her elaborate courtship rituals were in full swing. An addictive negotiator, she loved this part of the job and was constantly arranging for him to attend carefully stage-managed meetings, where commissioning editors from television networks and film executives would express their fascination with Appleby's work in front of potential publishers. If she had been as beautiful as she was clever, Appleby thought, she would have had a string of millionaires offering marriage.

One Sunday evening she rang him in York.

'When are you next in London, James? There's someone I want you to meet.'

At 1.00 pm on the following Thursday he presented himself at the Ivy in Covent Garden where, Phyllida boasted, she could always get a table at short notice. Appleby was nervous. He had heard about the restaurant's glamorous clientele, and he wasn't sure how to behave – or even what to wear. He was terrified Phyllida would introduce him to someone famous or important, and he wouldn't even know who they were.

Still, the Maitre D was friendly enough, and there was something comforting about the soft tones of the art deco furnishings. Someone took his coat, and he saw Phyllida waving from the back of the room. Her guest had already arrived and was sitting opposite Phyllida with her back towards him. As he approached the table she turned round. Appleby almost jumped out of his best Marks and Spencer suit. It was Claire.

'I believe you two know each other already,' said Phyllida.

'Yes,' said Appleby. 'You could say that...'

Stamford Hill

'All right! All right! I'm coming. I'm coming. Stop that infernal banging will you? Don't you know it's Shabbas?'

Aaron Abramsky staggered downstairs in his dressing gown, still half asleep. Through the small window above the door he could see the grey dawn light. As in many of the Victorian terraced houses in Stamford Hill the door still had its original panes of decorative stained glass, and he could see the dark forms of several large men on the other side. Suddenly he realised what the banging was. These men were not knocking; they were trying to break in. Only the extra security bolts and a large metal bar which he had fitted himself had held them back.

'What the...Sarah! Call 999! We've got burglars!'

But Aaron's wife didn't need to call the police, because at that moment they burst through the front door, ten of them, all wearing protective vests and helmets and carrying a variety of guns.

'Armed police!' shouted the lead officer. 'Put your hands over your head and face the wall! Now! Do it!'

'This is an outrage!' said Aaron, but he did as he was told. As the first officer pinned him against the wall, five more rushed past him and up the stairs.

'Where is he?' they shouted at Sarah. By now she was standing looking bewildered on the landing, desperately trying to put her wig on.

The men fanned out, each one taking up position outside a different bedroom door, before flinging it open and swinging in, gun pointing forward, cocked and ready to fire. The Abramskys' two daughters sat trembling in their beds as the men burst in, ordering them to get out of bed and lie on the floor.

'Shame on you!' shouted Sarah. 'This is like the Shoah! How dare you? And in England too! You think we don't pay our taxes, to treat us like this!'

Downstairs four more officers were rampaging through the ground floor, waving their guns around and shouting.

'Over there!' shouted one, startled by a cat in the kitchen-diner, where food had been prepared in advance and laid out ready for the Sabbath.

'Where?' shouted another, swinging his gun round suddenly and scattering bread, cakes, meats and crockery all over the floor, before letting off a round.

'It's a fucking cat, stupid!' said his colleague.

'Don't shoot my cat, you butchers!' shouted Aaron.

'They shot the cat?' wailed Sarah. 'Tell me it isn't true!'

An officer leaned over the banister. 'All clear upstairs!'

'Fuck! Fuck! Fuck!' said the lead officer. 'We've missed the bastard!' He turned his face back to Aaron's. It was centimetres away. 'Where is he?' he snarled.

'Where's who?' said Aaron indignantly.

'Don't fuck about with me, old man! Where's your fucking guest?'

'I want a lawyer!'

'Just tell him, Aaron,' said Sarah from the landing. 'Then perhaps they'll go.'

'I want to see my solicitor,' said Aaron.

'He left yesterday afternoon,' said Sarah, 'So he could travel before Shabbas. He's a sweet boy. Very devout. Not that you would understand that, with all your disgusting profanities!'

Finally the officers began to relax a little. The family were ushered into the front room and questioned. They were frightened and indignant but willing to co-operate. The young man was called Yitzak. A nice name. It means the one who laughs, you know. He was the son of a cousin who lived in a settler village not far from Jerusalem on the West Bank. (This much the Anti-Terrorist officers knew already). He was a nice boy. Very handsome. Very religious. He had come to England for a few days on business. (Unlike the Abramskys, they knew this was completely untrue).

He said he had to go up north somewhere. Where did he say? Sheffield? Leeds? They had lent him their car, a battered old Volvo estate. He said he'd be back by Tuesday. They gave the officers the registration number.

'You'll have to clear everything up in there, young man!' said Sarah imperiously. 'We're not allowed to.'

'What?' said one of the officers incredulously.

'It's their Sabbath day,' said the boss. 'They're not allowed to work. Listen,' he said turning to Aaron. 'You're all gonna have to come with us for questioning. I'm arresting the lot of you on suspicion of harbouring a terrorist. And nobody's touching anything. There's a forensics team waiting outside.'

There was a loud mew from the kitchen.

'Put that fucking cat out, will you, before it eats the fucking evidence?' said the boss. 'And block the fucking flap so it can't fucking get back in.'

'Such language!' said Sarah. 'Does your mother know you speak such filth? Shame on you!'

'I demand to see my solicitor!' said Aaron.

*

'Freek! Freek? Where are you? I'm home, Freek!'

Van Stumpe had told the taxi driver to wait outside the house when he arrived home from Schiphol. He wanted to be in and out as quickly as possible. The door was slightly ajar, and he assumed this meant Freek was emptying the rubbish, or doing something in the garden. But there was no reply.

He had gone to England with a mobile phone issued to him by the Institute, leaving his new personal phone, a neat little smartphone, charging up on a side table in the front room. He mustn't forget it.

'Vaartje! Vaartje? Are you in bed?' he called.

The lights were on, but the kitchen was empty. He went into the living-room and retrieved the phone. There was nobody there either. Had Freek taken his father out somewhere and carelessly forgotten to close the door? It didn't seem likely, even in an emergency. Especially when he had texted from the airport to say he was on the way and to make sure that he and Vaartje were ready to travel.

Something was wrong. Van Stumpe experienced a sharp stab of fear, a sensation he had not had since he was a small boy. It seemed to concentrate itself somewhere in the region of his prostate gland.

He called out again, 'Freek! Vaartje!' Still no reply.

He went into his father's bedroom. The old man was lying on the floor in his pyjamas. What little remained of his hair was clotted with blood, so dark it was almost black. He had soiled himself and the room stank. His face was a waxy grey. Van Stumpe did not have to touch him to know that he was dead. He cradled the old man's head in his arms.

'Poor Vaartje,' he said. 'Who has done this to you? So cruel. They didn't even let me say goodbye.' He began to sob gently. 'They didn't let me tell you how much I loved you or thank you for being such a wonderful vaartje.'

He sat there for nearly ten minutes, weeping and caressing the old man's head.

Then he stumbled into the kitchen, wiped his eyes, and poured himself a stiff glass of Schnapps. Outside the taxi was still waiting, ready to take them to a safe-house in Utrecht. From there he had planned to drive with Freek and his father to Zurich where an old friend ran a hotel in the mountains and had offered him the use of a small annexe. The taxi driver was growing uneasy and beeped his horn. Van Stumpe decided he would have to send the cab away now and call the police. Then the phone rang.

'Welcome home, Mijnheer.' The caller spoke in English, but the voice was muffled and disguised. 'You are probably wondering what has happened to your young friend.'

'Who are you? What are you wanting? Did you kill my father?'

'You have something we want. We have something you want. If you are prepared to co-operate we can do business. Then we can return your goods undamaged…relatively speaking.'

'Where is my little Freek? What have you been doing with him?'

'The boy is quite safe. But don't even think of calling the police or he definitely won't be. Is he a masochist, do you know? They say some sodomites enjoy physical pain. Now why don't you put that glass of Schnapps down and send that car away. Then return to the house and wait for us. Someone will collect you shortly.'

The line went dead.

It was all too much for van Stumpe: the shock of his father's death, his fear for Freek, the realisation that he was being watched at that very moment and the dread of what might happen next. He put down the Schnapps as the caller had instructed, staggered across to the kitchen sink and tried to pour himself a glass of cold water, but it slipped from his hand as he passed out.

York

Iris and Appleby did not sleep together that night at the conference in Leeds, but by the end of the evening they both knew it would happen. The affair started at her house in York and picked up momentum gradually over the next few months.

On the afternoon they made love for the first time, they lay in her bed afterwards, idly watching her little portable television. The old black-and-white war film 'Ice Cold in Alex' was drawing to its end. It had reached the scene where the crew of the British military ambulance, having struggled through the extreme heat and danger of the North African desert, have finally made it to Alexandria and are sitting in a bar, about to drink the ice-cold lager they have been fantasising about for days.

'That's what it's been like for me,' he said.

'What on earth are you talking about?'

'Before this…I was dying of thirst…emotionally speaking.'

'I'm not sure I appreciate being compared to a bottle of lager!' she laughed, feigning indignation and hitting him with a pillow.

*

Much to Appleby's surprise, they were still seeing each other on the same easy, non-committal basis three years later when the Dean of Humanities called him into his office.

Matthew Featherstone was a distinguished English professor who quite liked Appleby and shared his mistrust of post-modernism and his distaste for Andrew Howland.

'Ah! James!' he said as Appleby put his head round the door. 'Come in. Come in. I was remembering that television programme you made the other day. It must have been about fifteen years ago. Something about an unexplained massacre in Wiltshire, wasn't it? Did anything ever come of that?'

'Not really,' said Appleby wearily. 'Bit of a cul-de-sac, as it turned out.'

'Shame that. It all seemed rather intriguing. Anyway, do take a seat. Something's come up that might interest you...How would you feel about the prospect of spending six months as a guest lecturer in Cambridge?'

*

Two months later he had installed his picture of Sir Nicholas Harker on the wall of his quaint, but cramped rooms overlooking the Cam and was enjoying his first taste of J.D. Clovis's 'fabled Despenser hospitality'.

Seven Dials

Astonishment, anger, hurt, bafflement, curiosity: all these emotions crowded into Appleby's mind when he saw Claire Tenterden sitting opposite Phyllida in The Ivy. It induced a sort of psychological gridlock, but before he could disentangle his jammed thoughts, she stood up and slipped on a neat little black jacket.

'Don't worry,' she said quietly. 'I'm not staying.'

Her hair was different. She had had it cut shorter in a chic bob that made her look more mature. Her clothes were elegant but sober, without the flamboyant ethnic flourishes, the scarves, waistcoats and sashes he remembered from Cambridge. Her make-up had always been subtle, but now it was positively minimal. It was her face that had really changed. She was paler, almost puffy, and although she looked self-possessed, the spark of ingenuous fun that had played around her eyes had vanished. It was the first time they had seen each other since they had breakfast together after their night in Amsterdam. She could almost have been a complete stranger.

'I wanted to give you this,' she said, taking an envelope from an expensive-looking, soft leather handbag. 'You don't have to read it, of course, and I couldn't complain if you didn't. But I very much hope you will.'

As she passed him the letter, he noticed that the tips of the fingers were still an unusually dark pink, but that the nails had now grown forward over them to a normal length and were carefully varnished. Without waiting for him to reply she turned to Phyllida.

'Bye, Phylly. We'll talk soon…Goodbye, James.'

And with that she was gone.

'Was that who you wanted me to meet?' asked Appleby.

'She wanted to meet you, actually,' said Phyllida. 'She wanted to give you that in person, so I asked her along.'

'Do you know what it's about?'

'I'm not her confidante. If you want to know, you'll have to read it.'

'But I don't understand. How do you know her? And why invite me to lunch to meet someone who isn't staying?'

'Business, of course, dear boy. What else? Now let's order. I usually go for fish myself, but my carnivorous friends speak highly of the corned beef hash.'

Over the meal Phyllida explained that much the best offer had come from Shaftesbury, the venerable English publishing house, now owned and run by that global octopus, MediaCorp. As she had hoped, they would take twin volumes: 'Cranham's Journal' and 'The Collected Harker'. Apart from the 'ridiculously generous advance for what are essentially academic books', they would be able and willing to spend far more on publicity and marketing than most of their rivals. He would be an absolute idiot not to go with it, apparently.

'So where does Miss Tenterden fit into all this?'

'She's been working as a publicist at Shaftesbury for several months now, and I have it on impeccable authority that she's fucking good. Half the young women who do the press and PR for book publishers are absolutely hopeless, dippy young Sloanes doing the party circuit until they find a rich husband. Claire's superb, apparently. She has a real flair for it, my sources tell me, and she specialises in anything historical. Of course, I've known her Da forever.'

'I see.' Appleby thoughtfully masticated a mouthful of corned beef hash for a while. 'Do you know what happened to her doctorate, then?'

'She dropped it. Between you and me, I think she had some kind of breakdown.'

'Really? What kind of breakdown?'

'I'm not entirely sure. Why don't you just read the bloody letter, Jimmy?'

*

He read it that evening on the train back to York. It was written in that neat rounded hand they taught in girls' schools, which many women seemed to reproduce flawlessly for the rest of their lives.

It was strange to get a hand-written letter. Nobody wrote letters any more. She had even dated and addressed it, from her parents' place in Kensington.

Dear James

I am writing this because I simply couldn't face speaking to you on the phone. Emails can seem so horribly impersonal, and one never knows who else might read them. I'm afraid I was far too much of a coward to come and see you. Besides, conversations never follow the course we plan for them, do they? I was afraid I wouldn't say the things I want to say, or else it would all come out horribly mangled.

After that dreadful trick I played on you last year I shouldn't blame you a single bit if you never wanted to hear another word from me in your life. Even so, I hope you will do me the undeserved kindness of reading this.

I will never fully understand why I allowed myself to be used in that way by those terrible people at Despenser. The pitiful truth is that I have always been surrounded by powerful and controlling men. I know I like to tell funny stories about them and practice my skills in amateur psychoanalysis, but the truth is that I am not nearly as detached from it all as I try to make out. Confident authoritative men have always found it shamingly easy to get me to do things, even when my instincts scream at me that they are wrong.

You will have realised long ago that J.D. Clovis and Professor Skyne asked me to spy on you while I was in Amsterdam. Skyne knew I liked you, but he insisted it wouldn't do you any harm. He made it all seem like a clever little game, and I admit that I found it all rather flattering. To be honest I was jolly curious myself, and saw it as a bit of a challenge. I'm afraid I never believed your sweet little fable about Sir Philip Sidney and the film script, especially as we'd just had that conversation about 'cashing in' on historical knowledge.

Do you remember that, James? I always loved our little chats during my supervisions. You were the only man I knew who wasn't trying to manipulate me in some way or just get me into bed. It was so refreshing to speculate about 'life, the universe and everything', with such a clever, thoughtful man, without thinking you had some nasty hidden agenda.

What upsets me most is knowing that you must believe that I made love to you as a crude ploy to get you to tell me your secret. That makes me feel so ashamed, so cheap and dirty. I know that that is how things actually worked out, so it is very hard for me to deny it. But I would never have slept with you if I did not really really like you. If you can believe this, the fact that you had never made any attempt to seduce me only made the idea of going to bed with you all the more intriguing. I expect that sounds perverse, doesn't it? Perhaps it is.

When I told Clovis and Skyne about the diary and so on, I knew how much it all meant to you, but please believe me, I had no idea they intended to take the work away from you. When I realised what they were planning, I felt ashamed beyond words, James. I don't think I've ever felt as wretched as I did that week. It made me question who I was, and what I had become. I was so depressed that I became physically ill. I couldn't bear the thought of seeing you. On the day of our next supervision, I went home to my parents.

It turned out that this business was the cue for all sorts of unresolved personal 'issues' (I do so hate that word) to rear their ugly heads. The worst of it concerned a squalid little episode with one of my father's best friends when I was still only fourteen, but I'll spare you the details. My shrink said I was clinically depressed. My parents told their friends I had glandular fever and told Despenser I was suffering from 'nervous exhaustion'.

Mother took me to a cottage in Cornwall for two months. We went for long walks, ate nursery food, and I started to write a novel. Yes, you have guessed; it's a romance set in an Elizabethan country mansion, full of intrigue and scheming, with walk-on roles for Sir Walter Raleigh and Shakespeare. It's probably the most appalling tosh, but writing it has been wonderfully therapeutic. It also helped my recovery enormously when I learned that Skyne and Clovis's little scheme had back-fired. When I bumped into Jeremy Dilke in London, and he told me that you had got your gig back, I was absolutely overjoyed.

I've decided to abandon the PhD, I'm afraid. I hope you don't feel let down.

After my breakdown I no longer had the slightest desire to become a history don. I happened to meet an old school friend who's an editor at Shaftesbury and she said they were looking for an assistant in their PR department. They gave me a six-week trial. There's an awful lot of schmoozing involved, not to say pandering to writers with egos the size of cruise liners, but I seem to have learned all about that sort of thing at my parents' soirees.

The long and the short of it is this, James. Shaftesbury want to buy your wonderful books, and they would like me to look after the publicity. If you would let me, it would be a small way in which I could try and make amends for the shitty thing I did to you last year. I will understand totally if you never want to see me again, but I hope you can believe that I have always cared about you, and, if you do decide to sign with Shaftesbury, I would be honoured if you would let me handle your publicity.

And if you don't…well you can't stop me hoping that perhaps we can be friends again one day.

Yours remorsefully and with great affection,
Claire, X.

Appleby had read the letter three times before the train reached Grantham. He was astonished by her apparent candour. It also made him realise that he had been far more deeply hurt by Claire's betrayal than he had cared to acknowledge. It was as if a surgeon had appeared out of nowhere and dug out an old shell splinter from deep inside a limb. Between Grantham and Doncaster he stared out of the window, going over the events again and again. Was this confession just another deception? Was she just desperate for the work? She hadn't said what kind of contract she had with Shaftesbury, if any.

On the home stretch to York he read it twice more and convinced himself, not only that it was completely sincere, but that it was also extremely touching. That evening he rang Phyllida and agreed that they should go with Shaftesbury.

'And are you okay about working with Claire?'

'Yes,' he sighed. 'That shouldn't be a problem.'

'Good. She'll do us proud.'

But he made a resolution as he put the phone down. Whatever happened, the relationship would remain strictly professional.

*

The books were to be launched as two companion volumes the following spring. Phyllida was right about Claire. She proved exceptionally adept at whipping up interest. She began by dropping teasing hints to people she met at parties. Then she fed tantalising snippets to selected journalists, focussing on the more lurid elements of the story. This produced a series of small items in the news pages of several national and local papers. Then she arranged for Appleby to do a series of radio interviews, culminating in a long slot on a Radio Four history programme.

All this began to create a background buzz. She was softening the press up, hoping to get major features and profiles when the publication date arrived. She dangled the prospect of interviews and 'authored' pieces by Appleby himself in front of carefully targeted features editors, always promising a 'unique' angle, so that each believed they'd be getting something exclusive.

One evening in late November, Appleby and Jenny were just finishing their supper when Farnstable rang.

'My, my, James!' he trilled. 'I can't seem to open a newspaper without seeing some funny little teaser about my old friend from Brummagem. So you finally found out what happened at that place where we spent those happy times up to our knees in mud!'

Appleby hadn't seen Farnstable for three years. He told him the whole story: about the call from van Stumpe, the discovery of the chest, Clovis's scheming and the extraordinary revelations in the archive.

'This is amazing stuff,' said Farnstable. 'Why on earth didn't you call me?'

'I'm not sure,' said Appleby. 'I didn't really think about it. Anyway, you're so grand and busy these days. I hear you're running your own outfit now.'

'Ah yes. Box of Tricks. Never been busier.'

'I suppose I just assumed you'd have more glamorous fish to fry.'

'Well we must definitely do an update – a completely new programme I should think. I wonder if we can knock something together before your publication date. When is that?'

'Next spring, but you really need to talk to the people at Shaftesbury. I'll give you the publicist's details. She's on top of all that. I warn you, though, she's very sharp.'

*

The next afternoon Farnstable was visiting a shoot when his personal mobile phone rang. He did not recognise the number.

'Is that Tim?' chirped a young woman. 'My name's Claire. I'm looking after the publicity for James Appleby's books. I hope you don't mind. James gave me this number. So you want to make a programme?'

'Er, we're discussing the possibility,' said Farnstable. 'No more than that at this stage.'

'Well before you decide anything, can we meet for lunch? Are you free tomorrow?'

Farnstable hated being railroaded into anything, but there was something engaging about this young woman's chutzpah, and something intriguingly sexy about her voice.

'I suppose I might be able to squeeze you in. Why?'

'Because I have an absolutely brilliant idea, Tim. In fact, I think you'll agree it's a stroke of sheer genius.'

'Oh really?' said Farnstable dryly. He thought for a moment. He'd have to meet the woman at some point anyway. 'I'm checking my diary... Soho House at 1.00 then.'

Enfield

The man took a few simple precautions before he left the Jenveys' house. First he left a note written in Arabic script on the kitchen table, one of several he had been given before he left America. He couldn't read it. He was not even sure of the exact translation, but he knew that the message was along the lines of 'The soldiers of the Crusader state shall never be safe, nor shall their wives and children, not even in their own homes, as long as the infidel invades the lands of the faithful. God is Great!'

Next he went to the hall mirror, took a small bottle of fake tan from his pocket and rubbed it as evenly as he could on his face, neck and hands. Then he carefully attached a false moustache he had been keeping ready in his pocket, making sure there were no loose strands and that it was firmly secured at both ends. He retrieved the large sleeveless jerkin he had thrown down on the front room sofa and slipped it over his jacket. He was a stocky man anyway. This made him look positively corpulent. Finally he took the grey lambswool karakul hat he had been wearing when he broke into the house two hours earlier from the jerkin pocket and put it on again. It was rather fetching he thought, tilting it at a jaunty angle before he stepped out onto the street.

Several people saw him as he walked the hundred metres or so round the corner to his SUV. He even smiled at an old lady and said 'Good evening' in his best attempt at an Anglo-Pakistani accent. It didn't matter if he sounded like Apu from *The Simpsons*, and it didn't matter how many people saw him. The more the merrier, in fact.

He headed for an address in a place called Stevenage. On the way he stopped at some kind of roadside diner. He took off the hat and jerkin and threw them in the back of the SUV, before going inside for a typically tasteless coffee and a sub-standard English cheeseburger. The staff could hardly see the tiny entrance lobby from the restaurant, so none of them noticed that the squat Asian man who went into the

Gents' as he left had somehow lost his moustache and swarthy complexion when he came out again.

When he reached his rendezvous he swapped car keys and registration documents with a ferret-faced young man he had been told to call 'Jason'. Half an hour later the SUV's number plates had been incinerated, the vehicle and its contents were in a crusher, and the man was in a neat little Honda Civic saloon, heading west on the M25.

*

'It's not a pretty sight, is it?' muttered Appleby.

'You don't have to look,' laughed Jenny.

DI Kot had decided that, as there seemed to be no immediate threat of attack, and DS Handley was watching the monitors, he would take a dip in Angelini's indoor pool. As Handley had predicted his pot-belly was clearly visible through the glass sides, hanging beneath him.

'He looks like a fleshy version of one of those tubby old fishing boats,' mused Appleby. 'Except the hulls of fishing boats don't wobble.'

'Can we watch another channel for a while?' said Jenny. 'I'm sick to death of the way they repeat everything every half hour – and these constant "updates" from correspondents who haven't actually got any new information.'

'I just can't bear not knowing what's actually going on out there,' said Appleby. 'And when we pass stuff on to the police, we've no way of knowing if they're taking any notice.' He called across to Handley. 'Do your controllers back in London ever tell you what they're up to?'

'Only on a need-to-know basis, sir.'

'So they haven't told you if they've found my friend van Stumpe yet?'

"Fraid not.'

'Or if they even went to see those people in Swively, like I said they should?'

'Nope.'

'Or if they're anywhere nearer catching the maniac who tried to shoot me?'

'Oh, I'm sure they'll tell us as soon as there's a breakthrough there, sir. It's not cheap providing you with round the clock protection, you know.'

'Do you know I'd never thought of that. Now why don't I just wander out of the front gate and get myself shot. That should save the tax-payer a few bob.'

'It's a thought,' said Handley.

'I can't stand this much longer,' said Appleby. 'If we don't get out soon, I'll go mad. I'm going to talk to Kot. They've simply got to let me go to Guy's opening in Swively. They were always taking Salman Rushdie out to special dos, weren't they?'

By now Jenny was navigating the TV guide on the remote-control. 'Look, Jimmy. They're repeating that documentary de-bunking *The Da Vinci Code*. I missed that first time. Can't I watch it? Surely we can have just one hour's break from the bloody news?'

'Oh all right, then…What's that?'

'It's his phone,' said Handley. He called to Kot, 'Aren't you going to answer that, boss?'

There was a loud sploshing as Kot hauled himself from the water, and the ringing stopped. They heard a series of exclamations and urgent questions. A moment later he appeared on the balcony above them wrapped in a towel.

'Someone's shot Trev and his family! In their own fucking kitchen! They're looking for an Asian guy, probably a Pakistani.'

'Christ!' said Handley. 'Louise and the kids? Who'd do a thing like that? That's sick.'

'I don't like this,' said Kot, tight-lipped. 'I don't like this at all. This is getting a bit fucking personal.'

*

There were four civilian Scene of Crime Officers and two Special Branch detectives in the Jenveys' house. They were all wearing white coveralls. It was mid-morning, and they had been working in shifts for over twelve hours.

It was a daunting task. Finding the bullets and sending them off to the lab had been the easy bit. Within hours analysis of the microscopic scratches on the sides would enable them to match them to the killer's gun – if the gun was ever found.

The fingerprinting and DNA checks could take days, though. As in any bustling family home, there were prints, stray hairs and flakes of skin from dozens of individuals, from the family themselves, the parents' friends, the children's friends, the children's friends' parents, visiting relatives, and most were to be found in the kitchen.

'Did Forbes tell you they got that note translated?' a young detective asked his boss.

'I haven't spoken to him this morning,' she said. 'Anything interesting?'

'Well for a start it was in Urdu, not Arabic. Just the usual sort of Jihadist rant apparently, except there were three very peculiar grammatical errors. Not dialect stuff, mind – the sort of things a foreigner might get wrong.'

'So what does that tell us?'

'That it wasn't written by an Urdu speaker?'

Suddenly the young man took out a pencil and started scribbling lightly over the blank sheet on the top of the Jenveys' shopping-list pad.

'What the hell do you think you're doing?' said his boss, horrified. 'That's got to go to the lab, you idiot!'

'Look,' he said holding it up. 'What do you see?'

'Your scribble,' she said. 'And it looks like one of the kids must have been scribbling on the sheet that was on top of that one.'

'Look closer,' he said. 'See. There's a number.'

'Give me that,' she said, grabbing the pad from him. 'Is that a 4? No, it's more like an A. Then 39O? No, it's another 9. Could be some sort of code or a password, I suppose.'

'Or a road number,' said the young man. 'Anyone know where the A399 is?'

'Out west somewhere, isn't it?' ventured one of the SOCOs. 'Over Ilfracombe way, I think. My wife's aunt retired down there.'

'Oh my god!' said the woman. 'Exmoor! This is a set of directions!' She fumbled under her coveralls and whipped out her radio.

'Charlie? Is that you? It's Jayne at the house. Tell Forbes the killer knows where the safe-house is. Tell him he's got a fucking map!'

York

'You want me to do *what*?'

'To play Sir Nicholas Harker…in costume, of course.'

'You mean dress up in a ruff and wear a false beard? On national television?'

Appleby started to chuckle down the phone at Claire. Across the kitchen table, Jenny looked up quizzically. He caught her glance, grimaced to show he had just heard something humorously bizarre and shook his head to indicate that he wanted nothing to do with it. Jenny raised her eyebrows and returned to her copy of *The Times*.

'Now come on, James,' said Claire. 'You'd love it. You know you would.'

This was her 'stroke of sheer genius', her ultimate publicity stunt. She had just returned in triumph to her office, after eating a tiny salad lunch squashed next to Farnstable on a sofa in the crowded first-floor bar at Soho House.

'Let me get this straight. You're proposing a fifty-minute recreation of the *Common Rite* complete with a *Contemplation*, hymns and *Attestations*, the lot in fact, in front of an invited audience, with me leading it, dressed up as Sir Nicholas Harker…'

'Who better? You know I think you might actually look quite like him if you had a long beard.'

'…and you've actually convinced Tim Farnstable that he wants to film this…panto?'

'He loves it James! He's desperate to do it. He's already fixed a meeting at Channel 4. If that doesn't work out he'll take it to the BBC.'

'He doesn't really think they'll go for it?'

'Of course! He's totally convinced they will. The idea is sheer genius.'

'Claire, I'm flabbergasted…Let me think about it.'

After the call he sat back in his seat with a sigh.

'Did you get that?' he asked Jenny. 'Have you ever heard such tomfoolery? I'd be the laughing stock of every campus in the country.'

'Why do you say that? I think you'd be rather good at it, actually. I've always thought this Harker chap sounds a bit like your dad, if you don't mind my saying so. You could do it as if you were being him.'

'That's a bit Freudian isn't it?' He poured the last generous double from a litre of duty-free Irish malt over the remains of the ice-cubes in his glass. The smooth whiskey induced a mellow glow, and Jenny's words made him ponder. It wasn't as if he hadn't thought about the similarities between Harker and his father before. And as his work progressed his admiration for the slaughtered baronet had steadily deepened. On one level he wasn't sure he felt worthy to impersonate the man – on another he found the idea deeply flattering. 'I don't know,' he sighed eventually. '…I suppose I'll think about it.'

'I did tell you I'm off to London for the day tomorrow?'

'Did you? Remind me?'

'The funeral? Canon Dexter? The archivist at Lambeth Palace who let me photograph all that stuff for the book on psalters?'

'Oh God! I remember him! He's the snotty little shit who stonewalled me when I asked if they had the Cantwell correspondence. He's not still doing that job is he?'

'Well, he isn't now, obviously, because he's dead. That's why I'm going to his funeral.'

'Well spit on his grave for me.'

'That's not funny, Jimmy.'

*

The following evening he took a call from Phyllida. Her tone reminded Appleby of one of his mother's favourite words: she sounded 'shirty'.

'I've had Hermione on the phone again. She says you still haven't sent back the galley proofs and you're not answering her emails or returning her calls. What's going on? You've had them for a month, James!'

Appleby had always been bad with deadlines. As a schoolboy he was a past master at calculating exactly how much overrun time would be tolerated by each teacher before they brought down some form of disciplinary retribution. But then he would usually overshoot that anyway. He hadn't improved much since. He found it almost impossible to get anything in on time unless he was absolutely certain that lateness would have the gravest personal consequences, expulsion for instance, or summary execution. Explaining this to Phyllida, however, would do him no good whatsoever.

'I've nearly finished,' he squirmed. 'I'll ring her tomorrow and apologise.'

'You do realise that if you don't get the proofs back by the end of the week, we are in severe danger of missing the spring publication date, and all Claire's superb work will be completely undermined?'

'Yes. You're right. I know. I'm sure I can get it done in the next couple of days. Has Claire told you about her latest TV wheeze, by the way?'

'Yes, she has, but there won't be much point in doing it, if they can't publish the bloody books, will there?'

It was like being a student again. He would probably end up staying up all night, only this time there would be no raffish Old Etonian down the corridor selling amphetamines. They had just installed a new Freeview box, and he had been looking forward to spending the rest of the evening on the front room sofa, sipping red wine and channel-surfing. After the call he made himself a mug of strong coffee and headed up to his study. He had barely spread the proofs out on his desk when he heard the front door. Jenny was home.

'Jimmy? Are you upstairs? Come down! I've got you a present!'

He trundled downstairs, chuntering, 'I'm sorry, love. I can't talk for long. I'm really up against it. How was it? You really shouldn't have got me a present.'

'Oh yes I should. Check this out.'

He followed her through to the kitchen where she opened her shoulder-bag and handed him a thick A4 folder.

'It's not gift-wrapped, then,' he said with mock disappointment.

'Just open it!'

It contained a large sheaf of photocopies, separated into bundles.

Each had a small form stapled to the top, with an archive identification code and a brief description. The top sheet read, '*Interrogation of Sir Nicholas Harker by Bishop John Cantwell, Salisbury, Wednesday 1st to Friday 3rd May, 1594, Introduction and Transcript: Day One.*'

'Fuck me! The bastards had it all along! How on earth did you get your hands on this?'

'I had a chat to Dexter's successor at the funeral. He's a nice young chap called Philpott, a real sweetie, in fact. I told him about your little difficulty over the Salisbury correspondence, and he said he couldn't imagine what the problem was. We took a taxi back to his office, and he tracked it down in less than twenty minutes.'

'I'm gobsmacked. I don't know what to say. I don't know how to thank you.'

'You could start by making me a cup of tea.'

But she ended up making it herself. Appleby was flicking through the file with a degree of concentration that suggested he had just been handed Elizabeth I's private diaries or the manuscript of a lost Shakespeare play. After ten minutes he picked up the phone.

'Phyllida? It's James. Listen, I'm really sorry to spring this on you like this, but we're going to have to ask Shaftesbury if they can adjust their schedule. There's been a development...'

Amsterdam

Van Stumpe had no idea how long he had been unconscious. His chin was throbbing painfully. He must have caught it on the side of the sink as he collapsed. As the reality of his situation flooded back into his consciousness, he almost passed out again. His father lay dead on his bedroom floor. Freek had been abducted. There were horrible, cruel murderers out there, and they were about to come for him.

He staggered to his feet and into the hall. The front door was still wide open, and he could see across the little bridge that the taxi was no longer waiting in the road. Had the man just got tired of waiting? Surely he'd have been up to the house and seen that something was amiss? Had he alerted anyone or had he just beaten a hasty retreat? Or had someone sent him away?

Presumably they were still watching him. Were they listening too? When they first broke in, they could have had no idea where he had gone or when he was coming home. It would have been only too easy to keep tabs on him by planting a few listening devices around the house. Anyone could get hold of that sort of kit these days. He had read an article about it. As he stood in the hall he made a theatrical show of retching and staggered into the downstairs lavatory, closing the door behind him.

The house phone began to ring immediately, but he ignored it. He sat on the lavatory seat and took the new mobile from his trouser pocket. He continued making extravagant retching noises, while his fingers desperately fumbled across the keys. When he was sure the text had been sent, he set the phone to 'silent' and 'vibrate'. Then he opened the small cabinet over the hand basin, took a tube of haemorrhoid cream from a small plastic pharmacy bag, put the phone inside the bag and smeared the outside generously with the cream. It took a minute or two, and considerable discomfort, but eventually he managed to ease the package into his bottom, poking it as far up as he could. Then he pressed the lavatory flush, washed and dried his hands and stepped back into the hall. The house phone had continued to ring throughout this entire procedure. He picked it up.

'Next time you want to throw up go to the kitchen. Stay where we can see you at all times or your friend will suffer the consequences.'

Two minutes later a vehicle pulled up outside. It was dark by now, and he could not make out the make or model, though he could see it was larger than an ordinary car. Three men got out, all in dark jackets with the hoods up. As they walked briskly up the path, van Stumpe saw that they were all wearing sunglasses over woollen ski-masks which covered their faces. The first one to enter the house wore a purple mask. He pulled out a pistol and pushed it under van Stumpe's chin. He grabbed his upper arm in a steely grip and pulled him towards the door. The other two stood in front and behind as they marched him down the path. No-one spoke a word.

As they crossed the little bridge, van Stumpe was surprised to feel a vibrating sensation deep in his rectum.

*

All the news channels were filming live from the same event. The Ruling Council of the Tribes of Abraham had called a press conference at a hotel in Jerusalem. The international press corps were crammed into a large reception room. The place was bristling with every conceivable type of camera and microphone.

A group of twenty-three men filed in from a side door on the platform and sat in two rows at the back. Journalists muttered to each other, speculating as to who this unlikely assembly might be. A Ukrainian radio correspondent told his Spanish neighbour that he recognised a fire-breathing Russian Orthodox bishop; an American agency reporter thought she had seen a Presbyterian minister at an evangelical rally in Oklahoma, and an English war correspondent thought he had once interviewed one of the Shiite mullahs in Basra. But in general they were unknown. They might have been a group of twenty-three clerical tourists on pilgrimage to the holy city who had been pulled in off the street.

After a few minutes a rabbi stepped forward to a small lectern at the front.

'Ladies and gentlemen, thank you for coming to this conference and thank you for your patience. My name is Rabbi Elihu Binyamin and, as a representative of the first and oldest of the Abrahamic faiths, I have been nominated by my colleagues on the Advisory Council of the Tribes of Abraham to speak on their behalf.

'This conference, I promise, will be mercifully short. In a moment I will read a prepared statement, after which the proceedings will be closed. We will not be taking questions. If you have further queries about our organisation and its work, you may email them to us at our website. As you can see the address is now displayed on the screen behind me. I will now read the statement.'

The rabbi cleared his throat, took a sip of water and began to read.

'The Advisory Council notes that there has been much wild speculation about the nature and purpose of our organisation. It has been claimed that we are all fanatics and even suggested that we promote acts of terrorism and murder. These are vile slanders, and there is not a shred of truth in any of them.

'The Tribes of Abraham is a charitable foundation, entirely funded by donations and covenants from private individuals. We are an ecumenical organisation, which seeks to promote improved understanding among the three great monotheistic faiths. While we recognise that deep differences will remain among us, our purpose is to foster faith, piety and devotion in believers throughout the world. Above all, we seek to encourage the pure and steadfast love of the One True God.

'You may ask why our three faiths, so often the bitterest of enemies, should come together at this time. The answer is simple. We now have a common enemy so evil and so dangerous that our differences pale into insignificance. All around the world, faith is under siege by the remorseless forces of scepticism and unbelief. The immortal souls of countless millions are imperilled as whole societies turn their backs on God.

'This situation has been immeasurably aggravated by the spread of a new sham religion, an atheistical, some say "Humanist" cult which shamelessly travesties the mysteries and sacraments of Christianity. It creates among those who are foolish enough to fall for its lies, the delusion that they can enjoy the blessings and consolations of religious observation without accepting the word of the One True God.

'Ladies and Gentlemen, we stand at a crossroads. The Tribes of Abraham proclaim that our common purpose is to ensure that mankind proceeds down the paths of righteousness. We are men of peace. Our organisation exists solely to promote the love and understanding of Almighty God.'

Rabbi Binyamin coughed again and took another sip of water. 'That concludes the statement,' he said. 'I thank you.'

The room erupted as excited journalists began to lob questions towards the podium. A young Israeli reporter in the front row leapt to his feet and shouted.

'Rabbi Binyamin! Do you deny that Rabbi Katz was assassinated on the orders of your organisation?'

But Binyamin scooped up his script and left through the side-exit they had come in by, the other twenty-two clerics filing out behind him. Viewers of BBC News 24, including Appleby and Jenny, saw the BBC's Middle East correspondent collar a passing religious affairs reporter.

'So what did you make of that, Jocelyn?'

'It almost sounds as if the whole organisation has been set up to counter the effects of Harkerism, doesn't it? I know there has been a lot of alarm and anger about the way that cult has begun to gather a following over here, especially among some of the more extreme orthodox Jewish leaders, and of course, the Muslim militants hate it! To an extent this reminds me of the way the Roman Catholic church conducted fierce campaigns against communism during the Cold War – or indeed the Iranian persecution of the Baha'i.'

'But isn't it extraordinary to see hardliners from these three religious traditions apparently acting in concert?' asked the Middle East correspondent. 'Some of the Islamic groups represented here have a reputation for the most vicious anti-Semitism. And some Christian fundamentalist groups, especially the Americans, have spent the last eight years spitting blood about Islam!'

'Absolutely!' said the reporter. 'It's like the Reverend Ian Paisley teaming up with Gerry Adams in Northern Ireland…but multiplied by a factor of 100!'

'Could you explain to our viewers what that question about Rabbi Katz referred to?'

'Yes,' said the reporter. 'Rabbi Katz was a prominent member of an ultra-orthodox community here in Jerusalem who attended a Harkerite gathering. He told his wife he was just going to "check it out", apparently, but he seems to have been deeply affected by the ceremony and he ended up making an "Attestation" – that's a public confession – in which he said that he had repressed homosexual tendencies and that on several occasions he had abused young boys in his care. Worse, he claimed that the members of his community were "in denial" about paedophilia and that he knew of several other child-abusers in prominent positions in the group's hierarchy. The next day three masked men burst into his home and shot him in front of wife and children.'

'But is there any evidence that the Tribes of Abraham were involved in that killing?'

'As far as I know the Israeli police have found nothing yet, but it's worth pointing out that some of the rumours about their activities are said to have been leaked by sources close to Shin Bet. And we're not just talking about Israel. The organisation has been linked to several assassinations and bombings around the world.'

'So do you think this press-call will have done anything to scotch these rumours?'

'No, to be perfectly honest, I don't think it will.'

As the item ended Appleby called across to Handley who had been watching the report from the kitchen.

'Did you see that? Do you think these jokers have got anything to do with the attacks on me?'

'I believe that is one of a number of lines of enquiry, sir.'

*

'Are you absolutely certain that the house cannot be seen from anywhere along the perimeter fence?'

Even over a bad connection from the other side of England, Kot was slightly nervous when he talked to Commander Forbes. He always felt that he was about to be caught out in some elementary oversight. Forbes had a way of crushing you with a sarcastic aside.

'Yes, sir,' he said. 'Handley and I have both walked right round the perimeter to make sure. Apart from the odd glimpse of the roof, you can only see the house once you are some way inside the compound.'

'Good. Well keep a close eye on those monitors. Whoever shot Trevor Jenvey and his family knows where you are.'

'What?...You don't think Trevor told him?'

'It's worse than that. He drew them a bloody map. They may have been torturing his family, or threatening to. There were some very peculiar marks on the little girl's nose.'

'I hope the bastards do show up here. If I ever get my hands on them...'

'This is no time for Rambo impersonations, Kot. Whoever it is, they are exceptionally dangerous. When the attack comes, it will probably come when you least expect it. And don't get trigger-happy. I don't need to tell you they'd be far more use to us if you could capture them alive...So don't take any unnecessary risks!'

'We need back-up, sir, urgently. There are only two of us, and the compound is huge.'

'Don't worry. The cavalry is on its way. We couldn't hang about while the locals got their act together. Even if it's only one man, he's had about sixteen hours' head-start. He's probably outside the compound now, casing the place. The Home Secretary got the army to provide transport. There are twelve SO15 officers flying down in a Chinook. I gather they've just passed Bristol, so they should be landing on Angelini's croquet lawn in about fifteen minutes. If you go outside you can watch them arrive.'

Handley stayed dutifully in front of the monitors. Kot, Appleby and Jenny went up onto the wooden deck ready to watch the giant helicopter with its twin rotors descend and disgorge its cargo of heavily armed anti-terrorist officers. Within minutes they heard the whirr of the blades in the distance as the Leviathan approached.

The pilot had already identified Angelini's compound and soon spotted the croquet lawn. It was a relatively confined area, and he decided to take a pass around it until he found the easiest approach. He was particularly anxious to land gently. His original mission that morning had been to ferry a squad of infantrymen from Aldershot to an exercise on Salisbury Plain. They were already loading their kit when he was ordered to London to pick up a bunch of anti-terrorist police. One of these guys had just told him that the squaddies had left a case of live anti-tank missiles on board.

*

The stocky American was cursing his operators for not supplying him with another SUV. The Honda was nippy, responsive and reassuringly inconspicuous, but it was making very heavy weather of the rutted woodland tracks above Angelini's compound. Eventually he bumped and lurched his way to the brow of a low hill. He got out and surveyed the area through a small pair of binoculars. Ahead he could see the Bristol Channel, with tiny boats ploughing across a beautifully calm sea. To his right was heath and moorland, interspersed with copses and patches of deciduous woodland. To his left the ground dipped away. The roof of Angelini's house was just visible above the trees which surrounded the compound. This would be as good a place as any to assemble the rifle, test the sites and plan the attack.

He noticed a battered old diamond-shaped fire-warning notice down a track two hundred metres away. First he inserted a clip of solid ammunition. The stylised flames in the middle of the notice filled the scope. He took aim and carefully squeezed off a shot. There was a distant ping as the bullet struck home. Checking through the binoculars he noted with satisfaction that there was a fresh new hole at the tip of the highest tongue of flame, exactly where he had aimed. The scope needed no adjustment.

He was expecting to shoot Appleby from a considerable distance. To ensure a kill he would need to use the explosive-headed bullets. He filled a second clip with these and snapped it into the rifle. He decided he needed a more challenging target. About two hundred and fifty metres away he spotted a large herring gull on a tree-stump, looking out to sea. He rested the rifle on the roof of the Honda, took careful aim and squeezed the trigger again. The gull burst apart in a cloud of blood and feathers. A puff of smoke lingered briefly in the space where the bird had been, then dispersed.

It was at this moment that he heard the chop-chop-chop of the Chinook approaching from the East. As he looked up, it seemed to be heading straight for him and flying extremely low. Who were they? Police? The military? Were they looking for him?

The giant helicopter passed right over his position, then circled around Angelini's estate, before coming back towards him, still losing height. Suddenly the monster was directly above his head. Surely they could see the car! Had they seen him using the rifle? They must have. He was cornered. He panicked. He lifted the rifle to his shoulder and fired three shots in quick succession.

The first bullet merely blew out a small chunk of fuselage. The second hit a front rotor blade which shattered, causing the Chinook to dip and pirouette slowly in the air, like a tipsy ballerina. The third shot blew out the windscreen, sending a shock-wave of fragments into the pilot's chest and face. As he was hurled back in his seat, the pilot's hands locked over the controls, and the helicopter reared up like a horse. It hovered ominously in mid-air for a moment before plunging vertically back into the ground fifty metres from the Honda.

The man dived for cover as the fuel tanks blew up, followed seconds later by the case of missiles. He cowered behind the car as fragments of flaming debris and human body parts rained down around him.

*

The observers on the terrace heard all three shots quite clearly. They were toasting the imminent arrival of their new guardians in Angelini's champagne when they saw the helicopter gyrate, fall to earth behind the trees and explode. They stood in stunned silence for a few moments before Kot ducked back into the house and grabbed his phone.

'My God!' said Jenny. 'What just happened?'

Appleby's face was white.

'Jenny,' he said. 'I really don't think we should stay here. Things are getting completely out of hand.'

*

Forbes's deputy Charlie Drucker was walking to his office with a cup of coffee from the vending machine when he noticed something in a transparent evidence bag on DC Lambert's desk.

'Isn't that Dr Appleby's mobile, Debbie?'

'Yes, sir,' said the young DC. 'They've already downloaded everything.'

'I know. I saw the report. Did they put the SIM card back in?'

'Not sure. Why?' She slipped the phone from the evidence bag, and opened the back. 'Yes, it's there. Do you want me to check it out? The battery will be flat by now.'

'Did we keep his charger?'

'It's in my drawer.'

'We should have been monitoring it. Plug it in. See if anyone's tried to call him.'

She fished the charger out of her desk drawer, connected it to the phone and reached down to plug it into a socket under a metal flap in the floor under the desk. They watched impatiently as the screen sprang to life and the phone searched for a network. Eventually a small box appeared at the bottom of the screen. 'You have 1 new message'.

'Read it.'

'Message from Piet' appeared, followed by van Stumpe's mobile number. Lambert pressed READ: 'At hous. V murdered. F hostage. Bad men coming. Alert to Dutch police PLEASE!!!! pvs'

'Who is Piet? And who the fuck are V and F?'

'That'll be Piet van Stumpe, sir. You remember? The chap Appleby asked us to find. Christ! Look at the time! This was only sent ten minutes ago!'

'Call him back.'

She did.

'It rang a few times and went to voicemail, sir.'

Drucker roared to his secretary across the office. 'Cheryl! Get me Inspecteur De Groot in Amsterdam. The number's in my old rolodex. Tell him it's urgent! Debbie, get Kot back on the phone. Tell him I need to speak to Appleby.'

But Kot's phone was engaged. He was trying to get through to Commander Forbes.

York

NH: If e'er I waver in the Certaintie of mine own Uncertaintie, I have but to pass one half hour in company with a man of the cloth, and my Want of Faith is most perfectly restored.

TC: And yet thou darest not draw back the curtain to show him your Secret mind.

NH: Nay, Tom, alas, I dare not.

—The Colloquies, Vol IV, No 48

The publishers gave Appleby two more weeks. His editor agreed that he could make minor alterations to the introduction and include the transcript of Harker's interrogation as an annotated appendix.

He needed longer. To do the job properly he would have to spend weeks chasing up references, investigating ecclesiastical practices and checking points of Elizabethan law. But he was in no position to bargain. He would just have to do what he could in the time. Jeremy Dilke offered to help as far as he could. The rest could wait for a second edition – assuming there was one.

Over the last year Appleby had trawled through every document in the archive. He felt he knew Harker intimately. He could hear his voice in his head. But this transcript brought him much closer to the man than ever before. Its immediacy startled him. He felt he was in the room with him, wincing with anxiety at the old man's vulnerability.

Appleby tried to picture the events. How would Harker have travelled to Salisbury? Surely he was too old to ride. He must have taken his carriage, which Cranham once described as '*ancient and villainous ill-kepte*'. Country roads could be extremely dangerous. He would not have gone alone and unprotected. What was he thinking about on the journey? What did he expect to happen when he arrived?

The streets of the city would have been all-too familiar. Had his wife Grace asked him to buy things from the shops and market stalls while he was there? Or did she understand the gravity of his situation? Where would he have entered the Cathedral Close? The High Street Gate was presumably the busiest and the first you would come to from the Wolvington road, but both the St Ann's Gate to the east and the Harnham Gate to the south might have offered quieter paths to the grand entrance to the Bishop's Palace. Then he remembered the gates into the palace courtyard on what is now Exeter Street, a sort of tradesman's entrance. Had Harker gone directly in there?

Even in the shadow of the massive cathedral with its impossibly tall, narrow spire stabbing the heavens, the looming crenellated towers of the palace must have looked intimidating. When Sir Nicholas entered the building itself, he would have been utterly alone, without servant, friend or armed retainer.

The transcript was prefaced by a brief introduction. On his arrival at the Bishop's Palace, Sir Nicholas Harker of Farthingwell Manor in the Parish of Swively had been escorted to a reception chamber, not in Bishop Beauchamp's tower at the eastern end, with its magnificent hall, but in the early medieval gloom of the west wing. Had Harker visited the Palace before? Did his route take him through the old great hall where the Parliament of England once sat during the Wars of the Roses, intending to impeach John of Gaunt? Would he have even noticed?

The bishop had also seen fit to record that his private secretary, one William Rodaway, had asked if Sir Nicholas needed refreshment after his journey. When Harker said he had not eaten since sunrise, he was served a bowl of pottage with peas and boiled bacon, some 'manchet' (white bread) and a tankard of 'small beer', the weak ale everyone drank because, unlike the water, it was unlikely to poison you. Bishop Cantwell wanted it known that Harker had been decently, if not generously treated. After this meal, Rodaway returned with the bishop and an assistant of Richard Hooker's called Tobias Clift.

The transcript itself began with the bishop explaining to Harker that Rodaway would act as scrivener, taking down a verbatim record of the conversation using the *Characterie* of Rector Bright of Cambridge. The name rang a bell, and Appleby dug out some very old research notes. Timothy Bright's '*Characterie: an Arte of short, swifte and secret writing by character*' was the world's first known shorthand system. At the time of Harker's interview it had been in circulation for about six years.

Young Clift, said the bishop, was there only to observe. However, if any difficult questions of doctrine were to arise, he would refer them to his master who, as Harker surely knew, was in Salisbury completing his great work on the laws and policies of the English Church on behalf of Archbishop Whitgift himself.

If Harker still had any doubt that he was about to be interrogated about his unorthodox activities, this last piece of information must have removed it. Yet the interview seemed to have no formal status under ecclesiastical law, and he was not required to answer under oath. What did Harker make of that?

Appleby wondered if Cantwell was trying to work out what exactly it was that he was dealing with before initiating formal proceedings. Perhaps the whole purpose of the meeting was to obtain a written document he could send to the Archbishop and to Sir John Puckering in Whitehall. Perhaps he secretly hoped that the old man would demonstrate his innocence, in which case the record of the interview would provide insurance against the zealous pestering of Parson Mallaster.

If Rodaway had recorded the interviews in Rector Bright's cumbersome proto-shorthand, the document Appleby was reading must have been a transcription made later, and probably heavily edited. Rodaway introduced each participant's words with their initials: *NH* and *TC*, with *JS* indicating 'John Sarum' the *ex-officio* name of the bishop. When Harker was addressed in speech, Rodaway abbreviated his name to '*Sir Nic*'. Appleby thought the transcript read like the script of an extremely long and tortuous play.

On the first afternoon the Bishop seemed at pains to put Harker at his ease, speaking of his reputation as '*a good and kindly master*'. He asked Harker why he thought he had been summoned. Harker said he wasn't sure. '*I praye no deed or word of mine hath been the subject of false speculationne or maliciouse Rumor,*' he said.

Appleby wondered if feigning innocence was such a good idea. The two men continued to skirt around the subject until the 'observer', Tobias Clift lost patience and snapped at Harker:

'*I prithee do not take his Grace's questions as skittles for the juggling. Tell us, who is't that gathers at thy house on each Saturday morn, and to what end?*'

This quickly became the pattern: the Bishop courteous and emollient; Clift hostile and aggressive. Good cop, bad cop, thought Appleby. That must have been pre-planned.

At first Harker claimed they just met to discuss village matters and resolve disputes. He and Cantwell seemed like two fencers probing each other's reactions at the start of a bout, Cantwell tempting Harker to let slip his true beliefs, Harker desperately trying to gauge how much Cantwell knew already. When Harker admitted they discussed matters of morality, Clift jumped on him:

'*Matters of morality? Why, sir! In this thou dost most surely usurp the prerogative of the Church and of your priest!*'

The bishop reprimanded Clift for his rudeness. He was not yet ready to go for the kill. The discussion lasted several hours, covering the competence of Parson Wesson, the attitudes of the churchwardens and whether the bishop's representatives had been in any way misled on their visits to the parish. Cantwell knew that the Cranham family had once been Catholic recusants. What did Harker know about his neighbour's current beliefs?

Clift grilled Harker fiercely about the settlement of village disputes. Had he presumed to take upon himself the proper functions of the courts? If he had known of breaches of the law, ecclesiastical or civil, and had failed to report them, he must expect to answer for it.

At last the bishop said that Harker must be tired. He would leave him in the kindly charge of Rodaway who would feed him and accompany him to Evensong. The next day he would question him further about the Saturday gatherings. So Harker was left to stew for almost twenty-four hours, still unsure how much the bishop really knew.

When the interrogation resumed the following afternoon the tone had changed. The bishop pressed him fiercely with doctrinal questions. Who was to judge between good and evil and how? Had it ever occurred to Harker to doubt the mysteries of the gospels? The virgin birth for example? Did he, in fact, accept the majestic truth of the Resurrection? What did he expect to transpire at his own death? Would he not be judged, raised to heaven or consigned to the fiery pit?

As Appleby read on, it became increasingly clear that, like him, Harker really hated lying. Instead of telling Cantwell and Clift what they wanted to hear, he prevaricated. His answers became vague, evasive, circumlocutory. He tried to engage them in abstract philosophical hypothesising, which infuriated Clift.

Then as Cantwell asked for specific details about his Saturday meetings, it began to dawn on Harker that the bishop already knew far more than he had let on. He even asked Cantwell what he supposed was going on. Clift barged in:

'These "gatherings" as you would call them, Sir Nic., they are Services are they not? Liturgies! Blasphemous mockeries of those rites and Observances solemnly set down in our Book of Common Prayer, which every subject of Her Majestie must follow?'

'They are not "blasphemous mockeries", Master Clift. Nor are they Liturgies.' Harker replied, which, Appleby reflected, was legalistically just about arguable.

Then the bishop played his trump card.

'Then pray, Sir, I would fain know, Sir, what call you this?'

And at this point, the transcript noted, he threw down on the table a copy of Harker's *'Common Rite'*.

Game, set and match, thought Appleby. Harker now knew he had been betrayed. The bishop went through the pamphlet line by line, forcing

Harker to explain the meaning of each passage, sentence, phrase and individual term. They seemed to grill him for hours on what he meant by 'Spirit'. His answers evoked blasts of withering scorn from Clift.

Then something strange happened. Rodaway's account suddenly switched from verbatim transcription to summary:

> *'Then did Sir Nic seek to Justify his most damnable Blasphemies with reference to divers texts, the work of The Devil, no doubt, which he said he had not about him and of which His Grace, the Bishop and good Master Clift knew nothing.'*

Texts which the Bishop and Clift had never heard of, and which Harker did not have with him? What were they referring to? Harker's other writings? His collection of religious books? Or something else? Something so unspeakable that they were not even prepared to commit a description to paper? Appleby was mystified.

Eventually the bishop saw no point in further discussion and suspended proceedings for a second time, telling Harker he could send home for any document he thought might justify his actions. Meanwhile the Bishop would ponder the import of their dicussions overnight. Harker's manservant was sent back to Swively, accompanied by Clift and two of the Bishop's retainers. Appleby's heart went out to the old man. He must have been doubly shattered by the knowledge that someone very close to him, by accident or malice, had betrayed him, and by the shameful realisation that, in attempting to deceive the bishop as to the exact nature of his activities, he had dishonoured himself.

The four riders returned before Matins the next morning. *'His Grace read certain texts e'er he met with Sir Nic for the last time, but would speak of them with none save Master Clift.'* He told Rodaway that *'for the safety of his immortal soule, he may not even cast an eye upon them'*. They were not even mentioned in his final encounter with Harker.

This began with detailed questioning about the numbers attending the 'Rites', and more ominously demanding that Sir Nicholas provide their names. When Harker resisted, claiming '*If there be fault in this matter, then it lies entirely with myself*', the bishop revealed that he already had a list of names anyway, collected by Parson Mallaster, and merely sought Harker's confirmation. Inevitably, the Cranham family were at the top.

The Bishop then told Harker that he was free to return to his home and family while these heavy matters were considered, on his parole that he would not leave the boundaries of his parish until further notice. He was also warned on no account to hold any further gatherings or to use his 'Rite' in any way, private or public.

In a macabre final touch the bishop read something called *The Commination against Sinners*. It was an addendum to the Book of Common Prayer, a grand, formal denunciation of sin to which the congregation were obliged to respond. As far as Appleby could see, Cantwell's only reason for introducing it was to make Harker squirm. It included the line:

'*Cursed is he that putteth his trust in man, and taketh man for his defence, and in his heart goeth from the Lord.*'

To which Harker was obliged to respond, '*Amen.*'

He would have found the conclusion particularly chilling:

'*Let us... return unto our Lord, with all contrition and meekness of heart... For now is the axe put unto the root of the trees, so that every tree that bringeth not forth good fruit, is hewn down and cast into the fire. It is a fearful thing to fall into the hands of the living God; he shall pour down rain upon the sinners, snares, fire, and brimstone, storm and tempest... The day of the Lord... [would come] ...as a thief upon the night... Then shall [sinners] call upon me, saith the Lord, but I will not hear.*'

And so it was that Harker was released to go home, shaken to the core, no doubt, ashamed of his own weakness and convinced that grave repercussions were to follow.

*

Rodaway's report ended by noting that copies of the transcript were to be sent to Archbishop Whitgift and Sir John Puckering, though there was no reference to any material fetched from Swively in the middle of the night. To Appleby's surprise a third recipient was listed too: '*Sir R. T., Old Sarum*'.

It took a while for the penny to drop. The Member of Parliament for Old Sarum at that time happened to be one Sir Richard Topcliffe. Appleby had read something about this man, and it wasn't funny. He rang Jeremy Dilke.

'Topcliffe?' said Dilke. 'I've got stuff on him. I'll email it. By the way, I had a visit from Norman Skyne last week. He was pumping me for information about what you've found in the archive. Don't worry. I didn't tell him about the interrogation transcript. I ought to warn you, though, I think they're still looking for a way to discredit it.'

'Why?' said Appleby. 'I just don't get it. Oh well, let them do their worst.'

Dilke's material confirmed that Topcliffe was the most ferocious of the Queen's Catholic-hunters, claiming to be answerable only to Elizabeth herself. He had even boasted to a captured Jesuit missionary that the Queen had let him touch her up. He was deeply corrupt, extorting huge sums from his victims and their families, and a sadist who had set up a private torture chamber in his Westminster house. He had raped the daughter of one prisoner. If judicial procedure stood in his way, he simply ignored it.

'Sounds like the Elizabethan version of "extraordinary rendition",' said Phyllida when he mentioned the matter on the phone.

So why had Cantwell contacted this man? Had Topcliffe organised the attack on the house? The Reformation had seen numerous religious massacres on the continent, of course. Even England had had its moments of mass carnage. Edward VI's Lord Protector, the Duke of Somerset had sent murderous German landsknechts and Italian mercenaries, to massacre the men of Devon and Cornwall who had rebelled against the imposition of the new English prayer book.

Seven hundred had been slaughtered on behalf of Elizabeth herself after the Revolt of the Northern Earls in 1569.

Yet the attack on Harker's home seemed completely 'extra-judicial'. Cantwell, Whitgift, Puckering and Topcliffe had gone to great pains to make it disappear from history.

Only that semi-literate scrawl from Captain Hugo de la Zouche had remained, like the murderer's gun – or in this case matchlock musket – still smoking four centuries later.

*

At the end of his second week working on the transcript, Appleby had a call from Farnstable. Channel 4 had agreed to take the programme and were looking to screen it in an 8.00 o'clock slot on a Saturday night.

'When can you get down to London?' said Farnstable. 'There's a musician I want you to meet.'

Leicester

The man now known as Kerim Mehmet had been driven to the house of an unmarried civil engineer in the Highfields area of Leicester. A series of ever more obscure passwords took him to a web address where his new instructions were waiting for him.

All but one of the possible targets were British Muslims who had either stated publicly that Harkerism was not incompatible with Islam or who had actively embraced it. It was a surprisingly long list and included politicians, academics, writers, journalists, film-makers, two well-known actors, a stand-up comic and even three moderate imams. The man noted with disgust that a high proportion of the names were female.

There was a file on each with photographs, a short biography, details of their addresses and places of work and in many cases an outline of their daily routine. Some even noted functions or meetings they were likely to attend in the next few weeks.

He cursed Appleby for turning his head at the critical moment. Being taken off that mission was a deep humiliation. These local westernised apostates all deserved to die, of course, but they were minnows. Their deaths would bring little honour, and he would probably only be able to dispatch two or three at most before the police began to close in and he would have to flee the country.

Only one name stood out as a truly worthy quarry. This was a man who had nurtured the pernicious blasphemy from the earliest stages: a man of immense wealth and influence, whose putrid personal life and unspeakable practices were a daily abomination. He also presented by far the greatest professional challenge. He was protected by the most sophisticated security and would be permanently on his guard. He might take out one or two of the others on the way, if they presented targets of opportunity and he was sure he could slip away undetected after killing them. But his primary goal now was the destruction of the sole infidel on his list: the Italian sodomite, Giovanni Angelini.

His host issued him with a car, a pistol with a silencer and a contact address in Luton where he would be supplied with somewhat heavier ordnance.

*

At least Trevor Jenvey did not actually have to watch his loved ones being tortured before he died. Piet van Stumpe was not so lucky.

The three masked and hooded visitors had pushed him into the back of a van, bound his wrists and blindfolded him. They seemed to be driving for hours, sometimes at speed, sometimes stopping and starting as if passing through built-up areas. Finally the van began to bump and lurch and continued to do so for what seemed an eternity. Evidently they were on a rough track – and a very long one.

When the van finally stopped, they dragged him out and manhandled him over a surface that crunched lightly under foot. Then he was walking on some sort of hard, if slightly uneven floor. They did not remove the blindfold until they had thrust him onto a hard seat and tied his arms to the frame. As they pushed him down he was surprised to feel another series of vibrations near his prostate gland. Under the circumstances it was extremely disconcerting.

'Please!' he groaned. 'Please unbind my hands. My wrists – they are so very painful. I cannot have any feelings in my fingers.'

His captors did not answer. They stood behind him where he could not see them, waiting for him to realise what was in front of him.

He was blinking for several seconds before his surroundings came into focus. In front of him he could see a spotlight shining down. It was so bright he had to look away. Otherwise all around was darkness, although he could make out enough in the shadows to see he was in a large enclosed space, a barn perhaps, a warehouse or an empty factory building.

As his eyes gradually adjusted to the brightness he began to realise that a spotlight was shining down on the figure of a man about six metres away. His arms were held up tightly by chains attached to a beam above his head, so that the tips of his toes barely touched the floor, and his head had slumped forward. He was completely naked. Slowly the figure lifted its head and looked at him.

'Freek! Oh my poor Freek! What have they done to you?'

'Piet? Is that you? Please help me.' Freek's voice was so weak it was barely audible. 'It hurts so much.'

'Don't you want to help him, Mijnheer van Stumpe?' said a voice behind him. 'It is really very easy, you know. All you have to do is co-operate.'

Like the voice on the phone, the man spoke to him in fluent English. Van Stumpe thought the accent rather strange, though he could not place it. Whoever he was, he was not Dutch, but he did not sound like a native English speaker either.

'I don't know what do you mean? What are you wanting? Please let him down!'

'We were very impressed you know – what you did – it was remarkable. And an old man like you! That chest is very heavy, I understand. You must have worked very quickly to collect everything and re-pack it. How much did you manage to save, I wonder. Did anybody help you?'

'What are you saying? I don't understand.'

'Oh, I think you do. Dragging it all the way up that little back staircase and onto the roof, with the flames licking up behind you. I bet that flat roof was beginning to melt by then. Did your shoes begin to stick to it? Did you know it was about to collapse? It must have been such a relief when you made it across onto the next building. But there was quite a drop wasn't there? Well over a metre, I think. That must have been very awkward. And then all the way down the staircase in the other house! You're a bit like Spiderman, aren't you? What would you have done if their roof door had been locked, though? Had you thought about that? Were you going to shoot out a spider web and swing down?'

Van Stumpe said nothing.

'What's the matter, Piet, my old friend? Are you too modest to talk about these feats? And then when you got to the bottom you found there was a side entrance onto another street. You broke the emergency glass to release the lock, I believe. But that was risky was it not? What if it set off an alarm? And what if someone saw you? We would be bound to find out sooner or later. Better let everyone think you and your precious chest had gone up in smoke, eh? How did you know if you could even trust the police? Even they had better not know. Then you peered out through the door, and I bet you couldn't believe your good luck! At that very moment a taxi approaching! For hire! We heard that you leapt out of that door, waving your arms in the air! The driver was not happy when he saw that great big chest, though! You had to give him a big extra tip! It didn't do the upholstery on his car seats much good, did it? All those sharp corners! How am I doing so far, Piet? Have I got any of this wrong?'

Van Stumpe twisted his head away from the sound of the man's voice and stared at the filthy floor. He couldn't bear to look towards Freek who had fallen silent again.

'But do you know what, Piet?' the voice continued. 'You were so right that you could not believe your good luck. The taxi driver was a Muslim, you see, a good devout Javanese. He's not one of us, exactly, but mosques can be such terrible places for gossip, can't they? Or perhaps you didn't know that. It only took a few days for word to get around, but, of course, by then you had disappeared, and the chest with you! Where did you take it, Piet? That's all you need to tell us. Then you and your little friend can go free. Did you hide it somewhere here in Holland? Or did you slip across to your friends in England? Did you contact Professor Appleby? I bet that's what you did, wasn't it?'

By now the pain in van Stumpe's hands was excruciating, but for some reason he found that he was thinking with complete clarity. He knew with absolute certainty that whatever he said or did, these men would not let either himself or Freek out of that building alive. It was only a matter of how much physical pain they would have to endure before they died. He also realised that, whatever he told them, they would both be tortured anyway. These men would simply assume that his first answers were lies. Like Gestapo interrogators or the Spanish inquisitors of old, they would carry on inflicting ever more horrific torments, first on Freek and then on himself, until they had convinced themselves that he could stand no more and therefore might finally have told the truth.

'Aren't you going to tell me, Piet?' said the voice. 'That is so disappointing. You know, I think we should take a short break, while my friend here does a little decorating. Do you like interior design, Piet? I understand it is very popular with you people. But of course you can't repaint anything professionally until you strip away the old surface, can you? Fortunately my friend has brought his paint-stripper with him. It's so important to do these jobs properly, don't you think?'

As he spoke a man appeared from behind van Stumpe, carrying an object that looked like an outsized hair-dryer. He walked towards Freek trailing a long electric extension cable behind him. He turned the device on, and it began to whirr loudly as it heated up.

'Freek?' Van Stumpe spoke softly to his friend in Dutch. 'Can you hear me?'

'Help me, Piet! Please help me!'

'Freek, we must both be brave boys now. These men are going to hurt us both extremely badly, as much as they can, and then they are going to kill us both. You must believe me that nothing I say or tell to them now will make the slightest difference to that fact. But the agony will not last forever. We must try to think only about the good things in our lives before we die. Think about the people you have loved and who have loved you, Freek, and think of all the good things that you have done. That is what I shall try to do.'

By now the rim of the metal tube around the nozzle of the hot-air paint-stripper was glowing orange-red. The man stood in front of his naked victim for a moment, lifted Freek's head and smirked contempt-uously into his face. 'Think about all the good things, Freek,' he said mockingly in Dutch as he pointed the nozzle at Freek's right nipple.

The shriek was ear-splitting and went on for many seconds before it subsided.

'Piet!' he wailed. 'Tell them. Please tell them!'

'I'm so sorry, my sweet boy' said van Stumpe, 'but it wouldn't make him stop! There is nothing I can do to help you, my love.'

'Just tell them the truth!'

'I can't. And if I did, they would not believe me!'

This time the man moved the nozzle towards Freek's crotch. His yells of agony became guttural and harsh, deep rasping gulps from the depths of his belly.

'Be brave, my little Freek. I love you.'

None of his captors could see the tears rolling down van Stumpe's cheeks.

London

'For do we not harbour within each of us, a bodger who, to save a farthing, will knock together a stool with three legs, each one a different length. Yet in another berth beside him lurks a master mason, who will pass months in finely chiselling the perfect likeness of a saint, though his children starve before a cold hearth? How are we to contrive concordance between these two rascals? Aye, there's the trick…'

—*Sir Nicholas Harker, The Colloquies, Vol I, No 3*

Jenny persuaded him to wear a smart new pair of black brogues for his trip to see Farnstable, and they were rubbing painfully against his heels. The nagging discomfort set the tone for the day. The rendezvous was in deepest Chelsea, an awkward journey by public transport. Fortunately Farnstable had told him to grab a cab at Kings Cross and charge it to expenses.

They met at the studio of Gordon Fairview, the composer Farnstable had commissioned to write the music for the programme. It was a small, soundproofed flat in an Edwardian mansion block, neat and cosily furnished. If it hadn't been for the computers, electronic mixing equipment and the grand piano, you could have taken it for a rich man's pied-a-terre – or his wife's love nest. Fairview was a clean-cut, fresh-faced man in his early forties in clean jeans and a crisp, pale blue shirt. He radiated enthusiasm.

He turned out to be a musical polymath. He had written stage musicals, the theme music for sitcoms and numerous film scores, though his passion was writing church choral music, even though he was a professed non-believer. Above all, he was a brilliant pasticheur who could switch from one musical style to another with the ease of an impressionist doing his repertoire of celebrities.

'This is one area where we're going to put a bit of cash on the screen,' said Farnstable, as they sat in the kitchen drinking herbal tea. 'This show is all about atmosphere, and nothing brings atmosphere like music. Play Jimmy the opening theme, Gordon.'

Fairview had already drafted a short orchestral piece to open and close the show and had persuaded a small orchestra he was working with to play it.

'We'll record it properly when it's finished,' he said, as the lush music swelled through the kitchen speakers.

'Something about it seems familiar,' said Appleby.

'That's because it's based on the same theme by Thomas Tallis as the famous Vaughan Williams Fantasia. "*Why fumeth in fight the Gentiles spite*". It's one of the anthems in Tallis's *Tunes for Archbishop Parker's* Psalter. So the original is Elizabethan, but of course everybody knows the melody from the Vaughan Williams. I wanted something of the same general period as our friend Harker, which seemed quint-essentially English, something familiar, yet unfamiliar – something intriguing and haunting and a bit stirring.'

'You've succeeded,' said Appleby. 'It's perfect.'

They spent the session going through Harker's various services, identifying points where music could be introduced. Farnstable had already agreed to employ a small choir and an even smaller consort playing contemporary instruments. The consort would introduce the service, play at some as yet unspecified point in the middle, and again at the end. Some songs would be sung by the choir alone, *a capella* like anthems. Others would be sung with accompaniment and there would be three songs with stirring tunes, to be sung by the whole congregation like hymns.

They sifted through Harker's writings, with Fairview absorbing everything Appleby had to say, taking notes and making suggestions. He played them exquisite examples of Tudor songs and church music, suggesting ways they could be adapted or updated. Appleby was thrilled.

'If everyone on this project is as good as him it could be absolutely fantastic,' he said to Farnstable as they drove to their next meeting at Box of Tricks.

'Don't get carried away,' said Farnstable. 'Gordon's getting half the budget. The music is a loss-leader. Nobody else is getting that amount of backing, and that includes you.'

It was a timely warning. Appleby soon discovered that television production had changed a tad in the eighteen years since the Swively documentary. They had fancy, compact digital equipment now, and could film almost anything, anywhere with ease. But the real difference was that every process had speeded up.

Budgets got tighter every year, Farnstable complained, and time was money. Everyone was a hired gun, working on ever-shorter contracts. New technology was pounced on, not to improve programmes, but to make them more quickly and cheaply. Everyone Appleby met on the project seemed addicted to the ephemeral, to be high on instability. Cutting corners had become an art form. Cut and run. Fire and forget. The contrast with the methodical plodding of academic research could not have been greater.

Appleby had always thought of Farnstable as a magpie, a disconcerting mixture of opportunistic chancer and sharp, insightful cultural omnivore. Now he saw him as a surfer, riding the breakers of multichannel, short-attention-span television production, and apparently doing so with panache. Box of Tricks specialised in drama-documentary hybrids and had a shelf crowded with awards.

The offices were in a converted Victorian factory behind the residential streets of Kentish Town. 'Gritty urban chic,' thought Appleby as he limped up the cast iron staircase to the entrance. His hobbling gait felt emblematic of his lack of nimbleness among Farnstable's darting creative dragonflies. He had come armed with a sheaf of notes, but he might as well have thrown them in the bin back in York. The team were weeks ahead of him, and nobody seemed interested in his views on anything.

That included Farnstable who described himself as the 'exec producer'. Confusingly there was another 'exec', a chap from Channel 4 called Dick. Apparently any organisation with a stake in the show had to have an 'exec'. Maybe he should demand to be an 'exec' himself. The real work was being done by a plain old producer, a nervy woman in her thirties called Chrissie, who spent the meeting fielding the execs' questions.

Her answers always followed the same pattern: 'Meredith's across that,' she said regarding costumes, 'Yad's across that' (the catering) or 'Sophie's across the other' (the computer graphics). Apparently you didn't count in this feverish world if you weren't 'across' something. Appleby didn't feel he was across anything, until he heard Farnstable say, 'Jimmy here's across all that, aren't you, Jimmy?'

'Sorry? What am I across?'

'Historical accuracy – anachronisms – general goof-avoidance. All the nerdy stuff.'

'I suppose you could say I'm across that,' he mumbled.

'Excellent!' said Dick. 'Because every tight-arsed historian and mealy-mouthed theologian in the country will be on our case when this is shown, just itching to denounce Channel 4 in *The Telegraph* and *The Mail* as usual! They'll do it anyway, of course. Just don't give them any free ammunition!'

The commissioning editor at Channel 4 had been so taken with this unusual project that she had commissioned a two-hour show (about a hundred minutes plus gaps for adverts). 'She's ticking all their Public Service boxes,' Farnstable explained. 'They'll be citing it for years, whenever they're accused of dumbing down.'

Jeremy Dilke was to present and narrate, which was news to Appleby, as nobody had thought it necessary to tell him, and the 'service' would be topped and tailed with historical context-setting, including some new computer images (another big slice of the budget) and archive clips from the 1985 documentary.

The 'Rite' would be attended by an invited audience, including family and friends of the production team, Channel 4 executives, sympathetic journalists and broadcasters, selected academics, representatives of various faiths and humanist groups and a smattering of interested celebrities. The congregation would be 'cast' as soon as the date of the shoot was fixed. Only Appleby and the musicians would be in costume. His 'congregation' should respond to the event as modern citizens. The service would be recorded, but, as far as possible, made to look like a live event.

Chrissie announced that they were booking the magnificent half-timbered Merchant Adventurers' Hall in York as the most appropriate location. It was larger than the great hall at Farthingwell Manor would have been, but the architecture was of the right period, and the rental was within budget. They planned to film in early February. A production designer called Bilbo had made preliminary sketches of a possible 'look', which he passed round to general approval. His concept involved dozens of candles and strategically placed torches, so that everyone there could appear in livid chiaroscuro.

Two things bothered Dick. Firstly, he said, the atmosphere should be as gripping as possible. 'I'm not talking Hammer Horror, but it should be pretty intense. Bilbo's sketches look great, but make sure that the aesthetic is picked up in the sets and music. We have to draw the viewers into the experience. If it looks like *Songs of Praise* they'll flip like that,' and he snapped his fingers. 'Then there's these "*Attestation*" thingies. That really has to work dramatically. It's gonna stir a great big dollop of reality show into the mix. It'll make or break the project. Have you drafted those sequences yet?'

'Drafted?' said Appleby in alarm. 'You're not planning on planting people in the audience with scripted confessions, are you?'

He suddenly realised that everyone was staring at him. He felt like 'The man who...' had committed some dreadful *faux pas* in an H.M. Bateman cartoon. There was a short pause.

'Ooh, no, I don't think anything like that will be necessary,' cooed Farnstable soothingly. 'I'm sure we'll find there are people in the congregation with things they'd like to get off their chests quite spontaneously. We might discreetly "sex things up" a touch occasionally, but basically this is serious television, James. We wouldn't fake anything.'

'Good,' said Appleby. 'I'm relieved to hear it.'

He noticed that everyone else at the table seemed to be looking down at their note-pads, trying to conceal ironic micro-smirks, or exchanging sidelong glances, as if sharing a joke to which he was not a party. Did Chrissie murmur something under her breath? He wasn't sure, but it sounded like 'Bless.'

The incident made him realise how proprietorial he felt about everything connected with Harker. This ought to be *his* project, but he now suspected that he had no control over it whatsoever.

*

It was over a month since Appleby had seen Iris. They had spoken on the phone a few times, but he was yearning to be with her. There would have been plenty of time to get back to York that evening, but he rang Jenny and lied... yet again. He had grown used to that over the years, though it still made him cringe every time he did it. The production team were all going for supper at some place in Charlotte Street, he said. It was bound to go on late. Farnstable had invited him to stay at his Islington town house. Yet again he listened for a trace of suspicion or anxiety in Jenny's voice. Yet again he detected none.

'It's been a long time, stranger,' said Iris when he arrived at her flat. She didn't kiss him on the lips, but placed her cheek alongside his, cradling the back of his head in her hand as he enveloped her in his arms. 'I missed you.'

If he hadn't been so overwhelmed with the sheer pleasure of holding her he might have clocked that use of the simple past tense. Not 'I've missed you' or 'I've been missing you'. He might have wondered if 'I missed you' implied an emotion that had finished.

Iris had never been very domestic, and he used to tease her about her pitiful collection of kitchen equipment. When the meeting ended he had taken the tube from Kentish Town to Tottenham Court Road where he called at a posh cookware shop. He picked out a hideously expensive stainless steel sautee pan with a copper base and a glass lid, and headed back north to Crouch End. The Broadway was lined with delis and supermarkets. By the time he reached Iris's flat he was laden with bags, bulging with food and wine.

He took over her kitchen, pouring them both large glasses of chilled New Zealand Sauvignon Blanc as he seared corn-fed, free-range chicken breasts in Tuscan extra-virgin olive oil. He gabbled away as he stirred in diced pancetta, thinly sliced garlic cloves and shallots, chunks of yellow pepper, shitake mushrooms, chopped up cherry tomatoes and black Cypriot olives. He was still complaining about his new shoes as he seasoned everything with sea salt, crushed black pepper, mixed Italian herbs and chicken bouillon from a bottle. By the time he sloshed wine over everything, put the lid on the pan and turned it down to simmer, he was still describing Gordon Fairview's studio.

Nothing could stop his chatter about the theme music, the Box of Tricks offices and the way he felt everything had been whipped out of his hands by Farnstable and his team. When the chicken was nearly ready he stirred in creme fraiche and chopped tarragon leaves and put fresh ciabatta in the oven to heat through. Then he apologised for the long gap in seeing her, explained about the interrogation of Harker and the transcript and how, at last, all the elements of Harker's story seemed to have fallen into place.

All the while she listened to him indulgently like a mother with an excited, prattling child. She threw in questions at appropriate moments and said she thought it all sounded splendid and she couldn't wait to see the programme when it was finished. She was genuinely happy for him and didn't want to spoil his pleasure.

They ate the chicken and warm bread on their knees in her sitting room. She produced fresh pears, oatcakes and a wedge of runny brie for dessert and fished out a bottle of Cointreau one of her new colleagues had brought when she came for dinner. He did a little imitation of a cheesy old advert as he poured it over ice. 'Poot ze two togezair,' he purred in his best Charles Aznavour accent, 'an ze ass melts.' She chuckled, and he asked if he could hear one of her Joan Armatrading albums for old time's sake. They sat on her sofa, silently listening to the music as they sipped the sweet, spicy liqueur.

'That was lovely, Jimmy,' she said after a while, 'and after such a long day. You must be absolutely knackered!'

'I am,' he said, exhaling deeply. Anticipation suddenly coursed through his body as he thought of bed.

But Iris moved to the opposite end of the sofa, drew her knees up under her chin and clasped her arms around her shins.

'Jimmy,' she said quietly. 'Would you mind if we don't have sex or anything tonight?'

'Oh... right... sure... of course,' he mumbled, startled. He did mind, though. In fact he was hugely disappointed. He looked across at her for some sort of signal, but she was staring at her bare toes. He noticed again, with a sharp pang, how slender and perfectly shaped they were, like a teenage girl's feet, without a blemish on the smooth olive skin.

'Is something the matter? Are you all right?' he asked hesitantly.

'Yeah, yeah,' she sighed. 'I'm fine. It's just that I've been feeling really down for a while. I still haven't told you, have I? My father died three weeks ago. The funeral was last week...'

'Oh, Christ!' said Appleby. 'I had no idea. I'm so sorry. Why didn't you tell me? What happened?'

'He had a heart attack,' she said, her eyes filling.

He realised with shame that he had been with her for over three hours and beyond a cursory 'How are you?' when he arrived, he hadn't asked her a single question about herself.

'I'm so, so sorry,' he said. 'I know how close you were...How's your mother taken it?'

'Badly,' said Iris quietly. 'In fact she's devastated. She's gone back to see her sisters in Ravenna for a while. I've a feeling she might stay...'

There was a long pause while Appleby wondered what he could possibly say to console her. 'Do you want to talk about it?'

'No. Not really,' she sniffed. 'Not just now... Let's turn in.'

'My God, poor Iris!' he thought with a chill. 'And what am I like? I've been prattling away all evening. Fifty-one years old and I'm still as self-absorbed as a teenager.'

Exmoor

'No, sir, I haven't got a fucking clue. We heard three shots... No, sir, *three* shots... Christ this reception's bad!... It just sort of *reared up* on end... I said it reared up!... never mind... *the helicopter blew up*!... What!?... *I can't hear*... How would I know that?... I expect...*I would rather imagine they're all fucking dead - sir!*'

As Kot struggled to convey to Forbes what they had just seen, Appleby noticed that his Gore-Tex jacket was hanging over the back of a chair near the front door. Handley had given up on his radio and was on his personal mobile, desperately trying to summon local help. He couldn't get through to anyone. The emergency phone-lines and every police station switchboard in the area were jammed with calls from walkers, pony-trekkers, holiday-cottage-renters, local residents and several people in boats at sea who had seen the crash or heard the explosion.

The two officers were far too preoccupied to notice as Appleby took Jenny firmly by the forearm and put his index finger to his lips. She frowned as he picked up his jacket from the back of a chair and handed her her bag. Nor did the officers notice as he rummaged in the pocket of Kot's coat and pulled out the keys to the Discovery, along with the neat little remote-control unit which operated the compound gate. He mouthed the words, 'Come on!' and pulled Jenny towards the door. He managed to open it almost silently, and they tip-toed across the gravel.

Handley only realised anything was going on when he heard the car doors shutting and the engine start.

'What in heaven's name do you think you're doing?' said Jenny as they lurched down the drive. 'This is insane! Where the hell are you taking me? We were safe in there!'

'You think so?' said Appleby. 'I don't. I don't know what just happened to that helicopter, but whoever's out there, they are heavily armed and they'll be coming for us next. And I, for one, don't want to be here when they arrive. Now do up your seat-belt.'

'But what about the others? We can't just take their car and leave them?'

'Do you think they'd let us go if we asked politely? By the time we finished arguing with them, we'd all be dead! They're big boys. Big boys with guns. They can look after themselves. Anyway, I'm the one these maniacs want to kill, for God's sake!'

His right hand was already out of the car window operating the remote. The gates swung open obligingly briskly. They had almost closed behind them by the time he saw Handley and Kot in the rear-view mirror, chasing them down the drive, shouting and waving frantically.

They had gone about a mile down the unadopted road towards the A399 when Appleby noticed a track veering off to the right through some woodland.

'Maybe we can find a back route into Combe Martin down here,' he said, swerving violently onto the bumpy surface.

'Ouch! Watch out!' called Jenny as her head hit the car roof. 'You're such a lousy driver! I hope you know what you're doing.'

'To be honest with you, my love, I haven't got a fucking clue.'

In the distance they could make out the first sirens as police cars, ambulances and fire-engines raced to the crash site from miles around.

*

The Discovery had just disappeared from view when an extraordinarily dirty Honda Civic rounded the corner. Unlike Appleby, the driver had no idea who had been in the helicopter or how many people he had just blown apart or incinerated. Like Appleby, however, he realised that the game had suddenly and drastically changed. Immediate, decisive action was required. He had one last chance to complete his mission and escape.

The policeman's sketch-map was rough, but proved perfectly functional. The gates of the Angelini compound soon loomed into view. The rifle and the Glock sat beside him on the front passenger seat, both fully loaded. He dropped down from fifth into third gear, lined the car up with the middle of the gates and pushed the accelerator flat to the floor.

'Banzai!' he cackled gleefully as the Honda smashed its way into the compound. 'Japanese Automobile Engineering, One: British Security Gates, Nil!'

*

Forty minutes later Special Branch officers from the Devon and Cornwall police arrived at the house. They found the Honda in the drive. The roof, bonnet and boot were covered with small dents, scratches and scorch-marks. The front bumper, the radiator and the bonnet were all crumpled and the headlights were smashed. The driver's door was open, and the keys were in the ignition. The car's electrical systems were switched on, as though someone had tried to start the engine and failed. Forensics officers later found traces of blood on the soft plastic key-grip and on the key-fob.

The locks on the front door of the house appeared to have been shot away. Kot was sitting on the floor, slumped against a sofa about two metres from the door. Handley was facing the door on the swivel-chair by the bank of security monitors. They were both dead. That night the pathologist told his wife they were the worst gun-shot wounds he had ever seen. More than half of Kot's face was missing. Handley had been eviscerated and a large chunk of his spine was missing. He had virtually been cut in half.

The men were still holding their service pistols, both of which had recently been fired. A bullet from Kot's gun had gone through the floor and was found in a utility room beneath. Handley's bullet was embedded in the wall near the front door. The surrounding spatter-pattern of blood and some strands of human hair around the bullet-hole suggested he had wounded his attacker before he died. The blood was later found to belong to a third individual, and to match the blood on the Honda's key-fob.

The officers' Land Rover had gone. There was no sign of the Applebys.

*

An outsider in Forbes's office might have described the atmosphere as borderline hysterical. The army had agreed to follow a common public line that the Chinook crash was a freak accident during a routine training exercise. But only for the time being. They wanted to organise their own investigation. Forbes was determined to get his own people down there first. But who could he send? The job really needed military specialists.

The team who had died in the Chinook had been hastily assembled from several units in Specialist Operations. Their various bosses were clamouring for information, and it was only a matter of time before the dead officers' families began to get wind of the disaster. TV and radio stations were already broadcasting eye-witness accounts, and several of these witnesses reported hearing shots before the crash. Members of Parliament were demanding answers in the House. Throughout the day, half the world's media seemed to arrive behind a hastily erected barrier outside New Scotland Yard.

Forbes had barely finished trying to get some sense out of Kot when a new report had come in from a senior officer in Leicester. A prominent feminist professor of Political Science, a woman of Egyptian descent, had been knocked down on her way home from an evening meeting of her Muslim Professional Women's Group at the university. A small black four-by-four with bull-bars had mounted the kerb near her house and driven along the pavement straight at her at an estimated speed of forty miles an hour. Her pelvis had been shattered. She had suffered a fractured skull and severe internal injuries and died on the way to hospital. She was four months pregnant. A neighbour had seen the incident, but the car had disappeared into the night, and he didn't get the number. Did Forbes think this could be a terrorism-related assassination?

Then there were the possible sightings of the Abramskys' Volvo in Doncaster, Cheltenham, Stranraer and Aberystwyth. They would all have to be checked out, and would almost certainly prove to be red herrings. A fifth tip-off came from a fence in Golders Green who kept the local CID off his back by grassing up his clients. He had heard of a vehicle answering that description being stowed in a hired lock-up half a mile away, 'by a nice young Jewish boy,' apparently. That one sounded more promising and should be followed up smartly – except that Forbes had virtually run out of officers.

All the while more and more details were coming through about the events around Exmoor. The very thought of what had happened turned Forbes's stomach. Who the hell were they dealing with? One fat little Pakistani in a karakul hat or a team of Taliban insurgents armed with ground-to-air missiles? How had they got into the country? Where were they now? Forbes felt as if he was about to be completely swamped. A phrase about *'tiny vessels on a storm-tossed sea'* swam into his head, he couldn't remember where from. Then Charlie Drucker walked in.

'Just had a call from my old chum De Groot in Amsterdam, sir.'

'Go on.'

'They rang that chap van Stumpe's mobile. He didn't answer, but they got a fix on it. He'd been at some disused battery chicken shed near the Belgian border. The local police rushed over and found a body hanging from a roof-girder. Everyone else had vanished.'

'Who was it? Was it van Stumpe?'

'No. It was some young male nurse, apparently. He'd been shot in the head, but he was naked and covered in burns. Looks like someone really went to town on him before they finished him off.'

'So where's Appleby's pal now, then?'

'That's just it, sir. They managed to pick up the signal again somewhere to the west of Antwerp. They tracked it to Ostend before they lost contact.'

'Ostend? That could mean he's coming over here. Oh, my God. That's all we need. Alert the relevant ferry ports will you.'

'I already have, sir... One thing, though. If he's been kidnapped, how come they let him keep his mobile?'

'I dunno. Maybe he hid it.'

'But they'd search him, wouldn't they?'

'How the hell would I know, Charlie? For all I know he shoved it up his bum! Why don't you ring his number? If it's on vibrate you might give him a thrill.'

*

That night Forbes was called to a meeting with a group from the Assessments Staff of the Joint Intelligence Committee in Whitehall. He hated these occasions. Dealing with the competing outfits in Counter Terrorism Command was bad enough. The tight-lipped, over-educated spooks from MI5 and MI6, with their enigmatic utterances and secretive agendas gave him the creeps. The civil servants were even worse. As for the politicians...

A young MI6 officer called Giles Chalmers gave a briefing to this sub-committee of a sub-committee. He had a shock of blonde hair over his forehead. 'Where do they get these useless public-school twats from?' Forbes muttered under his breath as he took his seat. 'He looks about fourteen!'

The briefing was largely based on information received from Mossad and the CIA, said Chalmers. Britain had almost certainly been targeted by an organisation known as 'The Tribes of Abraham'. Their primary aim was to wipe out Harkerism and to destroy any documents or other artefacts that appear to give the movement historical validity.

A smug-looking junior Foreign Office minister introduced himself as Conrad Weekes. 'Christ!' muttered Forbes. 'Not another fucking boy-scout.'

'I think you'll find the Tribes of Abraham are just a bunch of over-enthusiastic God-botherers,' said Weekes. 'According to our information, it's an ecumenical organisation for the promotion of mutual understanding among fundamentalist bigots.'

'I presume you're referring to the collection of fellows with extravagant facial hair and comedy headgear,' said Chalmers. 'Unfortunately they are probably just a front, recruited to lend a veneer of respectability to the organisation. It's the people who are backing them who should concern us…and the people they've already sent over here.'

'I'm afraid our normal sources aren't proving terribly helpful as yet,' said Yvonne Wilberforce, the acting deputy head of MI5. 'There's no connection with Al Qaeda or any other known group, as far as we can tell. What can your people contribute to our grasp of this situation, Commander Forbes?'

'Nothing much, I'm afraid, Ma'am,' said Forbes, 'beyond the fact that the country appears to be crawling with heavily armed religious psychopaths, and they've already killed half my men.'

'Let's not forget the two army pilots either,' said Wilberforce. 'And the FBI are still convinced that the chap who shot their agent in Washington is on the loose over here somewhere. They're really pushing us on that one. They want blood.'

'And what about the good Professor Appleby?' asked Chalmers. 'I had the dubious pleasure of meeting him once, and I can't begin to imagine why anyone should think a nonentity like that is worth killing. But since they evidently do, who's looking after him and his wife at the moment?'

'I'm afraid to say they've slipped off the radar,' said Forbes sheepishly.

'So you've lost them,' said Wilberforce. 'Have they been abducted?'

'It's possible. One of our cars is missing. The killer, or killers might have taken them off in that, or they might have used it to escape. We've got every officer in the south-west looking for them.'

'No tracking device in the car?' asked Chalmers.

'No.' Forbes let out a sigh of almost infinite weariness. 'I sometimes think it would be simpler just to let these maniacs bump the bugger off. Then maybe they'd all go home.'

'That thought crossed my mind too,' said Wilberforce, with an icy little smile.

'I was joking,' said Forbes.

'I wasn't.'

York

'Is it not wondrous how that the pampered prizes of the garden, for all the artful husbandman's endeavours, must one day wither and rot, e'en to the farthest reaches of their roots, ne'er to bear bloom nor fruit again? And yet one tiny seed, carelessly dropt upon a wayside bank by the scurrying farmer's boy, might lie forgotten and asleep i' the heedless earth, through drought and flood, through fire and frost, for years unnumbered, until upon some bright spring day it will burst forth into the welcoming air, outbraving all around in the strutting vigour of its youth.'

—*Sir Thomas Cranham, The Colloquies Book II, Number 22*

'They've asked me to suggest some names,' said Appleby, '...for the congregation.'

He was in his study at home. Jenny had gone out shopping, and he had taken the opportunity to call Iris. He was telling her about the forthcoming re-enactment.

'Uh-huh.' Her tone was inscrutable. Appleby hated having conversations like this over the phone. He wanted to see her face, to gauge her feelings.

'Numbers are a bit limited, I'm afraid,' he said. 'They can't guarantee places for everyone. It's a bit awkward in a way...'

'Don't worry about it, Jimmy. I know you can't invite me. We've never been "official", have we?'

'Well, you could always come as an interested historian... as a colleague.'

'And skulk around at the back pretending we're just professional acquaintances? No thanks.'

'Look, I... It's just that you... you know... since that first trip to Amsterdam when this whole thing kicked off. Remember that dreary hotel?'

'Of course I do!' she chuckled. 'The breakfast was dreadful. The sex was good, though.'

'Thanks.' Appleby gave a happy little grunt. 'That weekend was special, wasn't it?'

'It was. But this time you should be with your wife. This is her gig.'

*

But Jenny didn't want to go either. That really threw him, not least because he had asked Box of Tricks to send invitations to most of her family. In fact Ralph and Zeta had already accepted before Jenny told him she wouldn't come. Then Lucy and her theatre director husband accepted, asking if they could bring their three children. Even more surprisingly, Toby and his second wife accepted. At least Toby's children couldn't come. They were away at school.

Jenny was in the kitchen stewing rhubarb when he finally drew an explanation from her. She told him the whole idea of the service made her feel profoundly uncomfortable. She knew how much it meant to him, but it was still essentially just a historical exercise for him, a bit of theatre. But from everything he had told her, she knew that Sir Nicholas Harker took these ceremonies deadly seriously, and she simply couldn't get away from the feeling that they were a calculated affront to her personal faith.

'But you've attended Catholic masses in the past,' he protested. 'And what about that Hindu wedding you went to? Or the time that woman took you to her synagogue?'

'Those were different. I was just getting a taste of a friend's form of worship. Besides, they have ancient traditions of their own…and they all believe in God!'

Her sudden vehemence startled him. She turned to face him clutching her wooden spoon tightly against her chest, almost as if it was a crucifix, providing spiritual protection.

'When it comes down to it,' she said, 'it feels to me that your Sir Nicholas Harker was deliberately setting out to supplant *my* church, to undermine *my* religion!'

After a moment she seemed to calm down. 'I'm sorry, Jimmy. I do know how important this is to you,' she said. He thought it strange that, having been so defiant a moment ago, she was now placatory, but clearly avoiding eye-contact. 'You probably think I'm being completely irrational, but it just feels *wrong*. I'm not going to come.'

Appleby was startled and hurt. However detached she had become in the last few years, Jenny had usually at least feigned mild interest in his research. She had actually gone out of her way to help him occasionally, like getting him the transcript of Harker's interrogation. He was sure there was more to this reaction than she was letting on. But in secular, tolerant, ecumenical, all-faith-and-no-faith, twenty-first century Britain, it seemed that his wife was as adamantly hostile to Harker's philosophy as the church authorities of 1594 – albeit without the threat of murderous violence.

Appleby would remember this conversation vividly for the rest of his life. It was the first time that he discovered that Harker's homespun, if unusually ritualised form of agnostic humanism could hit raw nerves among modern believers. It certainly wasn't the last.

*

Satisfied that Appleby was 'across' Harker's original texts, Chrissie had agreed to work with him devising the actual form of the service for the televised re-enactment. She even went with him to Amsterdam where van Stumpe found them office space at the Institute, and he spent three happy days taking her through Harker's manuscripts.

Cranham's chest had contained several of his '*Rites*'. One, for instance, roughly paralleled Morning Prayers in the Elizabethan '*Book of Common Prayer*'. The manuscript Appleby had found first, entitled '*The Common Rite*' (also the one Bishop Cantwell had got hold of, apparently) was loosely based on the service of the Eucharist. In fact the act of '*Attestation*' was scheduled to occur at the point where a church congregation would have taken Holy Communion.

Did Harker see it as some kind of equivalent? Appleby was sure he did and had written a long endnote suggesting why. There were also shorter ceremonies for special occasions: births, marriages, deaths and so on, though for the purposes of the programme, these could be put to one side.

Between them, Appleby and Chrissie put together a service which would last about an hour and ten minutes. It combined elements from both the longer Rites, including one of Harker's '*Contemplations*'. It included pauses for songs and instrumental interludes and would reach its dramatic climax in the live '*Attestations*'.

Having made Farnstable agree that none of these confessions could be scripted, Appleby now began to worry about what would happen if nobody came forward. He mentioned this to Chrissie. For some reason she didn't seem bothered at all.

*

As the day approached, Appleby was getting more and more nervous. He spent hours pacing his study, rehearsing his script, though he tried not to do this when Jenny was at home. For a man who enjoyed long conversations with his best friend and who seemed rather good at listening to others, Harker did an awful lot of talking during his services. Appleby was really going to be in the spotlight, and in more senses than one.

He was getting particularly anxious about how the service would sound. Anything written in the language of Shakespeare and the King James Bible has a certain resonance, especially for an English audience. But that didn't mean that some Elizabethan and Jacobean drama wasn't third rate. He often found himself swept along by Harker's rhetoric, but what if the sentiments came across as trite or banal? He would be declaiming this stuff before a highly critical audience. There would be people there who would enjoy nothing more than pouring scorn on Harker – and on Appleby himself. As for the extravagant costume and that false beard... well that didn't bear thinking about.

*

They filmed the Rite on a crisp, cold evening in early February. Appleby was told to be at the Merchant Adventurers' Hall by 11.00 in the morning. It seemed absurdly early given that the service wasn't due to start until 7.00 pm. The pale grey sky had a strangely luminous quality, and as he cycled through the city, past shops and cafes, all brightly lit, large powdery flakes of snow began to fall. It was a busy Saturday, but a hush seemed to descend on the narrow, quaintly irregular streets. It all seemed vaguely portentous.

As he arrived at the hall he was surprised to see a small film crew, complete with lights and a fur-covered microphone, conducting interviews by the steps. Two women in their late twenties were talking to a camera. He had no idea who they were.

'Hi,' said a buxom Goth in a broad West Yorkshire accent. 'My name's Karen, and this is my best mate, Donna. We both work at t'Raven Beauties salon in Leeds, and also we're both Wicca women with a general interest in alternative lifestyles.'

'So why are you here tonight, ladies?' asked the interviewer. Appleby realised with a jolt that it was Jeremy Dilke.

' 'Cause Diggory here said it'd be a right laugh,' said Donna, pointing to an assistant producer who was hovering sheepishly nearby.

'Sorry, you can't say that!' laughed Dilke. 'I'll ask that again. Why are you here tonight, ladies? Why are you interested in this event?'

Donna tried to look serious. 'We've come here tonight because we're right open-minded when it comes to spirituality, and we want to see if this new cult has owt new to offer us, spirituality-wise.'

'We want to see if it reaches t'parts t'other religions don't reach!' said Karen, whereupon they both collapsed in a fit of giggles.

'Thanks, ladies,' Dilke grinned. 'That was terrific!'

'6.15 sharp, please,' shouted Diggory as the girls tottered away. 'Don't be late, now!'

Appleby squeezed past as a runner ushered the next member of the congregation into position.

'Hi there! My mates call me Duke. I'm a chicken-sexer from Diss in Norfolk and I'm a born-again Christian…'

Appleby made his way up the steps into the hall where he met Farnstable. Farnstable handed him straight over to Chrissie. Chrissie introduced him to Jake, the director, before handing him over to Natasha who was doing costumes. Natasha took him downstairs to a side-room where Olga was waiting.

Olga was his dresser. She made him change into a doublet, hot itchy hose, a vast floppy shirt and a ridiculous ruff. He had shaved especially closely that morning, but it still rubbed uncomfortably under his chin. She produced a huge embroidered cloak, faithfully copied from the one in his treasured portrait. Finally she put a black woollen cap with square corners on his head. It came low over the back of his neck, was even hotter and itchier than the tights and had to be held in place with hair-grips.

Jake walked him through his movements during the service, marking the places he was to stand with tape on the floor. He told him to speak up clearly and not to gabble. And no, there would not be time for a rehearsal.

At 12.30 Claire arrived, accompanied by a bubbly publicist from Channel 4 called Andrea. They had an extremely fat journalist in-tow and took Appleby off to talk to him as they ate lunch in an adjoining car park. He was a freelance, writing what he called a 'colour piece' for The Times. The poor chap could hardly squeeze into the seats on the converted double-decker bus that served as the location canteen. It turned out he had read English at York when Appleby was doing his first degree, so they spent most of the time gossiping about common acquaintances. He had spent a year in a house on Appleby's square and had even seen one of his revues, which, he said, 'could best be described as dreadful'. The food from the 'honey-wagon' was heavy and stodgy, typical film-crew fodder, Andrea said, and Appleby found himself nodding off during the interview.

The afternoon passed fitfully. There was another 'blocking' session; they tested the lighting and did a sound check, and he went over his script three or four times. By the time he was called by the make-up girls, he was hot, itchy, bored, tired and listless. It seemed like the worst possible preparation for any kind of performance.

Then suddenly the audience were filtering into the hall. He peeked out from behind a screen at the back of the small stage and saw his sister Kate, her husband Rob and brother-in-law Kevin. They had brought his parents in. His father was sitting in his wheelchair at the end of the front row with his mother beside him, apparently oblivious of her surroundings. He had to pop out and say hello.

'You look a picture!' said Barbara as he bent down to kiss her.

'Hello, Jimmy!' said Tom with a broad grin. 'What's the fancy-dress for?'

'It's for the ceremony, Dad. I'm supposed to be Sir Nicholas Harker.'

'Who?'

'Oh God!' he groaned, grimacing at Kate who winked back at him. 'Sir Nicholas Harker! He's the man I've been writing the books about, Dad! Remember?'

'Oh aye. Well you look a right Charlie, if you don't mind my saying so! Is this the school play then? What is it? *Murder in the Cathedral?*'

'I'll talk to you afterwards, Dad. Okay?'

Tom beamed back at him.

When Appleby looked up he saw that Gordon Fairview was busy arranging his consort of musicians and the small choir by the wall to the left of the stage. They were all in Elizabethan costume too. Fairview turned round, caught his eye and gave a friendly little wave. 'Break a leg, James!' he called.

A small team of APs were getting the congregation to sign some kind of form as they came in. He must ask Farnstable what that was. Ushers, also in costume, were handing out the *Order of Service*, which was prefaced by a brief essay by Dilke explaining the historical background. Waiters, also in costume, were giving out drinks. 'Wassail cup?' they said. 'Spiced mead?' 'Mulled country wine?' Was Farnstable trying to get everyone merry so they would lose their inhibitions and respond more? That was risky. There was a smell of incense in the air too, and he noticed little clumps of joss-sticks burning around the room. Whose idea was *that*?

By now the candles and torches had been lit and the place had taken on a mellow glow, like... like what exactly? Then he remembered – that first Midnight Mass with Jenny in Norwich nineteen years ago. Once again that sense of warm communal well-being began to creep over him, until he was suffused with the glow of it. Suddenly everything felt all right. He slipped back behind the screen.

Ten minutes later Jeremy Dilke's microphone-enhanced voice rose above the chatter

'Ladies and gentlemen! Boys and girls...'

He began by asking them all to switch off their mobile phones and put away packets of sweets and snacks.

'...Ladies and gentlemen, we are about to enjoy a rare privilege! We are about to participate in what is probably the first truly Humanist ceremony ever performed in a Christian country, a ceremony which has not been enacted for over four hundred years!'

He reminded them that there would be responses for the congregation and asked them all to 'give it a bit of welly'.

'...And now it is my privilege to introduce our star and your Mediator for the evening! In the role of Sir Nicholas Harker of Swively, Wiltshire, please put your hands together and give a warm Merchant Adventurers' welcome to York University's very own...Doctor James Appleby!'

Gordon Farview raised his baton, and the consort struck up a brisk melody. It was pretty and rather catchy, perhaps a touch melancholy too, somewhere between a wistful anthem and a perky Tudor folk tune.

The First Assistant Director turned to him and gave the signal. Appleby was on...

The congregation applauded as he stepped to the lectern at the front of the small stage. As he waited for the music to finish, he surveyed the crowd. There were over a hundred people in the hall. He had been warned that some well known faces might be there, including nationally famous humanists, atheists and faith leaders, but it was the personal connections he noticed. Even without Jenny or Iris there, he felt like a drowning man whose life was passing before his eyes. His parents were in the front row. Beside his mother sat Ivor Gruffudd, also using a wheelchair by now, but smiling broadly. Kate and her family sat behind them. Behind Kate sat Ralph and Zeta with Toby and his wife. To their side were Lucy, the theatre director and their children.

Across the aisle sat Phyllida Trask and Hermione Green, his editor from Shaftesbury. They had been joined by Claire, Andrea and the fat chap from *The Times*. It was probably just as well that he did not know that the four people sitting behind them were all journalists too. To his delight he saw that Phyllida had brought Piet van Stumpe and the Director of the Renaissance Institute. Why hadn't Piet told him he was coming? The Director was whispering earnestly to Philpott, the Church of England archivist.

Further back he could see Pete Elyot with his latest boyfriend and Matthew Featherstone and his wife with a clump of other colleagues from the university. The Charltons were there from Swively sitting with Farnstable and his wife. Then right at the back he saw Norman Skyne from Despenser. Who had invited *him*? Not Dilke surely? What a cheek! He was talking to Andrew Howland, both getting ready to mock and sneer no doubt. Those two should get on like a house on fire! Hmm… maybe that wasn't the best choice of words under the circumstances…

The music stopped. Appleby looked down at his script and began. His voice surprised him. The hours of pacing had paid off. He was calm, confident, resonant and warm. The service opened with a communal affirmation of the *Ten Principles of the Goodly Life*, Harker's equivalent of the Ten Commandments:

Mediator:
*Beloved Kindred, let us open our hearts, one unto another, in the presence
of that common Spirit that is both within us and amongst us all...*

Appleby tensed. Would the audience respond? They did – most of
them – and with surprising gusto. Maybe that booze wasn't such a bad
idea after all.

People:
So let it be!

That was encouraging. He pressed on:

Mediator:
*The Spirit that is within us speaketh unto us all. Here is the truth that
guideth. Let us hear that truth and own it as ours, from the cock's crow at
the dawning of the day, to the guttering of the last candle at eventide, yea,
and through all the darkest watches of the night.*

People:
*For in the truth of the Spirit, mercy abideth. Let our Spirit know
mercy and show it unto all, that mercy may be shown unto us.*

Some of the congregation stumbled during the longer responses,
tripped by unfamiliar phrasing and syntax. Yet they kept going and,
for the most part, stayed in unison.

Harker began with an exhortation to avoid the worship of 'false gods',
Did he in fact mean *all* Gods? The congregation were then exhorted
to be temperate and avoid anger, to attend contemplative ceremonies
regularly, to honour their families, as well as their neighbours and not
to murder anyone.

Appleby was wondering how many of the audience had realised
how closely this sequence paralleled the Ten Commandments. As if to

answer his question, a young man in a tangerine cravat who was standing half way down the hall on the right, let out an angry and scornful 'Oh, for heaven's sake!'

Appleby had not noticed that there were two young women with camcorders on their shoulders hovering in the aisle, like the cameramen at awards ceremonies ready to get close-ups of audience reactions. One of them made a bee-line for Mr Tangerine-Cravat. But if anything his interjection seemed to spur the rest of the congregation to respond more emphatically. '*Let the Spirit incline us ever to walk in the ways of peace and justice!*' they chanted.

Appleby ploughed his way through being faithful (not his own strong-point, he realised), not stealing or cheating people and not lying (nor that). The last injunction was against envy and covetousness. He had been worrying about this: Harker could be very wordy:

Mediator:
Let the Spirit free us from all covetousness and envy, which do lie as a stagnant pond within the heart, smothering the Spirit in congregations of foul and pestilential vapours. Let us ever nurture within ourselves, and likewise within our neighbours, the will to diligence, to work with zeal, to artful invention and to proper pride in the craft of hand and mind, all of which shall bring joy to the heart and shall mightily feed the Spirit. Let us never be led by jealousy to slight the works of our neighbour, to belittle or to undermine those whose works, through their diligence, invention, pride in their craft or the uneven gifts of Nature, may surpass our own.

To Appleby's immense relief the audience seemed to be keeping up. They answered robustly: '*Let the Spirit so free us, and inscribe these principles within our hearts and the hearts of our Kindred for ever and always.*'

Mr Tangerine-Cravat could bear it no longer. Appleby found out later that he was a mature theology student, hoping to be ordained as an Anglican priest. He pushed his way to the aisle where he held up his Order of Service, exclaimed 'This is pure blasphemy!' threw it theatrically to the floor and stalked out.

His exit was accompanied by loud mutterings: 'How rude!', 'Really!' and 'Shame!'

Appleby heaved a sigh of relief. Apart from this minor outburst, he had cleared the first hurdle with barely a stumble. There followed a brief exchange from the opening of Harker's equivalent of Morning Prayers.

Mediator:
Let the Spirit open our lips.

People:
That our mouths may rejoice in the Spirit and give praise for it.

At the end of this sequence, Gordon Fairview turned to the choir and raised his baton. They sang unaccompanied:

As swift darts the martin i' the warm summer eve,
Let his quick flight and certain my Spirit achieve,
For thus with the wings of the birds of the sky,
Ever beauteous, unfettered, my Spirit shall fly.

As bold hops the robin when th'plough turns the ground
With his dexterous daring, my Spirit abound,
That with the quick eyes of the birds of the soil,
Courageous, my Spirit shall fruitfully toil.

As slow glides the swan on the smooth autumn stream,
Be my Spirit reflected in bright rivers' gleam,
And thus with the grace of the fowl of the lake,
Let calm contemplation, my Spirit awake.

As soft sings the dove in the dovecot each day,
Her harmonies sweet bless my Spirit at play,
As the birds of the household bring food, sport and joy,
Let labours and pleasures my Spirit alloy.

As high soars the lark in the clear summer air,
Let us strive ever upward our Spirits to bear,
Entranc'd by the flight of the birds of the sky,
Ever beauteous, unfettered our Spirits shall fly.

Appleby and Chrissie had nick-named this 'The Birdie Song'. They had selected it because they thought it was rather pretty, and hoped the congregation would enjoy the references to common English birds. Fairview's music, however, had turned it into something spine-tingling, full of subtle, haunting harmonies. In the last verse, a boy treble soared off into a descant which seemed to hover in the air like the lark itself. Appleby was entranced. The congregation burst into spontaneous applause at the end.

At this point in their highly truncated *Rite* they had decided to insert a *Contemplation*. These were Harker's equivalent of sermons, and about as preachy as he got. He generally avoided Bible stories. Most of his themes came from classical sources and English history. Aesop's *Fables* were particular favourites. In the end Appleby and Chrissie had settled on a familiar yarn:

Now, oh my Kindred, be ye seated in Contemplation of the deeds of man. The story is told that in those antic times, unnumbered generations e'er the coming of our English forefathers, when the Emperor of haughty Rome held dominion over the fair woods and waters, the fields and fells of these isles, there was a Queen among the British whose name was Boadicca...

Appleby pronounced the name according to Harker's peculiar spelling. There followed a long and lurid account of the Boudiccan rebellion, as recounted by the Roman historians, emphasising the Iceni queen's appalling maltreatment, but dwelling in graphic detail on the atrocities visited on the Roman inhabitants of Colchester and London, especially the mutilation of the Roman women. Appleby sensed that the boys in the audience were on the edge of their seats, while the girls cringed in horror. The final description of the slaughter of the British horde was worthy of a Hollywood blockbuster.

It was laced throughout with thoughtful asides and sharp psychological insights. Appleby felt the piece carried two separate morals. The first could be summarised as 'Don't lose your temper: you'll only make things worse', or as Harker put it: '*For burning rage will ever lay to waste the one who feedeth it within his heart.*' The second moral seemed to be: 'If you are going to take on a powerful enemy, get your preparation right and make damn sure you win.' This struck Appleby as pragmatic, rather than uplifting.

Appleby scanned the congregation's faces, looking for signs of inattention. He noticed a middle-aged woman in a chunky cardigan about ten rows back, apparently grimacing in pain. As he finished, she let out a loud strangulated gulp.

'Oh god! What have I done?' she cried in a middle-class accent. Appleby paused as the nearest camera-girl swung round for a close-up. 'I'm so sorry!' the woman continued. 'It's just that my daughter was being bullied at school.' Her words erupted like a geyser, 'and they started sending her these vicious messages on her mobile phone and writing vile obscene things about her on the internet, and she thought she knew who was doing it, and I went round to the girl's house and I just lost it! I just flew at her on her own doorstep, and now the police want to interview me, and I've just made everything much, much worse! I'm so sorry to interrupt! It's just that what you were saying really got to me...'

Appleby hadn't expected this. He would have to improvise. 'Be collected, good Sister,' he heard himself saying. 'Come thou before these thy Kindred at the time of Attestation and unburden thine heart, for through them shall thy Spirit perhaps find consolation.'

'Nice ad lib!' muttered Chrissie in her vantage point behind Jack's monitor in a side-room at the back. 'Where did *that* come from?'

'Thank you, Sir Nicholas,' said Mrs Chunky Cardigan. 'I will.'

And so the service proceeded. The first 'hymn' was a rather sombre little number about not fearing death, because the Spirit lives on in the love of others, but Fairview had come up with another hummable tune and most people joined in enthusiastically. In the middle of it all Appleby was delighted to hear the voices of Ralph and Zeta rising full-throated above the throng, blithely unconcerned about any incompatibility with their own beliefs.

Appleby delivered another mini-sermon, roughly when the priest would have read an 'Epistle' in a church service. It involved a story about some English privateers who fell into the hands of the Spanish and were tortured by the Inquisition. The moral was that you always have to stand up for your beliefs, even if that involves horrible consequences. Proclaiming something to be true just because someone was threatening you, said Harker, devalued the nature of truth itself. It did no one any good in the end. Appleby wondered if Harker had remembered that one during his own interrogation.

The consort played another short piece. Then Appleby read a rather complicated statement of faith in the Spirit, a sort of god-free equivalent of the version of the Nicene Creed in use in Harker's day. That provoked another walk-out, this time by three exasperated evangelicals.

The choir sang another poem as if it was a psalm:

Our lives are but frail earthen vessels. Within our hearts do we bear the love of the generations. Let us live well, that their lives may ever be held in honour...

Finally it was time for the *Attestations*. Picking up on a description in *The Colloquies*, Bilbo had designed an 'Attestation Stool', and placed it in front of Appleby's lectern, facing the congregation. It was like a short section of a pew where the *Attestor* could either sit facing the congregation or kneel, resting his or her forearms on a narrow shelf.

It was clear from Cranham's diaries that the business of *Attestation* had grown out of the informal discussions of disputes, grudges and grievances that had begun in Harker's early gatherings. Yet, as Appleby had explained to Chrissie, these acts of public confession did parallel an element in the Anglican service of Holy Communion. The instructions to priests in the Elizabethan *Book of Common Prayer* specified that no one who was known to be an '*evil liver*' should take communion lest it offend his fellow parishioners. He could only be allowed to do so if he had '*openly declared himself to have truly repented and amended his former naughty life*'.

Similarly '*those betwixt whom he [the curate] perceiveth malice and hatred to reign*' were not '*to be partakers of the Lord's Table until he know them to be reconciled.*' If either or both of the warring parties were prepared to '*make amends for that he…hath offended*' and to '*forgive from the bottom of his heart all that the other hath trespassed against him*', then they were welcome back. Harker had, in fact, simply incorporated an element of parish life, which, no doubt poor Parson Wesson was failing to provide. Once again, Harker's preamble echoed the language of the Prayer Book:

'*Let us hearken unto them, not with wrath or the cry for vengeance, but guide them that they may make true amends and restitution and their Spirit be healed.*'

The congregation replied and the dialogue continued:

We shall so guide them.
Let us understand the torment and the fear in the Spirit that is moved to confess. And let us console them in their moment of truth.
We shall so console them.

As Appleby concluded, the congregation seemed to have fallen into a hypnotic hush. He left a short pause for effect...

Let he or she that will do so, now come forth to Attest.

The moment of truth had arrived. Chrissie timed it: the silence lasted precisely ten seconds. It felt like ten hours. Someone near the back on the right stood up. It was the Goth called Karen. Appleby had an awful thought. Is she a plant? But then six-year-old Zoe, Lucy's third (and probably accidental) child, stood up. Appleby saw the assistant director waving frantically at the Goth to sit down. Zoe made her way to the front.

'I done something naughty, Uncle Jimmy,' she said.

The congregation tittered. Appleby decided he had to stay in character.

'And wouldst thou like to attest what thou hast done before thy Kindred, gentle child, that thou mayst make amends and they may forgive thee?'

'What does *attest* mean Uncle Jimmy?

'Tell these nice people what you did.'

'All right.'

'Then sit upon the bench and attest to thy Kindred, my child.'

Zoe sat down, looking back at Appleby for a cue.

'Speak, child. What hast thou done that is naughty?'

'My older brother wouldn't give me any of his big pack of Monster Munch, even though Mum said he should. But I know where he hid his magazine with bare women in, so I took it and I put it in the bin, right down at the bottom where it's wet and stinky.'

'You little bitch!' said a breaking male voice from somewhere near Lucy.

'Sorr-ee,' said Zoe. The congregation burst into gales of laughter. Zoe looked confused.

'How shall this child make amends to her brother?' asked Appleby.

'Make amends!?' Zeta called out imperiously. 'We should give her a medal!'

'It's still stealing, though, innit?' called a young man near the back. 'Them stroke mags cost money, you know.'

Before Appleby knew it the whole congregation was engaged in an impassioned discussion on pornography. It was all evil! Not if it was consensual! It exploited and degraded women! No it didn't; it exploited the saddos who bought it! Anyway it was only natural for teenage boys to want to look at the stuff! But it gives them completely false ideas about sexual relationships! The discussion went on so long and got so heated that Jake waved frantically at Appleby to cut it short.

'Peace my Kindred!' he called magisterially. 'Now how will you make amends to your brother?' he asked Zoe.

'What if I give him my pocket-money for two weeks so he can buy something else?' she said.

'So long as it's not more porn!' someone shouted.

'And he should give her her own packet of Monster Munch!' said Lucy.

'How say you to this?' said Appleby to his nephew, who looked as if he wished the earth would open up and swallow him. 'Wilt thou thus be reconciled?'

'Okay,' he mumbled, almost inaudibly.

'Then are we happily resolved,' said Appleby. 'Well done, Zoe!' and the congregation applauded delightedly as she scurried back to her seat.

'Who else will come forth to Attest?'

Karen the Goth started to get up again, but this time Mrs Chunky-Cardigan beat her to it. When she got to the stool she confessed to slapping the cyber-bully about the face, very hard indeed. Someone offered to go round and 'finish the job' with a baseball bat. Most of the assembled Kindred were sympathetic and felt that she had been right to confront the girl, but they also felt that like

Queen Boudicca, her use of violence had been foolhardy and excessive, and set a bad example. She should apologise to the girl and face the consequences. Was she sure she had got the right girl anyway? A young man announced himself as a computer hacker and said he could easily check that out. Then someone suggested that the bully should be shamed publicly for what she had done. The hacker said he could pass her details to the entire congregation and they should deluge her with electronic remonstrances. If that failed they would pin up notices describing what she had done all round her neighbourhood.

Appleby began to feel as if had let a genie out of a bottle. Poor Karen the Goth never made it as far as the aisle as the Attestations became increasingly serious. An elderly man had committed an act of spiteful vandalism in his neighbour's front garden. A sexually frustrated middle-aged woman had had sex with a male prostitute, paying with her husband's money. Entering into the spirit of things, one of the journalists got up and confessed to regularly inventing quotations from people he'd never even spoken to.

The urge to 'fess up' seemed infectious. Once they got the idea that the congregation would hear them with a degree of sympathy and make, for the most part, constructive suggestions as to what they should do, people couldn't wait to unburden themselves. Even Appleby's grown-up in-laws were not immune. Ralph and Zeta were astonished to learn, along with everyone else in the hall, that their son Toby had blown £20,000 in one night at a casino. At one stage the would-be confessors had formed a small queue. Finally Karen the Goth made it to the stool.

'I'd like to confess to being a fake!' she said. 'That lad Diggory,' and she pointed straight at the culprit, 'gave me fifty quid to come up and say that I've been shagging my best friend Donna's hubby. But I never would, and anyway he's dead ugly! So I took t'money to tell a big fat lie. And Donna got t'same to say she were nicking from t'till at t'shop when she never. So I'd like to attest that I were going to make a false *attestation*! So what you all got to say to that, then?'

In this case the consensus among the congregation was that the real fault lay with the production company. The Goths should buy themselves a drink and give the rest of the cash to charity. Box of Tricks should be reported to OFCOM. Appleby looked at Farnstable at the back of the hall. He seemed to be examining some cobwebs in the roof-beams and whistling.

Chrissie realised that it was time to wrap things up. She appeared at the back of the hall making increasingly frantic throat-cutting gestures to Appleby, who by now was only too happy to oblige. With a sense of relief he returned to his script:

Beloved Kindred, I pray you be of good heart. Let us now come together in song.

The congregation stood up. Fairview raised his baton again, and the choir cleared their throats. The consort struck up a rousing tune. Everybody sang:

Let ever bright the Spirit burn
That warms my earthly life
That guides me as the seasons turn
And turns my heart from strife

And when the winter's icy winds
My aching limbs beset
My Spirit, 'tis my hearth aglow
With pot o'er fire a-simm'ring slow
Where love of Kindred I shall know
And all my hopes beget
And all my joys beget

...and so on for three more verses, one for each season. When the secular hymn ended Appleby read the final blessing:

Peace be among us all, Beloved Kindred. Now, as we depart this our gathering, let us reflect in tranquility upon that which hath been said and sung here today, that it may help us all the better to live our lives. And let us ever sustain and succour, aid and comfort each other, forever guided by that Spirit that is within us and amongst us all.

And it was all over. The congregation burst into hearty applause. This quickly morphed into an excited hubbub as people started discussing the service, the music, Harker's rather innocent philosophy and, above all, what they had heard during the *Attestations*.

Jeremy Dilke and a small film crew waited near the exit, pulling celebrities and experts to one side for instant reactions. Diggory and another crew ambushed the 'ordinary members of the public' recruited by Box of Tricks for the same purpose, although they conspicuously avoided the two Leeds Goth beauticians. The computer hacker took up position by the outside door at the bottom of the steps, collecting email addresses from anyone willing to participate in his campaign to shame the cyber-bullies.

At the back of the hall Appleby spotted Farnstable deep in conversation with Claire. He saw him squeeze her hand, before leaning over and kissing her cheek. Was he hitting on her? For heaven's sake!

He tried to make his way to see Ivor Gruffudd and his parents but he was soon surrounded. Phyllida and Hermione pushed in briefly to say it was 'Extraordinary!' and they would call him. He could only wave at Piet van Stumpe as he disappeared with the director. Then Mrs Chunky-Cardigan bustled forward.

'Thank you so much, Sir Nicholas,' she blurted. 'I can't begin to tell you how much that has helped me!'

'I'm not really Sir Nic...' he began to say, but she had vanished into the crowd. He was barraged by questions, some from journalists, some from historians, some from friends and family. It was only when the crew started to shoo people out of the hall that the crowd finally thinned.

By then Farnstable, Chrissie and Jack had taken Dilke, Fairview, Claire and Andrea off for dinner in a restaurant. Appleby had declined the invitation to join them. The Webb contingent had occupied all the spare rooms at home, so his parents and Kate's lot were staying at a hotel on The Mount. He was joining them for a late supper.

When he finally stepped out into the night, the snow had settled in a thick blanket over every surface undisturbed by wheels or feet. He took a deep draught of the clear, cold air. He felt that something momentous had happened, though he wasn't quite sure what. As he wheeled his bicycle towards the street, a tall willowy woman came forward.

'I'm so sorry to trouble you, Sir Nicholas,' she said. 'You must be desperate to get home. But I belong to a Humanist group in Newcastle.' She handed him a business card. 'You probably know that we have all sorts of secular ceremonies and things, but I'm afraid there's nothing as impressive or as moving as this. Or as *old*! It was really inspirational.'

'Well I'm glad you enjoyed it,' said Appleby.

'It's funny,' she mused. 'My parents used to take me to church when I was little, and I absolutely hated it – all that stuffy ceremony, and those interminable boring sermons! But since I "lost my faith" – well I didn't really lose it, actually because I don't think I ever had it in the first place – but since then I find I miss that whole business of coming together, and all the aesthetics of it really. You know, the music – that was so beautiful by the way – and saying things all together. I'm sorry. I'm rambling, aren't I? It's just that your *Rite* or whatever you call it really hit the spot for me. Do you know, I felt like I had come home. Do you think you could come and do a performance for us in jolly old Geordieland? I could guarantee you an excellent turnout. At least twenty people!'

'I'm not sure,' he said, taking her card with a weary smile. 'I'll think about it.'

And he really *wasn't* sure. Playing Sir Nicholas Harker had been intoxicating, but he still didn't know how closely he wanted to be publically identified with this strange figure from the distant past. And despite his deep admiration for the man, how far did he *really* share his beliefs?

He was almost at the hotel when he was hit on the head by a snowball. A group of drunken lads were staring and pointing from the opposite pavement.

'Oy, wanker!' one of them shouted. ''Oo the fuck are you?'

Looking down he realised that he had forgotten to change out of costume. He was Sir Nicholas Harker, it seemed. And it was far too late to turn back.

North Devon

It was Jenny who found the back route into Combe Martin, using a 1:25.000 Ordnance Survey map Handley had left on the dashboard. From there they drove to Barnstaple, where they found a multi-storey car park near the town centre. Appleby drove to the highest level and left the Discovery in the farthest corner, buying a ticket for the whole day. With luck it would be hours before anyone noticed that it was there.

Then Jenny went alone into the first mobile phone shop they found. A young man in an ill-fitting suit tried to sell her a two-year contract for a device with built-in video, sat-nav and, in Jenny's words, 'a microwave oven and tumble-dryer too'. He became bored and grumpy when she insisted on the cheapest, simplest pay-as-you-go model they had. For some reason he demanded proof of her ID and address anyway. She produced her driving-licence and the bills from York which she had stuffed into her handbag and paid with a credit card in her maiden name. She was out of the shop in fifteen minutes. All they needed was somewhere to charge the battery.

They stocked up on sandwiches and bottled water at a mini-mart. Then they found the bus station. There was a bus leaving for Plymouth in twenty minutes, and they decided to take it. It was hot and stuffy, and they both fell asleep through sheer nervous exhaustion. When they finally arrived, they found a dingy B & B down a side-street behind Plymouth Ho, took a room and plugged in the battery charger.

The reception on the tiny TV set was dreadful, but they could just about hear the BBC news through the crackling blizzard. It was mostly about the disaster on Exmoor. The coverage was almost entirely speculative. There was no reference to the Applebys or the fact that they were missing. Eventually the newsreader moved on to the next story, the death of a middle-aged woman in a suspicious hit-and-run incident in Leicester.

When the bulletin ended Jenny made them a cup of nasty instant coffee from the 'hospitality tray', and they sat back on the bed to take stock. Appleby knew Jenny was feeling particularly wretched because she was fiddling with her hair, pulling strands forward over her forehead and looking for split-ends like a teenage girl.

'I don't think I can stand much more of this, Jimmy,' she said. 'I really think we should go back to the police. I've never felt so vulnerable and exposed in my life. Not even when...'

He tried not to sound impatient. 'Whoever it is that's so desperate to kill me, they found us *because* we were with the police. Apart from Giovanni and Iris, only the police knew. Kot said that poor sod Jenvey gave them a map, didn't he? Maybe they're getting inside information. Anyway, if they could get to him, they'll find a way to get to someone else. It's much safer if *nobody* knows where we are.'

'So what on earth do we do now, then?'

'We keep moving, I suppose. Pete's got a place in the Dales somewhere. Maybe we could go there. I'll give him a ring in the morning when the phone's charged up.' He paused a moment and lowered his voice. 'Maybe you should go home to your parents.'

'What! And put them at risk too? I don't think so.' She mustered a half-hearted smile. 'I'm afraid you're lumbered with me, chummy.'

Appleby turned to her with an earnestness that took her aback.

'Whatever happens I'm determined to get to Swively next week. I gave Guy my word I'd do it and I'm damned if I'll be intimidated into pulling out now.'

*

The stocky American couldn't believe his luck. He had stumbled dizzily onto a minor road near Combe Martin when a police car rounded the corner and stopped right by him. He was wondering if he had time to open the attaché case and pull out the Glock, when one of the officers wound down the window and spoke.

'You all right, sir? Had a bit too much to drink have we? Bloody hell! What happened to your head?'

'I was out walking, Officer, looking for a nice place to do a watercolour.' He lifted the case slightly implying it contained his painting kit. 'I slipped down a bank back there and gashed my head on a rock. I guess I'm a bit disorientated.'

'You American then?'

'Sure. I got cousins over here. We like to hook up every few years.'

'That looks nasty, sir. Hop in the back. We'll run you across to the A and E. There's no point calling an ambulance at the moment. You'd be waiting all week.'

On the way the officers explained that there had been a major incident nearby. He didn't happen to have seen an Asian-looking gentleman with a beard, did he?

The man had absolutely no idea where the hospital was. The tired young surgeon called down to A and E repaired the gash in his scalp using glue and tape.

'This is nasty,' he said. 'There's a tiny little groove in the bone here. I'll try to close it up without stitches, but you may have to come back.'

'You didn't ask for my insurance,' the man said groggily when the surgeon finished. 'Where do I go to pay?'

'No need for that, sir,' said the nurse. 'This is the NHS, you know.'

'You can pay for these,' said the surgeon, scribbling on a pad. 'I'm prescribing some strong pain-killers and a course of antibiotics. Take this to the outpatients' pharmacy. Come back here if you have any problems.'

The man wandered off a little unsteadily.

'Do you think he's all right?' said the nurse. 'What if he's concussed?'

Oh, he'll be okay,' the surgeon yawned. 'Mind you, he didn't gash his head on a rock.'

'Oh?'

'It was as clean as a whistle. Not even a speck of grit. If I had to hazard a guess, I'd say he'd been clipped by a bullet.'

'God! Shouldn't we tell the police?'

'If you really think so,' the surgeon yawned. 'Could you do it?'

'Did you hear all that fuss earlier?'

'No,' the surgeon groaned. 'I've been run off my feet all night. What fuss?'

'There was an incident on the moor. A helicopter came down or something. All the ambulances rushed off at once, but I just heard they've all come back empty.'

'Weird.'

'You know, I think I *will* tell the police about that American feller.'

Outside the hospital entrance the man was relieved to find that his smartphone was still working.

'It's called the North Devon District Hospital. The address is Raleigh Park – that's R-A-L-E-I-G-H Park. I know... I know... weird Brit pronunciation! It's in a place called Barn-staple... How long?... Okay. I'll wait in the lobby.'

*

Abbas Habibi was buzzing. He hadn't particularly wanted to do Northampton, but the night's gig had gone surprisingly well, and his agent had just called to say he'd been offered a regular slot on a new BBC Three panel show.

Stand-up comics of Iranian descent are a rare commodity in Britain, and Abbas's warm-hearted clowning had struck a chord with liberals of all ethnic backgrounds, including the more integrated sections of the Muslim population. Much of his act was about the absurdities and contradictions of Iranian family life. People said that it was the Islamic equivalent of Jewish humour, if such a thing were conceivable. He had recently developed a protracted riff on Muslims who wandered into Harkerite ceremonies by accident and the kinds of things they ended up confessing during the 'Attestations'. It had caused quite a stir in the community. The more relaxed members loved it; the traditionalists absolutely loathed it.

When he left the stage door of the Derngate Theatre he was wondering how quickly he could drive back to north London. With luck he'd be tucked up in bed by 1.30. As he pulled out his mobile to tell his wife the good news, he vaguely noticed the small black four-by-four with bull-bars a few yards away across the car park. He even saw that the driver's window was opening slowly and had time to wonder if that really was a silencer he could see poking out into the balmy night air. But he didn't hear the first of the four shots, the one that hit him in the forehead. He was already dead when he hit the ground, and three more bullets ripped into his torso.

The four-by-four drove slowly away. The driver was expected in Luton.

Camden

There was a brief interlude of calm between the recording of the Rite and the broadcast, which was scheduled to coincide with the book-launch. If Appleby had realised how completely his life was to change, he might have made more careful use of it, spending more time in Birmingham with his rapidly declining parents, perhaps. He might even have made another effort to sort out his becalmed, lifeless marriage – one way or another.

As it was he was struggling to get back in harness at the university. His old courses seemed excruciatingly dull now. Howland, who had been massively discomforted by his colleagues' enthusiastic response to the filming of the Rite and to Appleby's extraordinary performance, could hardly bear to look at him. Appleby seized any excuse to get away, especially to the post-production facility in Camden where Farnstable and his team were deeply immersed in the edit.

On one such visit he found them in an agitated discussion about the *Attestations*.

'Frankly, it's a fucking minefield!' said Farnstable. 'Did you know that cyber-bully girl was going to sue us?'

'I did see something in the local paper,' said Appleby. 'How did you sort it out?'

'Expensively,' said Farnstable. 'And we still can't use the bloody material.'

'I thought you made everyone sign release forms when they came in?'

'We did, but they're no bloody use when the *Attestations* involved people who weren't even there. And the ones who confessed to committing criminal offences are all desperately back-tracking. Somehow we managed to make them feel that they were in a safe, enclosed environment. Now it's sinking in that everything they said could be broadcast to the entire country. I knew it was a mistake doing it for real! Do you think those talk shows aren't meticulously stage-managed and legalled up to the hilt? Even your sister-in-law wanted to stop us using the bit with her kids.'

'Lucy? Really? She didn't say anything to us.'

'Well, we persuaded her to change her mind.'

'How?'

'Expensively.'

'You *bribed* her?'

'I gather EuroDisney is wonderfully quiet at this time of year. No queues for the rides, and the Disneyland Hotel is fabulous. Have you ever travelled first class on Eurostar?'

'Tim, you are outrageous!'

'Listen, James, my old mucker, would you do me a small favour?'

'What?'

'Would you just bugger off and let us get on with our work?'

*

A month later a complementary copy of Claire's novel arrived in the post. The title was taken from Shakespeare's sonnet No 94. It was called '*The Power to Hurt*'.

'Grace Cranston has barely passed into womanhood,' read the blurb, 'when she is forced to marry Sir Richard Tarker, an overbearing Devon aristocrat three times her age. At the tender age of fourteen she is torn from her idyllic childhood, only to find she has become the third Mistress of Halvingdene Manor...'

It was, as Claire had predicted, 'the most appalling tosh', but it was lively and entertaining tosh, and she knew how to rip a bodice with perfect historical accuracy.

He was reading it on the train when he travelled down to London for a press screening organised by Channel 4. It was held in an upmarket West End hotel with a small cinema in the basement. Afterwards Appleby, Farnstable and Dilke did a 'Q&A' session, fielding largely inane questions from the press, before Andrea ushered him into a plush sitting room to give individual interviews to three different television journalists.

He found himself using the same anecdotes, examples and phrases over and over again. The story began to coagulate into what became his 'official version'. When he mentioned this to Andrea, she smiled maternally and shrugged.

'Don't worry about it, James. All celebrities end up doing that, you know.'

'*Celebrity*?' he squawked. '*Me*? Please God, no!'

'You're so sweet,' she laughed. 'It may only be for fifteen minutes, but you're going to be famous now.'

The night before the broadcast, Claire organised a lavish launch party for the twin books at a club near Shaftebury's headquarters in Bloomsbury. Appleby drank far too much red wine on an empty stomach, talking nervously and compulsively to people he had never met or even heard of. By the time the party wound up, he was swaying.

'How'd I g't't'm' 'OTEL, m'dear?' he asked Claire. 'Uv FUGGUTT'N where ut uz.'

'You're in no state to go anywhere, Jimmy,' she said. 'You're coming back with me.'

'Funk-slot, m'dear,' he said as she bundled him into a black cab. 'Burra wan' yer... t'unnershtan' somink... Thuzz... t'be ub-slootely... no HUNKY-PUNKY thish tum!... Iz-zat unnerstoo...?'

'I can live with that,' laughed Claire, pushing him firmly to the far side of the back seat.

When he woke the next morning, dehydrated and dizzy, on the living-room sofa in her Clerkenwell flat, he was surprised to see Jeremy Dilke walking to the bathroom in what looked like a woman's dressing gown.

'Morning, Doc,' said Dilke breezily.

Appleby felt an unexpected stab of jealousy as he registered the implications.

'Aren't you a bit young for her?' he mumbled.

Dilke either didn't hear the remark or chose to ignore it. Oh well, at least it wasn't bloody Farnstable.

*

When the programme was broadcast it attracted four million viewers, outstanding for Channel 4's serious factual slot early on a Saturday evening. Research indicated that it had not only retained its original audience, but had actually grown during the broadcast as curious channel-surfers stayed with it.

Sales of the two books were also extremely brisk. Then came the reviews. Appleby read them with a mixture of delight, gratification, irritation and, in some cases outrage. But they were quickly forgotten. Phyllida was already organising his first tour.

North Devon

The driver of the Chrysler Voyager had no difficulty in spotting his contact in the hospital lobby. If the man's appearance had not been distinctive enough, the prominent dressing on his head would have given the game away.

'That was some stunt you pulled back there!' he drawled as they walked to the car. 'Did you know you just wasted twelve of Great Britain's finest anti-terrorist officers, plus two Royal Army chopper pilots?'

'Shit!'

'And then those two Special Branch personal protection officers. I'm assuming that was you too. That's neat shooting. The Taliban would be proud of ya.'

'Where to now?' said the man glumly as they drove off.

'You'll be holing up with me for a day or two. Your new orders will arrive when we're there. We've got you a neat new piece of kit, by the way. You're gonna love it.'

As they turned onto the main road, a police patrol car screeched past, siren blaring, blue lights flashing. They were responding to a tip-off from a nurse in A and E.

*

Extreme fear often loosens the bowels. Protracted anxiety, however, can have the opposite effect, a phenomenon for which Piet van Stumpe had been extremely grateful for several hours.

Blindfolded and with his wrists still painfully tied, he had been lifted out of the back of the van. The narrow slit of light just discernible under his left eye had vanished. Nobody had touched the blindfold, and he hadn't felt it slip, so he concluded that meant it was now dark. He could smell sea air and heard the gentle whoosh of waves on shingle.

Nobody spoke to him as they pulled him along, first over tarmac, then over wooden planking. He thought they must have gone about twenty metres when they steered him to the left, but how could he judge distances in these conditions? Now the wooden floor dropped away steeply and bounced a little under his weight. It must be a gangplank. Someone pushed his head under a doorway and almost flung him down a steep set of stairs. Then he was shoved unceremoniously onto a padded bench. Outside he could hear a noisy diesel engine idling.

So that was how he would travel to England, on a small motor-powered boat or yacht, vomiting copiously in the swell, no doubt, and racked by self-doubt. Watching Freek's agony, his steely resolution had finally cracked. Deep down he didn't believe it for a single moment, but he was still clinging desperately to the hope that somehow these men would keep their word and let Freek go once he had taken them to the chest. Why had he not just agreed to their terms, before they started...?

Five hours later the sickening voyage ended. A tiny grey slit had reappeared beneath his left eye. It must be dawn. They pulled him off the boat and up some steep stone stairs. Onto a jetty? There was a short walk and he was shoved into the back of another van. Not again! Why couldn't they kidnap him in a vehicle with seats? After an hour or so – he really had no sense of time by now – the van stopped, and he could smell petrol.

'Please,' he stuttered. 'Why are we stopping?'

'Gas,' said one of his captors tersely.

'Please!' said van Stumpe. 'Is there a restroom facilities here? I am so in discomfort. I fear I will soon be making a most horrible smell and mess. Can you not take me somewhere before I am having some accident?'

'Wait,' said the voice.

He heard someone get out of the van, then a muffled conversation. Footsteps. Then a pause of several minutes. Then more footsteps and the conversation resumed. Someone climbed into the back of the van next to him, removed the blindfold and released his hands. It was the man in the purple ski-mask. He pushed an automatic pistol painfully into van Stumpe's face.

'Now listen carefully, my friend. There is a W.C. at the back of this gas station. We will take you there so you can do what you have to do. But remember, if you so much as look at anyone else in the wrong way, your little friend will die. Do you understand that?'

Van Stumpe nodded as emphatically as was possible with the muzzle of a pistol pressing into his cheek.

It was early morning, and the van was parked at the side of an otherwise deserted forecourt. Out of the line of sight of the solitary cashier, two men walked him round to the lavatory, one gripping each of his upper arms.

'You can shut the door, but don't try to lock it,' Purple Ski-Mask snarled.

Once inside, van Stumpe let rip with the sound-effects, though his relief when he finally eased out the mobile phone was all too genuine. He slipped it out of its ointment-smeared polythene bag, which he buried under used paper towels in an overflowing waste-bin. The battery was worryingly low, and he was terrified it would start emitting warning beeps. He didn't have to simulate the explosive sounds that followed, but he grunted and groaned extravagantly as he pushed his numb fingers across the keypad.

He couldn't think of anyone else to alert; he would have to try Appleby again. Anyway, his was still the only number in the contact list. He made a series of mighty and protracted 'Oooorgh!' noises to cover the faint clicking of the keys. 'P 133 now v soon,' he wrote. Surely James would understand what that meant. The screen confirmed that the message had been sent. Then he dialled Appleby's number again. He had a feeling that if the phone was active, even for the short time before the battery died, it might help the authorities locate him. At least they would know he was somewhere in southern England. He had noticed the hinged lid on top of the toilet paper dispenser. He opened it and dropped the phone into the top. Without waiting for a reply, he pulled the flush, washed his hands and stepped outside.

Purple Ski-Mask took a deep breath and darted into the empty cubicle to check that van Stumpe had not written any messages on the walls. He checked under the lid of the cistern and pulled out the first sheets from the toilet paper and paper towel dispensers to make sure no messages had been scribbled there. Van Stumpe's mobile was still on silent, and the ringing of Appleby's phone was almost inaudible. Nor did the man hear the first forlorn little beep of the low battery warning as they walked away. Van Stumpe heard it and winced.

'Please, do not be covering my eyes or binding my wrists again,' he pleaded when they heaved him back into the van. 'It is so very painful and nauseous. I promise I will not be making any troubles, if only for my little Freek's sake.'

His two escorts climbed in next to him, Purple Ski-Mask was still brandishing the automatic, but this time they did not blindfold him or bind his hands. Van Stumpe massaged his wrists as he settled back on some old sacks. He found he was leaning against some kind of locker.

His mind was eaten up with dread and apprehension. Physically he had never felt so relieved in his life.

*

As France's brightest young expert on historical fashion, Florentin Bonneau was expecting to enjoy his spell as a guest curator at the V and A. The fact that his good friend Giovanni Angelini had invited him to house-sit his palatial home in Holland Park while he returned to Italy for a while, was the icing on the cake. Florentin also had free use of the BMW, or 'the town runabout' as Giovanni called it.

They had met five years earlier at a party in Venice and become occasional lovers. Florentin was all too aware of his own entrancing beauty. Giovanni used to call him 'My Parisian Narcissus'. He did not appeal to certain types of gay men, being somewhat modestly endowed, but he had the face of a Greek god, his body was as perfectly sculpted as Michelangelo's David (without the freakishly large hands), and he prided himself on being unusually inventive in bed and attentive to his lovers' desires. Giovanni, he felt sure, was completely infatuated with him.

The two men were almost exactly the same height and, despite the considerable age gap, had the same waist, chest and leg measurements. Even their shoe size was the same, and Giovanni had told him blithely that he could borrow anything that took his fancy from his many closets. So he had dressed himself in an unworn pair of Giovanni's hand-made shoes, an exquisitely tailored Milanese suit and an individually designed silk cravat, inspired by an LA period David Hockney, when he set off for a house-party in Berkshire.

There were only two things he disliked about this cushiest of billets. He was disconcerted by the occasional appearances of various servants. Giovanni had given him a list of their names and functions, and they were scrupulously courteous and discreet, but he never knew exactly when they were going to appear or where. Secondly he found the fiendishly complicated security systems utterly tiresome. In Paris he would just pull the door of his apartment shut behind him and stroll out for a baguette. Entering or leaving Giovanni's house seemed to take about half an hour and involved remembering endless codes.

Florentin had just made absolutely sure that he had secured the garage door properly and was climbing back into the driving seat of the BMW when he noticed that the end of the mews was blocked by a small black four-by-four. It had bull-bars. He rather thought he disapproved of that, especially in towns.

*

As Izzy Charlton rather unkindly put it, her husband Guy was 'going ape'.

Building the life-size, historically accurate reconstruction of Farthingwell Manor, along with the Visitors' Centre, including a small museum, café and gift shop, not to mention the adjoining Cranham Institute with its library, reading rooms and lecture theatre, had taken the best part of four years.

There had been many setbacks on the way. After a year Guy had dismissed all his English builders because they were habitually late, disappeared on other jobs for weeks on end and constantly made mistakes, while rare and expensive materials mysteriously disappeared. He had retained the architects and their project managers for the three buildings, but for the last three years eveything had been built by teams of eager and competent Poles, Estonians and Latvians. Guy referred to the mass dismissal of the natives as his private 'Baltic Exchange'.

Gradually the project had come together. Obviously nobody knew exactly what Harker's house had looked like, but they knew the groundplan of the building from the excavations, and enough other examples of large mid-fifteenth century timber-framed houses survived to allow them to reproduce the correct building materials and construction techniques. Some of the internal fixtures and furnishings were genuine antiques from the late sixteenth century or earlier; other items were hand-crafted replicas. They had even managed to make the floorboards look wonky and worn as they would have been in Harker's time, a hundred and fifty years after the house was first built.

The effect was stunning. Now that 'Farthingwell 2', as Guy called it, was finished, and much to Izzy's irritation, he spent hours wandering around the place, especially the long gallery on the first floor, in a delicious reverie, gazing through the uneven leaded windows. He delighted in the details and would spend happy evenings playing with the iron spit over the kitchen fireplace or sitting contemplatively in the garderobe, a lavatory projecting out from the corner of the master bed-chamber on the first floor, with a hole in the hinged seat that dropped directly down onto the midden below.

The builders had found this en-suite facility, a convenient location for the big telescopic rubbish chute they used to drop their debris into a large skip. To Guy's frustration both the skip and this hideous monstrosity in bright yellow plastic were still there, although the boss had sworn they would be cleared away before the launch.

The Visitors' Centre and Institute building were ready too. The plumbing, gas and electricity were installed and connected. Staff had been hired and trained; the gift-shop stocked, the café menus agreed, the projectors, screens and computerised white-board installed in the lecture theatre. The new library contained a copy of every book so far published on Harker and Harkerism (new volumes seemed to appear every month) and a mass of related material on Elizabethan history, religion and rural life. A car park had been built with its own access to the Wolvington road and its own lavatory block.

For the grand opening Guy had also hired an enormous marquee and booked a catering tent which would serve wholesome Elizabethan dishes. The numerous stewards and waiters, even the car park attendants, would all be dressed in period costume. There was a packed programme of events, including lectures, re-enactors dressed as Elizabethan soldiers and demonstrations of country dancing. There would be an Elizabethan service up at the church, and Gordon Fairview had agreed to come as guest conductor with a choir and another consort of musicians. The producer of a new British film with an Elizabethan theme had even agreed to hold the first public screening in the marquee. Every hotel, guest house and B & B for miles around had been booked solid for weeks.

There were two problems. Both Guy and Izzy had been badly rattled by van Stumpe's unexpected night-time visit. The thought that their house was harbouring an object that could make it the target of some unspecified, but violent attack was particularly unsettling. They were beginning to get as nervous as sixteenth century aristocrats would have been when harbouring a Catholic priest.

The second problem was more pressing. James Appleby had not only agreed to give a lecture on Harker and the history of the archive, but as the highlight of the whole weekend, he had promised that, for the first time since his performance at the Merchant Adventurer's Hall over four years ago, he would dress up as Sir Nicholas Harker and conduct a full-length version of *The Common Rite*. Now the grand opening was only days away, and Appleby had disappeared.

Izzy made the mistake of raising this point over dinner. After a day of fruitless emails and phone-calls, Guy growled at her like a dog psyching itself up to bite someone's leg.

'The silly bastard's gone to ground, hasn't he? Nobody knows where the fuck he is!'

York

'That man's taken over your life,' said Jenny. 'What on earth are you looking for now?'

It was a Saturday morning, and Appleby was sitting at the breakfast table, flicking through a well-thumbed edition of his collected Harker.

'Anything that sounds vaguely Buddhist, if you must know. Various people have pointed out that there's a strange similarity between some of his more enigmatic utterances and Buddhist philosophy. I said I'd give a talk about it to some people in Hull.'

'Pfff,' went Jenny. 'That's a new one. How could he possibly have known about Buddhism?'

'I don't suppose he did,' Appleby said wearily. 'I expect it's just coincidental.' He suddenly had a thought. 'Do you remember all those nutty letters I got after the first documentary?' he said.

'Vaguely,' said Jenny.

'One of them mentioned Buddhism – something about Jesus spending his missing years in India. I think he was suggesting Harker might have known something. Absurd, of course, but I might dig it out – if I've still got it.'

'If that's how you want to waste your time…'

He had grown used to Jenny's indifference, but there was a sour note in her voice these days. He noticed it more and more and he didn't like it.

Mind you, she was right about one thing: Harker had taken over his life. That publicist Andrea's prediction that he'd get at least fifteen minutes of fame had proved extremely conservative. Fifteen minutes had become fifteen days, then fifteen weeks and now fifteen months. A trickle of requests for interviews had become a stream of invitations to give talks and lectures, then a torrent of bookings at conferences and literary festivals.

Sir Nicholas Harker had become fashionable. Appleby had first heard of a group of Humanists in Brighton putting on their own

Rite only a month after the broadcast. A well-known gay actor had performed as Harker. Since then groups seemed to be popping up all over the country. Something was striking a chord. Features began appearing in the lifestyle supplements of the national papers. He even started getting calls from journalists on women's magazines and researchers from daytime TV shows.

He might have dismissed all this as just another middle-class fad, like Transcendental Meditation, macrobiotic diets or Feng Shui, but there seemed more to it than that. Had he accidentally stumbled on some unfulfilled spiritual need among people who had no religious faith? When a group started up in York, he resisted their pleas for him to perform, but he did give them a talk and attended one of their gatherings. He could see why people went. They were all very sweet-natured, if a little eccentric, and he found he enjoyed their homely version of a Rite far more than he expected to. There was something extraordinarily reassuring about it – and it was fun.

By now the backlash was well underway too. It began in the anarchic melee of the internet, but it was soon in the papers. What started as gentle mockery quickly turned into contemptuous dismissal. As the fashion for what was now called 'Harkerism' continued to spread, the contemptuous dismissal turned into strident denunciation. Every polemical columnist, especially the self-appointed guardians of public morality, jumped on this bandwagon, frequently targeting Appleby himself in harsh personal terms. It had reached the point where he hardly dared to open a newspaper.

Then Jeremy Dilke had rung to say that a man called Nicholson, a protégé of Norman Skyne, was about to publish a book denouncing Harker and all his works. Apparently he claimed to have evidence that the archive was a forgery concocted by a lunatic. He sought to discredit Appleby's research on a point-by-point basis. It was clearly nonsense, said Dilke, but mud might stick. Nicholson, he said, had been sponsored by something called the Phoenix Foundation. If Appleby looked them up online, he would see that it was a new inter-faith organisation devoted to reinvigorating religious belief. Dilke had heard that J.D. Clovis might be involved in some way, though he couldn't say how.

'You know what the worst of all this is?' Appleby had asked Kate on one of his ever-rarer trips to Birmingham. 'It's driven a wedge between me and Jenny. It hasn't been brilliant between us for years, but since she refused to come to the filming, she's become more and more distant. She hates what I'm doing, I can tell. It's like she's having this epic sulk. I've never been more in demand in my life, and I've never felt so lonely.'

'She'll come round,' Kate had said unhelpfully. 'She always does. All marriages have their ups and downs, you know.'

He had never been brave enough to tell his sister about how bad things had really become since the still-birth – let alone about Iris. As he flicked through his book that Saturday morning he realised he had barely seen Iris since the night she had told him about her father's death, and then only fleetingly. He felt a sudden surge of guilt.

'I'll have to go to London again next week,' he said.

'It's all the same to me,' said Jenny. 'Just let me know when you expect to be fed.'

*

Four days later Appleby was back in Crouch End.

'She called you a what?' laughed Iris.

'Apparently I'm an "addlepated peddler of morally toxic, brain-rotting slop",' said Appleby.

He had made the mistake of picking up a copy of the Evening Standard on the bus. The article in question was by a woman called Anne-Marie Philkins. He had often heard her on Radio 4, where she seemed to be employed to hector liberals on discussion programmes.

'That's quite good, actually,' Iris chuckled. 'You should be flattered.'

He was relieved to find that she had regained most of the old easy-going affection. Over dinner at Farfalli's he had regaled her with tales of his latest public appearances. Now they were side by side on her sofa, and she was getting a blow-by-blow account of a writers' dinner at the Cheltenham Festival.

She passed him her spliff, and he took his usual single drag. They gradually relaxed, talking more slowly as the dope took effect.

'It's funny,' he said. 'Both our lives have changed beyond all recognition in the last few months.... Do you think we'll last much longer, you and me?'

'Who knows?' Her tone changed. She looked at him with a sad little smile. 'Do you?'

'I do love you, you know,' he said, 'although...'

'Although what?'

'...to be honest, I've never really understood why you've carried on seeing me for so long.'

'I sometimes wonder that myself.' That sad little smile again.

'Seriously, you must meet loads of other men – younger, fitter, richer – not married...'

'You don't understand,' she said. 'You're rather special, actually. Maybe I've just been unlucky. All the guys I meet of my own age – apart from the complete losers and the one's who aren't already taken – I dunno – they're shallow or arrogant; they only want a quick shag – or they're just *dull*. You're clever and knowledgeable and funny and open – and you're *kind*. That's not so common these days...'

'Kind? That never did me much good when I was young!' he laughed. 'But thanks for that.' He kissed her and sighed reflectively. 'But wouldn't you like to have children? A family of your own? You really should find someone... before it's too late.'

'Tell me about it...' She took another deep drag on her spliff. '...and you still love your wife, don't you – despite everything?'

'I...it's hard to say...I try not to think about it, really. It's been getting very difficult recently...but we went through some terrible things together...she really suffered...'

'So – you're never going to leave her, are you?'

'What?' His voice dropped to a murmur. 'For you, you mean? You don't want that, do you? I just assumed...'

'Sure...' she said, '...so did I, I guess. Anyway, one way or another, it looks like we're doomed to part.'

'Let's not talk about it anymore,' he sighed. 'Not just now.'

'No, let's not.' She kissed him gently. 'Bed?'

Her melancholy seemed to melt away as they undressed. In fact she suddenly became so fervent that it startled him. She gripped him tightly to her as they made love and started rocking vigorously back and forth. He was dog-tired, and it began to feel like hard work. In the end he relaxed and let her move his body, as if she was manipulating a giant pillow on top of herself in powerful rhythmic movements. Her energy was astonishing. When he could contain himself no longer, she squeezed him inside her, trapping him with her legs so that he could barely move, long after she had reached her own climax. They lay in this tight, sweaty clinch, her pelvis pressed up hard against him, for what seemed like an eternity. Finally she released him, kissing him tenderly as he slid to the side.

'My God,' he gasped, turning to face her. 'What brought that on?'

'I dunno,' she sighed. 'All this talk about drifting apart, I suppose.' She laughed and tickled his midriff. 'Maybe I wanted something to remember you by, you daft old lump. Besides, I've never had sex with a *celebrity* before. It's quite a turn-on, actually...'

*

It was half past one on a Saturday morning when Appleby got home after giving yet another lecture, this time in Manchester. He let himself in as quietly as he could, hoping not to wake Jenny. The house was dark and silent. He turned on the hall light, slipped off his shoes and walked softly through to the kitchen.

But Jenny wasn't in bed. He found her asleep at the table, slumped forward on her arms which were folded over a book. It was the copy of Harker he had inscribed for her, though he had never expected her to read it.

'Jenny?' he said quietly. 'Are you all right?'

She stirred and looked up. 'What? What time is it? I think I fell asleep.'

He eased the book out from under her. The pages were damp. He turned the light on and saw that she had been weeping. He reached his hand around her, leaned down and kissed the top of her head. 'What's the matter, love? Has something happened?'

'I just read that,' she said.

Suddenly, without looking up, she turned and pulled him strongly towards her, burying her face in his midriff. Appleby looked down at the book, quickly scanning the page. It was a passage he remembered well, 'A Rite of Consolation upon the Death of an Infant':

'Beloved Kindred, we are gathered together in the presence of that Spirit which unites us...We meet in our common sorrow to mourn the passing of (Name the dead infant) and to love (him or her)....For (his or her) Spirit liveth as a flame, howsoever tiny, that burneth in our hearts...'

When Appleby had first come upon the text of this brief ceremony in Amsterdam he had hardly been able to read it. Some of Harker's phrases might seem commonplace, but they could be extremely resonant, and it was all too close to the bone:

'As Great Nature giveth, so doth She take away...For ever the lamb shall fall in the meadow and the unfledged chick shall tumble from the nest....Let us welcome their Spirits within our own, for they are as travellers seeking shelter from the tempests of the night. And let us love them ever...For thus may we triumph over the Shades of Death...the dead shall dwell as welcome Guests in the Spirits of the living...'

Jenny's whole body seemed to heave and shudder. He felt her hot sobs through his shirt. It was as though some great dam had burst in

393

her heart.

'I so wanted children!' she sobbed. 'When our baby died I thought it was the end of my world.' She looked up at him and then away again. 'It's made me dead and cold inside,' she said, 'and that was so unfair to you!'

Appleby felt his heart melt. In that moment he realised something strange. In all those long years when he had felt frustrated and shut out by her, he had never once felt resentment or anger. He wondered why.

'I know you've been unfaithful to me,' she said after a while, 'but I pretended not to notice because I didn't want to care about you any more. I did what I thought was my duty by you, but I daren't love you any more, not as a wife should, because I daren't let myself feel *anything*. You tried so hard to get me to talk about it and open up to you, but I couldn't. I daren't. And you've gone along with it all and stayed with me, and I'm not sure I deserved it. You could leave me now if you wanted. I wouldn't blame you if you did.' By now she was dabbing at her face with a fistful of crumpled tissues.

He was still wondering what on earth he could say to her when she spoke again. Her voice seemed to have dropped an octave.

'And there's something else – something even worse – for me anyway.' By now she was gazing out of the window with a look of almost infinite fatigue. 'I don't love God anymore,' she said eventually. 'I can't. Not after what happened. I tried to come to terms with it. I really tried. I spoke to that canon at the Minster. Tranter. Did you ever meet him? We spoke for hours and hours. He tried so hard to comfort me, and I prayed and prayed and prayed. But none of it helped. The truth is that for nearly fifteen years I've just been pretending. The truth is that I don't think I even believe any more.'

She blew her nose again loudly. 'There, I've said it. I've never said that aloud before, but I've been thinking it for years.' Slowly she released her grip on him. 'That's why I couldn't come when they filmed your ceremony. I was terrified. It would have made me face it.'

She turned back to the book. 'This is so simple. So beautiful. The next time there's a service or whatever you call it near here, will you take me?'

Eventually they crawled into bed and slept in each other's arms for the first time in years. She had put on weight, but not that much. Her body felt curvy and womanly and generous. When she got up late the next morning the sunlight streamed through her white cotton nightdress, and he realised how much he still desired her.

The next night they made love again. It was slow, comfortable and so intensely intimate it made him want to weep. After long, cold years in exile he had finally come home.

*

She didn't go to the Minster on Sunday. She drove them out to their old haunt, Rievaulx Abbey and they went for a leisurely walk instead.

'Daniel would be fourteen and a half now,' said Jenny after a long silence. 'I wonder what...' but her voice tailed away.

'Isn't it strange?' said Appleby. 'In all these years we've never talked about what Daniel would have been like, have we?'

'That's my fault,' she said, her eyes filling again. 'I couldn't...'

And so they had what turned out to be the first of many conversations, wondering what sort of young man they would have produced and which traits he might have inherited from each of them. They even managed to ease the sadness with grim humour.

'If he'd had my capacity for procrastination combined with your stubbornness, he'd have been in real trouble!' said Appleby. In the end they decided he would have been the most wonderful boy that ever walked the earth – even if only they could see it.

Appleby drove them back. As Jenny dozed in the seat beside him, he realised that he had already made a decision. It was time to see Iris again.

Kent

As the three kidnappers shoved van Stumpe back into the van, he wondered miserably if Appleby would ever get his message. Now he no longer had a phone, he had played his only card. If the ruse failed, he was done for. He was sure they would kill him as soon as he had led them to the chest, the contents of which they clearly intended to destroy. But he had to carry on while there was even the faintest shadow of a chance that they might keep their word and release poor little Freek.

*

The previous night DC Lambert had finally made it back to her pokey little flat in Wood Green after a long, draining, adrenal shift. Her clock-radio showed that she had lain in bed for precisely seventy-nine minutes, completely unable to sleep. She had tried her usual method of relaxing when insomnia struck, but somehow she couldn't achieve the moment of blissful nervous release which usually brought oblivion in its wake. She had only succeeded in making herself more wakeful and edgy when her alarm went.

She was back at her desk by 6.00 am, trawling through the Applebys' phone records, when his mobile gave a succession of staccato trills. It was still sitting on the desk beside her, plugged into the socket in the floor. 'You have one new message', said the screen.

It was sweet revenge to ring Charlie Drucker and wake him too.

'That Dutch chap's just sent Appleby another text, sir.' She read it out. 'P133 now v soon.'

'What the fuck does that mean? '

'Presumably Appleby will know.'

'Yes I'm sure he will,' said Drucker with heavy sarcasm. 'Pity we have absolutely no fucking idea where the fuck he is!'

She was so tired, and Drucker's scornful blast was so aggravating that it was several seconds before she realised that Appleby's phone had now started ringing.

'Wait. His phone's going!' she shouted, snatching it up and pressing it to her free right ear. 'Hello? Hello? Hello-o-o!'

'Whatever you do don't hang up, Debbie!' shouted Drucker in her left ear. 'Keep him talking.'

'But there's no-one there, sir. It's weird. It's still connected but all I can hear is... it's like water dribbling in the background – like a cistern or something.'

'I'll get onto Gupta. See if they can locate it. Just keep that fucking line open...'

*

The service station was on the A2070 south of Ashford. The Kent police got there within half an hour of Drucker's call, but they had been scouring the place without success for another forty-five minutes before one of the officers felt an urgent call of nature. The paper dispenser had a narrow window in the side to show the level of the stack of sheets. As he pulled a small wad from the base, a silvery grey object dropped into view at the top. When he lifted the phone out, the battery was dead and the screen was blank.

Another officer had been reviewing the station's CCTV. As instructed, she rang straight through to Drucker.

'It looks like an old Ford Transit, sir. Probably a Mark 4, I'd say. Dirty white. We think we've got part of the plate: M620... That might be enough for Swansea, anyway. Maybe the geeks will get the rest.' Her colleague walked into the shop, waving the phone. 'And we've retrieved the guy's phone for you.'

But by then the van had had well over an hour to make it to the M25 and beyond. As Drucker observed with a weary sigh, 'They could be bloody well anywhere by now.'

He was still puzzling over the meaning of van Stumpe's text. Then he remembered that Jenvey had mentioned taking a similarly enigmatic message from the Dutchman to Appleby. Had Appleby said anything about what it meant? If so, had Kot or Handley relayed it back to Forbes before they were murdered?

Now it was Forbes's turn to be disturbed in his bed.

*

According to Appleby's 'Third Law of Bed and Breakfast Accommodation', the overall quality of any establishment is a direct, mathematically calculable function of the quality of the sausage served with the full English breakfast. If the sausage is poor, for instance, the percentage probability of the tiny bedroom television having lousy reception and the shower-head in the en-suite bathroom emitting a pathetic dribble of tepid water is increased incrementally, according to a complex, yet reliable equation.

The Drake's Drum Guest House in Plymouth served a nasty pink pulverised-gristle-and-cereal-packed turd of a sausage from the economy range of a downmarket wholesaler. On the Appleby scale, it rated a wretched 2 out of 10. But at least the electric socket had worked, and Jenny's new mobile was fully charged. As they washed the greasy fry-up down with acrid, stewed filter coffee in the otherwise empty breakfast-room, Appleby rang Pete Elyot.

'Jimmy?' said Pete groggily. 'What sort of time is this to ring an ageing party-animal? How are you? *Where* are you? We've been hearing all manner of scary rumours.' Appleby heard Pete whispering to someone. 'It's just a friend, Bosie. Go back to sleep.'

'Bosie!?' exclaimed Appleby with a snort.

'It's a pet-name, James. Our little in-joke, *entre nous*. And yes, he does call me "Oscar". Now what could you possibly want at this unconscionable hour?'

Appleby explained the bare bones of his predicament, and asked if they could borrow the cottage, emphasising that it was critical that Pete did not say anything to anyone which could possibly reveal their whereabouts.

'Gosh,' said Pete. 'How terribly cloak and dagger! I'd be thrilled to help. It's on the edge of a tiny village called Thwaite in Swaledale. If you haven't got transport you'll probably have to get a cab from a railway station, and they're all miles away. Darlington is probably your best bet. It'll cost a fucking fortune, but the buses are hopeless. The keys are with a lovely old biddie called Ivy – Mrs Tench – who lives near the village shop in Muker. That's the last village along the dale before Thwaite. I'll tell her to expect you. I suppose you'll want me to give false names, then? Any suggestions?'

'How about Mr and Mrs Bunbury?'

'A Wilde reference! Ernest's non-existent friend! How appropriate! Try and ring ahead so she knows roughly when you and "Cecily" are arriving. She tends to go to bed at about half past eight. She'll explain about the gas canisters and the electricity and all that stuff.'

Appleby took down Mrs Tench's address and phone number. They were all set.

Back in their bedroom, he and Jenny began to formulate a plan. They had no idea what, if anything, had happened at Angelini's house after they left, but assumed the police would be looking for them. They might have found the Discovery by now, in which case they would know they had been in Barnstaple the day before. If they were checking CCTV footage they might know they'd taken a bus to Plymouth too, though they wouldn't necessarily assume they had stayed the night. If they were checking hotel registers it should be a while before anyone got round to this place. They would probably go through the bus and rail station CCTV footage first. Depending on how desperate they were to find them, they might be watching stations all over the south-west. They probably had a means of tracking withdrawals from their bank and building society accounts. If they hadn't already started doing that, they soon would.

Jenny said the police would be so busy with the helicopter disaster, and trying to find whoever had caused it, that they might not be bothering with the Applebys at all. After all, it was their own stupid fault if they wanted to run off. They might have decided to leave them to their fate. Appleby said he wasn't prepared to take that risk. And if the police did find them, the killers might find them too.

Jenny had always kept what she called her 'emergency fund' of about ten thousand pounds in an instant access account in a building society. She would go straight into the nearest branch as soon as it opened, tell them she was buying a car, cash-in-hand, and insist on withdrawing the lot. Under the terms of the account she was allowed to do this. They would hit a snag if there wasn't enough cash on the premises or the manager became suspicious, but she had her passport and all the other documentation she might need. And of course she looked and sounded utterly respectable. It was worth a try.

If it worked, they could pay for everything in cash, leaving no further electronic trail. They would then travel north in a succession of minicabs, thus avoiding both station CCTV cameras and watchful officers. They would do the entire journey in twenty-five to fifty mile hops from town to town, choosing places large enough to have cab services, but, wherever possible, with poor public transport connections between them, so that hiring a cab to go to the next town wouldn't seem so strange. It would be painfully slow and ludicrously expensive, but they should be able to make it to Thwaite without being caught on any CCTV camera which the police were likely to check.

An hour later Jenny walked out of the central Plymouth branch of the Priory Equitable Building Society, her handbag bulging with two hundred crisp new fifty-pound notes. Meanwhile Applebly had bought a road atlas of Britain.

'We can't really avoid Exeter or Bristol,' he said. 'They've both got good rail and bus links, but if we use them, we could find a welcoming committee at the other end. Exeter's smaller and nearer. Let's see if we can get a cab there.'

When they found a minicab office the controller was incredulous. 'You wanna take the train, mate! It's much quicker and cheaper.'

'My wife will only travel in cars,' said Appleby. 'She has a phobia of public transport.'

The driver was delighted. He'd take more in one half day than he normally did in three.

Tiverton – Taunton – Wells – Trowbridge – Swindon. Even with pit-stops for loos and refreshments, the journey seemed interminable. Cheltenham – Evesham – Warwick – Rugby – Hinckley. By the time they hit Burton-upon-Trent they had experienced every conceivable type of cab from spanking new people-carriers to smelly, battered old Japanese hatchbacks, and every type of driver from the silently morose to the irrepressibly garrulous. Uttoxeter – Buxton – Glossop – Oldham – Accrington. It was a strange way to pass through the heart of England. Under other circumstances it might have been rather interesting. They found another small B&B down a backstreet in Harrogate. They had to stop: if they pushed on they would arrive in Swaledale far too late to pick up the cottage keys. This time the sausage rating was a satisfying 8/10.

Appleby used Jenny's phone to make one brief call the next morning. He told Guy Charlton he was definitely coming for the launch. He could feel the surge of relief, humming through the ether. Guy insisted they should stay with them in Farthingwell House. Appleby told him to contact Box of Tricks. Someone there might know what had happened to his old costume.

At 11.23 a.m. they pressed a doorbell in Muker.

'Hello there. Mrs Tench? My name's Bunbury...'

*

The Kent police were not the only ones to swoop on a target a little too late that day. The officers who raided the lock-up in Golders Green found that it had now been abandoned, and there was no sign of the Abramskys' Volvo or its nice young driver. There was, however, evidence that someone had been transferring a liquid from several large plastic containers to something else. It had left a curiously insidious smell. 'A bit like glue mixed with cheap perfume,' said one officer.

*

Commander Forbes had three phone calls reporting on different forensic investigations that evening. The first concerned the blood samples from the wall of Angelini's Exmoor house and the key-fob of the Honda. They had circulated the DNA profile among several 'friendly' security organisations, and the FBI had produced a match. The man in question was not Pakistani at all, or any other kind of Asian for that matter.

He was called Garston Swilby. He was forty-three, five foot eight inches tall, of muscular build, with dark brown hair and eyes and he had a substantial criminal record. The file showed that he had been brought up in a tiny North Carolina sect called the Allingham Baptismal Brethren. Their world view was completely dominated by a homophobia so intense that they would loudly denounce any organisation, from the federal government to importers of foreign furniture, which countenanced any kind of tolerance for homosexuality. Their noisy and aggressive demonstrations were notorious and had caused massive offence for hundreds of miles around.

While still with the sect, Swilby had clocked up several convictions for minor public order offences and assault. He had drifted away as young man, though he was still thought to share the sect's basic worldview. His record was not bad enough to prevent him enlisting in the U.S. Marines, however. Eventually he had trained as a Navy Seal, assigned to covert operations in the first Gulf War.

On his return to America he had taken work as a 'private security consultant'. He had been convicted of several tax and motoring offences, but attempts to prosecute him for the bombing of an abortion clinic in Atlanta, the murder of three gay-rights campaigners near Memphis and an arson attack on the offices of a campaigning liberal newspaper in Charleston had all failed for lack of evidence. For the last two years he had been on the payroll of a Texas-based corporation which traded in global drilling rights. He was known to have adopted several aliases, occasionally posing as a Baptist pastor.

The second call concerned the chemical traces found in the Golders Green lock-up that morning. 'This is going to sound a bit odd,' said the man at the lab, 'but it's hair-lacquer -a rather old-fashioned type as well – used to be sold in hair-spray aerosols. Do you want the chemical name? Well names actually. There are several active ingredients.'

'No. I think I'll survive without that,' said Forbes.

'Were you expecting something in particular?'

'I was afraid you were going to tell me it was explosive fertiliser or a nerve-agent.'

'No,' the chemist chuckled. 'Nothing so sinister – unless someone's preparing a weapon of mass re-styling.'

The final call was from the team at the Exmoor crash site. It was too early to say with certainty, but they were more or less convinced that the Chinook had been brought down by small arms fire – possibly only one weapon.

Forbes was still trying to make sense of all this when he picked up the phone again. He had to ring Signor Angelini at his villa by the Lago d'Orta. There was yet more appalling news to pass on.

Crouch End

Appleby had always respected the moral principles by which his parents lived their lives, but there was one he had long regarded as arrant nonsense. Throughout his youth his mother had told him, when and if the subject of sexual relationships arose, that it was impossible to love more than one person at the same time, to truly love them, that is.

In Appleby's admittedly somewhat limited experience, love came like food or music in a vast array of flavours and rhythms. It brought an infinite variety of possible delights (or disappointments), and they were not mutually exclusive. He could easily have fallen head-over-heels in love with a score of the other women he had encountered in his life if the circumstances had been conducive or he had not actively stopped himself. Claire Tenterden had been the last addition to that particular list.

The catharsis of the previous week had demonstrated resoundingly that he still loved Jenny deeply and that he had never stopped loving her, even through the most emotionally paralysed stretches of their life together. But did that mean that he did not truly love Iris? Not a bit of it. The nature of their relationship had always been different, more sexually daring and vibrant, but somehow cooler and more tentative emotionally, at least when compared with his early years with Jenny.

Their last conversation had merely confirmed what had always been unspoken, that each regarded their affair as temporary, that Iris assumed he would never leave Jenny, and that he assumed she would find someone else. He had never asked her if she had slept with other men during their affair, though he would have been surprised if she hadn't. As long as she still wanted to see him, he really didn't want to know.

If anything his feeling that he could never fully 'possess' her had made his appreciation of her qualities as a human being all the more intense. The enforced distance made him imagine he could see her more clearly for what she was, and as he thought about it on the train down to London one Wednesday morning, he realised that he adored what he saw.

He was giving a lecture in the evening. She was working at home that day, so he had offered to join her at her flat and then take her out to lunch. He had resolved to end the affair, but his resolve was weakening by the minute. The closer the train drew to London, the more the thought of losing her distressed him.

Claire had just sent him a copy of the fourth novel in her rapidly expanding 'Halvingdene Saga'. After *Temptation Slow* and *Lords and Owners* came *The Steward of Excellence*. He tried to read, but his mind drifted away. He closed his eyes, and he and Iris were naked in bed together, their bodies melding, warm and sticky from sex.

When he finally reached her flat Iris gave him a quick peck on the lips, a friendly but cursory hug and said she'd booked them a table at Farfalli's. Her manner was so brisk that he wondered if she had somehow guessed what he intended to do.

She didn't waste time at the restaurant either. He had barely started his plate of bresaola with shaved parmesan, rocket and balsamic vinegar, when she leaned over and put her hand on his.

'Jimmy, my love, there's something I've got to tell you.' She looked him straight in the eye. Her voice was calm and affectionate, but decisive. She had never lacked moral courage.

'I've met someone else,' she said simply. 'I'm sorry.'

*

That night the audience at Queen Mary College noticed that there was something distracted about Dr Appleby's performance. His responses to the questions afterwards were particularly vague and ill-focussed.

He was the guest of a distinguished Professor of Renaissance Studies who had organised a dinner party for him at her house. Apologising profusely, he said he was feeling dizzy and unwell and crept off to lie down in the guest bedroom.

He pulled out his mobile phone, but realised miserably that there was nobody he could talk to about what had happened. He had never told anyone else about Iris, even though they had been seeing each other for five years, not even Pete Elyot.

Then he remembered another friend, a man to whom he had, on occasion, confided his most intimate secrets, and who had offered tough, but wise counsel in return. While the dinner guests chattered and laughed downstairs, Appleby rang Piet van Stumpe and poured his heart out.

Avon

'Boy, Garston, when you fuck up, you fuck up big time. They're gonna put you in the National Fuck-Up Hall of Fame.'

Garston Swilby's host had little use for tact. They were behind closed curtains in the comfortable sitting room of a large modern bungalow in the countryside near Bristol. Swilby knew him as 'Dean Wallen'. But that would not be his real name, just the one on his passport and the one he had given to the arms dealers he worked for from his office down the road in Bristol. Like Swilby, he was ex-Special Forces, one of an ever-growing global army of lethally-trained mercenaries, providing specialised services in the shadier reaches of the free market.

They had just seen a remarkably accurate PhotoFIT of Swilby's face (including the head injury) on the early evening news, along with a description of his height, build and American accent. His real name had been given, along with several aliases he might be using, including 'Pastor Davidson'. The Metropolitan Police were anxious to interview him in connection with the Enfield murders. No link had been made publicly with the helicopter crash. The official line was still that it was an accident on a training exercise. The murders of Kot and Handley had not even been announced yet.

'You're grounded until further notice, pal,' Wallen continued.

'I still haven't completed my mission,' said Swilby tersely.

'No shit!'

'So what next?'

'Nothin'. I've been told to expect your new instructions in the next two days. When you're through, they'll provide you with new papers so you can get your sorry ass back to the Home of the Brave.'

'I'm just wondering if they're gonna trace us here? We were surely filmed leaving the hospital. Didya see that camera over the entrance? Have you noticed the way they have cameras fuckin' everywhere in this fuckin' country?' Now he was no longer posing as a pastor, Swilby felt less need to moderate his language. 'It's as if they're trying to recreate that fuckin' book – *1984 – Big Fucker is watching you.*'

'Yeah, but fortunately the Brits aren't too hot on efficiency. Most of 'em don't work; and if they do, it takes 'em weeks to find what they need, 'cause they don't have the staff. Besides, I put false plates on the Chrysler when I picked you up.'

The next morning Swilby shaved his beard off and Wallen showed him his new toy.

'Ain't she a beaut?' he chortled, as he quickly and easily snapped the parts together.

The beaut in question was an AS50, the latest British sniper rifle, specifically commissioned and designed for use by U.S. special forces. 'This makes that piece of junk they gave you at Hallingham look like a third-grader's pea-shooter. 1.5 MOA, accurate up to two kilometers, but get this; it's semi-automatic, five rounds per clip. Free-floating barrel with a dual chamber muzzle-brake. You'll hardly know you've pulled the fuckin' trigger. She'll also take incendiary or explosive rounds that'll take out almost anything smaller than a main battle tank. Go on. Pick her up.'

Swilby lifted the gun rather suddenly. He had expected it to be a lot heavier than it was.

'Fourteen kilos,' said Wallen. 'Light as a feather, and she'll pack away in a hiker's back-pack. All ya gotta do is find the right vantage point.

That afternoon Swilby's new chaperone seated him behind the darkened glass windows in the rear of the Chrysler and drove to a secluded private estate. After two hours' tuition Swilby had dispatched a fox, two hares, four rabbits and a pheasant, besides cutting down three saplings over a mile away, incinerating a disused forester's hut and blasting an abandoned tractor to smithereens.

It was a most satisfying little outing. For the first time since landing at Heathrow, Swilby was in a really good mood.

*

Van Stumpe could just hear the driver's voice through the metal partition of the dirty white Ford Transit. As his two companions were in the back guarding him, he presumed he was talking on a mobile. Though almost inaudible, the cadences seemed familiar. He was sure it was Dutch, but maddeningly, he could barely make out one word in twenty.

Purple Ski-Mask had not replaced the gag or the ties on his wrists, but after a few miles, his partner, who van Stumpe mentally identified as 'High Voice', had decided it would be wise to put his blindfold back on. With the van on the move, he had done this roughly and carelessly, though, and van Stumpe had quite a wide field of view, this time through a patch of semi-transparent material over his right eye. The picture was a little fuzzy, but he could see something through the windows in the two rear doors.

Maybe it was his imagination, but fragments of the roadside landscape seemed familiar. After all, he had driven to Swively himself only three days before, though most of that journey had been in the dark. He was pretty sure they had been heading west on the M3 for some time, and had just passed the services at Fleet, when the van suddenly veered off on a slip-road. They turned left at the roundabout, and were soon in deep countryside. After a while they turned right, then left again down a bumpy track and stopped.

The driver threw the rear doors open and beckoned to High Voice who climbed out and followed him to a distance where they could not be heard. Van Stumpe thought he glimpsed some angry gesticulation.

After a few moments both men jumped into the back of the van. They grabbed him, pulled off his coat and frisked him, far more vigorously and thoroughly than they had when he was first abducted. They pulled off his shoes and inspected them, followed by his socks. Next he was being relieved of his pullover and his shirt. He had a dreadful feeling about what was coming next. Strong hands flipped him over onto his stomach. Down came his trousers, closely followed by his big comfy cotton briefs.

'Oh God, please no!' he groaned in Dutch, as he felt a hand thrust up his backside, the fingers squirming in exploration. Then it was out again, and the excruciating pain began to subside very slowly. He would be sore for days…if he lived that long.

'Yeuch! What's this white stuff?' asked the hand's owner. 'You disgusting old man!'

'Haemorrhoid cream, if you must know,' van Stumpe, muttered resentfully. 'I have piles, and you have just caused me excruciating pain.'

'I swear he's clean,' said the driver in English.

'Then how did they…?' said High Voice.

'Shut the fuck up!' said the driver. He lifted van Stumpe's blindfold an inch or two. 'Put your clothes back on, old man,' he said, reverting to Dutch, 'before we all throw up.'

As he fumbled with his clothes, van Stumpe's mind was racing. Why the intimate body search now? What were they looking for? A phone or some other kind of tracking device presumably. It must be related to the driver's phone call. Of course! The man had been talking Dutch. The trick must have worked! The Dutch police had been tracking his phone, and someone had tipped off his abductors.

Did that mean the Dutch police had found that horrible place where they had tortured Freek too? If so, Freek was either safe under guard in a hospital bed…or he was dead. Van Stumpe knew in his bones which it was. Either way, it changed everything.

The British police should have found his phone by now, and if Appleby had got his text he would tell them where to come.

'What now?' said Purple Ski-Mask.

'We wait here,' said the driver.

*

'There's a feeling that you're overstretched, Bill.'

The Commissioner was the only colleague who ever addressed Forbes by his first name, especially in its shortened form, and then only when telling him something he knew he wouldn't like.

'This situation has become extremely complex and volatile. Things need pulling together and quickly. You simply don't have the resources anymore. Anyway, it's out of my hands. Whitehall have decided to hand over coordination to Wilberforce at MI5. You're to liaise with her. Sorry, but you'll agree it's for the best.'

Normally this would have been a source of intense professional resentment. What Forbes actually felt was huge relief. News of fresh developments bringing fresh problems had been streaming in since the previous night.

First there was the murder in Northampton where another small black four-by-four had been seen. Coincidence? Surely not. But there was still no registration number or even a make and model. He suspected these murders must be the work of the Wahabi assassin the FBI had warned them about, the one who had tried to kill Appleby in Washington, but it was just a hunch. He had no evidence.

Next the Abramskys' Volvo had been left outside their house in the middle of the night, and the keys pushed through their letterbox. Nobody had seen it arrive, or who brought it. A forensics team was crawling all over it, but they had second-cousin Yitzak's DNA profile anyway, and the Israelis had already passed on everything they knew about him. There were traces of the hair lacquer in the boot, but all that told them was the rough size and shape of the new containers. Spotting the Volvo had been their main hope of finding him. Now they didn't even have that.

Then the American had slipped through their fingers. By a miracle the CCTV in the hospital forecourt had been working, and Forbes had been sent clear images of the two men driving off in a dark Chrysler Voyager, but it turned out to have false plates. They were desperately trying to identify the second man, but his face had never been in shot. Officers in Devon and Somerset had been checking traffic camera foot-age, so far without success. Others were trawling the DVLA records for any matching Chrysler which had changed hands in the last five years. Others were visiting Chrysler dealers in the south-west. It was worth a shot, but the man could have bought the damn thing anywhere. It might not even be his.

Oh, and poor old van Stumpe! There was enough information for the DVLA to come up with an exact reg for the white Transit, so they had the name and address of the owner. He had recently reported it stolen, of course. The Kent police were now leaning heavily on every dodgy second-hand car dealer in the county. There had been one sighting. Officers in a patrol car on the M3 had seen a driver using his mobile while driving and had radioed in the number, but they had taken off after a speeding Porsche and not pulled him over. The van was heading west.

As for the people they were supposed to be protecting, they knew Jenny Appleby had virtually emptied a building society account at a branch in Plymouth the previous morning. After that nothing...

At least they had IDs for two of these invaders and a partial ID for a third. The contingent from Holland, though, remained a complete mystery. Apart from the entirely innocent Abramskys, they still had no idea who was sheltering and equipping any of them, or even if their activities were being centrally coordinated.

As he told his wife when he finally got home that night, 'I'm glad they've handed the coordination over to that snotty cow Wilberforce. This business has been doing my head in. It's been like shovelling shit with a pitch-fork.'

York

Appleby and Pete Elyot had just sat down in the Langwith College Senior Common Room bar for the first time in – well, Appleby realised he couldn't remember how long. He had asked Pete to come for a drink because it was the anniversary of his break-up with Iris, and he was feeling deeply melancholy, not that Pete knew anything about that.

'Still drinking that vile red stuff, I see,' said Appleby. 'I don't know how you can swallow it. It looks like cherryade and tastes like a ruptured spleen.'

'That's why it complements my sense of humour so perfectly,' Pete grinned, 'not to mention my general approach to my fellow man.'

The beverage Appleby found so offensive was Pete's customary Campari and soda. Appleby himself was on the scotch as usual.

'So,' said Pete. 'How do you feel about your old nemesis becoming Dean?'

'Howland? I couldn't give a toss to be honest. I've got other fish to fry these days. I don't see how that man can hurt me anymore.'

'Actually, deary, I wouldn't be quite so sure of that.'

'Oh? What do you mean?'

'I'm not really supposed to tell you this, but what the hell? Before he left Matthew Featherstone was going to put you up for a personal chair. He rather liked having an international celebrity in the faculty and thought we should give you an upgrade before someone else snapped you up.'

'Really? That was nice…'

'Yes, well he'd put together quite a detailed proposal, I gather. It was in a file on his desk when Howland took over.'

'Oh. Right…'

'Straight in the bin apparently – literally. Sylv from the office actually saw him do it.'

'The cunt!'

'Quite. You do know why he's like that, of course?'

'Not really.'

'Because he's still in the closet.'

'Oh you *would* say that!' Appleby snorted.

'Believe me I can tell,' said Pete. 'He's self-righteous and superior all right, but he's also capricious, deeply manipulative, vain and bitchy. He has favourites; he can't bond with other men unless they're subservient and he has a seam of malice so thick you could mine it. I'm not saying all my un-out brethren are like that, but I promise you, these are all classic symptoms. He probably hates you because he secretly fancies you. Or at least he did when he first arrived.'

'That's the most preposterous thing I've heard all year!'

'You are still so unworldly, Jimmy. It's very endearing, you know. Talking of which, how's the lovely Jenny these days?'

'She's good actually – never better, in fact. She just sold a new book. You know, I'd say we're as happy now as we've ever been.'

'Excellent,' said Pete. 'I'm delighted to hear it…And what about the mistress?'

'What?' Appleby spluttered. 'What mistress?'

'That dark-haired siren from St John's.'

'Iris? How did you know about her?'

'Really, Jimmy! Half the campus knew. Didn't you realise? You really are unworldly.'

'Bloody hell. I had no idea. Anyway we split up a year ago today as it happens. I am now a faithfully and happily married man again.'

'So she dumped you.'

'Let's just say we both knew it was time to move on. She didn't waste any time finding a new man, either. Some rich young Canadian Adonis called Darius, apparently. They've got a baby now, I hear. I'm very happy for her, really…'

'Yes,' said Pete raising an eyebrow. 'I can tell… Still, at least you've still got Sir Nicholas to occupy your leisure hours. How's all that going?'

'It's extraordinary,' said Appleby. 'The whole thing just keeps on growing. It's been spreading abroad too, you know. I've been getting invitations from all over Europe. I've been invited to Geneva, Munich, Barcelona, Oslo, Bologna…I was supposed to be going on a tour of the States this summer, but my father's been ill, so I've asked my agent to try and reschedule.'

'I'm sorry to hear that,' said Pete. 'What's the matter?'

'He had a minor stroke about a month ago, but he's been recovering very well, and he's back home. My mother can't look after him any more because she's not in great shape herself, but my sister's organised all sorts of help, and they seem to be coping.'

'He's a great man, your pa,' said Pete. 'I've only met him a couple of times, but you can tell there's something very special about him. He told me all about his childhood in Stalybridge…'

'Yes, being orphaned at nine and brought up by his widowed grandma.'

'I remember him telling me about how the headmaster of his elementary school marched round to the education office with his English compositions when he failed the entrance exam and got him a scholarship to the local grammar school.'

'I know, I know…'

'Well, it's an impressive story,' said Pete. 'And a hard act to follow, I imagine…'

'Tell me about it.'

*

In fact, his father was much more seriously ill than Appleby had realised. Three weeks later Kate rang to say he was back in hospital after another stroke. This one had been devastating.

Appleby and Jenny raced down to Birmingham. Tom was barely conscious. At one point his eyes opened, and he seemed to focus on his son. He tried to say something but it was unintelligible. Appleby was holding his hand when he died.

Back at his parents' home, he and Jenny sat late into the night talking to Kate and Rob.

'He was really proud of you, you know,' said Kate.

'Was he?' said Appleby. 'It didn't feel that way sometimes. I always felt I'd let him down somehow.'

'No, Kate's right,' said Rob. 'He was always banging on about you, whenever I came round. I'd be down on my hands and knees unblocking their bloody sink and he'd be standing over me rabbiting on about your latest article or how lovely your house was. It was a pain in the arse to be honest,' he laughed.

'It's true,' said Kate. 'When you made that documentary he got all the neighbours round to watch.'

'Really?' said Appleby. 'I had no idea.'

'Oh you were always the special one, Jimmy' said Kate sadly. 'Don't get me wrong, they both loved me, but for that generation…well, I was just the daughter, wasn't I?'

They all sat in silence for a while.

'So?' said Jenny eventually. 'What about your mother? She can't stay here on her own, can she?'

'We'll take her in,' said Kate. 'Rob's already fixed up the spare room. And we're still entitled to help. It'll be fine.'

*

Despite Kate and her family's efforts, Barbara went into a steep and rapid decline. A few weeks later, she stopped eating as if, without her beloved husband, she had simply lost the will to live. She died a fortnight before Christmas.

*

The following April Appleby learned of the first Harkerism-related murder. There was a particularly large and active 'Kindred' which met in the old St Pancras Town Hall near Kings Cross. Inspired by the Box of Tricks televisation, they went in for long, elaborate rites, with a small chamber orchestra and a choir, candles everywhere and censers. They also met on Friday nights, believing that most of their congregation would be too busy to attend on Saturdays.

One week a small group of students from Bahrain had wandered in, simply out of idle curiosity. They were with a friend, the son of a Saudi prince living in an enormous stuccoed town-house in Belgravia. They had been drinking heavily, but as the effects wore off, the friend began to get agitated. During the 'Attestation' he had staggered to the front and confessed that his family had brought three young Bangladeshi women servants with them from Jeddah and kept them in the house as virtual slaves. They withheld their passports, made them work eighteen hour days, never let them out and frequently beat them. That very morning he had raped the prettiest girl, and not for the first time. What was more his father and his uncle had all done the same thing.

The service had ended in uproar. The next morning the women were all given their passports back and put on planes to Bangladesh carrying cheques for enough money to keep them in comfort for several decades. Two days later a man on a motorbike shot the prince's son twice in the head on his own doorstep.

Appleby had heard that the movement was recruiting briskly among the more moderate wings of several religious groups. He was sometimes asked about this issue, and would usually say that, although Harker had invented his own form of Humanism, he had always refused to deny the possible truth of Christianity. Given his long-standing fascination with comparative religion, it was reasonable to infer that he retained an open mind about religious belief in general. He was as close to a modern agnostic as it was possible to be in the sixteenth century and would probably have disapproved of dogmatic atheism as much as dogmatic religion.

But as the movement spread, it became ever clearer that there were religious factions, in Britain and abroad, who found it entirely unacceptable for any of their members to have anything to do with it. Appleby was horrified when violent, often fatal attacks were reported with increasing frequency.

He had no idea how much worse it would get.

Whitehall

'Have you eaten, Eevie? They do a tip-top breakfast here.'

'Let's just find a quiet corner, Dick. We can talk over a coffee.'

'Of course, my love. Follow me.'

Professor Richard Thorneycroft was an old friend from Yvonne Wilberforce's PPE course at Oxford. He murmured something to an attendant by the entrance, and she followed him through the heavy Victorian grandeur of the Reform Club lobby, up the wide ceremonial staircase and around the square first-floor gallery.

'I'll swear you've been wearing the same cord jacket for the last twenty years,' she said, 'and probably the same trousers.'

'Do try to get your facts right,' he said dryly. 'It's thirty years at least.'

He led her into an empty side-room, equally ornate and furnished with deep Chesterfield sofas. They moved to a corner near the fireplace.

'It's sometimes easier to sleep in a guest-room here than get the train back to Berkshire,' he explained. 'There are so many ghastly official functions now I'm head of faculty. Sit yourself down. The coffee will be here in two ticks.'

'The LSE are getting their money's worth, then?'

'I should say so.'

'So? My email?'

'Right. *The Tribes of Abraham*, eh? How do you think we can help? You're the ones with state of the art intelligence gathering systems.'

'Yes, and I also realise our limitations. We are overstretched simply keeping up with immediate threats. You academics have the leisure to look at underlying trends – "the wood and the trees" and all that. I know you have a research project looking at the organisation and funding of religious fundamentalist groups.'

'So we do. More specifically, we've been charting links between political power structures and spikes in fundamentalist aggression. Have you heard of "Warlord Theory" by the way?'

'I think someone alluded to it at a JIC briefing once. Isn't there some new book...?'

'It's a pet project of one of my colleagues, a psychologically orientated approach to the study of political power. Here's a handout he gives his first years. You only need to read that quote at the top really. It's from that great political philosopher, Genghis Khan.'

He handed her the sheet and she read it out: '*The greatest joy a man can know is to vanquish his enemies and drive them before him; to ride their horses and take their possessions; to see the faces of those who loved them wet with tears and to possess their wives and daughters.* Nice!'

'It's probably apocryphal, but that's beside the point. It distils a certain mindset in its purest form. What matters is not that all men who achieve power think like Genghis Khan, but that men who do think like this are grossly over-represented among the world's elites. It has always been the case: medieval barons, sub-Saharan dictators, Balkan ethnic cleansers, 19th Century American railroad barons – make your own list...'

A waiter arrived with a tray of coffee.

'Just leave it there, thank you,' said Thorneycroft. He poured the coffee. 'The point is that wherever they operate these "Warlords" do not change their essential character. They will lie, cheat, steal exploit, even commit murder – or at least have others commit murder on their behalf – in the pursuit of wealth and power. Once you get your eye in, men matching this behavioural profile pop up everywhere.'

'Forgive me, Dick, but this is hardly news.'

'Bear with me. In mature democracies, these characters have to develop aggressive philosophical self-justifications. They will co-opt economic theories or ideas of social morality which appear to justify their own behaviour, disguising the fact that their motives are essentially selfish and their methods ruthless. It's been called "Warlord self-validation". They commonly present themselves as pillars of respectability – they make generous and well-publicised donations to charities – but deep down they remain as ruthless and rapacious as

Genghis Khan himself.'

'You're beginning to sound like an old-fashioned leftie. I thought you'd abandoned all that anti-capitalist radicalism.'

'I have. I've been a convert to the free market for years. You know that. The whole point about the Warlord mentality is that it corrupts the free market. It distorts the delicate organic processes by which the free market functions. It makes it less efficient. It has also been demonstrated that, while these sociopathic types are skilled at attaining positions of power, statistically their performance in those positions is usually below average.'

'So manipulative, over-ambitious narcissistic maniacs fuck things up. I'm sorry, Dick, but where is this taking us?'

Thorneycroft took a sip of coffee and frowned.

'Two points,' he said. 'My own group's preliminary findings indicate clear, frequent and demonstrable links between interventions by Warlord types and the fostering of aggressive religious militancy. It seems these men (and they usually are men) find it extremely useful to recruit fundamentalism as their bodyguard and attack dog. I won't bore you with a list of historical precedents, but believe me, they are legion. First lesson: if there is a sudden burst of fundamentalist aggression, look for the Warlords backing it.'

'We're working on that as it happens.'

'Good. That brings me to the second point. Warlords are utterly ruthless in attacking anything they perceive as a threat to their position. Did you know my team has done an analysis of the killings of Harker-ites over the last three years, by the way?'

'No, I didn't.'

'It seems the murders fall into three distinct categories. Approximately fifty per cent were committed by religious fanatics – mostly poor and uneducated – who had been told the cult was a direct attack on their religion. Another fifteen per cent were executions or state-sanctioned assassinations carried out by the security forces in states with intolerant religious laws. It's the remaining thirty-five per cent that are really interesting. They were all related to what the Harkerites call 'Attestations'. The victims had all made public confessions which exposed immoral or criminal activities by powerful individuals or groups with whom they were connected. Warlords hate Harkerism because it has an uncanny knack of turning people into whistleblowers. Basically they want the whole damned movement to disappear.'

'Okay,' said Wilberforce. 'So how do The Tribes of Abraham fit into all this?'

'The TOA is a new phenomenon,' said Thorneycroft guardedly, 'but some of our researchers have been picking up chatter. It seems that the organisation is channelling a lot of new money into religious militant groups, and that this money is coming from individuals who fit the Warlord profile. More specifically, they are sponsoring a common anti-Humanist agenda. It would be a classic Warlord tactic to recruit such militants to lend a gloss of spiritual legitimacy to what are often simple acts of gangsterism. I expect most of the clerics who front this organisation are completely sincere in their way and genuinely believe that this new evangelical form of Humanism is a threat to religious belief. But I'd say the question you should be asking is who's been providing the cash and why? Warlords, Eevie my darling, look for the Warlords…'

Wilberforce got up to leave.

'Thanks, Dick. Food for thought, eh?'

'Do you know anything about an outfit called the Phoenix Foundation, by the way?'

'The religious pressure group?' said Wilberforce. 'Perfectly harmless as far as I know. Why do you ask?'

'Only because there seems to be some overlap with the TOA. If you do come across anything, could you possibly tip me the wink?'

'Sorry, Dick, you know I can't promise anything like that. Thanks for your time, though. Sometimes it helps to stand back from things for a while…'

*

'He's a bit tasty,' said DC Lambert. She was looking over Drucker's shoulder at his computer screen.

'Do you like swarthy types, then Debbie?' asked Drucker. 'Intimate relations with this particular Romeo might get a bit, shall we say, "explosive".'

'Who is he?'

'This, my girl, is our "Yitzak", the Abramskys' cousin's nephew or what-have-you.'

Forbes walked in, slightly more relaxed after a decent night's sleep, safe in the knowledge that the buck would stop on someone else's desk if this investigation got even messier than it was already.

'Take a look at this, sir,' said Drucker. 'A rare helping hand from the DCRI in Paris. Debbie reckons he's hot.'

'Go on.'

'He is an Israeli national. Lives in one of those fortified settler compounds near Jerusalem, but he does most of his dirty work in Europe. The French want him for bombing an apartment block in Marseilles. Blew up the flat of a Syrian with links to Hezbollah – it was very messy – twelve innocent deaths and thirty serious injuries.'

'Is he Mossad?'

'Nope. It was Mossad who gave us the ID, remember? They want him taken out. He's a loose cannon, apparently, an adventurer who hires himself out. They think he's done several hits for the Russian mafia.'

'Why on earth are these people descending on us? I just don't get it. See if the Abramskys will confirm this is our guy, will you? Then circulate the picture. I'm off to yet another sodding briefing in sodding Whitehall.'

*

Forbes was the last to arrive again. It was exactly the same group that attended the last meeting.

'Let's get started, gentlemen,' said Wilberforce crisply as Forbes sat down. 'We've a lot to cover, and time is pressing.'

Forbes promised himself that he would not allow himself to be niggled by anything she said or did today...

'We've been trying to set recent events in their international context – since that is something that seems to be beyond the powers of our Special Branch colleagues – Giles?'

...but it was going to be difficult.

'The picture's getting a little clearer,' said Chalmers. 'Certain patterns are beginning to emerge. We've been getting stuff from the CIA and Mossad – and from our own records, of course – about some of the people who attended that TOA summit in Beirut. It turns out that several of the non-clerical "delegates" are involved in a whole string of interconnected oil deals. These involve organisations based in Dubai, Texas and Uzbekistan. A huge network of Uzbek pipelines seems to be secretly controlled by an Israeli-based energy corporation with extremely dodgy Russian connections. Their CEO was at the Beirut junket too. We are only just beginning to untangle this ball of string, but it seems to involve astronomical bribes, rigged contract allocations, price-fixing on an epic scale, the circumvention of environmental protection regulations and the brutal suppression of political opposition. We've started digging a little deeper, and guess what? Each of these outfits has suffered some kind of embarrassment recently because one of their lackeys has had a fit of conscience after joining a Harkerite Kindred.'

'This is all absolutely riveting,' said Forbes, 'but I still don't see how any of it's going to help us catch the maniacs we've got charging around the country.'

'A little patience please, Commander Forbes,' said Chalmers. 'We've had some very interesting intercepts through from GCHQ in the last forty-eight hours. We now know that the various attacks over here are being co-ordinated from a seven-star hotel suite in Dubai. The geeks have transcripts of phone conversations from there to a woman in an office in Houston and a man in a Tel Aviv apartment. Coincidence? I don't think so.'

'You said something significant came through this morning,' said Wilberforce.

'Yes it did. We now know definitely that they are running four teams, each working independently with its own separate support network and targets. They may not even be aware of each other's existence. All we have at the moment are their code names: "Isaac", "Ishmael", "David" and "Solomon".

'Do they mean anything?' asked Weekes.

'Isaac and Ishmael were the sons of Abraham said to have founded the Jewish and Arab nations respectively,' said Chalmers. 'And of course Jesus was of the House of David, so presumably that could mean our Christian fundamentalist friend, Mr Swilby. Solomon was the builder of the first temple in Jerusalem.'

'And what's the significance of that?' asked Forbes.

'Well the first temple was built to house the Ark of the Covenant, the box containing the stone slabs on which God had written the Ten Commandments. So it would make a kind of sense if they were the ones who'd gone after our Dutch archivist…'

'…and his box, containing the laws of the new cult,' said Wilberforce. 'Quite.'

'I still don't see what they expect to achieve by this,' said Weekes.

'Victory,' said Wilberforce crisply. 'It seems their controllers think like Warlords. They regard Harkerism as a deadly threat and they are determined to detroy it. These attacks are designed to demoralise, intimidate and if possible, decapitate the enemy.'

*

'Ishmael' was back in his latest safe-house, a semi in Luton, when he discovered that he had killed the wrong person – again. It was humiliating and infuriating. He had taken a huge personal risk, driving to Holland Park and back with an RPG launcher hidden under an overcoat on the back seat. And the explosion had been a thing of beauty. The BMW had simply burst apart in a ball of fire. It was almost orgasmic. At least he had the consolation of knowing he had dispatched another filthy Sodomite.

But there could be no more mistakes. His next attack would be up close and personal, even if it meant he became a martyr himself in the attempt. Friends in Milan had just seen Angelini board a flight to London. He would watch his house until he made a move. And this time he would stay on his tail until he got the chance to finish him off.

In the meantime the 4 by 4 was having a makeover in his host's garage.

*

'Where the heck is Hilversum, anyway?' asked Jenny.

Pete Elyot's cottage was not quite what the Applebys had imagined. Far from being chic, minimalist, post-modern or ironically kitsch, it was like the set of a TV drama, set in their 1950s childhoods. There were doilies on the coffee tables and antimacassars on the three-piece suite. The bookshelves were stocked with Agatha Christies and small leather-bound editions of Victorian classics with black and white plate illustrations and little silk ribbons attached as bookmarks. There was also a set of the old pocket-size editions of Wainwright's fell-walking guides, with their spidery little illustrations.

It had small electric fires, a whistling kettle on the stove, a knitted tea-cosy, and the beds had heavy blankets and quilts instead of duvets. In a cupboard by the living room fire they found several jigsaw puzzles and a cribbage set, along with boxes of Ludo, Beetle and Snakes and Ladders. There was no television, just an old Bakelite radio with lines on the tuner marking the Home Service, Light Programme, Third Programme and Hilversum.

'Hilversum? It's a town in Holland,' said Appleby. 'I think they used to broadcast light music over here for a while. This place is something else.'

As they snuggled up under the heavy bedding that night, they concluded that this was Pete's refuge from his radical, bohemian, sexually experimental lifestyle, a place where he could regain his lost innocence for a few precious hours on quiet weekends.

It was high season and Swaledale was crowded with hikers, holiday-home-renters and day-trippers in cars and coaches. They decided to stay in the cottage until the the crowds had subsided, confining themselves to a short walk in the village in the early evening. The only food they could buy provided a ridiculously unhealthy fry-up, but even that had a comforting, retro feel.

To Appleby, Swaledale, with its pretty stone houses, dry-stone walls and iridescent green hills, grazed by shaggy sheep with big, curved horns, was a northern English Elysium. He had been several times as a child and he adored the place. He made Jenny get up early the next morning and they walked up a large limpet-shaped hill called Kisdon. The summit was rough and tussocky. A huge pale lemon-coloured sun shone through the early morning mist. They could only see a few metres ahead down the path.

'Look at that,' said Appleby. 'It's magical, as if we'd passed into another dimension.'

'You wish,' said Jenny.

They returned to the cottage and stayed put for the rest of the day. Appleby was delighted to find a copy of Harker sandwiched between 'The Thirty-Nine Steps' and 'Economical Cookery for the Newlywed Houswife'. Maybe Pete had brought it up one weekend and forgotten to take it back to York. He decided to look for a suitable Contemplation to use at the launch.

It didn't take long to choose. Tucked in at the back of the collection was one Appleby had found loose in Cranham's chest. It was a copy of the last one Harker ever wrote, intended for the Rite on the day of the massacre. Appleby assumed it had never been delivered. He found it unbearably poignant:

'Beloved Kindred all, I stand before you this day as one who should himself Attest to a great weakness and still greater folly...More than a fortnight

since I was summoned to Salisbury to be questioned by His Grace, the Bishop.'

Harker then looked back over their years of meeting together, the sad condition of the late parson and the bond that had grown between them all:

'Have our ceremonies been Heretickal? Perhaps, but only if 'tis Heresie to leave a space for Righteous Doubt…and to rejoice in the Spirit of man… yet the Bishop, I fear, is not of my mind.'

Harker went on to confess that he had tried to disguise the true nature of their activities, and that he had not stood up for his beliefs until it was too late. He had let them all down. He would be ashamed of this until the day he died:

'My hour of trial was upon me, my Kindred, and I had not the wit to see it. Now the moment is gone, and I can no longer defy that towering Spire, making it shake with the glory of the Spirit within us…of that which hath brought such joy and such comfort.'

He said he saw no value in a life of craven fear, of pretending to believe 'arrant and palpable falsehoods'.

He told them not to fear, for he had taken all responsibility for their actions upon himself.

'I fear me this must be our final Rite…soon you will learn that I have been translated to another, darker place from which I may never be suffered to return…I ask only this, my Beloved Kindred, that you keep my Spirit alive in your hearts…as I shall carry yours in mine, until the very moment of my end. May the Spirit burn bright within us all.'

How utterly appalled the old man must have been when the soldiers arrived, and he realised that, by holding this one last Rite, he had summoned his followers to their deaths. This was the *Contemplation* Appleby must read. He would also take it as the text for a 'Contemplation' of his own.

He had finished writing by late afternoon, and they took another walk, this time to the summit of Great Shunner Fell. Near the top, they sat on a rock looking back down the hillside. The dale was spread before them, bathed in the soft, early evening sunlight.

Jenny leaned against his arm. 'What are you thinking about?' she asked.

'Dad,' he said. 'He loved it here.'

'You really miss him, don't you? Once I'd have believed he'd be looking down on us…'

'Well,' said Appleby, 'if there actually is a heaven and by some bureaucratic oversight, they were ever to let me in, then I hope it's like this.'

'Why don't we just stay here forever?' sighed Jenny.

'Because we're not dead…yet.'

Back at the cottage, she heated up a home-made meat pie they had bought at a local bakery. Appleby rang Mrs Tench to ask if she had the number of a car service.

'Where do you want to go?' she asked.

'Wiltshire ultimately, but Richmond would be a good start.'

'When?'

'Tomorrow morning. Early.'

'Hang on.'

Appleby could hear muffled voices in the background.

'My son Clarke says he'll take you.'

'What? To Richmond?'

'No. To Wiltshire. He says he'll do it for a hundred pound plus the petrol and you're to get his dinner at one of them motorway service stations.'

'Done.'

*

Van Stumpe had fallen into a fitful doze in the back of the Ford Transit. He was awakened by the sound of doors slamming and rough, angry voices. Something was pressing painfully into the side of his right buttock. His captors were all outside the van for some reason, so he rummaged about. It turned out he was sitting on the handle of a medium-sized slot-headed screwdriver. He just had time to ease it, handle first, up the sleeve of his jacket when his captors came and pulled him unceremoniously into the fresh air. A glossy black Hummer and a small Fiat hatchback were parked by the track.

Purple Ski-Mask and High Voice pushed him into the back of the Hummer. At last! A comfy seat! The driver was arguing with two men who had presumably just brought these vehicles to this ad hoc rendezvous.

'You took your fucking time. Any fucker could have found us by now.'

'You gave shit directions. What do we do with the van anyway?'

'Torch it.'

The driver climbed into the Hummer, started the engine and pulled away. Van Stumpe craned his head round as they headed back towards the motorway. There was an orange glow in the trees behind them.

Bloomsbury

'I don't miss the sex or anything....Sorry, that sounds awful, doesn't it? That was all very nice while it lasted...I'm just trying to say that I really, really miss our friendship. You were such a big part of my life, and if I'm honest, I got as much out of our conversations and, you know...' she paused briefly, searching for the words, '...sharing stuff, ideas and experiences, as I did out of anything else. That's what I miss. I just wondered if maybe we could meet up from time to time and just talk. Like we used to.'

Appleby stared into the remains of his cappuccino. It was getting on for four years since he had split with Iris, three since he had learned who her new lover was, and that she and Darius had a baby. They had never quite lost contact completely. They had exchanged Christmas cards at their office addresses. They had even had a very brief chat on the phone once, but neither had thought it appropriate to meet.

So he had been surprised, intrigued and a little unsettled to get an email from her, completely out of the blue, asking if he'd like to meet up near her work the next time he was in London. She hadn't said why.

So here they were, a week later, drinking coffee and eating tasteless toasted paninis in a chain coffee-shop, and he had his answer. He stared out of the window, as if watching the passing tourists would help clarify his thoughts.

'I'm really not sure that would be a good idea,' he said eventually. 'I don't know how I'd react to prolonged exposure. Jenny and I...well we've been back on track for a long time now. I don't want to mess that up again. Not ever. How is Darius by the way?'

'He's good,' she said wistfully. 'Back in Canada.'

'Uh huh. How long for?'

'Indefinitely. We broke up last year. Don't get me wrong,' she added quickly. 'That's not why I asked to meet.'

'I'm sorry to hear that. What went wrong then?'

'It was me really. I think I kind of drove him off. It was great for a while. I did love him – still do if I'm honest. I just found the whole business of actually living with someone else really oppressive. I'd become so used to living my own life. It was difficult to share. That's what was so lovely about us. You never made any demands. You never wanted to influence the way I lived my life. And he was a real prig about the dope! He actually made me stop, which I have incidentally, and I'm glad I did now, but at the time I *really* resented it!'

'But what about your boy? Edward is it? He must be…how old is he?'

'He's three and a half.' Her eyes sparkled with motherly pride. 'He's gorgeous. Darius was never much use with him anyway to be honest. He's not the paternal type.'

'So how do you manage? Are you okay financially? Does he help?'

'I'm fine. My salary's okay, and he sends me a cheque every month which covers the nanny and so on. It's no skin off his nose. His whole family are rolling in it. And he comes and sees us when he's in London. I wouldn't want any more than that anyway.'

'I'd like to meet little Edward sometime.'

'I'd like that too. It would be really good if he got to know you. We're a bit thin on… especially since my mother died.'

'Oh no! When did that happen?'

'Last year. Not long after Darius left actually. She'd had undiagnosed bowel cancer for ages apparently. They found secondaries everywhere. It was all quite quick in the end.' She gave that sad little smile of hers again. 'I'm an orphan now.'

'Oh, Iris. That's awful. So you're on your own, you and little Edward.'

'Yeah. Pretty much these days…So does that mean we can become *just good friends* then?'

'Sure. Why not?

She took his arm as he walked back to the tube station across Russell Square. They swapped selected news-bites from their four years apart and agreed they would meet again soon, and Appleby would come back to Crouch End to meet her son. They hugged each other for a long, long time by the news-stand opposite the station entrance before she turned to leave.

*

He decided to tell Jenny about Iris. Since their reconciliation, she had never asked about his infidelities, and he certainly did not intend to inflict any of the details on her, but if he was going to start seeing Iris again, even if only as a friend, it would have to be completely open and above board.

In the end it was nearly five months before he did see her again, and he never got down to Crouch End to see little Edward. A week later Phyllida rang to suggest a summer tour of America. There was huge interest in his books, which were to be re-issued as a single volume, something she had planned for years. She'd had requests for signings and lectures from all over the States. She already had bookings lined up in Washington, Boston, Chicago, Atlanta, Seattle and San Francisco. The Smithsonian Institute was even offering to pay for business class flights.

This time he decided to go.

Swaledale

The morning after their walk, Appleby and Jenny got up at 6.00, show-ered, dressed and had breakfast. At 7.00 Clarke Tench and his mother arrived in their Ford Escort. Ivy gave the cottage what she called 'a quick once over', and they all headed back to Muker. She nipped into the house when they dropped her off and came out with a bag of cheese sandwiches and a big flask of tea, which she handed to Jenny.

'You look after these, Mrs Bunbury. You'll be needing something on the journey.'

Jenny burst out laughing. She had completely forgotten that they were travelling under an alias. Appleby sat in the front with his new script on his knee. Jenny stayed in the back and fell asleep.

'How long do you think it'll take?' asked Appleby.

'Long enough,' said Clarke.

*

Early that afternoon Forbes was summoned to see Wilberforce again.

'So,' she said crisply. 'Where are you up to? Have you found the American yet?'

Forbes looked glum. 'We're still trying to trace the Chrysler.'

'Or the jihadi? Or the Israeli?'

'We're following up every lead we get,' he said, barely disguising his resentment.

'Well, we're doing what we can here,' she said, trying to sound placatory. 'We'll let you know immediately if we get anything more from our own assets of course, or from GCHQ. I presume you've drawn up a list of likely Harkerite targets.'

'No.' said Forbes. 'I have neither the time nor the resources.'

'Well fortunately we have. You do realise that they're opening that big new Harkerite centre in Wiltshire tomorrow? At that village?'

Forbes did know, but he had barely had time to think about it, let alone make any arrangements. Now this patronising spook was making him feel like an idiot. He shrugged.

'Well I think you'd better get over there, hadn't you?' she said, suddenly alarmed. 'You still don't know where these people are, and it's the prime target! Go tonight – with your best team. I've already spoken to the organisers, and I've arranged for some airport security people with x-ray machines and metal detectors to cover the entrances. But you need to take as many armed officers as you can muster. I'll get the Home Secretary to press-gang extra muscle from the local forces.'

'What about your people?'

'They're intelligence specialists, not security guards. By the way, did you know our friend Appleby is due to give a performance?'

'Well that's not going to happen. He and his wife have gone to ground. Either that or they'll turn up in a ditch somewhere with a bullet each in the back of the head. Appleby won't be there.'

'Oh, I think he will. He rang the organiser two days ago and promised to go. We checked the number. He was using a pay-as-you-go mobile, but he hasn't used it since. And have you found the Dutchman?'

'The Transit's just been found in Surrey, just off the M3. It was burnt out, so they must have transferred to another vehicle. The Surrey police checked the tyre tracks. There was a big 4 by 4 down there, probably a Hummer.'

'The M3, eh? So they're heading for…'

'Who knows?' said Forbes. 'We're still checking the motorway cameras, but there are hundreds of 4 by 4s on that road.'

By now Forbes was sick of being put on the spot. He decided to turn the tables.

'And have your "intelligence specialists" turned up anything useful on any of these people? "Ishmael"?'

'Not yet.'

'Yitzak?'

'Nothing new, I'm afraid.'

'*Nothing?*'

'Not yet.'

Now it was Wilberforce's turn to squirm.

*

'You don't seriously expect me to ride in this heap of junk?'

'Special, ain't she? She's a twenty-seven year-old Leyland Princess! Ain't she just the shittiest lookin' motherfucker you ever saw?'

'Where in hell does a man acquire such a monstrosity?'

'There's a charming gentleman down the road goes by the name of Mr Wayne "Pikey" Doggler. Sells scrap metal and breeds ferrets or somethin'. Man, you should see his yard – just like you'd find in the backwoods of the Appalachians. Come to think of it, you should stroll on by, Garston. You'd feel right at home down there.'

'Why can't we take the Chrysler?'

'Too risky. They're probably lookin' for it by now. If we go in this thing, the cops'll assume we're just a couple of local losers, heading for a ferret-fuckin' convention or whatever they do for fun round here.'

Swilby's new orders had come through the night before. Appleby was due to attend the opening of a new Harkerite centre in Wiltshire. Swilby was to find an opportunity to take him out, but always to remain at a safe distance. Strictly no shoot-outs with the police.

'I found the perfect vantage point for ya,' said Wallen as they joined the A4. 'It's like a ruined castle on this big artificial hill thing. You have to climb through some underbrush to get to the place, but it's deserted and you can hide behind the walls. It has an uninterrupted view of the house where our friend will be doing his little number. And the main entrance is slap-bang in the middle of your field of vision. I marked it up for you on the map there. See – it's that place called Sneck-bridge. There's a print-out of the day's schedule there too, and a picture of your target in the fancy dress he'll be wearing. Study it carefully, my friend.'

'What's the distance?' asked Swilby.

'About a mile. Well within range. Is that a problem for ya? I was told you were recruited for your sniping prowess.'

'It's not a problem.'

'Tell me something, Garston. This mission – is it a matter of religious conviction for you? Are you, like, a true believer?'

'Damn right, I am. Ain't you? A believer?'

'Me? Sure I am?' said Wallen. 'But I go with Oliver Cromwell, you know, the dude who wasted their king. "Trust in God, but keep your powder dry!" That's my motto.'

'I'll tell you my motto if you like,' said Swilby ruminatively.

'Go on.'

'Kill every faggot, atheist, commie, Catholic, Jew, Muslim, nigger, towel-head and slit-eyed gook on this planet. That's my motto.'

'Well thank you for sharing that,' said Wallen. 'You know something, Garston Swilby? You are one twisted sonovabitch.'

Westminster

Two days after Appleby had left on his tour of America, Yvonne Wilberforce went to a meeting at the Italian Embassy in Three Kings Yard. The invitation had come from Gianfranco Borsetti, a senior member of the Embassy staff, who acted as an unofficial liaison officer between the Italian security services and the various British intelligence organisations. Wilberforce had no idea what he wanted to discuss. He had merely said that he wanted to introduce her to someone who might be able to help her.

Borsetti ushered her into a room with a colleague from Italian military intelligence, and another man she vaguely recognised.

'Thank you so much for coming, Yvonne,' said Borsetti. 'Marcello from AISE you know already, of course. Now allow me to introduce my friend, Signor Giovanni Angelini.'

The penny dropped. 'Of course, you're the publisher!' said Wilberforce. 'Didn't we meet at a reception here once? You have a house in London…'

'Quite so,' said Angelini, 'in Holland Park. London is my "home from home" as you say.'

'So how do you think you can help us, Signor?'

'I will explain that, but first I should say that I am very much hoping that you will be able to help *me*.'

'How?'

'I have not yet let this be known publicly, Signora, but I am the owner of a collection of documents currently housed in Amsterdam, known as the Harker-Cranham archive. As I am sure you are only too well aware, all those associated with Sir Nicolas Harker and his philosophy have become potential targets for attack in recent years. For some time now I have been receiving death-threats myself. It is evident that my identity as the owner of this material is already known to people who might wish me harm. I would be immensely grateful if the British security services could alert me to any potential threat you become aware of while I am a guest in your country, and perhaps offer some form of protection.'

'Well we would pass such intelligence to Signor Borsetti and his colleagues as a matter of course, anyway, but I will certainly alert my staff. Protection would be a matter for the police, I'm afraid, but I can put you in touch with the relevant officers at Special Branch. Now, how do you imagine you might be able to help *us*?'

'As you may know,' he said, 'the foremost expert on my archive is Doctor James Appleby. I have not yet had the privilege of meeting him, even though I have been, at various times, his "Fairy Godmother". He has recently travelled to the United States, has he not, where I understand he has been encountering considerable hostility. I fear that before long, my secret protégé may require protection himself. Now I have two fine properties here in the United Kingdom and they both benefit from the most sophisticated security systems...'

*

The FBI contacted Forbes's superiors as soon as Appleby started getting death-threats in America. Forbes was told to draw up contingency plans. When the threats turned into actual assassination attempts, he remembered a phone call from Yvonne Wilberforce at MI5 mentioning some Italian publisher. He gave her a call.

Then the FBI warned the Home Office that the Washington sniper might be on his way to the U.K. Forbes decided to get Appleby to a safe-house as soon as he landed. This would have to be done as discreetly as possible.

The simplest way would have been to have officers escort him directly from the 747, but Forbes had an almost paranoid mistrust of the Heathrow ground-staff, convinced they were riddled with thieves, organised criminals, spies and potential terrorists. Any unusual arrangements might be noticed by some undesirable and passed on to God knows who.

He decided he needed to enlist the help of a friend – someone who

Appleby would trust implicitly, but who would not be recognised, even by well-briefed attackers. That ruled out his family, of course, and close colleagues. Trying to build a more complete profile of Appleby's life and activities, he contacted a series of 'known associates', including a peculiar chap called van Stumpe in Amsterdam. That proved interesting. It turned out that Appleby had secretly had a mistress in London. As far as van Stumpe knew, nobody else knew about her. They had broken up several years ago, but were still in contact and on friendly terms. Forbes decided to pay Ms Tulliver a visit.

The following week there were two attempts on Appleby's life and the Renaissance Institute was bombed, apparently killing van Stumpe. The day before Appleby's return, Forbes sent Kot and Handley, first to check out Angelini's Exmoor property, then straight up to York to collect Appleby's wife. Later that day he picked Iris up in Crouch End and took her to meet Angelini at his house in Holland Park. As Appleby left JFK, Agent Keppler delivered his enigmatic instruction to look out for her at Heathrow.

A few hours later Appleby flew back into London and the rain, wondering why on earth Iris would be waiting for him and still expecting to get the train home to York.

Swively

'Some say the Historie of man runneth as a river, whose course is carved by Providence or the hand of God. Others do say the Bearings of our Voyage are set by the march of armies or the stratagems of the Mighty. This is not my estimation. Is it not made manifest daily that our Destinie is a rattling Dray, dragged behind two wayward and unbroken colts, one named Accident and the other named Error?'

—*Sir Nicholas Harker, The Colloquies, Book IV, No 32*

It was nearly 3.00 am when the black Hummer reached the edge of Swively. The driver turned towards van Stumpe.

'We're nearly there,' he said in a clipped voice. 'Now you're going to direct us to this house and you're going to tell us where to find the chest.'

'How will I be knowing that my Freek is alive and that you have released him?' asked van Stumpe.

'You won't,' said the driver. 'Not till we know we have that chest. Now direct me to the house.'

Van Stumpe told them to drive through the village and out again. After half a mile, they reached the end of the Charltons' drive. The gravel crunched quietly as they pulled up on the forecourt in front of the grand Jacobean porch.

'Okay,' said the driver. 'We're here. Now where do they keep the chest?'

'I am not knowing exactly,' said van Stumpe. 'Mr and Mrs Charlton will have found some place to put it securely. All that I know is they have assured me it is safely in here.'

'Now,' said the driver. 'My friend here and I are going to pay these people a visit. He picked up an Uzi machine-pistol and pointed it at van Stumpe. 'I feel sure that they will be only too happy to help us. In the meantime my other colleague here,' and he pointed to Purple Ski-Mask, 'will stay behind to make sure you're...comfortable. Only when we call his cell phone to say we have achieved our mission, will he put you in contact with your little friend back home. In the meantime you wait.'

The driver and High Voice pulled on ski-masks, jumped from the Hummer and set off across the gravel. Van Stumpe saw them ring the doorbell. A minute or two later a light came on, the door opened and they stepped inside, holding their guns in front of them.

Purple Ski-Mask was pointing his automatic at van Stumpe's chest. 'Tell me something, old man,' he said. 'Why did you ever let yourself get involved in this shit? I know you're a faggot and all that, but have you no God? No faith? No belief?'

'Of course I have,' said van Stumpe. 'I believe in history and I believe in truth.'

Purple Ski-Mask chuckled softly and shook his head. 'You know I really don't think we need to wait for that call. Why don't I arrange for you to join your friend right now? The two of you can cuddle up nice and warm…in the fires of Hell.'

'Freek was dead almost as soon as we were leaving that horrible place where you burned him, was he not?' said van Stumpe quietly. He gently shook his right arm until he felt the screwdriver slip down his sleeve. He clasped the handle in the palm of his hand.

'Sure. But you knew that all along really, didn't you? The human capacity for irrational hope is a miraculous thing.'

He leaned forward, pressing the gun against van Stumpe's temple. His face was inches away, smiling mockingly, pouting. 'Now why don't you just "think about all the good things", you perverted old queen.'

'Yes,' said van Stumpe, driving the screwdriver with all his strength into the soft underside of the man's jaw and sending him sprawling backwards. 'I am a queen! I am Queen Boudicca!'

It took two more thrusts to kill the man, one into the neck and the third through the heart. Van Stumpe was amazed by the magnificence of his own rage and by the strength and energy it gave him.

He wrenched the pistol from the dead man's hand, leapt from the Hummer and trotted as quickly as he could, round the side of the building and down some steps to the small door into the cellar under the original medieval wing. Please, please let them have forgotten to lock it again! They hadn't, but Guy Charlton had done something equally stupid. Van Stumpe could actually see the key in the back of the lock through a small glass pane in the door. How could they be so careless? Thank God they were! He smashed the pane with the butt of the pistol, reached in, turned the key and crept inside.

A back staircase took him up into the old kitchen. He could hear voices, but they seemed to come from the floor above. He took his shoes off and crept into the medieval hallway. Then he carefully pulled away the detachable section of staircase, pushed down on the stone slab, took out the small wooden board, reached for the iron lever and pulled. The door in the wall made an agonising scrape as it opened. Then van Stumpe replaced everything as neatly as he could before stepping behind the panel and shutting himself inside the first hiding place. Apart from a thin line of pale light under the panel it was pitch dark.

He didn't know how these men planned to destroy the archive, burn it presumably, but if he went into the main priest-hole and sat on the chest, he could shoot them dead as soon as they appeared in the doorway. He felt for the handle on the misericord, turned it and opened the second door.

'Argh!' he gasped. 'Who are you? Are you some ghost?'

A man with a torch was leaning over the chest. The spectre began to turn round.

'I have a gun here!' said van Stumpe. 'Stay in that place or I shoot you!'

'Hello, Piet,' said Appleby. 'Fancy meeting you here! Please don't shoot me. That was a clever little tip-off you sent, by the way. Page 133 – genius!'

'James!' hissed van Stumpe. 'Mine God! It's you! But, please, you must be completely hushed. There are two murderers in the house with those little Uzi guns. I have escaped from a third one. They are intending to make the Charltons show them to where this chest is hidden. But if they are coming I will be ready!' and he waved the automatic towards the door.

'Christ!' whispered Appleby. 'This is going to get interesting. There are two armed police officers in the house. I suppose it all depends on who sees whom first.'

Suddenly van Stumpe stepped across to Appleby and embraced him in the dark.

'Oh James!' his voice was barely audible. 'I am overjoyful that you are alive still. I had made myself convinced they must have assassinated you by this time.' Appleby noticed that van Stumpe still had his halitosis problem. This probably wasn't the time to mention it, though. 'Did you know they killed Vaartje and my little Freek?'

'The police just told me,' Appleby whispered. 'I'm so sorry, Piet.'

'And what of your nice wife? Mrs Jenny?'

'She's here, with the Charltons.' Appleby shone his torch on the chest again. 'You did an absolutely brilliant job in Amsterdam. You've saved almost everything. How the devil did you get it out?…Uh-oh! It's started…'

They heard a distant shout, followed by the muffled sound of gunfire. There were at least two bursts from machine-pistols and several single shots, all overlapping and almost indistinguishable. Then they heard a shriek followed by a heavy thud. It seemed to come from the floor above.

'And now perhaps they have killed the Charltons also,' van Stumpe groaned.

'Oh God! Jenny was upstairs too,' Appleby wailed. 'I must go to her!'

'Stop!' whispered van Stumpe through clenched teeth. Appleby was taken aback by his vehemence. 'You cannot be helping her now. We wait in here. If they will come through that door I shoot them. They take this chest over my corpse!'

The silence that followed seemed interminable.

'It's unbearable not knowing what's going on out there,' Appleby murmured. 'Now I know what those Jesuit missionaries felt like.'

They heard the sound of heavy footsteps, first overhead, then coming down the nearby stairwell. Then silence again.

The panel from the hallway made a faint creak as it swung open.

'Oh shit!' muttered Appleby. 'Here we go!'

'I am ready,' van Stumpe whispered.

Appleby turned off his torch. The door opened. A burly man peered into the gloom.

'Well, well, well,' he said, 'the famous Doctor Appleby, I presume. Commander Forbes, Metropolitan Police. We meet at last! And you must be Mijnheer van Stumpe. Delighted to meet you, I'm sure. Now do put that gun down, there's a good little archivist...'

*

Yvonne Wilberforce had commandeered The Kindred Spirit as a temporary headquarters for the security services, providing the disgruntled guests with alternative accommodation in a chain hotel several miles away. Forbes had arrived from London at midnight and gone straight to his room, but he had been woken by Drucker as soon as the Hummer was spotted in the Charltons' drive.

When the doorbell rang, Drucker told the Charltons to try to lead their unwelcome visitors upstairs, where he and another armed officer would wait out of sight on the landing. After a lot of agitated discussion, Guy managed to persuade the driver and High Voice that the chest was in a spare bedroom at the top of the stairs. They were following him across the landing when Drucker opened fire. He dispensed with the regulation verbal warning. The driver died instantly. High Voice got off too wildly inaccurate bursts from his Uzi before Debbie Lambert shot him in the chest.

By the time Forbes led Appleby and van Stumpe back to the Jacobean entrance hall, the two corpses were already being loaded into ambulances.

Jenny and Izzy were sitting side by side on the stairs, both white and trembling. When Jenny saw Appleby she sprang up and hugged him tightly.

'You made a thorough job of that chap in the Hummer, Mr van Stumpe' said Forbes. 'Anyone would think you'd had training.'

'I was in a most absolute rage,' said van Stumpe, 'like Queen Boudicca!'

'Ah, but you kept your head,' said Appleby.

'That's because I pay attention during sermons. Now, if you please, I would like to be washing myself.'

'I'll find you some clean clothes,' said Izzy. 'My goodness! Look at your wrists. They're raw! I'll get you some Savlon.'

Two minutes later she reappeared with antiseptic cream for van Stumpe and a letter.

'Sorry, I forgot about this,' she said, handing the letter to Appleby. 'This is for you. It arrived a couple of days ago. Someone's clearly been hoping you'd make it here.'

'Thanks,' said Appleby. 'Let's hope it's not another maniac.' Glancing at the envelope, he recognised the handwriting. It was from Iris. 'I'll read it later,' he said, stuffing it in his jacket pocket unopened.

'Thank God that's all over!' said Jenny. 'Maybe now we can start leading a normal life again.'

'Not over yet, I'm afraid,' said Forbes with a mirthless grin. 'It would seem that we have just dispatched Solomon. Unfortunately we still have Isaac, Ishmael and David to contend with…'

*

The Charltons put the Applebys in the same room they had slept in on their first visit. Appleby couldn't sleep. Jenny was in a state of nervous collapse and snored loudly beside him all night.

'James,' she said when she woke the next morning. 'Please don't tell me I'm mad, but I saw her again.'

'Saw who?'

'That woman. The woman I saw before. Susannah Cranham or whoever she is. Only this time I know it was real. I met her on the landing when I went to the loo.'

'Oh?'

'She was in the same white nightie. I'd just stepped out of the bedroom, and there she was. She looked at me and said, "Beware." I said "Beware of what?" She said, "*It will come again.*" I said, "What will come again?" She said "*The fire. The fire will come again.*" Then she walked away. This time I just know she was real.'

'Jenny,' said Appleby gently. 'I've been awake all night. I haven't slept a wink. You've never left the bed, my love.'

*

Everyone in the house except the Applebys and van Stumpe was up by 5.30 that morning. Forbes and Drucker were supervising the security arrangements. Most of the estate was surrounded by an eight foot stone wall anyway, but eight local officers had been detailed to patrol the perimeter. The Charltons' house had been cordoned off with temporary metal fencing, and the old public footpath to Swively had been closed, the entrance now guarded by armed officers. This left two other entrances, one leading from the Charltons' drive and the other on the edge of the car park by the Wolvington road. By the time visitors began to arrive for the 10.00 am start, these would both have armed guards too. All visitors would have to pass through the airport-style security gates organised by Wilberforce, complete with x-ray machines and metal detectors.

Meanwhile Guy was marshalling the vehicles which were allowed into the estate itself. These included three police minibuses the caterers' vans, several mobile lavatory units, two mobile generators and outside broadcast vans for a BBC news unit and Wilts FM.

There was also a van for the team who had erected the marquee which would act as an overflow auditorium for visitors who couldn't get seats for the events in the main buildings. Another team were installing a large cinema screen and sound system for this purpose. This team had their own van too. Izzy checked the people at the marquee had everything they needed and headed for the reconstructed Farthingwell Manor to make sure all the furniture had arrived and was in the right place.

Even she had to admit that her husband had done a wonderful job. The house looked stunning, except that, as she noted with dismay, the builders *still* hadn't removed the hideous yellow rubbish chute and skip from the side. She called Guy on her walkie-talkie.

'I know!' he fumed. 'I'll strangle that incompetent twat when I see him! It's too late to do anything about it now, dammit.'

When she went inside, Izzy found a young man in overalls with a large pressurised spray carefully coating the walls.

'Hello,' she said cheerfully. 'What are you up to?'

'Fire-prevention, Madam,' he said. 'It's only a retardant, but you can't be too careful in a wooden building like this.'

He had a slight foreign accent, but what worker didn't these days? He also had a deep, gentle voice and was a bit of a dish, swarthy with deep, dark, penetrating eyes and a five o'clock shadow. If only she were twenty years younger. Okay then, thirty. She could see his van outside: Adams of Swindon – Fire Prevention Consultants.

She went upstairs to the long gallery. Appleby and van Stumpe were due over at 8.00. They were to display the chest on a small platform and arrange the most significant books and documents in a long row of lockable glass cases. The chest and the cases would then be roped off, and visitors would file past as part of a tour of the upper floor. She adjusted a few signs slightly, but everything appeared to be ready and in its proper place. The early morning sun was streaming in through the long run of uneven leaded window-panels. No wonder Guy loved this room. It was fabulous.

*

The Applebys joined van Stumpe for breakfast in the Charltons' kitchen. Forbes had just returned Appleby's mobile and he was checking his messages.

'Page 133 again. You texted as well,' he chuckled. 'That really was inspired.'

Through the window they saw a chauffeur-driven Bentley swing round towards the front door. It was Angelini. He had flown in from Milan as soon as Forbes told him about the attack at his London house. He joined them in the kitchen. He was clearly in a bad way, deeply upset by the death of Florentin and blaming himself that it had happened at all.

'I should have known better, he said. 'I should never have left him in my home without proper protection. I had to speak to the poor boy's parents last night...' his voice tailed away miserably. 'Did you know about that? About the attempt to kill me in London?'

'Yes,' said Jenny. 'Forbes told us last night. I'm so sorry.' She put her hand over his and looked into his eyes. 'Giovanni, do you really think this is wise? You coming here, I mean?'

'Why not? It seems everybody knows about my role in the movement now. Why should I miss the party? Anyway, I want to see my precious documents before I sign them over to the Charltons' foundation.'

'Of course!' cried van Stumpe happily. 'Guy has asked myself and James to make them into a display in the new Farthingwell Manor house. You can be assisting us to do this. Will you come now?'

'Give the man a cup of coffee, first,' said Appleby. A thought struck him. 'I'm giving a lecture about the history of the archive this morning. Why don't you let me introduce you as the man whose generosity made all this possible?'

Giovanni sipped his coffee. 'Yes,' he said eventually. 'I think I would like that very much. Just don't ask me to say anything. I refuse absolutely to make speeches.'

*

Half an hour later the four men went to the priest-hole. This astonished and delighted Angelini. They retrieved the chest, took a corner each and marched it solemnly across the fields to the replica manor house. It would normally take weeks to plan an exhibition like this. As it was van Stumpe issued them with latex gloves, and they spent a frenetic hour arguing about what should go where, and making sure everything was as well displayed as possible, given the ridiculously short time they had. Finally van Stumpe made sure all the display cases were secured. Guy had given him a separate padlock for each one, and van Stumpe jangled the keys officiously, like an old-fashioned school caretaker.

*

Suddenly the estate was full of visitors, and the programme of events was under way. Appleby felt he was flying on auto-pilot when he gave his lecture in the new Cranham Institute. It was old, familiar ground, and he had passed beyond tiredness. At the end he introduced Angelini to the audience who gave him a warm round of applause. Angelini bowed slightly, beaming with appreciation, but remained resolutely silent.

They passed Jeremy Dilke in the lobby as they came out. He was about to give a lecture himself entitled 'Attesting Reality: Harkerism in the Media'. They exchanged warm greetings and agreed to meet later.

'Catch you at the screening?' said Dilke.

'Oh,' said Appleby, 'Is that...?' But he had gone.

*

Angelini headed back to the Charltons' to change. Appleby headed for the catering tent to meet Jenny and van Stumpe for lunch. He was amazed at how busy the place was, and at the number of people who had dressed up in period costume for the day. Van Stumpe and Jenny chose the spit-roast hog with mashed turnips from the 'Authentic Elizabethan Menu'. Appleby went for something called 'Condemned Man's Pottage' which was meant to be the pea-soup with bacon and rough white bread served to Harker before his interrogation. Appleby thought this particular bit of whimsy was rather tasteless, though it was nothing like as tasteless as the soup itself. He left most of it. Eating a lot would only make him drowsy.

*

Outside the marquee Charlie Drucker was worrying about the perimeter. A youngish man in a blue hoodie had been seen climbing over a fence near the car-park, avoiding the security checks at the entrance. It was probably just a student who didn't have a ticket and didn't want to pay, but even so...

*

Guy had told the Applebys how thrilled he had been when the producers of a new British film with an Elizabethan theme agreed to hold their first preview as part of the launch. This 'world premiere' was to be screened in the marquee at 2.00.

Appleby and Jenny thought they had better check it out and wandered across. As they walked in someone shouted and waved. It was Farnstable, furiously beckoning them over to join him. Appleby had heard a rumour that he was making a feature film, but he had no idea this was it.

The title sequence came as an even bigger shock:

A Greater Need

The Life of Sir Philip Sidney:
Warrior, Poet, Lover

Original Screenplay by
Claire Tenterden & Jeremy Dilke.

And the fun was only just beginning. Farnstable had negotiated a co-production deal with an American cable TV channel. Certain liberties had been taken with established historical fact to appeal to their American audience. The Duke of Parma personally tortured Dutch prisoners with red-hot implements. Sir Richard Topcliffe, who had somehow inveigled his way into the story, was seen behaving inappropriately with Elizabeth I as she sat in her bath, and Sir Francis Walsingham was shown *in flagrante delicto* with the Italian free-thinker Giordano Bruno during the latter's visit to London.

When the English army opened the Battle of Zutphen with a massed artillery barrage, sending computer-generated Spanish cavalry flying through the air in bursts of bright orange flame, Appleby dissolved in uncontrollable laughter.

He was also astonished to see that most of the scenes set in Sidney's London residence had been shot at Despenser College. At one point Sir Philip himself actually leaned out of the oriel window in Appleby's borrowed suite, though there was no sign of young men with flagons of ale wedged between their buttocks on the lawns over the river.

Then came the credits:

Historical Consultant
Hans von Biegen-Herzenslust

That had to be the Hamburger! It was an even greater surprise to read

With special thanks to Professor J. D. Clovis, CBE

But it was the very last credit that really knocked him out:

From an idea by Doctor James Appleby

He didn't know whether to laugh or sue.

*

While the film was in full flow, a new arrival in the car-park clipped the corner of a green Suzuki Vitara, damaging the tail lights and making a slight dent in the bodywork. A steward was taking down the offending driver's details when he noticed something odd. He called one of Forbes's officers over.

'Didn't you tell us to look out for a small black four-by-four?' he said. 'Well take a look at this. See, where the paintwork's chipped? It looks like it's been resprayed. It's black underneath. Nobody uses black undercoat do they?'

'Hmm,' said the officer. 'No bull-bars, though.'

'Maybe not, but the fittings are still there. It's had some at some point.'

'Good call,' said the officer. 'I'll get someone over. If anyone comes near that thing, you give me a shout.' And he walked off speaking into his radio.

Two minutes later Forbes relayed a message around his team:

'Eyes peeled please, everyone. It looks as if "Ishmael" may have come among us.'

*

Appleby was to perform the Rite at 5.00 pm. The master bedroom next to the gallery in the manor house had been set aside as his changing-room, so he went across to try on the costume, go through his script and take a short rest. The door said 'STAFF ONLY'. He closed it behind him, stripped off and pulled on Sir Nicholas's undershirt. The bed looked so tempting. He had to lie down for a while. It was not made up, of course, but there was a sheet over the mattress and a soft, warm counterpane on top. He soon dozed off.

He was awoken by a hand, gently reaching round his tummy, and the feeling of a soft woman's body pressing against him.

'Hello,' whispered Jenny as he stirred. 'You look so comfy. Mind if I cuddle up?'

'Hmm. Go ahead. That's nice.'

He turned to face her, and kissed her tenderly. She kissed him back. Was it the release of pent-up anxiety? The warmth and comfort of the bed? Suddenly he was flooded with love and desire.

'Do you remember our first night in Swively?' he said. 'In the inn?'

'Of course,' she said. 'How could I forget that?'

'You know what? Wouldn't it be... you know... here in a replica of his bed? In a replica of his bedroom? With me in a replica of his underwear? I mean, that would be a bit special, wouldn't it?'

'Have you gone mad?' she laughed. 'You don't mean it?... Really?' she grinned. 'Oh, go on then, but you'll have to be quick!'

'Thank you, that was lovely,' he said as he rolled away ten minutes later.

'This is ridiculous,' she laughed. 'I feel like a teenager at a party! And I'm amazed you had the energy.'

'So am I,' he sighed. 'But it's always important to get into the part.'

*

They knew from Cranham's journals that Harker's ceremonies had been held in the Great Hall on the ground floor. It was only on the day of the massacre that everyone had been forced into the gallery upstairs. At 4.30, now pleasantly relaxed, Appleby went downstairs in his full Harker costume. He checked that his lectern was in place, with a glass of water to hand and that his microphone was working. He pulled out the script he had completed in Thwaite and laid it in position, open at the right page.

As the audience filed in, Farnstable, Claire and Dilke came over to wish him luck, closely followed by van Stumpe and Angelini.

'Break a leg,' said Jenny, giving him a hug and a good luck kiss.

Within minutes the hall was full. Everyone was settled. It was time to begin.

He was hoping that, compared to his performance in York, this would be a relatively undemanding gig. Apart from a few press and broadcast journalists, the congregation consisted entirely of enthusiastic Harkerites. And so it proved. They lapped up everything with relish, reciting the responses in loud, sincere voices. Some of them even murmured his lines, which they evidently knew by heart, as he delivered them, which was really quite off-putting. And they sang as if to save their lives. Gordon Fairview had written a lovely new hymn and another anthem which the choir sang unaccompanied. Once again, it made Appleby's spine tingle.

The only source of disappointment for his audience was that Appleby had insisted that there should be no *Attestations*. 'If we start all that, we'll be here all week,' he told Guy, 'and it would be unfair to preselect a few people.' Instead Guy had organised an open 'Ceremony of Attestation' in the marquee the next morning, to be conducted by the Senior Mediator from the St Pancras Kindred. Three hundred people had signed up.

For Appleby the only part of the ceremony that really mattered was the *Contemplation*. Perhaps it was the potent hormonal cocktail produced by prolonged fatigue, intense relief, sexual release and the elation of performing, but as he read Harker's text he found himself overwhelmingly moved. He slipped into a reverie again, not unlike his experience at Midnight Mass in Norwich all those years ago. The audience became ghosts. He was in the original hall on a bright May morning, four hundred years ago. As he reached the end of Harker's last address to his Kindred, his eyes filled with tears.

'I'm sorry,' he mumbled, wiping them on the sleeve of his robe. 'That poor old man...'

A sympathetic murmur rippled round the hall. Appleby took a sip of water and regained his composure.

'Now if you will forgive me, I will step out of character for a moment. I would like to say a few words of "Contemplation" on my own account, as James Appleby. I will take as my text a line we have just read: '*My hour of trial was upon me, and I had not the wit to see it.*' Like many people in this room, I have had the rare privilege of living in a time of ease, comfort and prosperity. There have been wars aplenty, of course, and appalling violence but a few miles over the sea in Ireland, but not here, in this quiet corner of Europe. Few in human history have been so lucky. There have been ordeals of one kind of another for many of us, no doubt, myself and my wife included, but these have, for the most part been personal tribulations, suffered in privacy, and not catastrophes inflicted on the whole society.

'In my case, and I suspect my experience is not untypical, this has led to a certain detachment. And that detachment has led to a kind of moral inertia. We have seen cruelty and injustice rampaging elsewhere in the world, and we have tut-tutted and eased our consciences by signing petitions, writing angry letters or making donations to charity. Some us have even got involved and taken direct action to help those who cannot help themselves. But most of us, myself included, once we had dropped our coins in the charity envelope, have turned back to the petty preoccupations of our centrally-heated lives.

'Yet it has been at home that we have been found most wanting. I have been guilty of failing to see, or if seeing, of failing to act. I have been guilty of the passive bleating of the over-comfortable. After the last war, our parents' generation felt an overwhelming collective urge to build in this country a New Jerusalem, a 'Shining City on a Hill' where social justice, equality of opportunity, good health and education would be the birthright of all. Yet during my adulthood my own generation has slipped into a state of moral enervation, watching idle and inert as those ideals were slowly eroded, have dissolved and faded away.

'Britain is now a land eaten out from within by the rot of amorality. The mass media regularly, systematically and cynically distort the truth or simply lie. In our precious countryside, the supermarkets grind down the farmers, who respond by herding their "Corn-fed, free-range" chickens into toxic barns and stuffing them with chemicals. Priests molest children while their superiors turn a blind eye. Garage mechanics charge for work that did not need doing and which they may not even have done at all. "Loan-management" companies cheat the needy of their homes. "Carers" abuse the elderly in care-homes. Parents lie and cheat to get their children into the best schools. Banks sell loans or insurance plans they know their customers do not need and cannot afford. Private Equity groups cynically plunder the assets of thriving businesses which they then destroy, and our political masters betray us in secret deals we never even hear of. For decades now, we have lived in a world poisoned from top to bottom by cynicism, greed, chicanery and deceit.

'How did we ever let this happen? Why didn't we all fight harder to stop it? Why don't we fight harder now? Even if it does mean that we have to face unpleasant repercussions. Is the disease now so widespread that we have lapsed into fatalistic resignation? Have the forces of selfishness and cynicism convinced us that their norms are *the* norms? Have they actually won?

'I now believe that Sir Nicholas Harker's *hour of trial* comes to each of us, in tiny increments, throughout our lives, and if his tragic death, close by this very spot all those yeas ago, teaches us anything, it is that we must *have the wit to see it*. For me Sir Nicholas Harker's most profound and resonant belief was that we all possess an innate moral sense, that we all know right from wrong without the spurious authority of religious dogma. We should find the resolution to follow that instinct, our Spirit, if you will, and resist wrong-doing with all our might, on each and every occasion. Let the remembrance of Sir Nicholas's death, and the deaths of his family and neighbours, burn as a beacon in the moral fog, and guide us to a future where honesty triumphs over lies.'

'Fuck me,' Farnstable muttered to Dilke. 'This thing really *has* got to him!'

Claire leapt to her feet and applauded furiously, closely followed by Jenny, then the entire congregation. Cheers could be heard wafting through the air from the marquee.

Appleby sat back utterly exhausted. It was time for the final hymn.

*

'Bunch of *Guardian* readers!' muttered a pretty attendant dressed as an Elizabethan country wench who was standing guard by the entrance.

The main door to the hall had been left open because of the heat, and she had been directing latecomers to the overflow seating in the marquee. Guy and Izzy were leaning against the wall a few metres away, standing next to Forbes who was on his radio, desperately hoping that someone had spotted 'Ishmael'.

'He's finished the *Contemplation* now,' said Izzy, looking at her watch. 'Not long to go.'

'Honestly, some people!' said Guy indignantly. 'You see that oik in the overalls over there, chatting up that wench. He's right in the entrance and he's getting his fags out! Who is he anyway? He's been hanging around all day?'

Suddenly Forbes was paying attention.

'That's the chap who did the fireproofing,' said Izzy. 'He's a bit of a sweetie, actually. I thought *you* hired him.'

'Fireproofing? I didn't order any fireproofing!'

'Well that's weird. He was in there first thing this morning. He was terribly thorough – seemed to be spraying every surface in the place. Didn't you notice the smell? Like cheap perfume?'

'Shit!' said Forbes, pulling his pistol from the holster under his arm.

Yitzak had a particular spot in view, on the floor under the right-hand door-jamb. It looked dry now, but as he finished that morning he had soaked that area in odourless barbecue lighter fuel. Things had to get off to a good start.

Forbes's first shot missed, breaking a side window on an outside broadcast van. But Yitzak felt it whistle past his head, and was so startled that he dropped his match harmlessly on the ground. He was fumbling to light another one when Forbes's second shot hit him in the chest.

Forbes shouted into his radio. 'Charlie! I'm at the manor house. Get some paramedics and a stretcher over here now! I think I just dropped "Isaac".'

The attendant was hysterical, but inside the Great Hall, the congregation hadn't noticed a thing. They were too busy singing, '*Let ever bright the spirit burn*'.

*

'There's something going on down there,' said Swilby peering through the scope of the AS50. 'Some dude just collapsed in a heap.'

Perched beside him on the ruined castle wall, Wallen was watching through powerful binoculars. He had a much wider view.

'A guy shot him with an automatic,' he said, 'an armed cop, I'd guess. Could you see what the guy was doing?'

'Trying to light a cigarette.'

'Maybe they classify that as a terrorist attack over here. Uh oh, here come the medics. Now you just keep that scope trained right on the doorway. Mr Gopher should be popping out of his hole any minute now.'

'If they taught me nothin' else in the Seals, it's that a good sniper has limitless patience.'

'The apricot or the chest?' asked Wallen. 'I heard the guy they sent to Washington went for a head-shot and Appleby turned away. The Marine Corps's teaching new recruits to go for the upper body these days, I gather.'

'I guess you'd call me a traditionalist,' said Swilby. 'But I don't have to hit the apricot, anyway. This mother'll take his whole fuckin' head off.'

*

By the time the *Rite* ended, Yitzak's body had been removed and the attendant was being comforted in the medical tent. Forbes was acutely aware of the danger, but had decided against ordering an immediate evacuation. The service was almost over, and the last thing he wanted was the entire congregation scrambling out in a panic. He put officers inside the doorways, though with instructions to stop anybody lighting up. When the building was completely clear they would close it up and call the fire brigade.

Appleby was standing in a corner by the rear exit in a huddle with Jenny, Farnstable, Dilke, van Stumpe and Angelini as the congregation filed out of the front. A stream of people wandered over to say hello, offer congratulations or ask questions. He answered them with as much courtesy as he could muster. By now he felt completely spaced out. At last the hall was almost empty. He would make his excuses, stagger back to the Charltons', have a big tumbler of whisky on the rocks and go to bed.

He was turning to leave when a handsome, fresh faced young woman came up.

'Please excuse me, Doctor Appleby,' she said in an American accent. 'You seem to be a difficult man to contact these days, but I've come over to England specially to see you.'

'Oh?' said Appleby. 'That's very flattering. 'How can I help?'

'Well it's just that I have brought a few things over which I think you might be interested to see. I guess you'd call them family memorabilia, really. My people are of Dutch descent, you see. My ancestors settled in upstate New York in the mid seventeenth century. I only came across this stuff recently. I've got it all back in my hotel room in Wolvington if you want to stop by and see it later. It's all quite fascinating actually...'

'I'm sorry,' said Appleby. 'What did you say your name was?'

'Oh, my! Didn't I say? I'm Perdita – Perdita Spirit Krannem.'

'*What*? I...What sort of stuff is it?'

But a tall man was pushing in.

'Look, I can see you're busy,' she said. 'I'll catch you later!' And she was gone.

For a moment Appleby thought he must be hallucinating again. The man who had pushed in was dressed from head to toe in exactly the same clothes as he was. The only difference was that this second replica Sir Nicholas was a light-skinned black man. Appleby realised he had seen him before, and very recently.

'Hi there,' said the apparition, seizing Appleby's hand and squeezing it fiercely. 'Let me introduce myself? My name is Jay Ophier. I have the honour to be the Elder Celebrant of the North Manhattan Convocation. I just wanted to say what an absolute privilege it has been to attend your Rite, Professor Appleby. And as for your *Contemplation* – that was truly inspirational, sir! I shall remember this ceremony for the rest of my life.'

As it turned out, that would not be a particularly impressive feat.

'Thank you,' said Appleby. He was about to ask what 'The Purgation of Fire' was and what had become of the juvenile incestuous rapist, but Ophier was already walking away.

'Man!' said the Elder Celebrant as he stepped out into the sunlight. 'That was some occas...'

*

'Bull's-eye!' said Swilby. 'Mission accomplished.'

'Nice shot,' said Wallen. 'Did you catch that jet of blood? Whoosh!'

'You know what?' said Swilby, swiftly changing the clip on the AS50. 'I'd like to give the rest of that repugnant congregation of god-hating fag-lovers something a little bit special to remember me by.'

He aimed carefully and squeezed the trigger again. The incendiary round hit the doorway and exploded. Within seconds the entrance was engulfed in flames.

'Okay,' said Wallen. 'Recess is over. Let's split.'

'Man, that fire is spreading faster than crabs in a Cancun cathouse,' said Swilby, chortling with delight as they scrambled down the bank. 'That is so deeply satisfying.'

When they reached the Princess, Wallen opened the boot, held his hand out for the AS50 and clicked his fingers impatiently.

'So what now?' asked Swilby as he handed it over.

Wallen quickly stripped down the rifle and packed the parts away in the rucksack.

'It's back to my place now, Garston. Your new papers came through this morning. Then we'll sort out your route back to Home Sweet Home.'

'What about the rest of the ordnance? The other rifle and the Glock?'

'They're right here in the trunk, but don't you worry about a thing.

My instructions are to take care of all waste-management issues. No one'll even know you been here.'

As he said this Wallen picked up the Glock, swung around and put two rapid shots into Swilby's forehead.

It was not quite the return journey Swilby had envisioned. An hour later he was half way back to Bristol, travelling in the boot of a battered old British car, minus the back of his head, squashed up like a foetus, with a painful case of *rigor mortis*.

*

Swilby was not the only one to be surprised by the speed with which the blaze took hold.

'My archive!' shouted van Stumpe, and ran up the stairs.

'We must help!' said Angelini striding vigorously after him.

'Come back, you idiots!' Farnstable was calling. 'Get out now!'

Van Stumpe turned around at the top of the stairs. 'Help us!' he shouted. 'Please! All will be lost. These documents are priceless – completely irreplaceable! Please! We are needing help so badly!'

By now the flames had begun to spread briskly across the floorboards towards the rear entrance. The temperature in the hall was rising by the second. Appleby stood motionless, transfixed by indecision.

'Come out, Jimmy!' shouted Farnstable.

'If you go up there, you'll die!' called Dilke.

'Jimmy! Hurry! Come out! Please!' Jenny shrieked.

He had never heard her shout so loud. Her voice had become a piercing throaty screech. She lurched towards him but the two men manhandled her through the back door.

His last escape route was about to be cut off. Within seconds he would have to jump through flames. Time slowed to a crawl. Voices crowded into his mind like angry creditors clamouring for payment: '...harmless, but spineless and flippant... Every man thinks meanly of himself... your steadfastness and moral courage... gentlemen in England now abed will hold their manhoods cheap…My hour of trial was upon me…'

The flames had reached his feet. He charged up the staircase.

'Jimmy! No!' Jenny's cry was somewhere beween a roar and a wail. 'Jimmy please, *come out!*'

But Appleby hardly heard her. When he reached the gallery van Stumpe was moving from display case to display case, desperately fumbling for the right key. Giovanni had pulled the chest off its plinth. He was grabbing the documents and throwing them inside as van Stumpe opened each case. Progress was painfully slow.

Appleby tore a fire-extinguisher from the wall and strode from case to case smashing the glass. The three men reached into each one, seizing the documents, smearing them with blood as the broken glass nicked their hands. By now the flames had crossed the stairwell. They were cut off.

Appleby threw in the last document. It was the *Brief Rite of Consolation on the Death of an Infant.*

'We must push it out at the window,' said van Stumpe, slamming the lid shut.

'Lock it!' shouted Giovanni, 'or it will fall open, and the papers will fly everywhere.'

Van Stumpe grabbed one of the locks from a cabinet and closed the chest.

'Check the windows.' said Appleby. 'Maybe they're bringing ladders.'

Van Stumpe struggled to open one of the leaded panels, but it wouldn't budge. Appleby smashed it open with the extinguisher. The flames had burned right through the thickness of the walls below them and were already licking up the outside.

By now a large crowd was watching from a safe distance. Van Stumpe leaned out of the window and shouted desperately, 'Bring ladders! We have no way of exit! Please bring us ladders!'

Drucker was shouting desperately to Forbes on his radio when he noticed a man in a blue hoodie step forward and aim a pistol. He took two shots at van Stumpe and darted back into the crowd.

Appleby had no idea that fires could be so noisy, but he and Angelini still heard the shots. Van Stumpe fell back unconscious.

'Shit!' said Appleby. 'They're shooting at us! This is just like fucking 1594!'

'The window!' called Angelini. 'We must throw the chest clear of the flames!'

It was heavy, but there were stout handles at each end, and they both managed to get a firm grip. They swung it back and forth rhythmically, gradually increasing the momentum.'

'On the count of three!' said Appleby. 'One... Two... Three!'

The two men let go, and the chest sailed majestically through the broken panes and past the flailing arms of the fire. It landed with a crump on the grass beneath, but it did not break apart. Van Stumpe had always said it was well-constructed. Three men rushed forward and dragged it to safety.

Appleby thought he heard another shot as he crouched over van Stumpe. There was no halitosis this time. Was he dead? It was impossible to tell. He grabbed the fire extinguisher and sprayed foam all over van Stumpe's inert body.

'Help me!' he shouted to Angelini. 'He's been shot!'

The two men grabbed van Stumpe under the arms and dragged him across to the window. With a huge effort, they heaved him up and pushed him through, thrusting him as far from the building as their strengths would allow. They heard a horrible crunch as he hit the ground beneath them.

'Now I am going to jump!' said Angelini, and he hurled himself through the window too.

Appleby peered out through the smoke. He could see van Stumpe being dragged away, while a limping Angelini was helped away by bystanders. Suddenly a man in a blue hoodie burst from the crowd and ran towards him, but this time Drucker was ready. Appleby heard the shots as the policeman fired. That's the second time in twenty-four hours that man's fired without giving a verbal warning, he thought.

He was preparing to jump himself when a violent gust of flame shot up the outside wall in front of his face. He looked around desperately. Flames seemed to be leaping past every window. By now the floor was too hot to touch. Then he heard the staircase collapse. He was trapped.

Appleby knew the end was near. The heat was unbearable, and he was about to pass out. He staggered through to the master bedroom. There was a mirror on the wall opposite him, and he saw his head and torso in Elizabethan costume framed against a background of livid orange flames. It was as if the vague sense of dread he had felt when he had first seen that peculiar portrait had been a sort of premonition. He flopped onto the bed to get off the hot floorboards. He found his jacket and felt in the pocket for his mobile phone. Maybe he could just send Jenny one last text. Must keep it short. He keyed in a message and pressed 'SEND'.

That was when he remembered the letter from Iris, still in his coat pocket. He tore it open and tried to read, but he could hardly keep his eyes open. Words swam up at him: '...stomach cancer... consultant... chemo... six months if I'm lucky...Edward...his only family.' It was too much to take in. He had to make one last effort to get out.

Then he noticed the garderobe. Perhaps the fire had not reached that corner yet. He began to crawl towards it. His hands and knees were blistering. He thought he felt a gust of cooler outside air, but the room had filled with smoke. He began to cough violently. A blissful vision of a sunlit evening on a Yorkshire Dale appeared as unconsciousness descended...

*

It took the fire brigade over two hours to make their way along the narrow lanes, clogged with unusually heavy traffic. By the time they had found a suitable water supply and attached their hoses, the house had been entirely incinerated.

The investigators didn't even find any teeth. They said the blaze had been hot enough to reduce bone to fine powder, as efficient at destroying a human body as the oven of a crematorium. Anyone trapped on the upper floor would not have stood a chance. At least they would have passed out from smoke inhalation before the flames reached them.

The following morning the builders finally removed the skip and the molten remains of the rubbish-chute.

Cambridge

'I see our poor little train-spotter bought it,' said Norman Skyne, looking up from his copy of The Times.

Clovis took another Gitane from his case, crossed his study and sat at his desk.

'Yes. All very dramatic, I gather, and rather noble. Didn't he hurl someone out of a window?'

'Yes, that chap from the archive in Amsterdam. Bit of a wasted gesture, apparently. The fellow's not expected to live. I tried to get the low-down from Dilke, but he got very spikey with me.'

'That young man's gone soft,' said Clovis. 'He's no use to anyone.'

'The people behind it – the police statements have been positively sphinx-like. They're nothing to do with...'

'Oh, no no no,' said Clovis. 'Bunch of hot-heads. We'll just have to wait till this all blows over before we set things in motion.'

'That book you mentioned, J.D. – there were several possible references to something in the material Appleby published.'

'I know that,' said Clovis crisply. 'But nobody seems to have put two and two together, thank God. Not for now, at least.'

'By the way, J.D. I was surprised to see that you let them give you a credit on that silly film. Why ever did you do that?'

'To annoy Appleby, of course.'

York and beyond

Jenny didn't even realise that Appleby had sent her a text until Forbes returned her old mobile phone to her three days later. Lucy was already driving her back to York when she finally got round to checking her messages.

She read it aloud: 'U right. Larkin wrong. NOT almost.'

'I can't make head nor tail of that,' said Lucy. 'Larkin? What on earth did he mean?'

'Right,' said Jenny after a pause. 'I've just worked it out. We once had an argument about a poem. Oh, God…'

She bit the back of her fist, then wept inconsolably for half an hour.

*

They held a memorial service for Appleby in The Merchant Adventurers' Hall, conducted by the mediator of the local Kindred. It was meant to be a modest affair for family and friends, but so many Harkerites wanted to come that they had to organise another at the Conway Hall in London a month later.

*

In the following months news gradually filtered out about the police investigation. The engineer at RAF Hallingham who provided Swilby's first firearms was arrested in November. Swilby himself seemed to have disappeared from the face of the earth. Nobody had noticed the blood dripping from the boot when Pikey Doggler's clapped-out Princess went into the crusher. Three days later the cube of compressed metal was at the bottom of a cargo ship en route for China. 'Wallen' was arrested in Miami a year later.

A militant Zionist businessman in Golders Green was arrested for providing Yitzak with chemicals. He had been told they were for use in arson attacks on the offices of pro-Palestinian organisations in central London. An ultra-orthodox Israeli couple working at a new

Judaic Studies centre in Leeds had supplied the van and a gun. They were both killed in a shoot-out with Israeli agents in Jerusalem the following spring. No charges were brought against the Abramskys.

The network who helped the Wahabi were put under long-term surveillance, and proved to have connections with several other jihadist groups, including Al Qaeda. The following summer a total of thirty-four arrests were made in synchronised swoops at addresses in east London, Leicester, Dewsbury, Calais, Paris, Milan, Montreal, New Jersey and Baltimore. 'Ishmael' was eventually identified as the son of middle-class Palestinian refugees, brought up in Kuwait.

The men who killed Vaartje and Freek and kidnapped Piet van Stumpe were never identified, nor was anyone who had helped them. The two men shot on the Charltons' landing had been circumcised. The man in the purple ski-mask had not.

MI6 eventually identified three of the men who had initiated and bank-rolled the attacks. All had water-tight political protection. None could be arrested. Despite a few hard-hitting exposees by campaigning journalists, their deals went ahead uninterrupted.

*

The destruction of 'Farthingwell Two' had repercussions around the world. For some Harkerite groups, especially the American 'Flamers', Appleby became a martyr. They even coined a new term, 'The Eternal Righteous'. In his moment of death, Appleby had become the Harkerite equivalent of a saint. There were 'Meeting Houses', 'Kindred Centers' and 'Halls of Congregation' where gaudy paintings of him appeared alongside Harker himself in a sort of diptych, each enveloped in his own fiery womb.

Six months after learning of his death, a college in Wisconsin made Appleby the world's first 'Posthumous Professor' in their new School of Agnostic Studies.

'So he finally got a chair,' Jenny told Kate ruefully, 'and he'll never even know it.'

She had been offered a full-time job at a publishing house in London. She sold their house in York, bought a garden flat in Muswell Hill and began a new phase in her life.

Swively

On a warm summer evening, two women walked over Farthingwell Meadows. They were followed at a distance by a man with a pronounced limp pushing an elderly companion in a wheelchair. The site had long been cleared. The foundations of the original hall were now surrounded by a neat footpath, roped off and furnished with small weatherproof panels describing the layout of the building.

Fifty yards away, just beyond the site of 'Farthingwell Two', work had already begun on the foundations of 'Farthingwell Three.' Guy Charlton was never going to give up. His own funds were finally running low, but he now had a wealthy Italian sponsor.

Otherwise the site was now completely covered by a trim lawn. In the middle a small, but tasteful polished granite memorial had recently been erected. It bore one name, James Appleby, with his dates. Beneath was a simple inscription:

'His spirit burns within us.'

The women walked slowly towards it and stopped. Both carried a large bouquet.

'You go first, Claire,' said Jenny.

Claire stepped forward and laid a bunch of large, fleshy white lilies against the small stone plinth.

'You were a lovely teacher, Jimmy,' she murmured, 'a lovely teacher and an adorable man. Here's a little something just in case you've got nothing better to do.' And she laid a copy of one of her novels beside the flowers. It wasn't the latest and darkest in the Halvingdene sequence. That was called, '*Lilies that Fester*', and the title didn't quite seem appropriate. Instead she chose the last but one, '*To the Summer Sweet*'.

If Jenny said anything as she put her own bouquet down, she said it in the privacy of her own thoughts. She stood with her head bowed for so long that the others began to wonder if she was all right. At last she turned away, rummaging in her handbag for tissues. As the two women stood aside, the man in the wheelchair looked up at his carer and picked up a bouquet from his lap.

'It is our turn now, Signor, is it not? If you please…'

'Yes, Piet,' said Angelini, taking the flowers, 'it is our turn now.'

As Jenny looked up, she saw another woman walking down the path towards them, a young boy trotting by her side. She had a sallow complexion and sunken features, her hair covered by a large woolly hat.

'May I?' she said. 'I hope you don't mind. Giovanni told me you'd all be here today.' She turned to the little boy. 'Come on Eddie,' she said, crouching down. 'Let's put the pretty flowers down here for your daddy. Do you think he'll like them?'

'Yus,' said the boy with a giggle.

'Iris?' said Jenny. 'It's you. I hardly…And this must be Edward? I'm sorry… *What* did you just say?'

Iris stood up and faced her. 'Jenny, I think we need to talk…'

'Of course,' said Jenny quietly. 'I think we do. You must both come with me.'

She took Iris's arm. Claire, Angelini and van Stumpe followed a few yards behind as the little party slowly made their way to The Kindred Spirit.

Acknowledgements

I would like to thank all those who have helped me with their encouragement, advice, and constructive criticism, in particular my wife Elizabeth for her unfailing support, my brother Simon, sister Nicola and brother-in-law Richard and friends who commented on the first versions, including Rose, Peter and Barbara. For guidance and points of information on historical background I am indebted to Professor Richard Wilson and Canon Edward Probert. Finally I am immeasurably indebted to all associated with Pighog who helped knock this into some kind of shape: John, Meredith, Tom, Dina, Andrew, Chloe and Jennie.